FEAR'S JUSTICE

"A tense and muscular crime adventure. Olden lays down a hard-as-nails story that rings with savvy appraisal of halls of power and mean streets."

—*Publishers Weekly*

"A nonstop nail-biter and terrific read."

—*Lexington Herald-Leader* (KY)

"Tough, gritty, and compelling. . . . A cop to the core, the hero of Marc Olden's new thriller is politically incorrect and proud of it as he bulldozes his way through a blue wall of corruption and death."

—W.E.B. Griffin, author of the bestselling
Badge of Honor series

"Refreshingly realistic. . . . The first book I've read that tells it like it is. . . . Top of the line for pure reading enjoyment."

—*Chattanooga Free Press* (TN)

"Piano-wire writing: razor-sharp but oh-so-lyrical in a leather-tough sort of way. Dirty Harry with a heart of gold."

—*Kirkus Reviews*

Books by Marc Olden

The Ghost*
Fear's Justice*
Dai-Sho
Gaijin
Giri
Oni
Te
Kisaeng
Krait
Gossip
Poe Must Die
A Dangerous Glamour
The Book of Shadows
Cocaine
The Informant
Narc
Black Samurai
Choices *(as Leslie Crafford)*
The Harker File

*Published by POCKET BOOKS

THE GHOST

MARC OLDEN

POCKET STAR BOOKS

New York London Toronto Sydney Singapore

This book is a work of fiction. Names, characters, places and incidents are products of the author's imagination or are used fictitiously. Any resemblance to actual events or locales or persons, living or dead, is entirely coincidental.

 A Pocket Star Book published by
POCKET BOOKS, a division of Simon & Schuster Inc.
1230 Avenue of the Americas, New York, NY 10020

Copyright © 1999 by Marc Olden

Originally published in hardcover in 1999 by Simon & Schuster Inc.

ISBN: 0-671-00418-2

First Pocket Books printing June 2000

10 9 8 7 6 5 4 3 2 1

POCKET STAR BOOKS and colophon are registered trademarks of Simon & Schuster Inc.

Cover photo by PhotoDisc

Printed in the U.S.A.

QB / ✶

For my mother, Courtenay Olden,
with love always

Acknowledgments

I would like to thank Diane Crafford as always and for reasons too many to mention; Richard Pine and Lori Andiman for taking me seriously; and Carlo Fargnoli for being so unselfish. You are New York's finest.

And the wild regrets and the bloody sweats,
None knew so well as I:
For he who lives more lives than one
More deaths than one must die.
—Oscar Wilde, *Ballad of Reading Gaol*

THE
GHOST

1
The Watcher

He followed her for two days. Waited in the shadows across from her Manhattan apartment.

Tailed her to Central Park on a cool June morning then watched her jog around Sheep Meadow.

Tracked her car to Queens, to an empty Italian restaurant where she sat alone in a back booth for forty minutes. She seemed jumpy.

His guess: She'd been stood up.

He watched through the restaurant window and made entries in his journal. She used a cell phone—two calls—then ordered a salad that she ignored.

He kept a journal on each woman, his personal record of occurrences, reflections, and experiences.

She was the only one still alive.

He returned to his car. Waiting didn't bother him; he was a tenacious man, born with forceful willpower and a bulldog tenacity. He deliberately gave the impression of being indifferent and unconcerned, but his mind never stopped plotting.

He switched on the tape deck, sipped his black coffee, then slumped in the front seat. Head back, eyes closed. Listening to Pavarotti. Fat Lucy, if you will.

His love for the woman was like opera. Reckless and intense; all or nothing. He couldn't bear to have her out of his sight.

He'd done some reflecting and decided a bowlegged Dominican riding a mountain bike along Columbus Avenue was also following the woman. The "Domo" sipping Evian water; pretending he's only window-shopping. Cute.

He knew why the guy was dogging her. She'd put people in prison, and now someone wanted to get even.

The Dominican could have been a purse snatcher. A crack dealer making his rounds. He could have decided he liked the lady's butt and craved a closer look. Latinos, bless 'em, enjoyed going on booty patrol. Maybe the Domo was looking for a pickup basketball game: half court, five bucks a man. He could have several reasons for riding his little black bike from Columbus Avenue to Central Park West and back again.

The Dominican was actually a contract killer with seven, eight bodies on him. The Watcher had been in the station house when the Domo was being booked. Not for murder but for setting a dog on fire and throwing it from a roof in Washington Heights.

She was still in the restaurant. Sipping a cappuccino and looking at her watch.

The Watcher couldn't protect her against all of her enemies. She had too many.

He had a plan. It couldn't miss.

Leave New York. Just the two of them. With enough money to live comfortably for the rest of their lives.

He was confident and composed. Credit Tai Chi and origami. Tai Chi for conditioning and cool nerves; origami for patience and a sense of beauty.

Fold a thousand origami cranes and your wish will be granted.

He couldn't fold a crane without thinking of her.

She left the restaurant and drove to the Queens Public Library where she examined back issues of New York newspapers. She photocopied a few pages, arousing his curiosity.

He wanted a closer look but decided no. Too risky.

Good move. Minutes later who strolls into the library but her lover, a former NYPD homicide detective now in private security. They dined at a nearby Chinese restaurant, read fortune cookies out loud, and laughed.

Later they drove to a popular Cuban nightclub in Jackson Heights and danced to a live salsa band. He watched from a packed bar. His mouth went dry at the sight of her. She was a terrific dancer. Dazzling and seductive. Moving as though close to orgasm.

Midnight. She left the club with her lover and returned to his Brooklyn Heights apartment. They kissed in the lobby, then entered the elevator. The Watcher shivered in disgust. Why did they have to be so public?

He stared into the rearview mirror, thinking about today's actions and episodes. Examining and scrutinizing her every action. The lady was up to something. Yes, indeed.

He switched on a penlight and began reading his journal.

The Italian restaurant. The library.

He thought, *I sense a theme here*.

She hadn't been stood up. She'd gone to the restaurant for a meeting, a little singsong around the campfire, you might say. But nothing face-to-face.

She'd been talking to someone hiding in the kitchen or storeroom. It explained the cell phone and why she was a bit twitchy. Why she had no interest in food.

The lady was gathering information. The Watcher could read her like a book. He knew exactly where she was going. He'd committed a murder to protect one of the most important men in the city and the lady was going after him.

Score one for the Watcher.

2
Ross Magellan

It was almost three in the morning when she left her Manhattan apartment and drove to the Bruckner Expressway in the South Bronx. She parked behind a sagging billboard, took a gun from the glove compartment, and left the car.

She walked toward a second car parked facing the billboard. As she neared the car, a rear door was unlocked by a small man sitting behind the wheel. He was a thirty-eight-year-old Puerto Rican, five years her senior, and shorter, with a bald head and a ponytail. His eyes were hidden behind dark glasses. He held a cigarette between his thumb and forefinger.

Detective Ross Magellan slid into the backseat. The gun went into a pocket of her sweatshirt.

She said, "Morning, Freddy. What did you want to see me about?"

Detective Freddy Palacio stared at her in the rearview mirror and scratched the tip of his nose. "Dark as hell around here."

The expressway was nearly pitch black. Thieves had stolen the copper wiring from newly installed lights and sold it to scrap-metal dealers.

"You want privacy," Ross said. "You got privacy."

"Let's talk about what I *don't* want," Freddy said, "I don't want to do time. I'm giving you and Joe Labriola the biggest case of your lives. I want to be paid. Ain't nothing for nothing in this world."

"I see." Ross waved a mosquito from her face. "You kill a prostitute, wound her john, and you skate. Is that it?"

Freddy removed his dark glasses. His eyes were blinking nonstop.

He said, "I do for you, you do for me. That's all I'm saying."

Ross shook her head. "I don't remember you being this stupid when we were partners. But that was two years ago."

"Stupid?" Anger turned Freddy's face red.

"Employing two or more prostitutes is a felony, punishable by one to seven years. What were you thinking?"

"I'm paying on two divorces. And some bitch over in Brooklyn claims she just had my kid. I got her lawyer screaming, 'Show me the money.' I had to do something."

Ross said, "So you moonlight for an escort service as a chauffeur-bodyguard. Drive the girls to the session, wait outside till they're finished, then go in and collect the fee. Three-way split—the girl, the agency, and you. Except you get greedy."

He threw up his hands. "Could we *not* talk about this?"

"Greedy with a capital *G*," Ross continued. "One of the girls tells you she has a regular, a dentist who's loan sharking on the side. Putting money on the street with some Italians from Staten Island. Last week the dentist shows up for his date carrying a hundred grand in cash. You pull your gun, the dentist pulls *his* gun, and two seconds later, you find yourself in a world of shit."

She winked at Freddy. "Know what your problem is? You still think you're a cop. Still think the ball's in your court and you're holding all the aces. You don't want to let go of that. Every cop who gets jammed feels the same way."

She leaned toward Freddy and spoke in a sweet voice, gently tapping his forearm for emphasis. "But when they take away your gun and badge, and you're looking at five to fifteen for murder two, it's safe to say you're not a cop anymore."

Freddy said, "You're on the job twelve years. Labriola's got maybe fifteen as federal prosecutor."

"So?"

"So this case has glory written all over it. You're second grade now. You bring down Reiner, you got a shot at first. Labriola, he gets to quit the U.S. Attorney's Office and run for senator or anything else he wants to do with his life. I'm handing you the guy who's the chief judge of New York narcotics on a silver platter. Adam Reiner is yours for the taking. You get to nail a judge for fraud, suppressing evidence, witness intimidation, you name it. You ever take down anyone bigger? I don't think so."

Ross said, "If you're waiting to hear how benevolent and reverent you are, it's not going to happen. You were going away unless you got lucky. So you got lucky. You stumble across a judge who's a degenerate gambler, who covers his losses by taking bribes. Reiner may be a scumbag, but Freddy's out for Freddy."

He said, "Doesn't change a thing. Wasn't for me, you'd never know Reiner had a jones. The man's slick. Does his gambling out of town. Private poker games. Tells people he's traveling to legal seminars, law enforcement conventions, judicial conferences. Won't touch a card when he's in the city. I call that tricky."

"And you're handing him to me. Freddy, you're a regular Santa Claus."

He gave her a smile of ugly teeth. "Lucky or not, it still counts. Someone had to drive Reiner to those games. Turned out to be me."

Ross said, "You had help. You happen to know the shyster who represents Judge Reiner. That very same shyster hooked you up with the escort service. Like I said, you're a lucky man."

"Sometimes I wonder. Anyway, I'm throwing in a bonus. Or did you forget?"

Ross looked at the back of her hands. "I was wondering when you'd get around to that." There was anger in her voice.

Freddy held up a forefinger. "Reiner nearly got you killed. Now you get even. Payback, courtesy of Freddy. You'd never whack a judge. Not your style. But you can send his ass to college. Just remember who's making it all possible."

Ross stared at the new moon. Her eyes were bright slits.

She said, "I remember Judge Reiner freeing a psychopath, knowing that the guy had a beef with me. I remember this same psychopath deliberately running over Elizabeth Ruiz, hitting her at a hundred miles an hour. Ripping her head from her body and thinking he was killing me. There are times when I don't know if I'm remembering or dreaming. Either way, it's like carrying a graveyard around in your head. Not a nice feeling."

"And they never caught the guy."

"No. He's still out there somewhere. My guess is Albania or Serbia. He's from that area. Tried tracking him through Interpol, but they came up empty."

She leaned back. "Anyway, let's talk about you. I reached out for Labriola because you asked me to. Got him to give you a deal. A good one, if you ask me. I also agreed to go undercover and gather evidence against Reiner because you asked me to."

She shook her head. "Now you're asking me to be stupid. The answer on that is no. If I go back to Labriola, he won't renegotiate. He'll withdraw the offer and you're back to square one, with a reputation as a man who can't be trusted. Under those circumstances, I don't see people lining up to deal with you."

Freddy tapped the steering wheel with his detective's ring. "I don't like the idea of being inside with people who know I'm a cop. This could cause problems, know what I'm saying?"

Ross shook her head. "You're doing a year at Eglin Air Force Base in Florida. Not some hellhole but a military barracks. Warm climate, palm trees. Lots of oranges. You're with bank presidents, congressmen, computer hackers, accountants and the occasional mob informant. Nothing you can't handle. You work on your tan for a year, then relocate with a new identity. Labriola insists you do time. Soft time in this case. It doesn't get any better. Not on a murder beef."

Freddy said, "I'd like it better if I walked. Talk to Labriola. Get him to drop the time. Tell him you think I should go directly into relocation when the case ends. Lie to the man if you have to. You're the best undercover I ever worked with. And that's what undercovers do best. They lie."

Ross smiled at the fireflies outside the window. Muscle meant nothing in undercover work, whereas the ability to talk, particularly the ability to talk your way out of trouble, meant everything. Undercover work was about being an actress, about playing with a perp's head and manipulating people. She loved it.

She looked at Freddy. "By the way, I never lie. I just say things that allow you to mislead yourself."

"Is that what you call it?"

"And I never say too much. That's the secret, in case you're interested. You never say too much."

"I've seen you in action," Freddy said. "Seen you lie with a word, a look. Seen you lie with silence. You got to be good to pull *that* off."

"The goal is deception," Ross said. "To blind them with science. How I get there doesn't matter. Not to me. Not to the people I work for."

Freddy shivered. "You got the most dangerous job in the department. Still don't see how you do it. One mistake and your name goes on the wall down at Police Plaza. You and all the other cops killed in the line of duty. Come to think of it, I *do* know how you do it."

"And how's that?"

"You're hooked," he said. "Scared shitless, but hooked."

"Hooked on what?"

"On the high you get from leading a double life. You dig conning people. Especially people who'd kill you if they knew you were a cop."

Ross said, "You could be right. Meanwhile, Labriola wants Reiner. And like me, he has his reasons. With or without you, we're going ahead. You can help, or you can throw shit in the game. Your call."

Freddy started chewing his nails, and when he spoke there was a finger in his mouth. "We use to meet informants up here when we were partners, remember? It was your idea. No tapped phones to worry about. No bugged rooms or video cameras. Smart. We had some times back then, didn't we?"

Ross closed her eyes. Freddy was saying she owed him.

She did.

Ross and Freddy going after Jamaicans operating from an East Village funeral home, the Js dealing heroin and cocaine from coffin tops. Wearing hockey masks and surgical gloves to prevent ID. Ross as "uncle," NYPD code for undercover. Lying her way into the funeral parlor at midnight to make the buy needed for a warrant. Doing her "ho" thang in spandex, black lipstick, and hoop earrings. Freddy as "the ghost," NYPD code for backup. Standing across the street disguised as a wino. Freezing his buns off in knee-high snow. Listening to Ross through an earpiece and hearing the code word indicating she needs help. Freddy responding, barrel-assing through the front

*door and firing on the run, putting two bullets into a
Jamaican attempting to rape Ross at knifepoint.*

Ross said to Freddy, "Right now three people know
you're giving up Reiner—my lieutenant, Labriola, and
myself. The minute you start shopping for a new deal,
that number increases. Not good. Because the more
people who know, the more likely you are to get hurt."

Freddy stared at the lit end of his cigarette. He
chewed his lower lip. Finally he exhaled and said,
"You can sure talk shit."

Ross fingered the car keys in her sweatshirt pocket.
"Life is hard, Freddy. It's even harder when you're stupid. Labriola can keep you out of court and put you
into a witness protection program. You'll need that
because when Reiner goes down, he's taking people
with him. People with unmanageable criminal tenden-
cies."

"The Albanians," Freddy said. "Reiner and his
lawyer Lou Angelo are tight with that crew. Those
guys are crazy. They'll kill you for a shoelace."

Ross nodded. "You don't want to be around when
they get popped. Still think I'm talking shit?"

Freddy shook his head. "I don't know what to
think."

"Think about this. Cross Labriola and you'll end up
hanging by your tongue, waiting to die."

Freddy didn't answer for a while. Finally he said,
"Guess I'm going to Florida."

"Everything considered, there are worse places."

Freddy scratched the tip of his nose. "Now that you
mention it, going to trial is a gamble. And speaking of
gambling, Lou Angelo tells me Reiner dropped sixty-
five grand in a Boston poker game last night."

Ross waved a hand in front of her face. Freddy's cigarette smoke was getting to her. She opened the car door and stepped outside. She hadn't had a cigarette since she'd stopped working Narcotics with Freddy and transferred to OCCB—the Organized Crime Control Bureau.

There was a time when she didn't feel alive unless she was smoking. When she didn't feel she was living unless she was killing herself. These days it was black coffee or gum. Anything but the weed.

She yawned, then walked toward her car. Cigarette smoke was nothing less than nauseating. Why hadn't she noticed that before now?

Freddy followed Ross. Just as he'd done when they'd been partners.

Their relationship had been strictly business. Ross wasn't into short guys who smelled like a gym bag. At five nine, she towered over Freddy, which bothered him more than it did her.

And she was Cuban. Cubans looked down on Puerto Ricans, seeing them as little more than monkeys who spoke bad Spanish. Cubans, in fact, were snobs who looked down on everybody.

When they reached Ross's car, Freddy said, "Lou Angelo says the escort service is catching heat because of my problem. Plus, he's got Reiner to worry about."

Ross leaned against the car hood and gazed up at the stars. "Life's not easy when you're a lawyer, a bagman, *and* a sleaze."

Freddy said, "How you and Angelo getting along, by the way?"

"Mr. Angelo and I are getting along just fine.

Thanks for the introduction. Eventually we'll get around to discussing his role as a bagman carrying cash from Albanian mobsters to a certain top judge. He says he'd like me as a client."

Freddy chuckled. "Knowing Lou, that ain't all he'd like. Guy's in his sixties and still thinks he's a lover. And he bought your cover?"

"Believed every word. As far as Mr. Angelo is concerned, I'm in Latin music. My name is Ross Marino and I have my own company, G and E Records. I'm also in music publishing and artist management. You remember Gloria Paz?"

"She owns G and E. You kept her brother out of a drug bust. Good-looking kid. Lucky, too. Could have gone to prison a tight end and come out a wide receiver."

Ross said, "She'll do anything I ask."

Freddy lit another cigarette. "I was supposed to drive Reiner to last night's game. Two grand, round-trip. But given my present circumstances, Lou said I best keep a low profile. He gave me five hundred bucks as a show of good faith, then hired another driver. Also a cop."

"Who?"

"Black guy named Cleveland Nobles. Works in Street Crimes. Does security part-time at the Aztec Club over on Tenth, which is how he and Lou met. Lou loves to go clubbing. And he loves cops."

Freddy snapped his fingers. "Before I forget, the judge and Lou have a new hustle."

Ross said, "You mean their phony charity isn't paying enough?"

Freddy said, "Reiner needs all the money he can get.

Sucker can't win at poker to save his life. Get this: He's saying he plans to run for Manhattan Surrogates Court judge. Well, it's a scam. The man's not running for shit. He's got Angelo accepting campaign contributions. Guess where the money's going."

"Reiner's buying wool to knit socks for the homeless."

"Not quite. Most of the cash is coming from lawyers looking to crawl up Reiner's ass. Mainly because a surrogate judge gets to hand out the kind of assignments that make lawyers rich."

"Everybody talks," Ross said. "It's one of the first things you learn as a cop. My job is to get Lou Angelo talking about the right things."

"Shouldn't be hard," Freddy said. "When we went clubbing, you couldn't shut him up. Always bragging about who he knew. Who he beat in court. A couple lines of coke and you can't shut him up. Girls at the escort service call him 'Chatty Kathy.' That's how I learned about the policewoman. The one Angelo claims he's protecting. She's a murder witness who could nail a very fat cat *and* another cop. When I asked why he's doing it, he pretended like he hadn't heard. You check that out yet?"

"Yesterday," Ross said. "Drove to Angelo's favorite Italian restaurant in Queens and talked with his friend, Emilio the waiter. At least I think it was Emilio. He wouldn't leave the kitchen, so we talked by phone. Said he didn't want to be seen talking to me even if I was the policewoman's friend. He's afraid the guy who's after her might just come after him. I said I wasn't her friend, that I was simply curious. He wouldn't budge. Mentioning your name didn't help."

Freddy grinned. "Emilio scares easy."

"He tells me he's not dealing anymore."

"Bullshit. Emilio's still doing business. The restaurant job's just a cover. And it's safe because he meets his buyers in a public place. Less chance of getting ripped off that way. Plus Emilio gets to show the IRS a legitimate income. You think Angelo's driving to Queens for pasta? He's out there scoring flake from his main man."

Ross said, "Emilio says this policewoman, assuming she is one, has moved out of his building. Claims he doesn't know where she is. He thinks Lou Angelo might know, but I'd have to ask Angelo directly. I also checked old newspapers looking for anything involving Angelo and female cops. Came up empty. I've got Connie looking into it. Let's see how he does."

"You tell anyone else about this missing lady cop, whoever she is?"

"If you mean other cops, the answer is no. I'm suppose to be after a corrupt judge, not looking for a policewoman who's hiding out because some cop wants to kill her. Anyway, we only have Lou Angelo's word on this. The whole thing could be bogus. Angelo just might be blowing smoke. Besides, you have to be careful bringing up this stuff around cops. You don't know who you're talking to. For now, let's just keep this between ourselves."

Ross watched an airliner, wing lights twinkling, glide across a new moon.

"Speaking of talking to people," she said, "have you spoken to anyone about this case?"

"No. Why do you bring that up?"

"Because I'm being followed."

"Fuck." Freddy's hands went up in the air. "You tell me that *now?*"

"I thought it best to take care of business before you got stressed. Anyway, I haven't IDed the guy. I do know he's there. I just haven't spotted him."

"If you can't see him, what makes you so sure he's there?"

"I know when I'm being watched."

"Jesus." Freddy looked sick. "You talk to your backup?"

Ross said no. If the department knew she was being followed, she'd be taken off the case. Maybe put into protective custody. She wasn't ready to be held hostage just yet.

First things first. Judge Reiner goes. After him, it's the maggot who's bird-dogging her.

Freddy said, "Suppose this guy's with Reiner and he's following you in order to get to me. I blame your people, goddam it. Somebody gave me up."

"You're not thinking," Ross said. "Labriola knows your identity. So why have me followed? Same with my lieutenant. Neither has a reason to put a tail on me."

"So what about your backup? Reiner could have reached any one of them."

Ross shook her head. "We've worked together before, and I trust these guys with my life. If Reiner had reached them, this case would be over. He'd have shut us down in a heartbeat. Court order, subpoena, whatever it takes. We're trying to send him to prison, remember?"

Ross said Reiner would hit them with every trick in the book. He'd have Jews accusing the NYPD of anti-

Semitism and politicians threatening to hang cops from telephone poles. He might even have an Albanian sociopath drop by to say hello. So far none of this had happened.

Freddy exhaled. "So you're saying there really is a wacko following you. *You*, not me."

Ross said it looked that way, then got in her car. She didn't say there was no such thing as coincidence, that there had to be a reason Judge Reiner and the wacko had entered her life simultaneously.

3
Applied Technology

In the basement garage of an East Eighty-first Street apartment house, the Watcher used a stolen key. He opened the door of a green BMW parked near an elevator. It was 4:15 A.M.

Reaching under the front seat, he pulled out a microcassette recorder. The tape was still running. He pressed Stop, then Reverse.

He turned down the volume. Then he pressed Play and held the recorder to his ear.

He listened, then raised one eyebrow. Well, now.

Tonight when she'd met her snitch, Detective Ross Magellan had been driving this very same BMW. The car and an upstairs apartment, where presumably Magellan now slept soundly, belonged to OCCB. Both had been confiscated from an Israeli who'd run Manhattan's largest bootleg video operation prior to being tossed in the slammer. Magellan used the ride and the crib when she worked undercover and had to appear well-off. When she had to look *uptown*.

The Watcher slipped the recorder into a shirt pocket and tapped it with a gloved forefinger. Only a saint could keep a secret, and Ross Magellan was no saint.

But then neither was the Watcher.

He had a complete set of Magellan's keys—two apartments, two cars, a gym locker. And her office at OCCB.

He was just as thorough in collecting information about Detective Magellan's background. The Watcher knew she had a younger sister, now institutionalized out on Long Island. He knew she'd killed a man and that she'd do anything to bring down Judge Reiner.

He knew why Detective Magellan's husband had been murdered. And why she was using a false name. There was a self-made wall around the lady, and the Watcher was taking it apart brick by brick.

He closed the BMW's door. Quietly. The car alarm wasn't a problem. He'd disconnected it yesterday. Knowing Magellan, the Watcher had assumed, correctly, that she'd be too busy to have the alarm repaired anytime soon.

Tell your secret to the wind and the wind would tell the trees. The Watcher treated himself to a small smile. Not even the wind and the trees knew more about Ross Magellan than he did.

He also knew about Freddy Palacio. The Watcher and Detective Palacio had worked together once, very briefly. The problem with Palacio was stupidity. How else to describe a cop who took money from whores and exchanged shots with a pistol-packing dentist?

Magellan was smarter. Not smarter than the

Watcher but certainly smarter than Palacio. At least she wasn't the embarrassment to cops Palacio was.

Detective Palacio was at his wit's end. But then he hadn't had far to go.

When the Watcher first learned of tonight's meeting, he considered bugging the BMW. He rejected the idea almost immediately. His bugging equipment was limited; should Magellan drive out of range, it would be impossible for him to listen in on her conversation.

Nor could he move closer without being seen. Magellan, bless her, was delightfully devious. A very strategical lady. She'd set the meeting when the city's streets were empty. When she could spot surveillance with her eyes closed.

Electronic surveillance and moving cars presented other problems. Such as interference from car phones and high-rises. From television signals and utility crews working at night. Drive under a bridge, and reception from a bugged car was cut off entirely.

The Watcher wasn't one for complexity. The direct approach was always best. So he planted a microcassette recorder in Magellan's car, then waited for her to come back to the garage.

When she returned from the Bronx, Magellan drove around the block twice. Reassuring herself she hadn't been followed. The Watcher nearly laughed out loud.

He watched Magellan leave the BMW and stand in the garage entrance, eyeing the empty street.

Once, she looked directly at his hiding place and saw nothing. He stood unmoving, still as a stone. Observing her through half-closed eyes. Enjoying the pleasure of possessing her even as she turned from him and entered the garage.

The microcassette. The Watcher touched it again. For one person to succeed, another had to fail. Tonight he'd succeeded, while Ross Magellan had failed. Tonight was one more sign she belonged to him.

He removed his gloves. Time to head home and catch a few hours sleep before reporting to the precinct.

He left the garage, a silhouette moving through shadows. Unnoticed and unobserved. Into the deserted street and toward the fire-glow of dawn.

4
News You Can Use

Ross Magellan arrived at the U.S. Attorney's Office in Foley Square at 12:45 P.M., catching Joe Labriola in the middle of lunch. The door to the office was opened by the federal prosecutor who shook her hand and smiled without making eye contact.

Ross said, "Spoke to M last night. Reiner and Lou Angelo are working a new hustle. Appears we'll have another fraud charge to hit them with."

M was Freddy's code name. His middle initial. M for Manuel.

"God is kind sometimes," Joe Labriola said.

He was a forty-six-year-old Italian, no taller than Ross but heavier, with a hooked nose and a slight paunch. He wore a dark suit, gray shirt, and a brown tie decorated with yellow golf clubs. Like all prosecutors Ross had worked with, Labriola was aggressive and demanding, with an overwhelming need to be number one. People like that weren't out to make friends.

A second man stood at a window, staring at the back of the federal Metropolitan Correctional Center. He was Special Agent Frank Beebe of the FBI, a forty-five-year-old country boy from Georgia, with a bull neck and hair between his eyebrows. His size, along with a taste for corduroy suits and brown boots, had earned him the nickname "Bear." Beebe was liaison on the Judge Reiner case, the link between the NYPD who was running the investigation and the feds who were financing it.

In the five days she'd worked with him, Ross found Bear to be cheap with his money and not especially fun loving. What bothered her most were his hard blue eyes, which seemed to stare through a woman's clothes.

Ross seated herself on a leather couch beneath color photographs of the President and Attorney General, then told Labriola and Beebe about Judge Reiner's phony election campaign. As she spoke, Labriola sat at his desk and used a plastic fork to poke at the remains of a cheeseburger and fries.

"I like it," he said when Ross was finished. "I'd like it even better if you told me you've got a nut on Lou Angelo. That you have enough to force him to give up Reiner."

Ross said, "In five days I've done pretty well. Of course, that's only my opinion."

"I think things could be better."

"Mind explaining that?"

Labriola speared a fry with the plastic fork and popped it in his mouth. "By now Mr. Angelo should be saying to himself, 'I'm going to prison unless I give up Reiner.' Tell me if that's happening."

"It's not happening today," Ross said. "And it won't be happening tomorrow. But I am getting closer to that point."

Frank Beebe turned from the window and fixed his beady eyes on Ross.

"Close only counts in horseshoes, darlin'," he said. "You either got Angelo or you don't. Which is it?"

"We're going dancing tonight," Ross said, speaking slowly and holding Beebe's gaze. "Myself, a friend, and Lou Angelo with whomever. My guess is it won't be Mrs. Angelo."

Frank Beebe rested a meaty thigh on the windowsill. "I assume it was your idea to party at the taxpayers' expense." His tone said he wasn't too impressed with her decision.

Ross didn't answer. Instead she began doodling in her notebook. Let Labriola and Bear assume she was making notes. She needed time to think. To figure a way of dealing with the dick club.

She drew a horse's head—nostrils flaring, ears straight up. She'd been riding since she was ten. Her first job on the force had been as a mounted cop working parades, doing crowd control, and patrolling the "Enchanted Forest," cop term for Central Park. Someone had described a horse as dangerous at both ends and uncomfortable in the middle. Not if you knew what you were doing.

The dick club. For Ross, the trick was to be able to handle fear. To not give in to it. To refuse to let these guys intimidate her.

They were leaning on her pretty hard this afternoon. And she knew why.

She'd read it in this morning's *Times.* A follow-up

piece on one of Labriola's old cases. A year ago he'd
engineered the arrest, indictment, and conviction of a
Wall Street figure who later turned out to be innocent.
Just one more abuse of federal power, wrote the *Times*
columnist, linking this case to Ruby Ridge and to
Waco.

Labriola planned to go into politics. He needed the
Times column like he needed cancer. It was an unpleasant reminder that he couldn't afford to leave the Justice Department on a sour note.

On the other hand, nailing Judge Reiner meant
going out in a blaze of glory.

As for Bear, he'd failed to make the *Times*. He'd
also failed to make the team. Yesterday his FBI bosses
had passed him over for leader of an antiterrorist team
in favor of a younger agent. A black agent.

Ross was sure friends and relatives would bring this
up when next Bear showed his fat ass in Georgia.

She figured Bear needed the Reiner case to show his
superiors he still had it. Meanwhile, he was telling anyone who'd listen that he was just one more white man
victimized by political correctness.

Ross enlarged the horse's nostrils. Labriola and the
Bear wanted their careers back. Well, she had a piece
of advice for them: Anytime you want something, you
leave yourself open to being manipulated.

She spoke to Beebe without looking up from the
notebook.

"It *was* my idea to go dancing," she said. "Gives me
and Lou Angelo the opportunity to get to know one
another. Angelo mentioned he'd won mambo contests
in the Catskills when he was young. He worked there
as a busboy to help put himself through law school. I

also mentioned I have a husband who's in prison and refuses to give me a divorce. Angelo's offered to help. Which means the hook's in. The next step is to talk money."

She looked up from her drawing. "But first, let's talk about M. He wants out."

Labriola squeezed the plastic fork tightly in his fist. "The hell's that suppose to mean?" he said.

A frowning Beebe pushed himself away from the window and folded both arms across a sizable chest.

Ross looked at the horse. "I calmed him down. Bottom line: He wanted a guarantee he's only working with me."

Labriola said, "That deal's already in place. The NYPD runs the Reiner investigation. The federal government funds it. You arrest him. We try him in federal court."

Ross closed her notebook. "I explained to M there'd be no renegotiating. A deal is a deal. It did occur to me that if M backs out and you go after him, Judge Reiner is bound to learn he's under investigation. He'll come after us. The mayor and the governor backed his appointment, so they'll come after us too. It's a given we'll have problems with the Jews and every judges' organization in the state—"

Labriola covered his eyes with one hand. "And the point is?"

"We need M," Ross said.

Beebe snorted. "And I suppose we need *you* to run him *your* way."

Ross smiled sweetly. "You weren't thinking of coming with us tonight, were you?"

"As a matter of fact, I was."

"No, you're not."

"Tonight's dance party is being funded with government money. That being the case, missy, I intend to be there."

Ross looked at Labriola and waited.

The prosecutor eyed Ross while speaking to Beebe.

"It's Detective Magellan, Frank," the prosecutor said. "Not 'missy.' We live in PC times, remember? And she has to look like a player. Since the NYPD can't afford to finance this investigation, we have to. The FBI will be with Ross only when money changes hands. As in a direct payoff to Angelo or to M. You're there as a witness only, to make sure the money doesn't end up in the wrong hands."

Beebe said, "Or in the offshore bank accounts of NYPD detectives."

Labriola looked over his shoulder at Beebe. "Detective Magellan is running the investigation. If she needs you, she'll let you know. End of story."

Beebe fixed his hard eyes on Ross. "Just doing my job, Miss Magellan."

"It's *detective*," Ross said. "Starts with *D*. The letter that comes after *C*. You have a problem working with women?"

Beebe looked down at the floor. "I have a problem working with a woman who's economical with the truth. Whose entire life, as far as I can tell, is propelled by intrigue."

Ross said, "You make it sound psychopathic. As though I'm genetically programmed to be a compulsive liar."

"You said it. I didn't."

"I think you should loosen your hair net. Your brain needs oxygen."

"A real smart mouth."

Labriola cleared his throat and spoke in a low voice. "You're pushing it, Frank. I've worked with Ross. She wouldn't be here if she wasn't good."

Beebe said, "If she's so goddam smart, how come she got a witness killed?"

Before Ross could answer, Labriola held up both hands in a stop signal.

"That's enough, Frank," he said. "You're losing it, and that could be a problem. For you."

He looked at Ross. "Let me handle this."

Labriola spoke slowly to Beebe, as though talking to a dim-witted child.

"Ross was working an Albanian crew out of the Bronx. The guys had been doing jewel robberies. Making big scores in the diamond district and scaring people shitless. Ross got to one of them, a guy named Sammy—"

"Sali," Ross said. She glared at Beebe. "Sali Korat."

"Sali," Labriola said. "Anyway, Ross cons this Sali. Tells him she's in the market for hot stones. Says she's lined up some South Americans with money to burn. Sali thinks this means Colombians. Ross plays along. After the bust Sali learns Ross isn't what she appears to be. I should mention Sali also had the hots for Ross. So what you have here is a double whammy. Ross not only lies this guy's ass into court, she breaks his heart as well. Anyway, along comes Judge Reiner who refuses to close his courtroom when Ross testifies against Sali's crew. Judges do this to protect undercovers from identification and reprisals. It's a given. Not with Reiner. He keeps his court open, and Ross gets made by Sali and his people. Plus Reiner cuts Sali loose on low bail."

The prosecutor reached for his diet soda and said, "Ross had a friend in the jewelry business. Elizabeth Ruiz."

Ross said, "Elizabeth was family. We were very close."

Labriola nodded. "Miss Ruiz had her own shop. She and Ross looked alike. People took them for sisters. To help nail Sali's crew, Ruiz pretended she was Ross's partner. Ruiz even agreed to testify she saw Sali bring hot rocks into the store. Unfortunately, before any of this occurs, Sali does a hit-and-run on Ruiz, then skips the country. Turns out Ross, not Ruiz, was the target. Albanians are crazy people, and Sali was one of the craziest. The man just didn't like women leading him on."

Labriola drank the last of his soda and said, "Ross didn't get Elizabeth Ruiz killed. It was Reiner, and he's still doing favors for the Albanians. Only now, thanks to Ross and her friend M, we have a chance to prove it."

Ignoring Ross, Beebe spoke directly to Labriola. "My ass is on the line with this thing. You understand?"

Ross said, "I don't work for you, and I don't report to you. As long as you understand that we'll get along just fine. You leave M and Angelo to me."

The FBI agent looked at the ceiling. "Lord help us all."

Ross's beeper went off. She checked the caller number then pulled a cell phone from her bag. She said to Labriola, it's my lieutenant. This is one call I have to take.

The prosecutor nodded.

Ross's lieutenant was Carlo Fargnoli, an ambitious

man who was prone to depression and interested only in useful friendships.

Ross dialed his number, put the phone to her ear, and said, "Loo, what's up?"

"Sorry to interrupt," Fargnoli said. "Got some news you can use. It's about the guy who's been following you for the past few days. You didn't happen to notice anything out of the ordinary?"

Shit. Ross closed her eyes. Fargnoli was nobody's fool. The man could smell a con job a mile away. If he learned Ross withheld information, she was off the case.

He'd have no choice. A dead undercover wouldn't look good on his resume. Especially a dead female undercover.

Ross told the truth.

"I haven't seen a soul," she said.

"Doesn't matter at this point," Fargnoli said. "They found him this morning. Vacant lot in the Bronx. Handcuffed and burned to a crisp. Whoever whacked him had serious intentions. Before torching the guy, they jumped up and down on his back until his spine snapped."

Fargnoli said we could be looking for a dancing fool on this one, maybe Fred Astaire or Gene Kelly, but he didn't think so. Anyway, he'd appreciate Ross dropping by the office as soon as possible so they could talk.

5
Poochy

The drug dealer lived in a decrepit Queens apartment building on 107th Street, within sight of Our Lady of Sorrows Roman Catholic Church.

It was just after midnight when the Watcher, carrying a new attaché case, knocked on the door of the drug dealer's eighth-floor apartment. Inside, a dog began barking furiously. The Watcher wasn't surprised.

He also wasn't pleased. Any dog in the company of a drug dealer was most likely a pit bull or a Rottweiler, either of which was a killer.

He touched the Glock worn in a left-handed Hi-Ride belt holster under his jacket. He'd prefer not to use the gun, but that would depend on the dog, now barking its lungs out. A year ago the Watcher had taken part in an East New York drug raid and looked on while two cops fired a total of ten shots into a charging pit bull owned by a drug dealer. The dog, a nasty piece of work, continued its attack until a state trooper with a baseball bat finally ended the drama.

The Watcher held the attaché case up to the peephole. Allowing Emilio Albert, waiter and part-time dope peddler, to see the initials *L.A.* on the case. Since Lou Angelo spent lavishly on himself, the Watcher had bought the best, laying out money for a top-of-the-line case, plus an extra few bucks for a rush job on the monogram. The case was a bit heavy, but it looked good. Good enough, hopefully, to persuade Mr. Albert to open the door.

Meanwhile, the Watcher waited in a hallway where the only light came from a pair of grimy bulbs in a deteriorating ceiling. From what he'd observed, most tenants appeared to be Hispanic. Illegals probably. Clutching their phony green cards and living on the drug of optimism. Waiting around for the future while they ate mystery meat and pissed in hallways, conduct which did little to heighten the Watcher's reverence for foreign culture.

On the other side of the door, a male voice said, "You the guy I just spoke to on the phone?"

"I'm Mr. Angelo's driver," the Watcher said. "Are you Emilio from the restaurant?"

"You tell Mr. Angelo, next time I don't do no business from my crib."

"I'll make sure he gets the message. At the moment he's not interested in talking. He's downstairs entertaining two ladies in the backseat of his limousine."

"Damn. No wonder he can't come to the phone. Somebody ought to tell him he's too old to be doing two women at the same time."

"He'll sue if he gets hurt. Mind giving me the package so I can be on my way?"

Emilio Albert snorted. "What's the matter, you afraid of Spanish people?"

"Not really. They're afraid of me, actually."

True. Oh, so true.

"Why? You some kind of crazy driver or what?"

"That's me. A regular wild man behind the wheel."

The Watcher rubbed the back of his neck. He wasn't buying that "no-business-from-my-crib" crap. Drug dealers were greedy, and Emilio Albert was no exception.

The Watcher said, "Mr. Angelo appreciates your taking care of him on such short notice. He's authorized me to pay extra for your time and trouble."

"OK, but after tonight we don't do this no more."

"After tonight you won't see me again."

Count on it.

The Watcher heard an iron bar being lifted from the door. Locks were unsnapped. A command in Spanish from Emilio, and the pit bull stopped barking.

The Watcher exhaled. He touched his upper lip with the tip of his slim tongue. His green eyes were mean and unforgiving.

The door opened into a studio apartment with a low ceiling and worn carpeting. Videocassettes, compact discs, comic books, and clothes were scattered over the floor, chairs, and a sagging couch. A fragile-looking card table held drug paraphernalia—scales, glassine envelopes, cocaine, crack vials, and cash. There was no air-conditioning; fresh air came from a window facing the street.

A young Puerto Rican male stood in a tiny foyer, cradling a sawed-off shotgun. He had short legs, a turned-up nose, and wore his dark hair in a greasy samurai top knot. He was dressed in droopy khaki shorts, white espadrilles, and a T-shirt reading, WHEN IT ABSOLUTELY, POSITIVELY HAS TO BE DESTROYED OVERNIGHT: U.S. MARINES.

Emilio Albert had never served in the marines. Of this the Watcher was sure, having been a jarhead himself. He could, in fact, spot one even before the guy so much as opened his mouth. That's why he knew Emilio was nothing more than a marine wanna-be. A trash-talking loudmouth trying to impress the girls. He didn't look strong enough to lick a postage stamp, let alone survive twelve weeks of boot camp hell.

Emilio scares easily. So said Freddy Palacio.

Still, it behooved the Watcher to be careful. Emilio had a weapon *and* a pit bull. The animal stood at its master's heel, studying the Watcher. The dog appeared suspicious. No surprise. Suspicion was a guard dog's first defense.

Lowering the shotgun, Emilio motioned the Watcher inside and locked the door behind him.

Emilio was alone, his only company being a boom box playing the omnipresent and ubiquitous merengue so beloved by Latinos and absolutely loathed by the Watcher.

The Watcher aimed his chin at the pit bull. "Poochy makes me nervous. How about locking him in the bathroom till we finish?"

Emilio looked down at the dog. "You said Mr. Angelo authorize you to pay me extra. How much we talking about?"

"Twice the usual price for the coke." The Watcher held up a roll of bills. "Plus a hundred for disturbing you at home."

Eyeing the money, Emilio leaned over and scratched the pit bull's head.

"Make it two hundred," he said. "Yankee, that's my dog, he likes ice cream. Häagen-Dazs."

The Watcher played along. "You're taking advantage of Mr. Angelo."

"Yeah, well if he don't like it, let him go someplace else."

The Watcher shrugged. "Guess I don't have much choice."

"That's right, you don't."

"Two hundred it is."

"Cool." Emilio laid the shotgun on the card table. Then after a few words to the pit bull in Spanish, he led the way to the bathroom. The dog followed and was locked in.

The dealer turned, stopped dead, and threw his hands in the air.

The Watcher, now wearing black gloves, was pointing his Glock at Emilio's head.

"This isn't a robbery," the Watcher said. He inched backward until his legs brushed the card table.

Emilio said, "If you don't rob me, why you got the gun?"

"We're about to get to that." Using the Glock, the Watcher motioned Emilio closer. "On the floor. Face down."

Emilio followed orders.

The Watcher said, "Where's the policewoman? The one you've been supplying with drugs."

Emilio lifted his head from the floor. "I don't know no policewoman."

The Watcher turned up the sound on the boom box.

Then he placed the Glock on the card table, leaped in the air and came down on Emilio's spine with both feet.

The dealer screamed. In the bathroom Yankee barked wildly and head-butted the door.

"We can do it easy or hard," the Watcher said. "Your call."

A weeping Emilio said, "I swear on my mother, I don't know where the policewoman is. She moved, that's all I can tell you."

"Where to?"

"She didn't say. If I don't know, I can't give her up. That's what she tell me."

The Watcher nodded. "Sounds like Jenn. She was a good cop before she became a dope fiend. One of the best undercovers I ever knew. What did you two talk about, other than the price of pharmaceuticals?"

Emilio stared up at the Watcher. "You the cop who tried to kill her. The one she's scared of."

"Jenn Sanchez and I have some unfinished business. Let's leave it at that. Did she mention my name or identify me in any way?"

Emilio shook his head. "No. She just said you both were cops, that you had worked together and that one time you tried to kill her. She said her only chance was to let you think she was dead."

"She almost pulled that off. Almost."

Emilio let his head fall to the floor. "You going to kill me too."

It wasn't a question.

The Watcher leaned down and said, "I want you to repeat, word for word, your last conversation with Jenn Sanchez. *Word for word*. Don't leave out anything."

Snap. It was the sound of wood being split. The Watcher looked up to see Yankee push his head through the bathroom door.

The Watcher reached for the Glock without taking his eyes off Yankee. At the same time Emilio attempted to raise himself from the floor. He grabbed the card table and brought it down, spilling drugs, food and guns onto the carpet. The Watcher spun around, tripped over the upended table, and fell onto Emilio, who shoved him aside and crawled toward the window. Rolling onto his stomach, the Watcher grabbed for Emilio's shorts. He missed, caught the dealer's ankle and pulled, turning him on his back.

Kicking with his free leg, Emilio drove a heel into his attacker's forehead. Despite the pain, the Watcher refused to release his grip. Emilio shifted targets, repeatedly kicking the Watcher's hand and weakening his grip. A final kick and he was free. Scrambling to his feet, he ran for the window, the Watcher in pursuit.

Suddenly the Watcher stopped, alerted by the barking. His mind sent a warning and he turned to see Yankee squirming through a newly made hole in the door. Once free, the pit bull bared its teeth and ran straight for the Watcher.

6
You Forgot Something

The pit bull was ugly. Stocky and muscular, with a short, broad skull and black nose. Its dark, round eyes were set to stare straight ahead. The ears were small and pink, the front legs set far apart.

Yankee weighed less than fifty pounds. But like all pit bulls, he was the strongest of all dogs for his weight.

"Kill him!" Emilio yelled to the pit bull. "Bust him *up!*"

Emilio saw that his attacker was between him and the front door. Get past the attacker and there was still the problem of opening a steel-enforced door secured by an iron bar and four locks. Too much time involved.

The window. Now that was the quick way. Yankee could tear this cop's ass out of the frame while Emilio went through the window. He'd chill awhile in Puerto Rico or Santo Domingo, then return to the Apple and go back into the business of selling dreams.

He stepped through the window and onto a narrow ledge. Arms spread to either side, he faced his building.

Then he stared straight ahead and whispered, "Don't look down. Whatever you fucking do, Emilio, don't look down."

He crossed himself, took a deep breath, and began inching his way toward freedom.

The Watcher had to act quickly. Emilio had seen his face. He must not be allowed to escape.

But first, the pit bull.

The most direct way of dealing with the animal: Shoot it. Except there wasn't time to fumble around on the floor for a gun, be it the Watcher's Glock or Emilio's shotgun.

Snatching the attaché case from the floor, the Watcher crouched and extended his arms, keeping the case between him and the pit bull. The dog sank its teeth into the hard leather. Now it was a tug of war. The Watcher versus Yankee.

The Watcher was slim and muscular, in excellent physical shape. But he wasn't ready for a test of strength with a pit bull and probably never would be. Sooner or later, probably sooner, Yankee would win this tussle, and the Watcher would find himself in one king-size jackpot.

Improvise. Plucking a metal fork from a pizza carton, he jabbed the pit bull in its nose. The dog, dripping blood from its snout, backed off, stepping onto video-cassettes. It slipped on the plastic containers, losing balance momentarily. A break for the Watcher. In those few seconds he found the shotgun and gripping it by the barrel, he rained blows on the dog's head and back, swinging the weapon in a murderous fury, not thinking about any danger to himself. Only when the dog collapsed and lay still did the Watcher stop his attack.

One down. One to go.

Breathing heavily and still holding the shotgun, the Watcher walked to the window.

Well, now.

Emilio hadn't gotten far. He'd panicked. Or decided to backtrack. Either way he was still within reach.

Not that the Watcher had any intention of going after him. There was a new moon and the temperature was in the seventies. The ledge, however, was not meant for a stroll. Barely six inches wide, it was cracked in places and caked in pigeon shit.

And there were no fire escapes. Not on this side of the building.

The Watcher decided Emilio was being true to his nature. The man was rooted to the spot by fear.

At the sight of the Watcher, he whimpered and edged away.

"I ain't coming back in," he said.

The Watcher said, "Have it your way."

Shooting Emilio was out of the question since it meant leaving bullets in the corpse. Bullets to be traced by Forensics. On the other hand, the Watcher couldn't have this little twerp running free.

An earlier check of the building by the Watcher had revealed a fire escape on the eastern side of the building. It could be that desperation would push Emilio into going for it. The Watcher didn't intend to wait around for that to happen.

It was time for Plan B.

He returned to the room. The pit bull was still breathing, be it ever so slightly. He picked up the limp Yankee in his arms and returned to the window.

"You forgot something," he said to Emilio.

He tossed the dying pit bull at its master.

Emilio lifted a hand to ward off the dog. The dog struck him in the shoulder, knocking Emilio off-balance. His foot slipped from the ledge and he fell backward, and then man and dog were in midair, Emilio screaming, and in an instant he and the dog had disappeared.

The Watcher didn't wait to see the end. Returning to the room, he holstered his Glock, then picked up the attaché case. After satisfying himself he was leaving nothing behind, he slipped a couple of crack vials into a jacket pocket and left the apartment.

He drove from Queens to Manhattan, crossing over the Triboro Bridge, then driving down the FDR Drive. At East Ninety-sixth Street he turned right and drove across Central Park to the West Side. On Columbus Avenue he stopped for a red light, using the time to study his face in the rearview mirror. He saw a slight strain. Not enough to dull his spirits but enough to make him look fatigued.

A man surprised is a man half beaten. Tonight he'd been surprised. By a damn dog, no less.

The Watcher didn't use profanity but tonight was an exception. Damn dog, indeed.

Man's best friend had prevented him from locating a woman the Watcher thought he'd killed. A woman who, by some miracle, was still alive.

Had the Watcher not kept close tabs on Magellan, he'd never have learned about Jenn Sanchez, the policewoman who'd been there when he'd killed a man. He owed Magellan, so why not thank her.

This very night.

In his own way.

7

A Florida Tale

Attorney Lou Angelo was a big, balding Italian of sixty-two. His round, smily face projected honesty, friendliness, and uncertainty at the same time. His clothes were those of an old-time mob guy—expensive double-breasted suits, handmade white-on-white shirts, gold bracelet, and pinkie ring.

It was nearly midnight when he waved to Ross Magellan from a table at Club Típico in Manhattan's Washington Heights. Ross was on the dance floor with Connie Pavlides, an ex-cop she'd been seeing for a year. Pavlides was a forty-year-old Greek with dark eyes, prematurely gray hair, and a perceptive and intuitive mind. He'd been a Manhattan homicide detective until a gunshot wound forced him into early retirement. He was now a vice-president with the New York office of a national private security company.

Angelo sat at a ringside table with Mercy Howard, a young black woman he described as "my personal trainer." Not according to Freddy Palacio, who had described twenty-two-year-old Mercy as a professional escort, a hooker for hire. One of the agency's most popular girls, in fact.

Lou Angelo was besotted with her. But then Ross didn't need Freddy to tell her that. Tonight while Mercy whispered in his ear, Angelo rested a hand on her shapely thigh and hung on her every word. When she finished, he nodded in agreement.

Ross and Connie slow-danced near the bandstand, within sight of Lou Angelo but far enough away to avoid being overheard. They'd picked a spot in front of the *conguero,* the conga player. Ross played the conga to ease the stress that came with police work.

She also played the cowbell, the sexiest of all Latin percussion instruments, and she could fake it on the bongos. The conga, however, was her favorite. Her palms were callused from years of pounding the tall, single-headed drum.

A short-necked Cuban, carrying a silver trumpet, left the band to walk to the microphone. He didn't play. Instead he sang "The Shadow Of Your Smile" in Spanish. He sounded better than he looked.

Ross watched Lou Angelo and Mercy Howard touch champagne glasses, then link arms. The two seemed unaware of any age or cultural differences. Lou Angelo was white, a grandfather with three children. He was also a politically connected lawyer and forty years older than Mercy Howard, who was barely old enough to vote. She was, however, brown-skinned and busty, with dark silky hair and a little girl voice that seemed to bring out the protective instinct in men.

In the case of Lou Angelo, Miss Mercy brought out that and more. She had him starry-eyed and walking on air. She also had him spending extravagantly. Tonight she wore a silver cocktail dress, spiked heels, and a blue blazer with gold buttons, all paid for by Lou Angelo. He'd proudly announced the price of the blazer—two grand. He'd gotten a smile from Ross when he said to her, "Watch me, kiddo. I'll show you how to be old."

Ross visited Club Típico at least twice a month. The place was so tacky, it was hip. She loved everything about it, from the colored shirts and three inch heels, to the chrome, mirrors, and strobe lighting. The music—salsa, mambo, merengue—was strong and beautiful and never left her mind.

Management knew her as Ross Marino, a Cuban businesswoman who tipped extremely well, taking care of the manager, captain, and waiters. She also tipped the guys at the door for letting her double-park in front of the club and for watching her car. She dressed up the house by looking great and by being an expert dancer. The result was excellent service, including free champagne. Anytime Ross brought the bad guys here, they were impressed.

Mercy Howard had been dazzled, telling Ross, "Girl, you got it going on."

Tonight two bands played for a mix of Latinos, blacks, and a few adventurous whites. Security was tight, as always. Washington Heights, with a quarter of a million Dominican immigrants, had the city's highest crime rate. Club patrons passed through two metal detectors, underwent a body search, and were photographed by a video camera. As a convenience to law enforcement, management kept the tapes for six months.

Ross kissed Connie's neck and stroked the back of his head. Arms around each other, they danced in place. Her love for Connie provided the only rest in her life. It was something she spoke of to no one but him.

They danced well together. He knew how to lead and move his hips Latino style. He danced on the beat and wasn't afraid to try new steps, new rhythms. And like any good dancer she'd ever slept with, Connie was good in bed. How had the son of a Greek butcher from Astoria, who'd joined the Navy at seventeen and been so clumsy he'd *twice* fallen overboard at sea, managed to learn the difference between merengue and merengue *típico*?

He learned it on the firing line, as an undercover cop in New York City social clubs, dance halls, and after-hours joints. Boogying with perps until he could make an arrest. He'd been in a Red Hook bar the night he'd taken a bullet in the side, chasing down a trigger-happy Jamaican who'd killed a loan shark for calling up his pregnant wife and threatening her.

He said to Ross, "You're off the hook. No more looking over your shoulder. Tell me about this Dominican who'd been following you. The one who was set on fire after somebody broke his back. Wonder what his horoscope said that day?"

Ross said, "His name was Juan Rivas. Street name: John-John. Twenty years old and an illegal. Hit man with *Las Muñecas,* a Dominican crew specializing in ripping off drug dealers. Tough kids. Everyone meaner than a rattlesnake. Lieutenant Fargnoli says John-John had been hanging around my West Side apartment building. Except I never saw him."

"What's *muñeca* mean?"

"Doll. As in baby doll. All gang members are young—late teens, early twenties. The crew was started by a woman named Graciella Catala and her brother Ricky. Both Dominican, both nutcases. Graciella's now running things by herself. Ricky's away at college."

Connie said, "What did he do?"

"Raped an eight-year-old boy. He's doing twenty to forty upstate. I put him there."

Connie took a deep breath. "I didn't know that."

He went quiet.

Ross knew why. He wanted her to confide in him, and she couldn't bring herself to do it. Secrecy was her daily habit, and a habit was a hard thing to break.

Connie said, "Mind telling me why you popped Ricky?"

Ross looked into his eyes. "A Haitian woman who cleaned my apartment said her son had been raped by a Dominican who had her scared shitless."

"Mom was probably an illegal."

Ross nodded. "That's why she hadn't gone to the cops. She feared they'd kick her and the boy out of the country. We spoke woman to woman. Then I spoke to Immigration. Upshot was, she didn't get deported, and I nailed Ricky. That was two years ago."

Connie looked at the ceiling. "I'd say Ricky just had his final appeal turned down. He's run out of miracles. He knows he now has to do the full bit, and he's angry. So he has Big Sister send a shooter after you. Next question: Who iced John-John?"

Ross said, "Lieutenant Fargnoli thinks the killing was drug related. That's because the Dolls have cranked up the volume. They're now robbing *caletas*."

"That is not smart. In fact it is enormously and gigantically stupid."

Ross couldn't have agreed more. *Caletas* were suburban safe houses used by Colombians to stash drug money before moving it out of the country. The houses were watched over by Colombian families who lived like normal suburbanites. They mowed the lawn, walked the dog, and bought their kids Barney dolls for Christmas. What the Colombians didn't do is invite the neighbors in to see the cardboard boxes of cash stockpiled in every room.

When it came to protecting their money, Colombians went in for bloodbaths. They tortured and killed entire families, including dogs. There were cases on record where they even killed the chickens in an enemy's backyard. To mess with their money, as Graciella and the Dolls were doing, was the height of madness.

Ross said, "Graciella's better off forgetting payback and concentrating on staying alive. I can't worry about people coming after me. Every detective in the NYPD is working an average of two hundred cases. Missing cats, multiple murders—little stuff, big stuff. There'll always be people who don't like what we do. Like I said, I can't worry about it."

She and Connie had talked about this. About dealing with fear. Ross handled it in her own way. She pushed it as far back in her head as possible.

Tonight Fargnoli had insisted Ross's rented limousine, the one being charged to the FBI, be driven by a member of her backup team. Which is how she'd ended up with Glenn Ford, a thirty-five-year-old black detective with large hands and feet, and an unwavering belief that the best way to get close to a woman was through casual sex. He was out front in the car, presumably thinking of new and better ways to get laid.

Ross would have preferred someone else. Someone more low-key and soft-spoken. Like Detective Harry Earles, a quiet and knowledgeable professional. He'd passed on tonight's driving assignment; a sick wife had needed his attention.

Connie was watching out for Ross in his own way—as a cop *and* a lover. She appreciated his concern. But he'd been on the job; he should know undercover work called for caution. For counting the risks. You couldn't expect someone to keep your secrets if you couldn't keep them yourself.

He knew she was going after Judge Reiner. He knew she was playing Lou Angelo to get him. And that's all he knew.

"Reiner deserves to go down," he said. "It's no secret the man's dirty."

"How dirty?"

"Word is he got paid for giving up two informants to his Albanian friends. Both informants were later found dead. He's also supposed to have thrown out a videotape confession made by the Albanian godfather. As you know, toss the video and you toss the investigation. Search warrants, interviews, arrests based on the video—everything has to be thrown out. I've also heard he takes photographs from files so there's no hunt for wanted criminals."

Ross said, "What's with him and the Albanians?"

"He spent time in Albania. His father was a diplomat there. I also assume the Albanians are paying him pretty well."

"Jesus, why is this man still on the bench?"

Connie shook his head. "Haven't you learned by now that New York has the worst judges in the country? Not to mention the most arrogant. They ignore the state legislature, rewrite the Constitution and act as the law unto themselves. Do I really have to tell you why he's still on the bench?"

Ross put her arms around Connie's neck. He didn't have to tell her anything. She knew.

Look no further than the New York State Commission on Judicial Conduct, which was supposed to protect the public from bad judges. That wasn't happening. The commission, in fact, wasn't doing shit.

Eighty-five percent of complaints against New York judges, no matter how serious, were rejected without so much as a second glance. Of 1,400 judges with recent complaints against them, only six had been censured. Only one had been removed. Judge Reiner could dress up as a drag queen, parade in front of City Hall riding a broom, and the judicial commission wouldn't say a word. When it came to bad judges, New York State was deaf, dumb, and blind.

That's why Ross had to come up with ironclad evidence against Reiner. Joe Labriola wouldn't settle for less. Give him what he needed, and it would be full speed ahead. He'd be playing on his turf where the rules were in his favor. Federal court took precedence over state court. Sentences were longer, there was no parole, and most important of all, the state judicial conduct commission had no power here. In federal court, Reiner would be toast.

The Cuban with the small ears and short neck began singing Ivan Lins's "The Island," one of Ross's favorite songs. This time he didn't sound quite so romantic. Ross remembered reading that swans sang before they died. Some people were better off dying before they sang.

Connie held her closer. "I know a judge who's into teenage hookers. Anytime one shows up in his court, she's almost certain to walk. He doesn't screw her. He gets his jollies pouring wine on the kid's feet and sucking her toes. From that point on, she's innocent of all charges."

Ross said, "It works for me."

She glanced at Lou Angelo. The lawyer was yawning and looking at his watch. He'd danced until his legs had given out. He wasn't half bad. Ross had danced with him a few times, and he was passable, though he'd needed to be brought up to date on the new merengue.

When he wasn't shaking his booty, he'd found time to put away a good-size steak and wash it down with a nice amount of champagne. He'd talked a blue streak, mostly about himself, and he'd thrown in a dirty joke or two. Now it was time to go beddy-bye. Lou Angelo wasn't a kid anymore.

Taking Connie's hand, Ross led him from the dance floor. She'd learned about Lou Angelo's love life tonight. About the last three cases he'd won. About his plans to win a surrogate judgeship for Judge Reiner. She wanted to hear more before Angelo passed out or decided he was too tired to talk.

He'd mentioned Freddy Palacio but only in passing, bringing up the subject while Connie was dancing with Mercy Howard. He hadn't wanted to dwell on Freddy's problems. Freddy was an embarrassment to the escort service, which was paying Angelo to keep it out of trouble. If Angelo didn't want to talk about Freddy in front of Connie, that was just fine with Ross.

When Ross and Connie reached the table, Lou Angelo and Mercy Howard had their heads together, the two of them giggling like sorority girls at a slumber party. Grabbing Ross's hand, a red-faced Angelo pulled her onto the chair beside him.

"You gotta hear this," he said. "True story. Happened last week when I took Mercy and my wife to Florida. I'm buying a condo in Fort Lauderdale so we—"

"Whoa," Ross said. "Back up. You took your wife *and* Mercy to Florida at the same time?"

"Why not. I got no secrets from my wife. Anyway, we had two suites overlooking the ocean. My wife's in one, Mercy and me in the other. Well, right after the closing, we all go down to the beach to relax—me, the wife, Mercy, and the real estate lady. Her name's Lauren. We're sitting around and Lauren's telling us she's taking care of some old Jewish woman's fish tank while the woman's in New York for the summer. Lauren's husband, he didn't come with us. He's in the bar with some friends. Anyway, we're on the beach and Lauren sees an old high-school boyfriend. Guy she hasn't run into in years."

Lou Angelo laughed until he nearly choked. Ross slapped him on the back until he recovered.

Angelo said, "Right away the sparks go off between Lauren and this guy. I mean you could see it. Right, Mercy?"

Mercy squeaked, "Right."

Lou Angelo leaned forward. "Lauren invites this guy back with her to the old lady's apartment to help her feed the fish. They're leaving the elevator when the guy puts his hand under his T-shirt to scratch his stomach. Happens another old Jewish lady is passing by right at that moment, and she thinks this guy's got a gun and Lauren's being kidnapped. She tells the cops. Next thing you know, cops, SWAT teams, and the FBI are clearing the beach. You got guys in black crawling all over the place. Inside the building, they clear the floor where Lauren and this guy are. They get this old Jewish lady to point out the apartment and they listen outside. They hear moaning and groaning. Sounds like Lauren's being raped. Cops blow the door and they find Lauren sucking this guy's cock. Well, all they can do is leave. They go downstairs for a drink and they're hysterical, telling this story and laughing like lunatics. Meanwhile, who overhears them but Lauren's husband. He goes upstairs looking for her and her old boyfriend."

Lou Angelo started laughing uncontrollably. Connie was laughing too. So was Mercy Howard.

Not Ross. Her eyes never left Angelo's face.

"What happened?" she said.

"I hear Lauren got a divorce and left the country," Angelo said. "Depending on who you believe, she's in Hawaii or New Zealand. My back teeth are floating. Gotta see a man about a dog."

He stood up. "Be right back."

"Me too," Mercy said.

Ross reached for her purse. "I'll get the check."

Angelo reached for his wallet. "Sure I can't help you with that?"

Ross smiled. "The company's paying." She patted a brown envelope near Angelo's drink. "Just give me an answer on this stuff as soon as you can."

The envelope contained legal work for Gloria Paz's record company. Tonight it was part of Ross's cover. There was a copy of a standard recording contract, contracts with ASCAP, and a rough draft of a severance agreement with an executive the company wanted to drop. Every item in the envelope was legitimate.

Angelo patted Ross's hand. "I'll get back to you before the week is out. Promise." He brought her hand to his lips. "Thank you for tonight. You've made a happy man very old and I thank you from my bottom." He laughed, showing a tongue colored purple by strobe lighting.

With Angelo and Mercy gone, Ross and Connie sat listening to the band play a salsa version of *The Flintstones* theme song.

Finally Connie smiled. "His wife *and* his girlfriend. The guy's got balls."

"And money," Ross said. "Lots and lots of money."

"Any lawyer with a judge in his pocket is going to be loaded."

"That's not what I'm talking about. I'm talking about the money he's stealing."

"How do you figure that?"

Ross twirled the stem of a champagne glass in her fingers.

"He's just bought a Florida condo," she said. "He travels with his wife and a girlfriend who happens to have expensive tastes in clothes. On the subject of clothes, those Bugsy Siegel threads Mr. Angelo is so partial to are costing him as well. And last but by no means least, he's getting ready to set up his girlfriend in an apartment not too far from my place on the East Side."

"He never mentioned that."

"Someone else did."

Freddy Palacio.

Connie said, "So you think he's stealing to pay for the good life."

"I know he is," Ross said. "He wouldn't be the first lawyer to help himself to other people's money."

"Who's he stealing from?" Connie said.

"Reiner," Ross said. "Who else?"

She reached for Connie's hand. "If the judge gets wise, things could turn ugly. He contacts his Albanian friends and Lou Angelo's got a problem. Even the Mafia doesn't mess with the Albanians."

"Then you've got your nut on the guy. He deals with you or he gets hurt."

Ross said, that's about the size of it. She didn't mention that Angelo was protecting a policewoman who feared for her life and that if he helped nail the cop who was trying to kill her, he could deal himself out of having to give up Judge Reiner.

8
The Next Five Minutes

One A.M. The Watcher, carrying the damaged attaché case, used a stolen key to enter the lobby of a five-story brownstone at Seventy-fourth Street and Central Park West.

Despite a poorly lit lobby and no doorman, the building was in good condition. The elevator service wasn't much, consisting of a small car with an earsplitting bell. The Watcher considered taking it to the top floor. He'd had a long day and could use the rest.

He backed away from the lobby door and into the shadows. There was little chance he'd be seen at this hour. Both the street and lobby were empty. So why move? *Instinct.* It didn't always tell him what to do. But it did tell him what *not* to do. Tonight it told him not to be careless.

He popped three chunks of bubble gum into his mouth, dropping the wrappers into a jacket pocket. He decided against riding the elevator. Too risky. If it broke down he'd be trapped inside, forced to wait for tenants and elevator mechanics to come rushing to his rescue. The world would know he'd been in the building, thereby raising any number of questions. He could lose Magellan, along with fifty million dollars. He could also end up on death row and all because he'd chosen comfort over safety. To force the mind to obey you was the ideal of mental discipline. He took the stairs.

Fifth floor. The Watcher, chewing bubble gum, sat on the top step in the empty hallway and opened his attaché case. Gum chewing was a vulgar habit. Ugly and without a hint of grace. Thank God no one was here to witness this low point of his life.

He put on his surgical gloves. There were just two apartments on this floor. One belonged to an accountant and his wife now vacationing in Brazil. The other, a nice-size condominium, belonged to Ross Magellan.

Neither apartment was cheap. The neighborhood was one of young, affluent professionals—offering designer children's clothing, upscale bed linen, and skiing outfits computer-measured to your body. The Watcher found the neighborhood pompous and showy, filled with self-loving yuppies, all of whom were as proud as peacocks and too clever by half. Magellan's detective salary hadn't been enough to purchase the condo. She'd bought it with money inherited from her late father.

The Watcher opened Magellan's front door with copies of her keys. However, he didn't enter the apartment. Not immediately.

Instead he removed scissors and a roll of duct tape from the attaché case. He cut two pieces, each an inch square, from the roll. Then he pasted a square over each keyhole. Next he covered the squares with bubble gum, completely hiding the tape. Then he entered the apartment and locked the door from inside.

He stood in the foyer, letting his eyes grow accustomed to the darkness. He smelled the sweetness of Magellan's perfume and the freshness of potted plants. His eye went to a moonlit window overlooking Central Park, then to the window's reflection in a wall mirror. In front of the fireplace, a leather couch assumed a nearly human form. He remembered touching her clothing and bringing it to his face. He felt a warmth in his groin. In the darkness, his fantasies and fears possessed him, and he clenched his teeth until his jaws ached.

He took a flashlight from the attaché case, switched it on, then walked into the living room. He'd been in the apartment before. Magellan's condo was sparsely decorated, with an eye toward simplicity and comfort. Brick walls, parquet floors and ceiling fans indicated a personal taste minus any frivolity. One bedroom featured a Victorian brass bed and an antique wooden rocking horse, both of which cost a few bucks. Couches were covered with hand-painted silk and velvet pillows. Magellan's medals from the NYPD were displayed on a mantelpiece. She'd won meritorious-service awards, medals for excellent police work, and a number of commendations. Impressive. But then she was unique. How many cops received their gold shield at the age of twenty-two?

Her conga drums were clustered in the corner of a sunken living room, directly below a large skylight. Near the drums, on a small table, stood a silver-framed photograph of Magellan's sister Francesca. Francesca

Linda Dominica Moniz. Chessy for short. Seventeen and round-faced, with dark hair long enough to sit on. Chessy was in a mental hospital on Long Island where doctors were trying to help her get back on her feet after a hellish childhood. Chessy was Big Sister's big secret. To the Watcher she was Magellan's tragic flaw and most vulnerable point.

He brewed himself a cup of herbal tea, working in darkness by the glow of the flashlight. Following a pattern set in previous visits, he took only one teabag. One wouldn't be missed. Two might set off an alarm in the ever-alert mind of Detective Magellan.

He never touched her food. Never used her phone. Never used her bathroom.

He wore gloves and cleaned up after himself. When he finished his tea, he would rinse the cup and saucer, drying them with a pocket handkerchief. The handkerchief was also used to dry the sink.

The Watcher, flashlight on his lap, sat in front of a teakwood coffee table and waited for his tea to cool. His journal was in one hand, the crack vials in the other. The vials, light blue in color, were initiated *B.D. B.D.* for "Blue Death," one of the most popular brands on the street.

Your average citizen shied away from anything with the word *death* on the label. However, your average crack head ran toward the word with open arms. In the drug world there was no more effective marketing tool than the promise of extinction. The slightest hint that an illegal drug might be fatal made it seem more potent and therefore more attractive. You had no idea what stupidity was until you talked to a dope fiend.

The Watcher knew the distributor of Blue Death by

reputation. The man who supplied Emilio Albert with product. Had he and Mr. Albert discussed Jenn Sanchez? The Watcher would look into that soon enough.

He thought about the possibility of Magellan coming here tonight. He didn't expect her. She was with her lover, after all. The Watcher figured she'd finish up with Lou Angelo, then spend the night at the Greek's Brooklyn apartment. Magellan was taking Mr. Angelo dancing in one of those Latin clubs she liked so much. The Watcher loathed those dumps, seeing them as little more than cesspools where people publicly indulged their grossest habits.

There was always a possibility Magellan and the Greek might invite Angelo to the East Side apartment for a drink. It would allow Magellan to do a little styling, to play the successful executive and convince Lou Angelo she was good for a few bucks. The Greek, being devoted to Magellan, would play his part. As an ex-cop, he could be depended upon to make all the right moves. Figure him to be in on the masquerade. But only up to a point. Magellan wasn't the type to tell her lover everything.

She certainly wouldn't bring Mr. Angelo here. Not with her police awards sitting on the mantelpiece. She herself might show up, with or without the Greek. If so, the Watcher was prepared for that contingency.

He'd come here tonight on impulse. Strictly spur of the moment. The near disaster with Emilio Albert had left him wanting to be comforted by Magellan. Since that wasn't possible, he'd snuck into her apartment. Within these walls he was alone with the sum and substance of her life. In his mind, however, he was with her. He was a lover, *her* lover, with access to all she owned, no matter how private or personal. Yes, his love was a secret. But like Magellan, he'd learned there was pleasure in secrets.

The Watcher sipped his tea. It was time to thank Magellan.

He placed the journal on the table. The flashlight went beside it, beam trained on the open page. He wrote in red ink, in small neat letters on an unlined page. He used small margins and his writing was level, leaning neither left or right.

He thanked Magellan for leading him to Emilio Albert, thus putting him on the trail of Jenn Sanchez. Juan Rivas's murder was described in three words: *dictated by reason.* Prodded by the Watcher, Mr. Rivas had admitted being ordered to kill Magellan, the order coming from Graciella Catala. With these words, Mr. Rivas became perishable goods.

Would Graciella Catala send another shooter after Magellan? Probably. After all, Ricky had been the focus of her life, the be-all and end-all of her existence. By sending him away on a sex rap, Magellan had not endeared herself to the unforgiving Graciella. Was the rumor true? Had Graciella and Ricky been having an incestuous affair? If so, Graciella wasn't just pining for her brother but for her one and only beloved.

The Watcher thought about another "beloved," one Mr. Connie Pavlides. Mr. Pavlides didn't know it, but he was a living dead man.

The Watcher stopped writing and leaned back, disappearing into the darkness. Then he leaned forward, his face hard. He wrote, *Set me as a seal upon thine heart, as a seal upon thine arm: for love is strong as death; jealousy* is *cruel as the grave; the coals thereof* are *coals of fire,* which hath *a most vehement flame.* He wrote the verse several times, filling the page, and he had started on another page, obsessed with these words from the Song of Solomon, when he heard the elevator ring.

He picked up the flashlight, walked to the front door and looked through the peephole. He could see the entire hallway. He heard the elevator rattling on its cable. Instinct told him it was headed for this floor.

Well, now.

The elevator stopped at the end of the hall and out stepped Magellan stifling a yawn. She carried a single yellow orchid, her favorite flower. She looked tired. But as always she looked beautiful. So beautiful that he wanted to take her into his arms and tell her she was in his care, that he and he alone was responsible for her well-being. Instead, he whispered the words, his lips barely moving.

He pressed his eye closer to the keyhole. Magellan was quick. Tricky and full of ruses. It was the only way to survive in undercover work. The Watcher, however, found her predictable. To tell her this would shatter her confidence. However, facts were facts.

He switched off the flashlight. There was only one way in or out, through the front door. And the building had no fire escape.

He smiled. The next five minutes were going to be interesting.

9
Gaslight

Ross Magellan stood in front of her apartment and reached in her purse for a gun.

The locks had been jammed with bubble gum. It was a burglar's trick, designed to keep home owners from walking in on a robbery.

She checked out the staircase, looking up and down. It appeared to be empty. But she couldn't see the door leading to the roof. To know whether or not it was open, she'd have to walk up one flight. Which could mean walking into an ambush.

She looked into her bag. Her mouth went dry and there was a sudden tightness in her chest. *She was unarmed.*

In her excitement she'd forgotten she wasn't carrying a gun. Her guns—a Glock and a .380—were at the East Side apartment, locked in a floor safe in the bedroom closet.

She rarely carried a gun undercover. Perps were too paranoid. Too suspicious. In their eyes, a stranger with a gun was "Five-O," a cop. To build up trust, an undercover had to go unarmed around psychos who, if they suspected betrayal, would kill you in a nanosecond.

There were exceptions. Ross carried a gun whenever she bought drugs undercover in the South Bronx and East New York. These were high-risk areas where a female addict, her cover, faced the near certainty of rape or being ripped off.

She'd bought from small-time dealers out to become big-time, and she'd managed to stay alive in the process. She'd been good enough to move onto bigger cases, like nailing cop killers, serial rapists, Russian art thieves, and wiseguys who dumped medical waste on public beaches. She still worked without a gun. And, as in the small cases, if she was caught, she was history. Dead and gone.

Her gaze was glued to her apartment door. How had the intruder gotten past locks that were supposedly impregnable? They'd been installed by one of Connie's people, an Israeli intelligence agent turned locksmith. All of the city's top locksmiths were Israelis, many of whom had learned the business while fighting terrorists. Connie's guy had recommended Ross install a metal door with a dead bolt and a multilock.

Both locks were covered with steel plates to prevent them from being pried from the door with a screwdriver and pliers. The Israeli had warned Ross not to lose her keys. He'd need two hours to open one lock and that was with using the best equipment in the world.

Did someone have a copy of Ross's keys? She dismissed the idea as too scary to even think about.

She took her hand from her purse and drew her

shawl around her shoulders. She was shivering. The intruder had heard the elevator stop at this floor. He had to be eyeing her through the peephole. And he knew she was alone. Son of a bitch.

Ross looked at the elevator. It was still on this floor, but if someone buzzed from the lobby, she'd be in trouble. The elevator would be on the move and without it, she'd have to use the stairs. Another trap. The academy had taught her to avoid bad positioning. Starting with not letting herself be caught in doorways and on stairways.

She ran for the elevator. *Made it.* In the car she closed the door behind her and pushed the lobby button. She then looked through the door's glass panel at her apartment. She saw her front door open slightly then close quickly, as if the intruder had stepped back to avoid being seen.

Inside the elevator the second door slid shut, cutting off Ross's view. As the car began its descent, she took out her cell phone and dialed her local precinct. Her call was answered by a Sergeant Nelson Pedroza. Ross identified herself as a police officer and reported a robbery in progress at her apartment. She gave her address, unit, and badge number.

The elevator reached the lobby just as Pedroza said a car was on the way and for Ross to do nothing until the officers arrived.

The inner door slid open and Ross froze. Had the intruder raced downstairs to wait for her in the lobby? She had to take her chances. Anything was better than being trapped in an elevator without a weapon.

She stepped into the lobby and ran from the building.

She was alone on a deserted street of brownstones and expensive high-rises. Directly across from her was a music school for children, its doorway as dark as the mouth of a tunnel. It was a place to hide until the police came. From there she could also see anyone leaving her building. Gripping her shawl tightly, she crossed the street and stepped into the darkened doorway.

The sound of breaking glass made her flinch. The noise came from the end of the street, in front of a high-rise facing Central Park. *Ross wasn't alone.* Leaning forward, she peered out of the darkness to see a black homeless male in a shower cap and army blanket, rummaging through garbage cans. All swag went into a shopping cart. He was too busy to notice Ross.

Leaning against the school's gated door, she stared up at her apartment. The windows were jet black. She saw nothing to indicate she'd had a break-in. But she had seen her front door open. *Or had she?*

Ross stepped from the doorway, into the glare of a streetlight, and looked at her watch. It was 1:45 A.M. She returned to the protection of the darkness. She wanted a cigarette, and God knows she wanted a gun.

Tomorrow she was visiting Chessy at the hospital. That's why she hadn't gone home with Connie tonight or invited him here. The plan was to hit the road early and come back before evening rush hour. To see Chessy, Ross was taking an "E-Day," an emergency day. The department gave each cop five E-Days a year for personal affairs. The time was yours to use as you saw fit, no explanations necessary. Ross had spent her last E-Day with Connie in Atlantic City where they'd won seven hundred dollars at blackjack, then blown it on dinner and champagne at Dock's Oyster House, the oldest restaurant in town.

She stamped her feet, more out of frustration than to keep warm. Where in hell were the cops? And what was she supposed to do if some mope walked from the building, carrying her stuff? She was mulling that one over when a patrol car, red and white roof lights flashing, turned the corner. No siren. Smart.

She ran into the street, waving her arms. As the car slowed down, she pointed to her apartment building. The car stopped in front of Ross, and two uniforms got out.

One was a square-faced black man with dimples. His name tag read DYEHOUSE, and he was in charge. His partner was McAvoy, a white female with large thighs and a thin upper lip. Both carried long, black flashlights. Ross told them she was working undercover and that her badge and ID were in her apartment. She said no one had entered or left the building since she'd come outside.

Dyehouse said, "Elevators make too much noise. We walk. Where's your apartment?"

"Fifth floor," Ross said.

McAvoy, the white woman, stared up at the building. "Shit, that's the top floor."

Dyehouse grinned. "You got that right. Let's get going."

McAvoy unbuttoned her holster. But not before giving Ross a dirty look.

Ross opened the lobby door and let the uniforms enter first. Inside she pointed at the staircase.

Fifth floor. "Detective Magellan, would you come here please."

Dyehouse stood in front of Ross's apartment, his flashlight trained on the door. McAvoy stood to one side, arms folded across her chest. Eyes closed, she shook her head. Ross felt the vibes; McAvoy didn't like her. No surprise. Cops were as prone to backbiting as anybody else. And with back biting came brownnosing. *How do you get twenty cops in a squad car? Promote one and watch the other nineteen crawl up his ass.*

Ross and McAvoy hadn't yet reached the brownnose stage. Whether it was about Ross being prettier or having made detective while McAvoy was still in uniform, the woman had no use for her. In the hallway she stood her ground, forcing Ross to squeeze past her.

Dyehouse said to Ross, "Look at the locks, and tell me what you see."

What Ross saw made her want to scream. The bubble gum was gone. Not a trace of it remained. Both locks appeared to have been untouched. Ross felt a slight dizziness.

Dyehouse switched off his flashlight and took a deep breath.

"Mind telling us again what you saw when you arrived here tonight?"

Ross touched the locks with her fingers. "I saw locks covered with bubble gum. I couldn't use my keys."

McAvoy examined her flashlight. "You look as if you've been partying, *Detective*. You didn't happen to have a few drinks, by any chance?"

Dyehouse looked at his partner and shook his head ever so slightly.

He said, "Let's go inside."

Ross unlocked the door, entered the foyer, and

turned on the light. Dyehouse and McAvoy each rested a hand on their holsters. Dyehouse pointed to McAvoy, who nodded and hung back, remaining just inside the door. The black cop followed Ross into the apartment.

He said to Ross, "Check to see if anything's missing."

Ross checked every room. Nothing was missing. Nor was there any sign that an intruder had entered the apartment.

Hands over her eyes, Ross sat in front of the teakwood coffee table. It was back. That nasty-ass feeling. The one she got when she realized she was being watched by someone so good that even she couldn't pick him up. For a few hours, right after Juan Rivas's murder, the feeling had disappeared, and Ross felt good. Now it had returned with a vengeance.

The invisible man, the one who'd entered Ross's life with the Reiner case, was still around. He'd been here tonight.

McAvoy said to Ross, "You look dressed for a night on the town. How much did you have to drink?"

Ross said, "I was working." She pulled a drawer from the coffee table.

McAvoy said, "Is that what you call it? Maybe somebody's gaslighting you. Messing with your mind like they did with Ingrid Bergman. But that was just a movie. Meanwhile, I'm still trying to figure out what *this* is all about. By the way, we still haven't seen any ID."

Dyehouse looked at his partner. "Chill. She's on the job. Check out that stuff on the mantel."

McAvoy shrugged her shoulders. "Just doing my job. The lady here could have stolen a key from the rightful owner. Maybe she's gaslighting us. I mean, it could happen."

Ross took her ID and shield from the coffee table drawer, then handed them to Dyehouse.

Dyehouse read the ID, then looked at the awards on the mantelpiece. "Grade two and working Organized Crime. Definitely makes you a star." There was a respect and a deference in his voice. "Pleased to meet you, Detective."

McAvoy examined the ID in silence, then handed it back to Ross without looking at her. The air seemed to go out of her. When a woman as young as Ross made second grade, it meant she was very good or she had a "hook," a powerful patron guiding her career. Either way, she had more juice than any uniform. One phone call from her and McAvoy could spend the next twenty years guarding a Black Muslim mosque in Harlem.

Ross said to Dyehouse, "Check the roof. Look for signs of anyone having entered or left the building."

The black cop nodded at his partner, who exited the apartment. Ross looked around the room. Nothing was out of place. But someone had been here.

McAvoy returned in minutes, shaking her head. She said that the roof door was locked from the inside. And it didn't appear to have been forced or tampered with.

Dyehouse said to Ross, "We have to report this, Detective."

She nodded. In their place she'd have done the same. No matter what kind of spin she tried to put on it, she was going to look like an hysterical woman who'd filed a false report of a crime. Was the invisible man out to make Ross look like a goddam headcase?

Dyehouse spoke into his radio, checking in with the precinct. Minutes later he and McAvoy took the elevator to the lobby, leaving Ross alone. She walked to the window overlooking the street. There were now three squad cars in front of the building. Three times the embarrassment. Three carloads of cops who wouldn't believe she was telling the truth.

Ross watched the blue-and-whites drive off, followed by a taxi flashing an OFF DUTY sign. Then the street was deserted. Talk about feeling like a complete and total asshole.

Too pumped to sleep, she went to the kitchen. A cup of herbal tea might soothe her nerves. Unless she got some Zs she wouldn't make it through tomorrow.

She was wondering how to explain the break-in to Fargnoli when her hand touched the kettle.

She leaped back from the stove. The kettle was warm.

10
In Secrecy and in Silence

He stood in the bedroom doorway and watched the nurse attach iron braces to his wife's withered legs.

Braces secured, the nurse tied the woman's orthopedic shoes. The nurse, a young black woman named Grenada Bratt, was warm, kind, and deeply caring. She was costing the Watcher a small fortune and worth every penny.

He rubbed the knife scar on the back of his neck. This morning he wore a terry cloth robe, pajamas, and open-toed sandals—anniversary gifts from his wife. He stifled a yawn. He rarely slept more than five hours a night. Sleep was a death, and death an unknown. Something he couldn't control. For that reason the Watcher spent as little time in bed as possible.

Raising a forefinger, he caught his wife's attention, then pointed to the small Christmas tree at the foot of her bed. The tree, white and artificial, was decorated with strings of blue lights. His wife smiled, then mouthed the words, *Thank you.*

The Watcher kept a tree all year round. Helene, his wife, liked it.

When he'd arrived home this morning from Magellan's apartment, he hadn't gone straight to bed. Instead, he changed the tree lights so that Helene could wake up to something new. She hadn't heard him moving about her room. She'd been in a deep sleep brought on by painkillers. Nevertheless he was careful not to awaken her.

He worked in his stocking feet, removing colored lights, ornaments, and tinsel from the tree. Then he put on two strings of blue lights and a single ornament at the top, a jolly Santa rocking back and forth in his sleigh. Helene had few periods of happiness. Looking at the tree was one of them.

They lived in a two-story red-brick house in Long Island City, in a dark area of railroad yards, factories, and public-housing projects. To spare his wife the strain of being carried up and down stairs, the Watcher had turned their living room into her bedroom. This allowed Helene wheelchair access to the dining room, kitchen, and backyard. She could also lie in bed and wave to her neighbors through the front window.

Her greatest pleasure was bridge-watching. The house was at the foot of the Queensboro Bridge, which connected Queens to Manhattan. At night Helene would spend hours propped up in bed, staring at the well-lit bridge and listening to Bach.

The Watcher walked to his wife's bedside and looked at her breakfast tray. She'd hardly touched her food. He'd prepared it himself, as he did every morning. Fresh orange juice, cream of wheat, and a sliced banana sprinkled with cinnamon. A three-minute egg, whole-wheat toast, tea, vitamins, and a yellow rose now in Helene's blue-veined hands.

The Watcher rubbed his neck scar. It was starting to tighten, a sign that rain was on the way. He wasn't happy with Helene's lack of appetite. It meant she was drinking again. Doctors had forbidden any liquor, citing possible liver damage and the danger that came from mixing alcohol with medication.

Helene, however, was headstrong. She was also intelligent and resourceful. Her drink of choice was vodka. Smuggling it past the Watcher and Grenada allowed her to be insolent and successful, rare victories for a cripple. The vodka would now have to be found and thrown out. The game was afoot.

Helene was in her early forties, with large eyes, sloping shoulders and a thick waistline. She was paralyzed from the waist down. She'd worked as a bookkeeper for the New York Public Library until ten years ago, when a speeding fire truck hit her car, severing Helene's spinal cord and killing their unborn child.

While doctors fought to save Helene's life, the Watcher fought for compensation, filing a multimillion dollar lawsuit against the city. He was certain he had a case. A dozen witnesses said that the fire truck had sped through a red light. What's more, the driver admitted losing control of the truck just before the crash. The Watcher should have won his suit hands down. Instead, he lost.

The suit was dismissed without coming to trial. Helene received a paltry ten thousand dollars from the city and was told the matter was closed. She had a history of drunken driving and traffic accidents, and it had come back to haunt her. Those cases had never gone to court. The Watcher had seen to that. But when she'd needed to go to court, he had been powerless.

Her insurance had covered some medical costs. But not all. Home nursing care, for example, came out of the Watcher's pocket. He borrowed from the union, dipped into his pension, and cashed in his insurance. When that money ran out, he found ways of getting more.

He did it without philosophical pretensions or ethical rationalization. At the moment, he had a hundred thousand dollars in cash hidden in the basement.

Basically he was cold and cared very little about people's feelings. Helene and Magellan were exceptions. His affections were always deep and lasting. Drinking aside, Helene had been a good wife. Understandably she had days of self-pity and depression. A fierce pride alternated with a sense of helplessness. But there were times when she was cheerful and easily pleased, when she was as lovable as ever.

His passion for Magellan was all-consuming. However, Helene still had a place in his life. A very important place. He wasn't about to throw her to the wolves. When he left the city with Magellan and fifty million dollars, Helene would be coming with them.

The Watcher knew what it was like to be betrayed. He'd worked with women cops who'd held a knife behind their backs, waiting for the opportunity to stab him. He'd trusted these women. Given them everything while they smiled and played him for a fool. A clean glove often hid a dirty hand. The Watcher wasn't going to do that to Helene. Not when she needed him most.

He said to her, "You've hardly touched your food."

She retreated into her little-girl voice. The one she used whenever she tried to get over on him.

"Medication can be an appetite depressant," she said. "Didn't you know that? You're working late again. Something big?"

"Could be. We'll see how it pans out."

"Sounds promising. Maybe you'll catch a break on this one. Get the credit you deserve for once. It's beyond me why the department doesn't see how good you are. When do Grenada and I get to hear about it?"

Grenada stopped combing Helene's hair. "Now you know he can't tell us nothing while the investigation is going on. That's not how the police work. You're right about one thing, though. If it was up to me, your husband would be police chief by tomorrow morning."

The Watcher grinned. A bit far-fetched on Grenada's part but she meant well. She was a slim black woman in her late twenties, with high cheek bones and a wide mouth. She was soft-spoken and sensitive, with a need to be needed. Her record as a nurse was impeccable, especially among rich white women in need of home care. She had a love for vulnerable human beings and treated Helene with loving care. Despite the expense the Watcher considered himself lucky to have found her.

He finished the last of a handful of raw cashews. It was time to entertain Helene.

He cleared a space on the night table, pushing aside Helene's reading glasses and a plastic bottle of mineral water. Then he took a rolled piece of blue paper from a pocket of his robe and spread it on the table. As the women watched, he slowly and methodically folded the six-by-ten-inch piece of paper into the shape of a frog. His thoughts were of Magellan.

A difficult art, origami. One had to fold objects out

of paper without cutting, pasting, or decorating. Complex to the point of madness. But it was that very complexity that held the Watcher's interest.

Finished, he placed the paper frog on a pillow beside Helene, then gently tapped its back. The frog hopped. Helene's eyes lit up, and she clapped her hands. The hopping frog was one of her favorites, along with the bird which flapped its wings when its tail was pulled.

The Watcher caught Grenada's eye and jerked his head toward the kitchen. He left the bedroom. Grenada followed.

In the kitchen she spoke first. "I know what you're going to say. Your wife got hold of some vodka. I found it and dumped it in the garbage. Somebody who thinks he's smart; he put it in a shampoo bottle. That's how it got in the house. She decoyed me. Delivery come and she sends me off somewhere for another pillow. I come down and the shampoo's hid. Took me two hours to find it."

The Watcher patted Grenada's shoulder, then looked through a kitchen window at his backyard.

He said, "She probably worked out something with one of the delivery boys from the supermarket. Slipped him a few bucks and he brought in the booze."

Grenada nodded her head in a manner that signified she intended to take measures.

"You leave him to me," she said. "I know the Haitian who made that last delivery. When I get through with him, he's going to wish he'd rowed his boat to some other country."

The Watcher smiled. "I'll leave it to you."

"She's your wife, but she's my patient. I'm proud of

what I do, and I don't feature no immigrant coming in here and messing up my work. I'm on that Haitian. The boy don't know it, but Grenada is definitely on him. Me and him are due to have a little talk. When we finish, I guarantee he won't be delivering nothing round here 'cept what's good to eat. I can't thank you enough for what you did for Levell. Like I said, you leave that Haitian to me."

Levell Bratt was Grenada's husband, a twenty-seven-year-old high-school dropout who'd fed his dope habit with a series of push-in robberies in the Bronx. He'd terrorized a Morrisania housing project, attacking old people as they entered their apartments. One victim, a ninety-two-year-old concentration-camp survivor, had died of a heart attack. Levell ended up doing hard time for involuntary manslaughter.

The Watcher's background check on Grenada revealed she'd loved Levell since they were teenagers. They had two children, an eight- and a nine-year-old, both girls. Levell's moral defects aside, Grenada remained faithful to him at all times, whether from true love or a lack of imagination, who could say. One thing was certain: Her efforts to win Levell an early parole had failed miserably.

To be paroled, Levell needed a job. Unfortunately most businessmen were reluctant to hire ex-cons. Enter the Watcher. He'd had no choice. Helene had become dependent upon Grenada, and as long as Grenada was worried about Levell, her nursing would suffer.

The Watcher contacted the parole board and promised Levell a job as a cab driver. Levell had now been hacking in Manhattan for three months, joining Pakistanis, Bengalis, and Sikhs in running red lights and cutting each other off for fares. He no longer did coke and was back with Grenada. For the moment everyone was living in the best of all possible worlds.

The Watcher said, "Any idea how we can get Helene to eat?"

Grenada filled the kettle with fresh water and put it on the stove.

"She loves soap operas," the nurse said. "Can't get enough of *All My Children* and *General Hospital*. What I do is, I wait till she gets real caught up in the plot. Then I feed her while she's looking at the TV and she just eats."

The Watcher nodded in approval. Grenada was a pearl beyond price.

She returned to Helene, leaving the Watcher alone in the kitchen. He sipped herbal tea and eyed the birds pecking at his cherry tree. He had no use for the fruit and couldn't be bothered to pick it. When Helene had had her legs she'd climb the tree, collect cherries, and make a halfway decent wine. But all that was in the past.

He watched two crows fighting over a branch, wondering why one or the other didn't simply move to another branch. Obviously each felt he was in the right. They were fighting toe-to-toe, neither giving an inch, sending leaves flying in all directions, and scattering the birds around them. The Watcher thought, *There you have it. Anger brings out power.*

He went upstairs to his room, locked the door, and began writing in his journal.

Magellan/June 9
There are times when your lack of gratitude brings out an anger in me. With that anger

comes a destructive power, one I never hope to use against you. You are alive because of my protection. Therefore I have the right and the responsibility to direct your life along lines I think best. Your attitude toward me now is one of indifference. But given time I know you will love me. For our love to exist, I must isolate you from the world. Take you from this city and from everyone you know.

In the past forty-eight hours I have twice killed for you. Emilio Albert is dead because he could have led police to me. My imprisonment would then have removed your only protection, leaving you to your enemies. As for Juan Rivas, he was your enemy. That was reason enough to kill him. Unfortunately the people who sent him after you are still alive, and you are in as great a danger as ever. Perhaps one day, I will ask the same of you, that you kill for me. It would demonstrate your commitment to me, a fidelity I deserve without question.

I am not a violent man by nature. I am forced into defensive actions. Under pressure from others, I act as I would not act. I kill to protect myself and more important, to protect you.

We will live or die together. I watch you in secrecy and in silence.

The mental hospital known as Oakes Institute was located in the rolling hills and secluded estates of Long Island's North Shore, sometimes called the "Gold Coast" because of its mansions and millionaires. Ross Magellan, driving a blue Audi, pulled into a parking lot at 10:30 in the morning. She wore a gray sweatshirt, dark glasses, and black jeans tucked into riding boots. The 380., tucked in the small of her back, was hidden under her sweatshirt.

The .380 was her "funny gun," cop name for a backup piece. She used it when working undercover, when she had to look like a perp. She'd bought a new gun, then done a number on it. Thrown the piece against a brick wall. Dragged it on the sidewalk. Left it out in the rain until the gun looked like something carried by a sorry-ass crack head. After cleaning and oiling the inside, she'd gone to the range for some test firing. *No problema.* The .380 worked just fine. It was ugly as hell, but functional. The perfect undercover gun.

Ross left the Audi, and, avoiding a pair of revolving sprinklers, walked across a well-cut lawn. The Oakes Institute was a three-story redbrick building with an ivy-covered front, white columns, and French doors. The name disguised its true function. Oakes Institute was a hospital for wealthy mental patients. One without barred windows or razor-wire fences. It did have pine groves, trimmed hedges, and tennis courts, making the Oakes Institute again resemble the estate of the original owner, a nineteenth-century millionaire who'd livened up Easter-egg hunts by slipping thousand-dollar bills into the eggs.

Ross reached behind her back and felt her gun. She didn't wear a holster; rubber bands around the grip kept the gun in place. The solid heft of the .380 was comforting. Last night's break-in at her apartment had left her jumpy as hell. *The intruder had let himself into her apartment with keys.* He could have caught her sleeping and defenseless. Just thinking about it gave Ross the shakes.

When you joined the NYPD, you became a cop twenty-four/seven. All day, every day. On or off duty, you had to carry your gun.

At the moment Ross was only too happy to follow the rules.

She entered a spacious lobby with a gleaming wooden floor, leather couches, and murals of sailboats cruising Long Island Sound. A gray-haired black woman with small ears stood behind a buffet table, dispensing coffee, tea, and finger sandwiches. Several patients played cards while others watched a television talk show hosted by two women sitting on high stools. Male and female staffers, wearing starched whites and plastic name tags, hovered over patients, speaking softly and smiling like proud parents. The score from *The Phantom of the Opera,* the only Broadway show Ross had seen in years, was being piped in through invisible speakers.

She stepped up to the front desk and was greeted by a short man in his mid-forties with a thick lower lip. He wore a corduroy suit with matching vest and an orange-red tie. A name tag said BRUNO SLOMA. His watch was beeping. He silenced it, popped a pill in his mouth, then took a sip of water. Ross had seen him on previous visits to the institute, but the two had never spoken.

He gave Ross the same wide-mouthed smile he gave the clients.

"Good morning and welcome to Oakes. I'm Mr. Sloma. How may I help you?"

Even with the smile, his face was rigid and controlled. Mr. Sloma had trained himself never to give anything away. Ross wasn't surprised. He was working in a mental hospital that didn't want to be known as a mental hospital.

Ross said, "I'm Detective Magellan. I'm here to see my sister, Francesca Moniz."

"Yes, I know who you are, Detective. You've been here before. One moment please."

Sloma picked up the receiver on a house phone, punched in a number, and announced Ross's presence. He listened a few seconds, then hung up.

"Doctor DeCarlo is on his way," he said. "Miss Moniz will join you shortly. Some friends are braiding her hair. Seems she's having it done especially for your visit."

"My God, is she really? I can't wait to see it."

Bruno Sloma gave Ross his frozen smile. "I'm sure she'll be uncommonly pretty. A star of the first order. Just have a seat and I'll direct Doctor DeCarlo to you."

Ross found a leather chair beneath a wall aquarium. Doctor DeCarlo ran the Oakes Institute, and it was costing Ross plenty to have him treat Chessy personally. Ross had money but it was disappearing fast. Their parents had left her and Chessy nearly $900,000. Chessy's hospital expenses and legal fees had taken $500,000, money well spent since it had kept Chessy from going to prison. Ross's condo had taken another $250,000. The rest was earmarked for Chessy's continuing treatment. When that ran out, there were going to be problems.

Ross looked up at the aquarium. The brightly colored tropical fish were keeping their distance from a miniature octopus half hidden by its own inky cloud. Ross also wanted some space. Some distance between her and the zoned-out patients with their ever-watchful attendants. Both gave her the creeps.

The patients at Oakes Institute—the hospital called them clients—were supposedly nonviolent and therefore no threat to the community. Ross, however, was guarded and watchful. But then she was distrustful of just about everybody. Being a cop did that to you. You began by being suspicious of bullshit artists and ended by looking for something bogus even in good people.

This morning she had stopped off at Connie's office and left her apartment keys. The sooner new locks were installed, the better. And since cops really didn't have off-days, she checked Connie's copy of the green sheet. This was the list sent to precincts each morning, detailing all crimes committed in the city during the previous twenty-four hours.

That's how Ross learned Emilio Albert had jumped from his eighth-floor apartment, accompanied by his favorite pit bull. Talk about weird. Since when did people kill themselves and take a house pet or anything else along for the ride? True, the Egyptian pharaohs did it. And then there were those California wackos who'd packed suitcases, stuck a roll of quarters in their pockets, then suffocated themselves with plastic bags. Police were calling Emilio's death a suicide. Ross wondered what Freddy Palacio would call it.

"Detective Magellan? Good to see you again."

Doctor Rolland DeCarlo extended his hand. He was sixtyish and thin, with a round protruding chin and full head of white hair. He wore tweeds, a silk bow tie, and tortoise-shell bifocals perched on the end of his nose. He conveyed sincerity, kindness, and compassion, qualities which hid a ruthless business sense. The Oakes Institute had been founded by DeCarlo and several partners, but it was DeCarlo who called the shots. Ross admired him for being direct and not wasting her time with unessentials.

She rose and shook his hand. "Good to see you, Doctor."

"Detective. How goes the world of crime?"

"They're keeping us busy."

"The usual outing for you and Chessy?"

Ross nodded. "Lunch in town. Some shopping. And if we have time, we may go riding."

"I understand Chessy likes pizza."

"That's an understatement."

"We serve it here sometimes. Nothing to write home

about. When you visit our thriving little town of Old Whaler, try Manello's. It's new. Right across from the bank. Since we have only one bank, it shouldn't be too hard to find. Everything's cooked in a wood-burning oven. I recommend the seafood pizza. Comes with a thin crust."

"Works for me. How's Chessy doing?"

He looked over his shoulder to make sure they were alone.

"Fine," DeCarlo said. "Or maybe I should say she's coming along. She's still quite fragile. At the moment her resilience is more on the order of an eggshell as opposed to something firmer. She still suffers from disordered thinking, hallucinations, and a withdrawal from reality, all common to people with schizophrenia."

Hesitating, he tugged on his earlobe. Finally he said, "She also remains subject to catatonic behavior."

Ross looked down at the floor. "First time I saw it, I didn't know what to do. One minute Chessy's hysterical. Out of control. Waving her arms and shouting. Next minute she's a statue. Frozen still. Not talking, not moving. I thought she'd had a stroke."

DeCarlo nodded. "The catatonic state can be disturbing, especially to the layman seeing it for the first time. The patient goes into a statuesque position. A complete absence of any and all voluntary actions. All of this in conjunction with what we call 'mutism,' the inability to talk. Total inactivity. Unfortunately, Chessy still remains subject to this affliction. The good news is, it doesn't happen as often. When it does occur, it brings on flashes of paranoid schizophrenia. Delusions of persecution accompanied by hallucinations."

Ross inhaled. "Doctor, in this case I don't think the word *delusion* applies. My sister was regularly and systematically abused by our father. He also tried to kill her. He put Chessy here. No, I wouldn't say she has hallucinations. She's been through hell, and it comes back to haunt her. I'm not a doctor but I think these hallucinations, as you call them, are very real."

"You have a point. All the more reason to be careful around her. Don't discuss your work and don't become angry with her. Above all, don't bring any violence into her life. She must never see your gun. I assume you're armed."

Ross nodded.

DeCarlo said, "The sight of a gun could trigger memories of the way your father died. It could undo any progress she's made."

Ross touched DeCarlo's forearm. "Chessy's here. We'll talk about this later."

Chessy ran across the lobby and threw herself into Ross's arms. The two hugged for long seconds. Finally Ross said, "Let me look at you."

She stepped back and held her sister at arm's length. At seventeen, Chessy was nearly as tall as Ross but thinner, with a chubby face and slanted eyes. Her hair was in waist-length braids interwoven with colored ribbons. She wore overalls, a flannel shirt, and clunky suede shoes with silver buckles. A sweater was tied around her waist, and the edges of her ears were dotted with silver studs. She wore a different Swatch watch on either wrist. She was affectionate and loving, but her own insecurities made her too sensitive to other people's feelings. She'd been at Oakes Institute for two years.

"Your hair's fantastic," Ross said. "I love it."

"You do? Oh, I'm so glad. We worked hard to get it right."

"We?"

"Fingers. That's Alice, my new roommate. Her father owns one of the biggest automobile dealerships on the island. She has this shoplifting problem, except she keeps getting caught. Fingers has money, but she says stealing's more fun. She just got arrested again. Third time this year. Instead of sending her to jail, they stuck her in here. Her dad pulled strings. Like you did for me."

DeCarlo lifted one hand and fluttered his long fingers in farewell.

"You two have a nice day," he said. "And don't forget Manello's. It's *the* place for pizza if you ask me."

A wide-eyed Chessy said, "Did someone say pizza?"

Old Whaler was a ten-minute drive from the Oakes Institute. Surrounded by woodlands, it still had the quaint flavor of a nineteenth-century whaling town. Shops on Main Street sold hand-dipped candles, antique prints, old maps, and beaded pouches from Long Island's two Indian reservations. City Hall and a whaling museum were housed in a single white clapboard building.

There were art galleries, real estate offices, and pasta restaurants. There were no traffic jams, highrises, or nonwhites. In fifteen minutes you could walk from one end of town to the other. Crime wasn't an issue. Other than the occasional shoplifter and joyriding teenager, a two-man police force had little to do.

Ross parked the Audi in front of yet another white

clapboard building, which served as a museum for Long Island sea life. Then she and Chessy shopped for nearly two hours. She bought Chessy a backpack, earrings, a denim jacket, and two Swatch watches for her collection. Chessy bought Ross a belt and a silk blouse.

At one P.M. they went to Manello's, a red-tablecloth, movie-poster-and-candlelight type of place. The customers, tanned, thin and dressed by DKNY and Versace, whispered into cell phones between sips of Mexican beer. All exuded the sense of vanity and power that came with money. Ross wanted a drink but decided it was too early. She ordered club soda, telling herself she was setting a good example for Chessy. And she let Chessy do most of the talking.

Chessy was proud of her long hair, which was still growing. School was OK but the kids still weren't allowed to have dances. She and Fingers were having their room painted, Finger's father had just given her a twenty-five-thousand-dollar Rolex, and Doctor DeCarlo had a new boyfriend. Chessy and Fingers were planning to take guitar lessons and maybe get nose rings.

Ross kept it light. She made no mention of Judge Reiner, the bloodthirsty Graciella, or the invisible man who was starting to get to her. Instead, she told Chessy about the Bronx perp who'd gotten arrested for knocking on apartment doors, pretending to be delivering pizza while carrying an empty pizza carton and wearing just a baseball cap. And the guy who shot holes in chairs, then sold each one as *the* chair a famous gangster had occupied the night he'd been gunned down in a Greenwich Village restaurant. And the one-legged burglar who'd been frightened off a job by a dog and

ran away, leaving behind a wooden leg with his name
and address carved on it.

At 2:30 they left Manello's and walked to the edge
of town, to a riding stable run by a former jockey, a
wizened looking Panamanian who'd done time for race
fixing. His name was Gus Chaco, and he flirted with
Ross in courtly Spanish while stroking his graying
mustache with a gnarled thumb. Ross deflected his
passes with a smile and a slow shake of her head. Gus,
married with grandchildren, had been playing the
Latino seducer too long to quit now.

Ross selected a horse she'd ridden before, a gentle
palomino mare named Miss Evita. Gus saddled the
mare but Ross insisted on fitting the saddle and adjust-
ing the length of the stirrups. She borrowed a pair of
blunt spurs from Gus and then it was time to ride.

She approached Miss Evita quietly, speaking softly
and patting the mare's neck to give her confidence.
Horses were testy. Always on edge. For your sake and
theirs, you had to talk to them. Talk, not shout. Horses
didn't like shouting. Nor did they like silence, which
for some reason upset them just as much as shouting.

Ross mounted Miss Evita from the left side. She
moved slowly, easing into the saddle, taking care not
to drop her weight on the animal's back. Mounted, she
stood in the stirrups and continued talking to Miss
Evita, patting her neck and gathering the reins. Then
she began walking the mare in a circle, controlling the
animal with voice and hands, legs and heels.

From a walk Ross pushed Miss Evita into a trot,
then a canter. Chessy enjoyed watching her ride, so
Ross left the stable and galloped along a dirt road leading to the woods. The wind was in her face, and soon

she was one with the power of the most beautiful animal God had ever created.

Away from the stable, she reined in the palomino, dismounted and put her gun in a saddlebag. Chessy mustn't see the weapon. Nor must she feel it when she climbed into the saddle behind Ross.

Back at the stable, Gus helped Chessy to mount behind Ross. Then shading his eyes, he stared at the sky.

"Rain," he said.

The sky was clear. There wasn't a cloud in sight.

"I can smell it," he said. "Use to do that in prison. Bet guys I could smell the rain. Won every time."

He smiled at Ross. "Smell you too. You smell better."

Ross said, "Goodbye, Gus. We won't be long."

They took to the dirt road, Ross, Chessy, and Miss Evita, Chessy with her arms around Ross's waist, shouting, "Awesome!" She wanted to go faster. Ross said no way. She alternated between a trot and a canter. She needed to control Miss Evita and watch the road for holes and logs.

She left the road a half mile from the stable and entered the woods. She guided Miss Evita onto a narrow bridle path and down an incline, through trees, shrubbery, and undergrowth, toward a brook flowing into an algae-covered pond. A pair of large boulders, standing side by side, guarded the pond like stone sentries. Quail, woodpeckers, owls, and squirrels seemed to be enjoying themselves. And not a drop of rain in sight.

Ross dismounted and tied Miss Evita's reins to a tree branch. Oakes wasn't the worst place in the world. Chessy, however, loved the outdoors. She was something of a collector—rocks, leaves, acorns, and pieces of wood. With her room being repainted, she was in the market for new forest stuff.

Suddenly the sun disappeared behind dark clouds. The forest turned chilly and became filled with shadows. Chessy slipped into her sweater. Ross shivered under her sweatshirt. They had to get back to the stable before the roads became too muddy for Miss Evita. Chalk up one for Gus.

Snap. The noise came from behind the boulders. To Ross, it sounded like someone had stepped on a dried branch. She heard the sound of small rocks being dislodged. Ross froze. She and Chessy weren't alone in the woods.

Ross thought about the man who'd entered her apartment last night, who'd been following her for days, and she was afraid. For herself and for Chessy. She stepped to the mare, pulled the .380 from the saddlebag and aimed at the boulders. "Police officer. Come out with your hands up. *Now.*"

The rain started to fall. Big drops. *Cold*. Scattered at first, then stronger, and in seconds a light shower had become a downpour. Ross and Chessy were quickly drenched. Lightning lit up a nighttime sky. The crack of thunder caused the mare to pull free and whinny. Nostrils flaring, she backed away from Ross.

Eyes on the boulders, Ross spoke to the horse and attempted to calm it. Up ahead, something moved. Biting her lip, Ross used a hand to wipe water from her eyes. She was ready to fire, to empty a clip. Cap the bastard, whoever he was, before he got to her and Chessy.

Then she saw it. A deer. Young, skinny, and terrified. Head and antlers peeking from behind the boulders. When it came into the open, Ross lowered her gun hand. The deer was scared shitless. More frightened than Ross. Funny, really.

Head high, the deer sniffed the air. Then Chessy screamed and the deer hopped sideways, turned, and in a burst of speed, disappeared among the trees.

Ross looked at Chessy. Now soaking wet, Ross's sister pointed at the gun.

Ross remembered DeCarlo's warning. She dropped the gun and ran toward Chessy.

12
Disclosures of a Sort

Ross Magellan sat in the living room of her West Side apartment and swallowed the last of her cognac. She hadn't had this much to drink since she'd gone undercover to nail a psycho suspected of killing an insurance agent for not settling a claim fast enough.

The last time the psycho met Ross he'd shown up with his wife's head in a box, promising Ross the same fate if she betrayed him.

She refilled her glass, then poured more coffee for Connie. He stood at the window, smoking a thin cigar and watching the rain. A carriage clock on the mantel struck 5:00 P.M. Two hours had passed since the sight of Ross's gun had sent Chessy into shock.

She'd told Doctor DeCarlo about being followed. But not about last night's break-in at her apartment and how it had left her on edge. She expected him to understand why she'd panicked today. He didn't. Or rather he had no interest in understanding someone who wasn't his patient.

DeCarlo's response was characteristically blunt. His responsibility, he said, wasn't to Ross. It was to Chessy. Explanations didn't change facts. Chessy was in a catatonic state because she'd seen Ross's gun.

For Ross, the pain of his words was as real as a blow to the face.

She felt Connie's arm around her shoulders.

"Chessy will come out of it," he said. "She always does."

Ross took a tissue from a pocket of her robe. "DeCarlo says right now she's *unreachable*. That's how he put it. He has no idea how long this will last. Damn it, he warned me about the gun. I should have listened."

"You told me she saw your father shoot himself."

"She was fifteen when it happened. High-strung, hysterical. Totally confused. My father had been raping her since she was twelve."

"If he hadn't killed himself, someone should have done it for him."

Because Connie was checking his watch, he never saw Ross eye him, then look away.

"Have to leave soon," he said. "I'm supposed to be at the convention center at six o'clock. Toy fair opens tomorrow. One of our clients is exhibiting some dolls."

"Thanks for changing the locks."

"What are you planning to do with the extra set of keys?"

"Same as usual. They go into the office safe."

"Any chance somebody got to the old set?"

Ross shook her head. "Fargnoli's the only one with the combination and I don't think he's the stalker type."

"You sure?"

"For one thing, he's into black women."

"Him, Lou Angelo, and Robert De Niro. What's with Italian guys and black women?"

"You're asking me? Another thing about Fargnoli. I'm not one of his favorite people. He doesn't see me as the ideal team player. Says I'm too much of a free spirit."

She touched Connie's cheek. "I can't picture you playing with dolls."

"The client does the playing. He's a Japanese businessman from Osaka, and he deals in antique dolls. Each one is worth a fortune. My job is to see they don't disappear. Last year's fair, one guy brought in some handmade dolls from Italy. Real beauties. Medieval costumes, human hair, tiny jewels, the works. Five grand a pop. Second night, they disappear right off the floor. With the guards standing there."

"Inside job," Ross said.

"One of the guards owed money to a shylock with ties to some wiseguy. Security company protecting the dolls ended up paying the owner three hundred thousand dollars. We don't want to pay out anything if we can help it."

"You've worked undercover."

"Still do. These days it's all corporate stuff. Embezzlement, missing office supplies, copyright theft. Your job's more dangerous."

"Did it ever get to you at some point?"

Connie picked up his coffee cup. "Only when I was a cop. The department doesn't like you staying under too long, as you know. You get weird. Start forgetting **who yo**u are. You do three, four months. Then they pull you out before you end up talking to walls. The problem with undercover work is it demands you think like the bad guys. Act like them too. Which is dangerous because the bad guys have all the fun. Money, women, guns, drugs. They have it all. Including the power of life and death over anyone who crosses their path. I've seen undercovers throw away their badges and become a bad guy full-time."

His eyes were glazed, remembering. "Even if you don't cross over, you find yourself thinking of nothing else but playing that role. Wife, family, friends. Forget it. You just can't wait to get back to undercover work. Hell, you're doing things normal people only dream of doing. You can really get into that shit. When the case is over, you find yourself looking around for another one. Is this normal? No. Does it affect your sanity? Yes."

He looked at Ross. "What bothered me most was setting up people so you could send them to prison. Gaining their trust so you could take away their freedom. Like you're doing with Lou Angelo. Over and over I asked myself, 'Is this right?' I still don't know the answer."

Ross rolled her empty brandy glass between her hands.

"If I think about that, I can't do the job," she said.

"So you don't think about it."

"Know what I think about? I think about going to court and confronting people who've come to trust me. People who now hate my guts and want to see me dead."

Connie stretched out his long legs. "You are human after all."

"Human enough to want to stay out of the rain. Thank God I don't have to leave the house tonight. DeCarlo's calling me the minute Chessy comes out of shock. What do I do if he says I shouldn't see Chessy again?"

"He won't. You're paying the bills, and he doesn't want you to stop. He'll probably recommend next time you don't bring a piece. Other than that, what else can he say? He's not Chessy's legal guardian. *You* are. You're being paranoid, as usual. I say stay home, get drunk, and watch *Jeopardy!*"

A cordless telephone rang on the coffee table. Ross covered her face with both hands. Then hugging herself, she rocked back and forth before snatching the receiver and putting it to her ear. "Yes?"

She listened, clenched a fist against her forehead. After a few seconds she put a hand over the mouth of the receiver and looked at Connie.

"Fargnoli," she said.

She took her hand away and spoke into the phone. "Yes, I'm with someone. Who? I'm with Connie."

She forced a smile and spoke to Connie. "Lieutenant Fargnoli wants to know if you'll let me come outside and play in the rain."

Connie waved. "Tell him I said hello and ask if he's still farting in the bathtub and breaking the bubbles with his nose."

Ross smiled. "I think he heard you. He's actually laughing."

Ross had caught Lt. Carlo Fargnoli in one of his rare, upbeat moods. He was a forty-one-year-old Italian, twenty years on the job, with chipmunk cheeks and a graying crew cut. He was demanding, temperamental, and could get nasty if he thought he wasn't being taken seriously. He put in long hours and fought depression by chewing ice cubes.

Ross put her hand over the receiver. "I think I'd better take this in the other room."

Connie rose from the couch. "No problem. I have to hit the road anyway."

Ross shook her head violently. "No, no. Stay. Please stay."

She hurried to the bedroom, phone to her ear.

Minutes later she returned to the living room, hung up the phone, and joined Connie on the couch.

"Sorry," she said. "Fargnoli wanted to talk about last night's break-in. He was contacted by the cops who responded to my report of a crime."

"Did he believe you?"

"You never know with Fargnoli. He's either at your feet or at your throat. He did suggest that after we take down Judge Reiner, I put in for vacation. He also called about something else. Seems while I was out trying to shoot Bambi, he had two of my team following Lou Angelo. Need I say Fargnoli's hot to bring down Reiner?"

Connie said, "Ain't every day you get a chance to nail the chief judge of New York narcotics. Any cop would be a glory seeker on this one. Who'd he have on Angelo?"

"Art Franzese and Harry Earles. Good cops."

"I know Artie. Weird little dude but he knows his shit. Earles I've heard of but never met. They say he wrote the book on ghosting."

"He's the guy you want watching your back. All three—Harry, Art, and Glenn Ford, have ghosted for me. Saved my butt more than once. Angelo's having a fund raiser tonight at his Park Avenue apartment. Starts at seven. Harry heard about it and got me an invitation. The man is smart."

Connie said, "What did he say? 'Hi, I'm Detective Earles and I'm ghosting for an NYPD undercover and would you please invite her to tonight's fund-raiser so she can nail you and Judge Reiner for election fraud?' "

Ross said, "Tonight's not about politics."

She tapped her temple with an index finger. "I told you Harry was smart. He called Lou Angelo's office, said he was from G and E Records, and asked about the legal papers I gave Angelo last night. Harry assumed I'd be invited to the fund-raiser, and he was right. He even talked them into letting me bring some G and E staffers."

"That covers your backup. You said this isn't about politics. What is it about?"

"Don't laugh. Lou Angelo supports a home for battered black and Latina women."

"You're shitting me. Does he really?"

"For real. Fargnoli ran it through the computer. The whole thing's legit. Not only did Angelo found the home, he's raised over half a million dollars to keep it going. Regardless of any scam he's running with Reiner, he's straight on this thing."

Connie scratched the tip of his nose. "There are a few things I have a hard time believing. Such as the idea that lawyers are capable of honesty, compassion, and pity. Other than that, everything you've said about Lou Angelo sounds solid to me. Something tells me you're going out in the rain."

Ross squeezed his hand.

"The police department is a man's world," she said. "Women aren't wanted and aren't welcome. I can't afford to wimp out. Not if I want to be a player."

"I wish I could say you're wrong but I can't."

"We get what you guys call 'tit jobs.' Fingerprinting, typing, making coffee. Body searches where we get to dig our fingers in some perp's asshole that hasn't been washed in weeks. Then there's sexual harassment—that can be downright frightening."

Connie scratched his head. "Not all cops are into that harassment shit. Unfortunately, you speak out against it and you're a wimp."

Ross said, "What about the other extreme? The cops who are confused by a changing world. When I was a rookie I rode with one old guy who was polite to the point of making me want to run him over. He was afraid of offending me. So he held doors, wouldn't let me drive, and offered to buy me lunch. I wanted to slam his hand in a car door."

"Hell, you've made your bones. You've won the respect of a lot of cops. They're lining up to work with you. You make big cases, and everybody on the team looks good. If I was still on the job, I'd kill to be a part of the Reiner investigation."

"There's something I have to tell you."

Connie's eyebrows went up.

Ross smiled. "No, I'm not pregnant."

Connie exhaled. "Thank you, Lord."

"It's about how I got my gold shield. I think Fargnoli knows. That's why I have to be careful around him."

"You've told me the story," Connie said. "Besides,

it's public knowledge. You nailed a cop killer. Happened ten years ago. They found a young cop named Eddie Hackett stabbed to death in his car on Grand Central Parkway. Had a wife, new baby. Needed extra money so he worked weekends at a Long Island flea market."

Ross said, "I was twenty-two, female, and a rookie. And I solved a cop killing. You'd think I'd make gold shield easy. Except it didn't happen. Why? Because I was twenty-two, female, and a rookie."

"What are you talking about?"

"You were a cop. You know how competitive the department is. And the backstabbing that goes with that? *Please.* I made a big case when I found Eddie Hackett's killer. But I was a woman, and I'd also made a lot of detectives look bad. Guys with twenty, thirty years on the job. They let it be known that if the department gave me my gold shield, I'd have problems."

"What kind of problems?"

"I could find myself alone on the street without backup. Confiscated drugs and cash could turn up in my locker. The word could get around that I was a rat and spying on other cops. Try and live through that at any age, let alone twenty-two. It was okay if I received a commendation or a plaque. But no gold shield. Not on the Hackett case."

"That wasn't right. You'd earned your shield."

"Hackett, by the way, was no shining light. The guy was stealing from the police property room and selling the stuff at the flea market. He was also screwing a woman he met there, a lady who sold kitchen utensils. Guess who slit his throat with a Ginsu knife when he told her the magic was gone?"

Connie winced. "Ouch. You needed a snitch to make that case. Who tipped you?"

"Someone I'm still using."

"I understand. So how *did* you make detective and what's this got to do with Fargnoli?"

Ross said, "Around this time I was doing B and B. Buy-and-bust in Harlem. Taking dope and guns off the street. One night I popped a dealer as he was making a sale to a sixteen-year-old white girl. Her name was Johanna Linder."

"Any relation to Deputy Commissioner William Linder of the NYPD?"

"His daughter.

Connie's eyes widened. "Uh-huh."

"Exactly."

Ross stuck her hands in the pockets of her robe. "The second I popped Johanna Linder, I knew she'd never be booked, fingerprinted, or body-searched. Pigs would fly before you'd find any record of her being arrested. She'd never see the inside of a courtroom, let alone do time. Somebody was going to call Daddy that very night, and before you could say 'the fix is in,' little Jo would be out and about. Case closed."

Connie said, "I see it coming."

"I decided to make the call myself. If Commissioner Linder was going to be grateful, let him be grateful to me. What I didn't count on was Mrs. Linder. A week or so later I made detective for solving the Hackett killing. Between you and me I got it for saving little Jo's ass. I got it because Ivy Linder pulled strings."

Connie said, "How did the old guys take that?"

Ross grinned. "What they thought didn't matter. I had Ivy Linder backing me."

Connie shivered. "Ivy could make an onion cry. That is one tough lady. And smart. They say Linder made commissioner because she told him whose ass to kiss and whose to kick."

Ross said, "She let it be known that speaking out against me would be a mistake. The kind of mistake that affects promotions and retirements. After that the old guys ignored me. I didn't make any friends among that crowd, not that I gave a shit."

She reached for Connie's hand. "I've never told this to anyone."

"You say Fargnoli knows."

"One of the old-timers could have tipped him about me."

Connie said, "Is that why you feel you have to prove yourself to him?"

"It's the reason I'm being careful on this Jenn Sanchez thing."

"In other words you haven't mentioned Sanchez to Fargnoli."

"Before I talk to anybody I need to know who's after Sanchez and why. No matter what I bring Fargnoli on this, he could still shit-can it. Cops cover for each other, even when it comes to murder. Anyway, the Judge Reiner case is mine. Nobody's bringing him down but me."

"Emilio Albert's suicide," Connie said. "What do you think?"

"I have one word for it: *timely.* I ask Albert about Jenn Sanchez and ten minutes later he and his pit bull go bungee jumping without a cord."

"Too bad Linder's not alive. You could use him right about now. What did he die of again?"

"Two years ago he went on vacation to the West Indies. Ate some toxic fish. Instant retirement."

Ross sipped more brandy. "I've still got Ivy. We're in touch. She knows everybody in the department and at City Hall. She's a big political fund-raiser. A lot bigger than Lou Angelo will ever be, and that gives her clout. Cops are her first love. Screams her head off at police hockey games and boxing matches."

Connie said, "You reached out for her lately?"

"Twice. She got Chessy into the Oakes Institute. One phone call and it was done. Second time was a year or so after Linder died. A female officer, a good friend, was taken to the roof of her station house and raped by her male superior."

"I'm sorry."

"A sergeant. Some lard-ass who walked around wearing an I LOVE POONTANG T-shirt."

"A world-class academic."

"Amy was terrified," Ross said. " 'Sergeant Poontang' told her not to bother pressing charges. Said it would be her word against his. He had a dozen cops who'd swear he wasn't in the house when the rape occurred. He had the 'Blue Wall of Silence' going for him."

"And Amy had you."

"I reached out for Ivy Linder. She was appalled, but she knew the department. Knew they didn't want a scandal and would only give her so much. The best she could do was have the guy busted to patrolman and assigned to a fixed foot post."

"Bet he loved that," Connie said. "You stand in one place and you don't move until there's face-to-face relief. Even if the temperature's fifty below, you stay put."

"They put him on a Washington Heights street corner. A hellhole. Had him checking the license plates of people coming off the bridge to buy drugs. He got shot in the knee and ended up taking early retirement."

Connie rose from the couch. "They should have aimed higher. So you think Fargnoli knows about your gold shield and about you zapping Sergeant Poontang."

"How do you keep a secret in the department?"

"You don't. Doesn't Fargnoli know you're a good cop?"

"Women cops have to prove themselves every day. Its a fact. It's also a fact I'm not letting Fargnoli hand over the Reiner case to the dick club."

"DeCarlo?"

"He can reach me anytime. That's what cell phones are for."

Connie said, "I'm having a late supper. Around ten or so. Why don't you drop by the convention center and we'll grab a bite?"

"Love to."

"Great. Front entrance. I'll leave word with the security guard. By the way, were you followed today?"

Ross shook her head. "I don't think so. I didn't get that creepy feeling out on the island."

Connie took her in his arms. "Sooner or later you'll have to tell somebody about the invisible man. Don't wait too long. This guy's too smart to suit me. Way too smart."

13
The Right Color

Lou Angelo lived in a Park Avenue high-rise facing the Seventh Regiment Armory, a popular site for Manhattan's charity balls.

His twenty-third-floor apartment featured an oval-shaped dining room, a library with a chandelier, and a bathroom outfitted with two color television sets, a fax machine, and stationary bike. A glass-enclosed terrace ringed the apartment on three sides.

At nine that evening the Watcher stepped onto the terrace, relieved to have escaped an apartment crowded with supporters of Angelo's shelter for abused women, something called Harborage. Many attendees were black and Latina women who claimed to have suffered greatly at the hands of brutal males. Tonight they were going public with their agony.

The Watcher listened as one misery princess after another told the crowd what a rough time she'd had of it. How much she'd been forced to endure. He had no use for public confession. It was the worst kind of weakness. Better to keep your secrets and suffer in silence.

Also lending their presence to the evening were politicians, reporters, and community activists, all ranting and posturing in support of a *good cause*. The result was an earsplitting noise level. By contrast, a minute on the terrace was like a month in the country.

A press release touting the fund-raiser had promised celebrities galore. Angelo, however, had played fast and loose with the truth, something that came naturally to lawyers. The only big guns seen by the Watcher were an aging actress escorted by her doorman; a former pro basketball player now running a third-rate Manhattan restaurant: a lesbian pop singer who'd gone twenty years without a hit, and a forties big-band leader recovering from a stroke and reduced to getting around in a wheelchair.

Rubbing his neck scar, the Watcher walked over to a small garden beside a dining patio. The scar was still tight, a sign the rain wouldn't end anytime soon. Driving home was going to be hell. He'd have to contend with stalled cars, washed-out roads, malfunctioning traffic lights, and incensed motorists backed up at tollbooths. A nightmare. At least Helene wouldn't be alone. Grenada, bless her, would stay put until he arrived.

A trio of Latina women, fanning themselves with bejeweled hands, stepped onto the terrace. The Watcher barely glanced at them. He had no reason to hide. All he had to do was look inconspicuous. Just present himself as one more kindhearted soul ready to whip out his checkbook and set the world to rights.

Still, he stepped closer to a trellis covered with tiny yellow roses, into the shadows. Instinctively hiding as much of himself as possible. He was and always would be an enigma, closed and cut off from the world.

He popped a raw cashew into his mouth and looked into the library. An obese black woman wearing a red turban was being wildly applauded for an impassioned speech in which she'd demanded that all men, for all time, stop beating up on women for as long as they both shall live. The Watcher thought, when hell freezes over. Fatty had lavished her love on an absolute fool who'd kicked her in the head at some point, thereby opening her eyes. Having survived her own stupidity, she now expected to be commended. And throw in a few bucks while you're at it.

The Watcher shook his head. It wasn't his responsibility to give money to abused women. They weren't *his* abused women. They didn't belong to him and he didn't belong to them.

He plucked a rose from the trellis and stuck it in his lapel. His eyes went to the dining room. A manic Lou Angelo was being interviewed, a process consisting of him and a broad-shouldered female reporter shouting in each other's faces. Angelo appeared to be in his glory, laughing at his own quips and playing to the crowd as though it were a packed courtroom. The Watcher found him clever but shallow, constantly in overdrive and tending to scatter his energies, giving him the attention span of a three-year-old. He did, however, have a way with words and a personality that could charm snakes.

"For me, it started back in Harlem's jazz days," Angelo told the interviewer. "When I was young, I spent more time uptown than down. It was the music that got me. Best years of my life I spent up there. I saw Billie Holiday at Poor John's. Honi Coles and the Copacetics dancing at Showman's. The Mills Brothers, Billy Eckstine, and Basie at the Baby Grand. I did Willie Bryant's radio show from the front window of the Baby Grand. Me, a dumb-ass white kid from Astoria. Small's Paradise, Palm Café, Shalimar, Sugar Ray's Lounge. I was everywhere."

He paused for breath, then resumed. "The people up there were my first clients. The first to hire Lou Angelo as a lawyer. I never forgot that. I figured the best way to pay them back was to start this women's shelter. Black woman are wonderful. Black men? God forgive me, but they don't treat their women right. Don't appreciate them. I started this shelter to give black women somewhere to go after being thrown out on the street. I put my heart and soul into this thing and so far, knock on wood, we've managed to help a few women who really needed it."

The Watcher touched his scar. Angelo was putting a Band-Aid on a cancer. Any woman he helped would eventually prove ungrateful. Of all human feelings, gratitude had the shortest memory.

He fingered the blue crack vials in his jacket pocket. The man who'd supplied them to Emilio Albert was here tonight. In fact, three known traffickers were at the fund-raiser, which said something about Mr. Angelo's choice of friends. The one who mattered to the Watcher was the one selling Blue Death. This particular dealer knew Angelo, and Angelo knew the whereabouts of Jenn Sanchez, who could put the Watcher and his very important friend on death row.

Had he shared that information with the dealer? Inquiring minds wanted to know.

Why hadn't the Watcher forced Mr. Angelo to give up Sanchez? Because Mr. Angelo was being protected by Judge Reiner. Touch a hair on Angelo's balding head and Judge Reiner would be forced to launch an investigation, one that would eventually come down on the Watcher like a hard rain. A little patience was called for. After that Angelo would belong to the Watcher.

He brought the yellow rose to his nose. Sweet. Just like Magellan. She was here with her backup, doing her best to charm Lou Angelo. As always Magellan was pleasing to the eye and lovely to behold. Almost goddesslike. She seemed to have recovered from today's business in the woods where she'd unwittingly pushed Chessy closer to becoming permanently gaga.

He closed his eyes, remembering the delight he'd felt at being in her apartment. Tonight he'd seen the way men looked at her. Seen their willingness to make fools of themselves over her. Watched them find a promise in her beauty, one they could never have since she belonged to him. *Behold thou* art *fair my love; behold thou* art *fair.*

He left the rose garden and walked along the terrace, watching the rain pound the glass enclosure. He'd always found rain peaceful and cleansing. No wonder primitive people worshiped the elements as God. Certainly the weather was kinder than any divinity the Watcher had ever known.

Having had the Bible beaten into him as a child, he wasn't too keen on the Almighty. He saw the Master of the Universe as a fabrication, a symbol of all that was useless and grotesque. The Bible, with its total lack of humor, had produced more bigots than saints. He'd sooner shoot off a toe than pick up the "Good Book" again.

He found Magellan in the living room, talking with Mercy Howard, Lou Angelo's bimbo of the moment. The Watcher stayed on the terrace, out of Magellan's range of vision. Her backup wasn't visible, but never fear, they were on the set. They could be anywhere—here, the room next door, or out in the hall, munching on soggy canapés.

He fished a cashew out of his pocket, then stopped before putting it in his mouth. Magellan was on the move. Excusing herself, she turned her back on Mercy Howard and pushed through the crowd. She appeared to be heading toward the door.

Other men in the room joined the Watcher in following Magellan with their eyes. One in particular was of interest to the Watcher. He was a muscular black man in his mid-thirties, with an upturned nose, processed hair, and five-inch sideburns. His smile switched on and off too quickly for it to mean anything. He stood in front of the fireplace, holding court for an all-female audience. The ladies hung on his every word, apparently finding him charming. One woman fingered the sleeve of his powder-blue suit, then nodded approvingly. He was dressed in blue—shirt, tie, pocket handkerchief, and alligator shoes. He also wore blue fingernail polish, a fashion fad which mystified the Watcher.

The Watcher popped the raw cashew into his mouth. When the man in blue checked his beeper, the Watcher smiled.

Well, now.

Returning the beeper to his pocket, the black man bid his female audience farewell and left the room.

The Watcher fingered the crack vials he'd taken from Emilio Albert's apartment. Then he went after Magellan and *Mr. Blue Death.*

14
Jackie Blue

"As usual you had the ladies going tonight. If you ask me it's the shoes. Definitely the shoes."

"It's the man inside the shoes. You are looking fine as wine yourself, Detective Ross. You are everything a man could want, with a side of fries."

"I guess that's a compliment. Just to be on the safe side, I don't think I'll inhale."

Ross was in a small bathroom near the kitchen in Lou Angelo's apartment. She was talking by cell phone to one of her informants, a drug dealer named Jackie Blue.

Jackie, who only dressed in blue, had left the fundraiser and was now being driven around the block in the rain by his chauffeur-bodyguard, a 410-pound Jamaican named Big Mac. Ninety percent of a cop's cases were made by informants. The better the snitch, the better the cop. How did Jackie Blue rate as an informant? Ross put him right up there. Top of the line and head of the class.

He worked exclusively with Ross, who'd used him

to make drug cases, confiscate guns, catch a serial rapist, and nail a Mexican addict who'd killed nine cabbies. It was Jackie Blue who'd tipped her to Eddie Hackett's murderer. In exchange Ross left Jackie Blue alone and arrested his competition.

Charming and ruthless, Jackie Blue enjoyed being the center of attention. Anything that didn't concern or affect him was of no importance.

At the age of sixteen he'd tried to hold up a 7-Eleven in his hometown of Charlotte, North Carolina. The heist ended abruptly when an elderly night clerk pumped seven bullets into Jackie's chest. In an eight-hour operation he died twice, to be revived by a doctor with blue eyes. A blue-eyed nurse assisted the doctor.

From then on the saving power of the color blue fixed itself in the teenager's mind. As he told Ross, the whole thing was nothing less than God's own sign. Lying handcuffed to a prison hospital bed, Reilly Jackson Simpson, chicken thief and failed stickup man, became now and forever Jackie Blue.

Ross placed her purse on the edge of the basin. She hadn't stumbled upon this bathroom by accident. She never entered an undercover situation unprepared. Before she set foot on the set, her backup checked out the building, hallways, streets, rooftops and, of course, the players. The information was then passed on to Ross.

Tonight the first thing Ross's backup had done upon entering Lou Angelo's apartment was to walk through it, then report to Ross on the physical layout and the guest list. Harry Earles had even given her a copy of the guest list. Ross's guys were good. Better than good.

"You ain't working crack houses and street corners no more," Jackie Blue said. "You got too much talent. Anywhere you go, something's happening. All them ugly-ass women in that crib? Shit, you ain't there 'cause you afraid to go out in the rain. One sister I talked to, she so ugly her shadow quit."

"These are women who've been hurt," Ross said. "Angelo deserves credit for trying to help."

She heard the disgust in Jackie Blue's voice.

"Shit," he said, turning the word into two syllables. "Woman follow the natural plan, she don't get hurt. She do like she's told, everything be copacetic, know what I'm saying? I see Angelo got himself a fine brown sister. Young too. The hell she see in that old white man, anyway? The only way he can run a finger through his hair is to cut a hole in his pocket."

Ross said, "You don't strike me as a women's-rights advocate. Mind telling me what brought you here tonight?"

"Angelo handles my legal business. We hooked up the last time I was inside. He got me out early."

"How early?"

"Five years. That's a lifetime when you in prison. He said he could get me out, and he did. Spoke to some people and just like that, I get put in work release. You need a job for that so Angelo got me one. Put me in his women's shelter as a cook. I do some mean rice and beans. You want to fall by my crib some night? Let me cook for you?"

"I don't think so. Mind telling me what makes Mr. Angelo such an humanitarian? He seems to have gone to a lot of trouble on your behalf."

"Humanitarian? Shit, I give him a hundred thousand reasons to help me. All of it in cash. I'd have paid ten times that to get my ass the hell out of Attica."

"Half for Angelo, half for Judge Reiner. That how it went down? Or was Reiner's cut bigger."

"Well, check this out." Jackie Blue sounded pleased with himself. "You playing Judge Reiner, am I right? Working Angelo to get to the big man. Well, *goddam*. I mean *goddam*."

"Jackie, we never had this conversation."

"I'm hip. *Damn*. Judge Reiner. That is something. You know, I seen two members of the po-leece upstairs. One is that nigger with the big feet—"

"Detective Ford."

"Yeah, him. Always bragging on what a big dick he got. Man even has a name for his dick. He call it the 'Anaconda.' "

"Please. On a need-to-know basis only, OK?"

"Other cop was that quiet guy. Man never say much. Wears bow ties all the time."

Ross fingered a towel hanging from the shower. "Detective Earles."

"The one they call 'Duke.' He ain't all that big, but he suppose to be tough. Three cops in the same place, same time. Something's happening."

"There's four of us," Ross said. "You missed one."

"Glad I quit the set before y'all try and hang something on me."

"You know anything about a policewoman named Jenn Sanchez? She worked Vice."

Jackie Blue hesitated. "I heard about her."

"What did you hear?"

"She's supposed to be hiding from some cop. Lookee here. I do not involve myself in disputes between the police and their own people. A man can get hurt that way."

"She used to be an undercover," Ross said. "Then something happened and she disappeared. Know anything about the cop who's after her?"

Ross heard Jackie Blue tell Big Mac, "Nigger, don't be running no red light with me in the car!"

He said to Ross, "Emilio told me you come to see him about Sanchez. She bought drugs from him. Had him scared, talking about some cop trying to set her on fire. Emilio wasn't stupid. He knew Sanchez was trouble. He didn't trust anybody who come looking for her, especially cops. That's why he wouldn't talk to you. I said you were cool but he didn't care. Right after we talk, Emilio and his dog set out to prove they could fly."

"You think he killed himself?"

"I think it ain't none of my business."

"Jackie, you know how the game's played. First one on board gets the best deal. That means whoever comes to me first with Jenn Sanchez wins the lottery. Meanwhile, let's assume I am playing Judge Reiner."

"Let's assume that. We can also assume you ain't forgot the sumbitch nearly got you killed."

"This is a big case. The cop who makes it is going places."

"Man be a fool not to want a cop like that on his side."

Ross said, "You're not a fool, are you Jackie?"

"I was a fool for love one time. Ain't been a fool since."

There was a knock on the bathroom door.

Ross said, "I'll be out in a minute."

A female voice said, "Sixty seconds and counting."

Ross said to Jackie Blue, "You heard from Reiner since he got you out of prison?"

"Happened a year after I stopped cooking. I was back on the street, doing my thing. Starting to reestablish myself. Everything's cool. Then I get a visit from Angelo. He say from now on, I have to do business with some Albanians in the Bronx. He don't *ask* me. He *tells* me. Tells me if I wanted cannons to put on my front lawn, I'd have to buy them from the Albanians too."

"Drugs and guns," Ross said. "One-stop shopping."

"Whatever. All I know is Angelo says Judge Reiner would appreciate my cooperation, these Albanians being friends of his and all. Matter of fact, first time I get together with these Albanians was at the judge's summer house out in the Hamptons. He wasn't there, but it was definitely his crib. Pictures of him, his wife and kids all over the place."

Ross flushed the toilet. "You're saying the chief judge of New York narcotics hooked you up with drug traffickers? That he let you meet at his place?"

"I'm saying I was in no position to argue with a judge, that's what I'm saying. The man got me out of prison. I figured he could just as easily send my ass back. My daddy always said to get along, you got to go along."

"So you went along. How much was the judge getting from this deal?"

"Nothing from me. But he so damn greedy, I figure he got something from the Albanians. Probably took a taste from what I was paying them. Six months I do business with them. Then I found a better deal. Didn't have to look over my shoulder no more."

"What do you mean?"

"Albanians are *intense*. Kill you just like that. And they never forget. Takes them twenty years, they get your ass you play them cheap. Robbery, that's what they good at. Supermarkets, ATM machines, banks, jewelry stores. They big on high tech—scanners, police radios, electronic doodads. They don't hit a place 'less they film it first. Want to know what they getting into. Back home the secret police and military intelligence teach them that shit. They got this thing they use to burn through safes and ATM machines."

Ross said, "What thing?"

"They call it a 'slice pack.' Has burn rods that heat up to ten thousand degrees. Safe get so hot, it got to be cooled down with a fire extinguisher. One time, they learn one of their people is talking to the FBI. They catch him. Use a slice pack on his ass. Dude was toast in no time. You do not want to mess with these people."

Ross turned on a faucet.

"So how did you get out of your arrangement with them?" she said.

"Same way I got out of Attica. Lots of dead presidents. This time I paid out *two* hundred thousand dollars. Gave the money to Angelo. Ain't heard from the judge or the Albanians since, which is fine by me."

"Jackie, I have to go. Help me out on Sanchez. I won't forget it."

"You know I will, sweet *thang*. Maybe you can do me a favor. Somebody who was retired is now thinking about getting back into the business. For that to happen, Jackie Blue got to retire or be retired, know what I'm saying?"

"One of your competitors quit. Now he's planning a comeback. But first, he wants you out of the way. He's given you a choice: you either quit or he'll kill you."

"He can damn sure try. Except I ain't going nowhere. Jackie Blue be here till Judgment Day. Let me ask you something. Why you so interested in Sanchez? What she got to do with Judge Reiner?"

Ross turned off the faucet. Why the obsession with a female undercover she'd never met? Was this a way of pressuring Lou Angelo to give up Judge Reiner?

Or was it something else?

Freddy Palacio and Ross meeting in Riverside Park at 3:00 A.M., the two alone in a children's playground. Meeting one day after Freddy tried to rip off a dentist for 100K, proving the rumors were indeed correct, that Freddy wasn't too swift. Freddy telling Ross about a female undercover being hunted by a cop she watched commit a murder. Telling Ross the undercover was being protected by Lou Angelo, patron saint of women in extremities. Ross at OCCB the next day, sitting in front of a computer and pulling up a photograph of Jennifer "Jenn" Sanchez, the female undercover. Seeing a tall, dark Latina Ross's age. Ross feeling as though she were looking in the mirror. Ross thinking, Sanchez is me and if she dies, so do I.

More pounding on the bathroom door. The woman outside now more insistent. "Hey you in there. While we're young, OK?"

Ross said to Jackie Blue, "Why I want Sanchez doesn't matter. Find her. Just *find* her."

15
A Surprise Guest

Back on the terrace Ross sipped a club soda and looked into Lou Angelo's bedroom.

The room was all paneled walls and gilt mirrors, with wall-to-wall floral carpeting and a steel four-poster bed wrapped in plaid raw silk. Lou Angelo sat on the bed, yellow legal pad and attaché case on his lap. In fifteen minutes he was to deliver a speech on behalf of Harborage.

"Make 'em feel guilty," he told Ross. "That way they won't forgive themselves till they write you out a check."

He asked Ross about Freddy Palacio. Was Freddy going to use a top criminal lawyer or stay with an attorney provided by the union? Ross said she didn't know. She was too busy running a record company to think about Freddy and his problems.

Angelo dropped the subject. But not before mentioning problems *he* now faced because Freddy had taken it upon himself to put three bullets into a

Westchester dentist. The victim's family was planning to file a lawsuit against the escort service. And police were investigating the service to see if it had a record of violence toward its customers.

And there was the question of the service's ownership. Cops wanted to talk to the real owners, not to front men and holding companies listed on the lease. Ross could have made the real owners with a phone call; their names were on file at OCCB. The service was owned by the Vendritto crime family which also had interests in topless bars, peep shows and triple-X bookstores. Thanks to Freddy Palacio, Lou Angelo now had to work full-time protecting wiseguys from cops, negligence lawyers, and the media.

Ross chewed on some ice. She'd opened the sliding glass door on the terrace, giving her a clear view into the bedroom. Three black women stood in front of her, talking about their children and blocking the doorway, allowing Ross to watch Lou Angelo without being seen.

Angelo's concern for battered women appeared to be genuine. Earlier he'd been approached by a small Hispanic woman with a bandaged forearm and bruised face. They talked and held hands, the two weeping as though a loved one had just died. Minutes later a tall black woman with missing teeth took the lawyer in her arms, calling him her "Angel Man," saying he was the only reason she wasn't turning tricks in some crack house.

Ross fished a lemon slice from her drink and bit into it. She was starting to like Angelo. The old fart was a bagman and a blowhard, not to mention a chaser. He wasn't a total shit, though. Which wouldn't stop Ross from taking him down. She intended to do her job, which was to worm her way into Big Lou's confidence and then send his ass to prison.

Mercy Howard was seated beside Lou Angelo on the four-poster. She listened attentively, arm in his, as he read parts of his speech aloud. She was dressed in silver—miniskirt, blouse, and jacket, with black stiletto heels adding inches to her already long legs. Mercy had the kind of looks that inspired men to make fools of themselves. Still Ross suspected Angelo and Mercy weren't just knocking boots. Mercy Howard was giving him something only young women could give old men—a reason to stay alive, with something to live for.

And where was Mrs. Angelo tonight? According to Mr. Angelo, she was in Fort Lauderdale, decorating the new condo, visiting her grandchildren, and playing golf.

"My wife took off for Florida," he told Ross, "because she felt I didn't need her tonight. Actually every man needs two women. One to appeal to his finer instincts and another to help him forget them."

Ross had her own opinion, which was Mrs. Angelo had gone to Florida rather than share her home with a hooker who was also her husband's mistress. There were some things a woman should be ashamed of. Allowing your husband to flaunt his mistress in your face was one of them.

Ross looked at her watch. Nine-thirty and still no word from Doctor DeCarlo about Chessy. He should have called by now. If she didn't hear from him soon, she was calling the Oakes Institute.

She looked at a Dutch painted-leather screen in the

bedroom. Detective Glenn Ford stood near the screen, hitting on a young black woman with a pointed chin and a nose ring. The beefy, thirty-five-year-old Ford wore a size-fourteen shoe, could bench-press four hundred pounds, and palm a basketball in one hand. He was ballsy, direct in his approach, and at times unsubtle, putting himself first. Just the sight of him was enough to chill the average perp.

Only minutes ago on the terrace, a goateed young Puerto Rican in fatigues and Timberland boots had tried putting the moves on Ross. Glassy-eyed and on weed, he sported gelled hair and gold hoops in both ears. "*Leche*'s my name," he said. "They call me 'Milk' 'cause I'm good for your body. I already know your name. It's *Satellite* 'cause your ass is out of this world."

Ross turned her back to him. He moved in front of her. "Baby, you got a nice smile," he said. He giggled. "Smiling is the second best thing you can do with your lips, know what I'm saying?"

Ross thought, *I can't believe this shit. And it's happening* here. When she tried to walk around him, the Rican grabbed her wrist. "*Mamacita,* you can't quit me now. We just getting started."

Ross smiled. She was still smiling when she caught Glenn Ford's eye. Seconds later, Ford was toe-to-toe with the Rican. Neither man spoke—Ford because he didn't have to, the Rican because he was scared shitless. The Rican refused to look Ford in the eyes. Instead he stared at the detective's large feet, plainly awed by their size. Finally, he shook his head in disbelief and walked away.

At the far end of the terrace, Detective Art Franzese, thirty-seven, small and balding, sat on a lawn chair, popping Advil and scowling at the falling rain. Franzese wasn't an easy man to know. He was energetic, quick-witted, and impatient with any situation he didn't like. Prone to frequent headaches, he took more risks than anyone on the team, making him dangerous to be around. Like a lot of cops, he gambled and owed money. Ross figured him for a total burnout in the not too distant future. Since taking a bullet for her, he'd become very protective. Too protective sometimes.

The team leader was Detective Sergeant Harry Earles who reported directly to Lieutenant Fargnoli. Ross took orders from Harry but didn't share her informants with him. For safety's sake, the fewer people who could ID an informant, the better.

At forty-two Harry Earles was blond and slim, with clean-cut features and wide-apart eyes. Ross had never worked with anyone so at ease and unruffled. Tonight in Lou Angelo's apartment he'd pulled his usual disappearing act. He handed Ross the Harborage guest list then vanished into the crowd. She couldn't see Harry, but she knew he was keeping an eye on her. Ross was counting on it. Harry was her rock. Her first line of defense.

Something in the apartment had obviously caught his eye. Instead of ignoring it, he'd done an immediate follow-up. He wasn't one to put things off. Not Harry.

"Too many people turn their lives into one long postponement," he told Ross. "I've never lived that way, and I don't intend to start now."

He was one of the smartest cops Ross had ever worked with. And fearless. Totally, utterly fearless. With his talent, Harry should have risen higher in the department. But after twenty years he was only a sergeant. And he was going to stay a sergeant because as far as Ross could tell, Harry didn't have a hook, a department VIP willing to pull strings on his behalf. If Harry's career wasn't dead, it was certainly on life support.

He'd saved her life twice—once when she was after some Russians who'd taken over a Wall Street brokerage firm and again when she was investigating a lawyer running a child-pornography ring. Without Harry Earles she'd be as dead as the female undercover who burned to death four years ago in a crack-house fire. If there was one cop Ross wanted watching her back it was Harry Earles. He wasn't just her protection. He was her luck.

Whenever Ross went undercover to make a buy— drugs, guns, stolen securities, jewelry—her team blocked off the surrounding area, covering the street, building, roof, and hallways.

One team member had a special job. He was the ghost and his job was so important, it exempted him from anything else. He watched the undercover's back. Period.

To do this, he had to ignore everything else around him. Muggings, fires, shoot-outs and multicar accidents. The ghost's orders: Let it happen. Let it go down. Absolutely, positively do not lift a finger to help. The ghost was on the set to keep uncle alive. Everything else was irrelevant, not to mention beside the point. Ignore the undercover for even a second and the result could be a dead cop.

To do his job the ghost had to stay close to the undercover. And do it while remaining invisible. Which wasn't easy. The bad guys knew the 'hood and every homey in it. Strangers stood out, and they weren't welcome.

It took imagination to become invisible. A ghost did it by hiding in a hallway or in a car. In a phone booth or a Dumpster. Depending on the deal, he could tag along as uncle's bodyguard.

He could also "blend." The homeless guy in a doorway. The UPS guy with the clipboard. The cable guy in the green overalls. It was the ghost working his show, and nobody worked it better than Harry Earles.

Ross and Harry had been a team for three years. Her relationship with him and the others was strictly professional. Harry had never made a pass at her. Glenn Ford and Artie Franzese, on the other hand, had taken a run at Ross, who'd wasted no time letting both know she wasn't interested. Ford ("Got any black in you? Would you like some?") had been his usual, upfront self. Franzese had once asked her out for New Year's Eve. When she said no, he'd sulked for days. Harry, thank God, minded his own business and went home to his wife.

All three were married, with Glenn Ford having the most trouble with marital fidelity. "Marriage is like being in the bathtub," he told Ross. "Once you get use to it, it ain't so hot." Ross wasn't surprised to see him macking a woman at the fund-raiser, preparing to once more betray his wife.

She watched as a large bald-headed man with bushy gray eyebrows entered Lou Angelo's bedroom. Baldy headed straight for Angelo. He looked familiar. Ross tried to place him. She'd seen that long, baggy-eyed face before. But where?

She snapped her fingers. Of course. Baldy had been in the papers, on TV talk shows, and in news magazines. She'd even seen his mug on a couple of book covers. Baldy was Moses Rousseau, a sixty-two-year-old ex-prosecutor turned criminal lawyer, now defending drug dealers, wife murderers, child rapists, and any dirtbag willing to pay him six hundred dollars an hour. What was he doing at a fund-raiser for abused women? Rousseau was a prick. If shit could float, he'd walk on water.

Ross had never met the man. But there was always a chance he'd seen her around the courthouse or in the D.A.'s office. She considered the risk factor and moved out of the doorway.

Moses Rousseau ignored Mercy Howard's outstretched hand. She simply didn't exist for him. Instead, he shook Lou Angelo's hand. At the same time, he whispered in Angelo's ear and slipped him a white envelope.

Ross raised both eyebrows. As a cop, she knew a payoff when she saw one. Moses Rousseau and Lou Angelo were, as they say, doing business, the business being fattening the war chest for Judge Reiner's "surrogate election campaign."

Angelo didn't check the envelope's contents. He simply dropped it into the attaché case, then whispered a few words to Rousseau who left seconds later.

Ross smiled. Was this worth coming out in the rain for or what? It wasn't every day that you saw a top drug lawyer hand an envelope to a judge's bagman. For Moses Rousseau, the payoff was simply business as usual. "Mighty Mo," as reporters called him, always tried to get the edge. Jury tampering, intimidating witnesses, framing cops, and encouraging clients to commit perjury. Mighty Mo hadn't missed a trick.

The black women left the doorway for a stroll along the terrace, leaving Ross without a shield. She stayed put, her eyes on Lou Angelo's attaché case. She wanted a look at the contents. Big Lou would be speaking in a few minutes. Would he take the case with him or turn it over to someone else? The smartest thing Ross could do was stay close to Angelo and see what happened.

She entered the bedroom.

Mercy Howard smiled. "Girlfriend, how you making it?"

Fanning her face with one hand, Ross sat down beside her.

"I'm warm," she said. "How about you?"

Mercy Howard shook her head. "Don't say a word. I'm about ready to take off my clothes and walk around buck-ass naked."

Lou Angelo peered at her over his bifocals. "You can do that if my speech goes into the toilet."

Ross removed a shoe and massaged her foot. "How's the speech shaping up?"

"We'll know soon enough." Lou Angelo looked at his watch. "Fifteen minutes till show time. My wife wrote a check to Harborage before she left. Five hundred dollars. Forgot to sign it. Think she's trying to tell me something?"

"I'm good for a five-hundred-dollar pledge," Ross said.

Lou Angelo grinned. "My speech is working already and you haven't heard a word."

Ross put her shoe on. "I'll messenger a check to

your office tomorrow. By the way, do you have something for me?"

Angelo bounced a heel palm off his forehead. "Totally forgot. It's right here. Contracts, severance letter, the works. So much going on."

He removed a manila envelope from the attaché case, handed it to Ross, then closed the case. But not before Ross saw white envelopes, one of which revealed a wad of cash.

Angelo tapped the manila envelope held by Ross. "My bill's included."

Ross peeked into the envelope. "*Muchas gracias.* How's the money coming in for Harborage?"

Angelo shook his head. "So far, it's been nothing to write home about. I have to juice 'em up with my speech. We're getting zilch from the city and the state. Everybody's cutting back. Try telling that to a woman who's just been kicked out of her home in ten-below-zero weather. Without Harborage, she'll end up living in a cardboard box."

Mercy put a hand on Ross's shoulder. "I gave fifty dollars. I wish I could give more but I can't. I'm not with the service anymore."

"Damn right she's not," Angelo said. "She's retired."

Ross said to Mercy, "Good for you. Maybe I can find something for you with us. Know anything about computers?"

Mercy shook her head. "No."

Ross touched her forearm. "Well, let me look around and see what I can come up with."

Mercy smiled. "I'd like that."

Ross had just finished her drink when a young black

man with a broad forehead and a weight lifter's body entered the room. He walked over to Lou Angelo and whispered in the lawyer's ear, causing him to frown and rise from the bed. Angelo started to leave the room, then remembered he was carrying the attaché case. He handed it to Mercy Howard.

"Guard this with your life," he said. "Don't let anyone near it. I'll be right back."

The black man winked at Mercy. "Heard you retired, sweet thing."

Nostrils flaring, Mercy Howard looked away.

Lou Angelo glared at the black man who shrugged as if to say, *What are you getting so worked up about?* Angelo said, watch your mouth, then left the room, followed by the black man who moved with a bouncing walk.

When they were alone Ross said to Mercy, "Who's the brother with the attitude?"

Mercy Howard shook her head. "Cleveland Nobles. He's a cop. Sometimes he lets that badge go to his big head. He does weekend security at the Aztec Club over on Tenth Avenue."

"What's he doing here?"

Mercy Howard shrugged. "That nigger don't interest me. Lou got him to drive some judge up to Boston. That's the only reason he's around far as I can see. Judge likes to play cards. That's what him and Lou talk about. Cards, gambling, money. Judge always needing money."

"Rich or poor, it's nice to have money. Love your shoes."

Mercy extended a long leg. "Lou likes me in high heels. Took me shopping this morning. Bought these for me to wear especially tonight."

"Anybody's plastic but yours, right?"

"Honey, I don't own no plastic. And they ain't about to give me one either. What's wrong?"

Ross had opened the manila envelope and was examining the contents. "Something's missing. A severance agreement Lou was suppose to draw up for me. I don't see it."

"You don't?"

"We're firing this guy. To keep him from suing us, we're giving him a going-away package. He signs this severance agreement and he gets a check, company car, and medical benefits. Lou was suppose to work that out for me. Take a quick look in the case. See if the agreement's there."

Mercy Howard never hesitated.

"Sure." Keeping the case on her lap, she opened it and looked inside. Ross thought, *My kind of woman. Sweet and clueless.*

Mercy Howard said, "Girl, I must be crazy. I don't know what I'm looking for."

Ross said, "I'll find it."

A quick glance at the door. *Lord, keep Big Lou occupied for another minute. Make that two.*

She counted six white envelopes. The unsealed one held a wad of fifty-dollar bills. Two more also appeared to be fat with cash. So far Judge Reiner was doing better than Harborage. Three remaining envelopes were sealed and flat. Contents? Correspondence, perhaps. Maybe checks. Each of these envelopes had been mailed to Lou Angelo at his Madison Avenue law office. Each had the same return address and a Dutchess County postmark.

Ross closed the attaché case.

"The agreement isn't there," she said.

She looked inside the manila envelope. "I'll check in here again. Well, what do you know? It was behind the music publishing contract."

Mercy said, "Thank God you found it."

Ross removed the legal papers from the manila envelope and glanced at them. After flipping through a few pages, she returned the papers to the manila envelope. Then taking a pen and small notebook from her bag, she quickly jotted down the return name and address on the envelopes in Angelo's attaché case.

She rubbed the back of her neck. Score one for Harry. He'd gotten Ross into the fund-raiser, and it had paid off.

She'd confirmed Lou Angelo was a bagman. She'd identified a lawyer making payoffs to Angelo. And she'd learned Mercy Howard didn't have credit cards. Which meant Lou Angelo was leaving a paper trail anytime he paid Mercy Howard's bills.

Finally, Ross knew where to find a witness who could testify about Judge Reiner's very serious gambling habit. That witness was Detective Cleveland Nobles, who was driving the judge to out-of-state card games.

She looked at her watch: 9:45. She was meeting Connie at ten and looking forward to it. She'd had nothing to eat since sharing a pizza with Chessy early this afternoon.

She looked up to see a grinning Lou Angelo heading toward her. He was a man with a passion for improvement. At least as far as battered women were concerned. Show him a woman in trouble and Big Lou's social conscience went into overdrive. Let's hear it for the Park Avenue Soul Searcher.

He took Ross's elbow. "Your lucky day. I want you to meet somebody. That divorce you're having problems with?"

Ross looked at her watch. "Lou, can we do this another time? I'm meeting Connie."

Tonight Lou Angelo was being a true Christian to every woman in his apartment. Now it was Ross's turn. He guided her toward the door.

"Got just the man. He dropped by to help out Harborage. A surprise guest, you might say."

Ross tried to pull away from Angelo who held firm. Not in a painful way, but in an I-know-what's-best-for-you grip.

He said, "You are serious about wanting a divorce, right?"

"Yes, but—" *What else could she say?*

"But me no buts. I've explained your problem to my friend, and he's willing to help."

"Who is this *friend?*"

"Judge Reiner. He's next door waiting to meet you."

16
To the Rescue

She remembered something Harry had said. *A general will nearly always be forgiven for being beaten but never for being surprised.*

Tonight Ross had allowed herself to be surprised. A mistake.

Cleveland Nobles, Judge Reiner's driver, hadn't wandered into the fund-raiser by accident. He'd brought Reiner here to get paid. To pick up money to feed his gambling habit.

Only he wasn't getting a dime from Angelo. Not until Big Lou had skimmed the "campaign funds" and taken a little something for himself. That's why Mercy Howard was holding the attaché case.

Judge Reiner was in Lou Angelo's apartment. Close enough to reach out and touch Ross.

The minute he saw her, he would ID Ross as a cop. The investigation would come to a screeching halt, making her the laughingstock of the department.

Ross Magellan. The undercover—*female* undercover—who'd blown a case by tripping over the perp.

Her palms were sweaty, and her mouth was dry. How the hell had she allowed herself to get jammed up like this?

A tap on the shoulder increased her panic. She turned to see Harry holding out a cell phone to her.

She exhaled. *Harry.* God bless him.

He winked at her.

Follow his lead, Ross thought. *Same as always. Ride with the tide and go with the flow. Take what he gives me and run with it.*

Her heart was hammering.

She waited.

Harry's first move.

"Trouble," he said.

"What kind of trouble?" Ross felt the rush.

"There's been a break-in at the office."

Harry, his back to Lou Angelo, handed the phone to Ross. Giving her the Harry look. Head down, hooded eyes, half smile. Harry getting into the game.

"Our building security just called," he said. "They caught Ray Espinosa stealing files and correspondence. He was loading boxes of stuff into his car. Contracts, financial statements, computer tapes. Security says the cops are holding Espinosa, who's claiming it's all a mistake. They want us to come to the office and ID him."

He turned to face Lou Angelo. "I'm Harry Edwards, head of security for G and E Records."

It was something Harry had taught Ross. The art of picking a phony name for undercover work. For a first name, go with your own. Easy enough to remember.

For a last name, go with the same initial as your surname. Again, it was easy to remember. Plus it allowed you to wear monogrammed items, like jewelry and clothing, without arousing suspicion. As Harry pointed out, when you're with the bad guys your name and initials had better match or complications may ensue.

"Espinosa," Lou Angelo said. "I just drew up a severance letter for him. He's the guy you're firing."

"That's the one," Ross said. "And he has a temper. Which is why Harry's with me tonight. Espinosa's threatened me twice."

Actually Espinosa was a mousy little guy whose wife outweighed him by eighty pounds. She wore the pants in the family, telephoned him at work several times a day, and, on occasion, smacked him around. From what Ross heard, the wife had pushed Espinosa into stealing. He'd handled foreign sales for Gloria Paz until she'd grown tired of his thievery and dumped him. He'd been allowed to "retire," with a nice severance package thrown in. In return he was to sign a letter pledging not to sue G&E for unfair dismissal.

Where was Espinosa at this point in time? Vacationing in Cancún with his fat-assed, bossy wife.

Ross put the phone to her ear. "Espinosa has another job. That's why he's walking off with our stuff. And he's at the office?"

"Him and his cardboard boxes. I don't see this as anything that should end up in court. But cops won't cut Espinosa loose until we confirm his identity and formally drop all charges."

Ross nodded. "Who's the officer in charge?"

"Sergeant Hurston. Manhattan South."

Phone to her ear, Ross turned her back to Lou Angelo. The line was dead. Not even a dial tone.

A quick smile then, "Sergeant Hurston, this is Ross Marino. I run G and E Records."

She pretended to listen. Then, "Yes, Ray Espinosa works for us. That is, he used to work for us."

She faced Lou Angelo, a look of frustration on her face. Acting the part. Speaking into the phone with one of New York's finest.

"We terminated his services as of this week," she said. "Everything's spelled out in a letter of severance drawn up by my attorney."

Lou Angelo nodded in agreement. Ross thought, *Gotcha*.

She said, "Sergeant, I'd appreciate it if you didn't arrest Mr. Espinosa. May I speak to him please? All right, we're coming down now. My security chief and myself."

Closing the phone, she handed it back to Harry.

She said to Lou Angelo, "I can't meet the judge or anyone else right now. As you may have gathered, we've got a problem."

"I understand," he said. "Look, now's a good time to get Espinosa to sign that severance letter. He's in no position to refuse."

Ross nodded. "Good point."

Angelo said, "Let me know what you intend to do about the divorce. The judge and I, we're ready anytime you are."

Ross said, great, and waved goodbye to Mercy Howard.

She looked at Harry. "Lead the way."

He said, don't I always, and headed for the hallway. Ross was hard on his heels.

17
Forgetfulness of Favors

He watched as Magellan stepped from the convention center and stopped to stare at the rainy sky. It was 10:30 P.M.

Behind Magellan, Pavlides opened an umbrella and took her hand. Together they hurried across the darkened, rain-soaked street.

Pavlides seemed agitated. Hot under the collar about something.

He and Magellan didn't go far. They entered an all-night diner opposite the convention center, a 1930s knock-off with Art Deco posters, stainless-steel bar, and a jukebox offering swing music from the forties.

The Watcher was parked within sight of the diner, behind a Ryder truck delivering toy dinosaurs to the convention center for tomorrow's exhibition.

The convention center was an enormous building, running five square blocks from Forty-fifth to Fiftieth Streets along Manhattan's Tenth Avenue. To some the center may have been an industrial showplace; to the

Watcher it was a fifteen-story, glass-and-metal monstrosity. A blot on the landscape, not to mention an offense to the eyes.

He wasn't here to look at ugly architecture or even to spy on Magellan and Pavlides. Not this time.

He was meeting one of Pavlides's coworkers, a man with whom the Watcher had something in common. Both hated Pavlides. Out of this hatred had come an alliance, one with a lot riding on it.

First and foremost, there was money. Fifty million dollars to be exact.

Then there was the Watcher's future with Magellan. Not to mention his plan to send Pavlides to prison.

Was it possible the coworker would see this alliance as too dangerous and try to pull out? Not very likely. The Watcher believed you kept people in line by making them afraid of you. By letting them know that the only way to escape this fear was to obey you on all counts, no questions asked. People reacted to fear. Not to sympathy or to amiability but to fear. Had the Watcher instilled this fear in Pavlides's coworker? Absolutely.

He bit into a turkey sandwich bought from the diner. The meat was slightly dry, the lettuce a bit wilted. He washed it down with cranberry juice and finished with black coffee. Not exactly haute cuisine, but it would hold him until he got home.

He switched off the windshield wipers. Their noise threatened to drown out Maria Callas on the tape deck. She was singing an aria from *Tosca,* his favorite opera. And as usual she was dazzling. Absolute perfection. Not even her Medea and Norma could top this.

He bit into a slice of pickle and watched Pavlides.

The Greek was starting to calm down, but his anger hadn't completely subsided. Pavlides sat in a window booth across from Magellan, shaking his head in frustration. At one point he threw both hands in the air before slumping back in his seat. The Watcher allowed himself a slow smile. Nothing was more amusing to him than the Greek's unhappiness.

The Watcher dropped the empty cranberry juice carton into a paper bag. Magellan had angered him tonight. More than she had in some time.

She'd left Lou Angelo's fund-raiser thirty minutes ago, rushing here to meet Pavlides. That's when the Watcher had found himself in a raging fury. Why? Because Magellan had barely taken the time to thank her backup team for protecting her, so anxious was she to throw herself into Pavlides's arms. Call it a forgetfulness of favors.

The Watcher's mother had been right. We live in a thankless world.

It was a dangerous feeling, his love for Magellan. But then he'd felt the same way about the other women. He'd been obsessed with each one, and in time he'd lost control, caught up in something too powerful to understand. At that point he'd given into his most violent instincts. Any introspection made him uncomfortable. But on those occasions when he did look within himself, he managed to catch a glimpse of the truth. There was a dark complexity in his relationships with women, and he'd become addicted to it.

His cell phone rang. It lay on the dashboard, within easy reach. He made no move to pick it up.

Instead, he kept his eyes on the diner. Two more rings, then the phone stopped.

The Watcher moved his lips, counting off the seconds. When he reached twenty, the phone rang once then stopped.

The man said, "What's so important you couldn't tell me over the phone? You got me sneaking out the side door and walking around like a thief in the night. Fuck is this, a James Bond movie?"

The man, Denny Rinko, was in his late twenties, with a slanting forehead, threadbare beard, and tiny, flat ears. One eye was higher than the other. His hooded green poncho was slick with rain, and he wore jeans with the knees cut out. He carried a bulging briefcase. A strand of blue barbed wire had been tattooed around his neck.

Rinko was a computer programmer with Connie Pavlides's security firm. When it came to computers the Watcher found Rinko to be intelligent, creative, and blessed with a robust imagination. In most other matters, Rinko was totally clueless. He possessed a weak character, was unforgiving and too easily flattered. His worst trait was a tendency to upset others with unthinking comments while remaining oversensitive to criticism himself.

The Watcher said, "There's been a change in plans. And I never talk on the phone. You should know that by now. As for this being a James Bond movie, I wanted to make sure you weren't being followed. It was also a matter of saving your life."

Rinko said, "Excuse me?"

"If anyone besides you had entered my car, he'd have gotten a bullet in the head. It was in your best interests to let me know you were coming."

Rinko rolled his eyes. "Jesus. Is that what cops do? Kill people?"

"There are hurtful individuals among us, Denny. Occasionally you have to thin the herd. For the most part, I manage to restrain myself."

"Right. There are twelve-step programs for people like you."

The Watcher nodded toward the diner. "I see you and Pavlides have been at it again. You have a talent for annoying him."

Rinko shook his head. "Pavlides is a self-righteous prick. The man's been on my case since day one."

"Why can't we all just get along."

"The company doesn't bug me about my personal life. Why should Pavlides?"

"Well, you do like them young. I'm surprised you're not out cruising a school bus. The girl in question was only fourteen."

Rinko scratched his thin beard. "It's still my business, man. The chick was a runaway. I took her in, gave her a place to stay. Hey, she told me she was seventeen. I believed her."

"You're one in a million."

"Pavlides should mind his own fucking business. I don't report to him. Besides the company's happy with me. They think I'm a genius."

"Pavlides is a cop," the Watcher said. "Retired, disabled, it doesn't matter. Once a cop, always a cop. He makes a phone call to his friends and you, as they say, are in deep doo."

"Man, I loved Rita. She was special. I was thinking of marrying her."

"Of course you were. Then Pavlides put in his two

cents, thereby ending one of the great love stories of our time."

"He gave me a choice," Rinko said. "Send Rita home or do time for statutory rape."

The Watcher smiled. "Bye-bye, Rita. On the upside, you won't spend the next ten years holding hands with some black con who's got a twenty-inch johnson."

Rinko spat out the open car window. "Want to hear what Pavlides did to me today? I had a consulting offer. Five grand to program computers at Juba Records. Two days' work. Pavlides said no. Said this toy exhibition was too important. No outside work until we finished with the show. So I end up working my buns off for him and for this fat little Jap with his fat little dolls."

"Let's see if I have this right," the Watcher said. "Pavlides wants you to concentrate on Philbin Security which is paying your salary. You, on the other hand, feel you should be allowed unlimited outside work while collecting your full salary."

Rinko pushed out his jaw. "When I signed on, I told the company I wasn't giving up my outside work. Now all of a sudden Pavlides is acting like he didn't know. I ain't getting paid enough to drop my outside clients. Philbin don't like it, they can fire my ass."

The Watcher held up a forefinger. "Not just yet. Speaking of outside work, how's it going down at police headquarters?"

Removing a plastic bottle of Evian water from his briefcase, Rinko unscrewed the cap and brought the bottle to his mouth. He swallowed once then belched.

He said, "Fucking burritos, man. Burn a hole in your stomach. Police headquarters is a madhouse. I'm there three days a week. Two, three hours a day. Me and a shitload of consultants working with the department's own computer people. Upgrading software, writing new programs, setting up different databases, coordinating shit with the precincts. Crime pays, man. Leastwise it does for me."

"Thanks to Pavlides. He recommended you for the job, remember? He's making it possible for you to piss away money on film school. 'What I really want to do is to direct.' Isn't that what they say?"

"And I'll do it, too. You'll see. I'm out a hundred grand, that's how serious I am. Tuition at NYU, plus the money I put into this film I'm doing as my school project. I need another fifty K to finish it. That's where you come in."

"How so?"

"The five hundred thousand I'm getting from our deal. I'm counting on that."

The Watcher scratched the side of his nose. "So you are."

"I do this film for my course," Rinko said. "Then I take it to L.A. and show the big boys I can direct a movie. Far as Pavlides helping me, hey, I got the NYPD gig 'cause I know my shit. When it comes to computers, I'm the best."

"Give some credit to your boyish bashfulness and retiring disposition."

"I can't help it, man. I was born great."

"Be that as it may, it's looking good for us. The more computer people working at police headquarters, the better. After we make our move, everyone will be under suspicion. You won't be singled out."

Rinko said, "Whoa. That ain't what the kid wants

to hear. You're suppose to fix it so I'm not a suspect, remember? This thing ain't suppose to come near me."

The Watcher looked at Rinko. "It won't. Trust me."

"*Trust me.* In other words, 'Fuck you, Denny.'"

The Watcher turned down the volume on the tape deck.

"Let's go back in time," he said. "To when we first met. You were mouthing off. Making a nuisance of yourself. Eventually we reached an accord. Remember how that came about?"

Rinko massaged his shoulder and leaned away from the Watcher.

"I locked you in the trunk of my car," the Watcher said. "Then I shifted into Reverse and backed into a brick wall at fifty miles an hour. Did that three times. Any of this coming back to you?"

Rinko said, "You almost knocked the fillings out of my teeth. I ended up with a bitching headache lasted a month. Look, what's your point?"

"Don't argue with me. *That* is the point."

"It just slipped out, OK? Why'd you bring me here anyway? You said something about a change in plans."

"Forget next month," the Watcher said. "We go in five days."

Rinko's jaw dropped. "Holy shit. Why so soon?"

"You have your laptop with you?"

Rinko touched his briefcase. "Never leave home without it."

Reaching inside his jacket, the Watcher removed a folded sheet of paper and handed it to Rinko.

"Scan this," he said.

He handed Rinko a penlight. "Use this for light.

Anything stronger might attract attention. When you finish, give me back the paper."

Rinko read in silence. Finally, he grinned.

"No disrespect," he said, "but this is some nasty shit. I like it. Where did you get the idea?"

"It all goes into Pavlides's computers," the Watcher said. "Home and office. Wait two days, then do a follow-up. Contact the companies involved to make sure everything goes the way we want it to. And use Pavlides's credit card."

"No sweat. I can access it anytime. I work with the guy, remember?"

Rinko looked at the page. "So why the change in plans? Why three weeks earlier?"

The Watcher looked at the diner. "We live in a thankless world."

"Want to run that by me again?"

"Some things are going to resolve themselves within the next five days. An investigation I'm working on. A missing persons case. That's all you need to know."

Rinko nodded at the Ryder truck. "Know what they call a lesbian dinosaur?"

"No, but I'm sure you'll tell me."

"A lickalotapuss."

"A lickalotapuss. Well, what can I say to that?"

Rinko jerked his head towards the diner. "She ain't no lesbo."

The Watcher wiped his fingers on a paper napkin. Three things in life were unavoidable—death, taxes, and Denny Rinko putting his foot in his mouth. The Watcher knew exactly where Denny was heading with this lesbo business. But since there was no stopping the little toad, why not bow to the inevitable. Allow

Denny to proceed, then punish him. One learned by doing. Denny was about to learn the hard way that there was something to be said for keeping your mouth shut. One vital experience coming up.

Denny said, "You don't like Pavlides. You're out to *zap* the guy. Cool. That's you and him, and as long as I get paid, I don't give a fuck one way or the other. At first I thought, this is about you and him being cops. You know, a beef over some cop thing. You never told me what the beef was about, and I never asked. Again, long as I get paid I don't give a shit. Except it ain't just a cop thing. This page I just scanned. The way you're looking at them right now. It's her, right? Pavlides's lady."

The Watcher said nothing.

Rinko placed his briefcase on the dashboard. "Can't say as how I blame you. She's definitely a babe. She can play army with me anytime."

The Watcher turned to look at him. "Army?"

"Yeah. I lie down and she blows the hell out of me."

The Watcher attacked without warning. He jammed a heel down on Rinko's ankle, then thumbed him in the eye. A quick strike to the throat followed, fingers digging into the larynx—cut off any sound Rinko might have made. Rinko's head snapped backward, to hang out of the window. His eyes were bulging. The rain plastered his thinning hair to his skull. Still holding on to Rinko's larynx, the Watcher pulled him back into the car.

The sneak attack had weakened Rinko, not that he'd had a chance against the Watcher. But now all he could do was hold on to the Watcher's wrist in a vain attempt to pull the hand from his throat. Then he felt his fingers slipping away and the darkness overtaking him and the hellish pain in his left eye began to recede. His eyes turned up in his head.

And then the hand was taken from his throat. His throat was on fire. For minutes he hung his head while sucking air into his lungs.

"Insult her again and you're a dead man," the Watcher said.

He released his grip.

Rinko spoke in the softest of whispers. "I'm out. Get somebody else. I'm not taking this."

The Watcher looked straight ahead at the Ryder truck. "Stolen computer chips have become the cocaine of the nineties. Did you know that? Easy to get rid of. Hard to trace. As a matter of fact, stealing computer chips is safer than drug dealing these days. Penalties are much less severe."

Rinko stopped massaging his throat.

The Watcher said, "Not too long ago, around the time you went to work for Philbin as a matter of fact, three armed men in ski masks robbed a SoHo computer chip firm. You were doing some consultancy work for the firm. As luck would have it, you missed out on the actual robbery. They said you'd come down with some sort of virus. Anyway, the thieves got away with a million dollars in new, untraceable chips. In the process they killed a security guard. Cops never found the inside man. There's always an inside man, isn't there Denny? Someone who tells the thieves about security, when supplies are unloaded, when shipments go out. What chips to take. And of course the inside man is paid for his information."

Rinko said, "How'd you find out?"

"It's important to know people's secrets. I know

everything about the folks I work with. And as luck would have it, I caught the case."

"You never told me that."

"Slipped my mind. I tied the heist to a Vietnamese gang working out of Chinatown. Never caught them. Informants tell me they're bouncing back and forth between Hong Kong and China. They're still in the wind. Well, not all of them. One stayed behind."

Rinko chewed a corner of his mouth. "Did you arrest him? I mean did he mention any names?"

"As a matter of fact he did. Poured out his heart. Told me everything. Not to worry, Denny. Your secret's safe with me. His name was Han, by the way."

"Petey Han. Where's he now?"

The Watcher turned up the volume a tad on the tape deck.

" 'Big-Eared Petey,' they called him. The kid had the largest ears I've ever seen. If a strong wind came along, it would blow him away."

He smiled, remembering. "Big-Eared Petey had a girlfriend who lived in Flushing. I sat on her. Three days of around-the-clock surveillance in front of her parents' home. Then one night, lo and behold, who should appear but Big-Eared Petey looking for love in all the wrong places. We talked. You were the inside man, Denny. Makes you an accessory in a felony murder. You could go away for a long time."

Rinko closed his eyes. "Where's Petey now?"

"Scan that page into your computer. I'd like to get home at a decent hour."

Rinko worked in sullen silence. Finished, he handed the page back to the Watcher, then returned the computer to his briefcase.

The Watcher turned the key in the ignition. "You can leave now. I'll be in touch."

Favoring his damaged ankle, Rinko gingerly stepped from the car and closed the door behind him. On the sidewalk, he turned and faced the Watcher.

"You didn't answer my question," he said. "Where's Petey? I never heard about him getting arrested. So where is he?"

The Watcher said, "There are two rules for success in life, Denny. Number one: Never tell everything you know."

The Watcher drove off, leaving Rinko holding his throat in the rain.

18
Phone Calls

The call came into her West Side apartment at 5:00 A.M. She was asleep and didn't get the message until two hours later.

Lt. Fargnoli had telephoned to say the feds were aware of the near disaster with Judge Reiner at Angelo's fund-raiser. Had Ross fucked up, Fargnoli wanted to know, or had she just been unlucky?

He wanted to hear her side of the story. In his office, 10 A.M. sharp.

The feds had a pipeline into OCCB. Fargnoli didn't say it. He didn't have to. To Ross it was as clear as day.

Labriola had learned of the Reiner incident right after it happened. He had to have gotten the word from one of Fargnoli's people.

Face it, girlfriend. Someone you're working with is ratting you out to the feds.

Did Labriola have her under surveillance? Anything was possible. She'd been watched ever since the Reiner case started. And there was the break-in at her apartment, a job marked by an expertise associated with the FBI in general and a Georgia lard-ass named Frank Beebe in particular.

Labriola was no fool. He knew any prosecutor who took down Judge Reiner had a future so bright he'd have to wear shades. Labriola also knew that when you went to kill the king, you had to kill the king. Go after Judge Reiner and there was no margin for error. No second chance. Nail him the first time and nail him good. Otherwise he'd kick your heinie until the toe of his wingtips got stuck.

Ross didn't give a shit about Labriola's ambition. Let him dream the impossible dream to his heart's content. But if Labriola had sent his goons to break into her apartment, he'd crossed the line.

The break-in had scared her shitless. Worse, it had touched Chessy. Thank God Sis was OK. They'd spoken late last night, with Chessy sounding surprisingly normal and not blaming Ross for anything. At Doctor DeCarlo's suggestion, Ross said nothing about the gun incident. But she wasn't about to forget his warning anytime soon. *Don't push your sister over the edge again. Because the next time she just might not come back.*

Ross was ready to forgive Labriola for breaking into her crib. After she got even.

At 10:15 A.M. she walked into Fargnoli's office. They were all there. Fargnoli glaring at Ross for being late. Harry Earles, Glenn Ford, and Artie Franzese on chairs scattered around the office. And Special Agent Frank "Bear" Beebe of the FBI, in pointy-toed cowboy boots and eating a breakfast of Mexican chili with a side of corn chips. Looking at Ross as though he'd trade his mother's wedding ring for one sniff of her panties. Creep.

She considered asking Bear if he'd pulled any black-bag jobs lately but decided against it. Accusing him without proof was only asking for trouble.

OCCB was attached to police headquarters but kept branch offices throughout the city. Ross was assigned to a branch located over a Seventh Avenue chess shop in Greenwich Village. OCCB had the second floor of a six-story wooden building that had seen better days. Some might have called the building decrepit. In the Village, it was seen as colorful.

Fargnoli's private office was a cubbyhole with red upholstered walls, and a view of Christopher Park, the view consisting of statues of two gay couples. The statue couples—one male and standing, the other female and sitting on a park bench—had been erected in 1991 to commemorate the Stonewall riots. The riots, considered the beginning of the gay-rights move-ment, had taken place across the street at the old Stonewall Inn, which was now gone.

Fargnoli said to Ross, "Glad you could join us."

Ross took the only empty seat in the room, a wooden folding chair in front of Fargnoli's desk. *The hot seat.*

She opened a container of coffee. "Sorry I'm late. I had a few things to take care of."

Fargnoli ran a hand over his graying crew cut. "They wouldn't have anything to do with this case, by any chance?"

"As a matter of fact, they do. Labriola thinks the case is going south. That's why I'm here, right? I think he's getting panicky over nothing, but that's just my opinion."

Fargnoli said, "We'll get to that in a minute. Harry's already told me about last night. He calls it bad timing, nothing more. What's your version?"

"Same as Harry's," Ross said. "Reiner's name wasn't on the guest list. He made a surprise visit to collect gambling money. Otherwise, he wouldn't have shown his face. I can't see him supporting battered women unless they play poker."

Frank Beebe looked into his chili. "You know this for a fact, do you? I mean he couldn't have shown up to ID you, by any chance?"

Ross sipped her coffee. "I know for a fact he didn't ID me. Like I said, he was there for the money. If Reiner had made me as a cop, he'd have told Lou Angelo who would have told me."

Beebe grinned. "Well now, hearing you say that makes me as happy as a clam at high tide. I mean, you and Angelo getting on so well. He bring you breakfast in bed or what?"

Ross blew into her coffee to cool it. "Agent Beebe, I need some help with my thoughts here. Are you accusing me of sleeping with Lou Angelo?"

Beebe looked around the room for support. None was forthcoming.

Nor did the detectives speak up for Ross. Which is precisely what she wanted. Some things you took care of yourself.

Beebe said, "Don't go putting words in my mouth, *Detective* Magellan. I don't need you getting smart with me this early in the morning."

Ross didn't look at him when she spoke. "*Am* I getting smart with you? How would you know?"

Glenn Ford winced in mock pain and exchanged

high fives with a smirking Artie Franzese. Harry Earles permitted himself a slight smile before staring at the ceiling. Fargnoli covered his mouth with one hand. With the other he picked up a ballpoint pen, then immediately dropped it on his desk.

He said to Ross, "I take it you've talked to Angelo since last night?"

"This morning. It's one reason I'm late. Everything's fine between us. Actually I called his apartment to speak to Mercy Howard. I'm setting up something for her. Lou Angelo answered the phone."

She looked at Beebe. "It'll cost the federal government, but I think it's worth it."

Fargnoli said, "What are we talking about here?"

"A photography session," Ross said. "Totally bogus. Mercy's looking for something to do since Angelo's 'retired' her from the escort business."

Fargnoli said, "He's getting ready to stash her in a crib near the East Side place we use. You told me that yesterday. Now tell me something I don't know."

"She'd like to keep busy. So I've arranged for her to pose for a G and E record cover. Gloria Paz is going along with it. The session is phony, but neither Mercy nor the photographer know that. It's being done at a studio with a stylist, hairdresser, makeup artist, the whole nine yards. Mercy doesn't know we're just going through the motions, that the photographs won't be used. Gloria doesn't care what we do so long as she doesn't get billed. The following week Mercy's doing publicity work for G and E. Gloria has a salsa singer opening at a Brazilian club in TriBeCa. Mercy will be working the door, handing out press kits, CDs, and checking the guest list. We, that is to say the federal government, will pay her. Right now she's like a kid in a candy store. All worked up about getting into show business."

Glenn Ford said, "We're going to break that child's heart and ruin her life."

Ross brought the coffee to her lips. "That's what we're here for."

"Ain't it the truth," Ford said. "Well, she can cry on my shoulder any day."

Artie Franzese tapped the black detective on the knee. "You serious about letting her play with your anaconda? I mean, she could go wild and smack it with a hammer. Do you really want to take that risk?"

Ross said, "Is there a sensitive side to you guys I'm missing here?"

She turned back to Fargnoli. "This scam will bring me closer to Mercy. She was so grateful for the 'album cover deal.' It was enough to make you cry. Lou Angelo thanked me too. I mentioned the divorce again. He said give him the word and he'll take it from there. What he didn't say was, 'It'll cost you.' "

She looked at Frank Beebe. "I'll need money for Angelo, and I'll need it soon. The minute Mercy and I start our 'public relations work,' I look for Big Lou to make his move."

Beebe nodded. "Long as I'm there to watch you hand it over."

Fargnoli scratched an eyebrow. "Speaking of money, Harry tells me Angelo collected a few bucks last night."

Ross nodded. "Big time. Envelopes *and* cash. This surrogate scam looks to be a gold mine."

Artie Franzese held up a hand. "I saw people slipping Angelo cash. Both were known associates of Angelo and Reiner."

"Names," Fargnoli said.

"Julio Prado. He's with the Bronx borough president's office. And Mayron Goldman, that dyke on the City Council. She's also involved with some big Jewish charity."

Fargnoli grinned. "This one's looking better and better. Take down Reiner while pissing off Puerto Ricans, Jews, and dykes. I love it. Anything else?"

Harry Earles said, "Ross managed to get a look inside the case."

Ross took her notebook from her shoulder bag. "I came up with a name. Park Lee Kim. It was on three envelopes in Angelo's attaché case."

Harry Earles said, "Mr. Kim is the city's richest Korean businessman. Worth millions. Very big on payoffs to the right people. And to the wrong people. Three envelopes means he's using different donor names to slip money to the judge. I'm betting these names belong to dead people, which is a preferred way of laundering political contributions these days. If Mr. Kim's into that, he's breaking the law. Meaning we've got him no matter what happens with Reiner."

"Check this out," Ross said. "All three envelopes had the same return address. That address, believe it or not, belonged to Mr. Kim."

Artie Franzese said, "You're shitting me."

"It's called arrogance," Ross said. "People with too much money very often get that way."

Fargnoli pointed to Frank Beebe. "Could you run Mr. Kim through Immigration?"

Beebe nodded. "Consider him run."

"And check out his resident status. Citizen, permanent resident, whatever. Let's see what's up with Mr. Kim. If he has a green card, see if it's legal. Look into his tax situation and his love life. If he's married, find out if he's a player. If he is, get the other lady's name. If he's a closet queen, so much the better. Gives us a chance to make him nervous."

Fargnoli handed Ross a computer printout.

"Yours," he said. "Everyone else has their copy. We ran with your information about Lou Angelo's expensive lifestyle. That printout says you were right. Mr. Angelo is the last of the big-time spenders. He's treating little Mercy like a queen. At the same time he's taking care of number one."

Fargnoli held up six fingers. "Last week he springs for six handmade suits at five grand a pop. He also dropped five grand on shoes and shirts. Then there was the ten grand on new computers for his office. He's got this new condo in Florida, and I'm hearing from you intrepid crimefighters that Angelo's Park Avenue crib ain't too shabby either."

Ross looked at the printout. Angelo was running up five figures in charges every month. And he always paid on time. No late charges, no partial payments.

Big Lou was riding the gravy train. He was either stealing or billing more hours than any lawyer since Perry Mason.

Ross folded the printout. Her instincts had been right. Big Lou had his hand in the cookie jar, and that's why she was going to own him. This week, next week, it didn't matter. Once he took the FBI's marked money, it was cut a deal with the federal government or go inside.

Ross couldn't see Angelo doing time. Not at his age. And not when he had Mercy Howard to cuddle up to at night. Big Lou knew how the game was played. He'd do the right thing.

Ross said to Fargnoli, "If Angelo's cheating Reiner, he's also cheating the IRS. I don't see him declaring this money."

Fargnoli said, "So we've got him on tax evasion. You just make sure he comes to you with his hand out."

"The minute he does that, he's gone."

"By the book," Frank Beebe said. "You make two separate payments, and I witness both of them. I want this boy hurtin' for certain."

Glenn Ford nodded. "Hurtin' for certain. Damn, I like that."

Fargnoli placed his hands palms-down on the desk. "OK, people, meeting adjourned. Now let's slam Reiner before he slams us. If he even suspects we're trying to send him away, he'll jackpot everyone in this room. Ross, nice work. That publicity scam idea is a winner. The closer you get to Mercy, the closer you are to Angelo."

Tearing the top sheet from a small notepad, Fargnoli handed it to Harry Earles.

"Came in late last night," he said. "Guy I know in the Two-O precinct says they've got two cars you might want."

Harry took the note. "Thanks, Loo."

Harry bought used police cars dirt cheap, then resold them to cab companies for use as taxis. Cops often took side jobs to make ends meet. One of Ross's former partners had made jewelry and sold it in the station house. She'd known cops who moonlighted as security guards, sold penny stocks over the phone, and peddled real estate on weekends. Harry was in the used–police car business.

Outside of police work Ross and Harry had little in common. He liked opera. She didn't. He spent quiet evenings at home with his crippled wife. Ross loved to go Latin dancing with Connie. Harry practiced Tai Chi. Ross preferred playing the conga. She respected Harry but couldn't quite warm up to him. He was a loner. Even other cops couldn't get close to the man.

Her office at OCCB was little more than a closet with a desk, two chairs, and a view of a rusty air vent. She'd just entered it, printout in hand, when the phone rang. The caller had caught Ross at a bad time; Harry was dropping by to discuss the scam they were running on Mercy Howard. Harry liked the idea but wanted to add a few improvements. Typical Harry.

Ross brought the cordless phone to her ear. "Detective Magellan."

"Listen up. 'Cause we're not gonna hang here too long."

Jackie Blue. Talking in that high voice blacks used when they were excited.

He said, "Got somebody here wants to speak to you."

A woman said, "You're Detective Magellan?"

"Who's this?"

"Jenn Sanchez. I understand you're looking for me."

19
One Word

Jenn Sanchez. Calling Ross.

She closed the office door and put her back against it. She cleared her voice before speaking into the phone.

"Where are you?"

"That's not important," Sanchez said. "I'm only talking to you as a favor to Jackie Blue."

She had an addict's speech. Soft-spoken. Slurring her words, the voice trailing off as though she were falling asleep. Underneath it all, fear and anger. Ross thinking, in ten years this could be me. Fighting to get through each day.

"I'm alone," she said. "We can talk."

Jenn Sanchez's laugh was short. Harsh. A bullet speeding past Ross's ear.

"You're *alone*," Jenn Sanchez said. "Is that what you think? Lady, where you been? Your problem is you're *not* alone. You're with cops and you think you're safe. I'm here to tell you that's bullshit. You're so wrong it's pathetic."

"What do you mean?"

"Let me ask you something: Why are you looking for me? Do we know each other?"

"No, we don't. But I've seen your picture. We could be sisters. And we're both cops. Both undercovers. We have a lot in common."

"Oh, baby. You don't know how right you are. If you did, I guarantee you'd run for your life. Just like me."

Ross felt her throat tighten. A tiny knot of pain formed behind her eyes. "What do you mean by that?"

"I mean the guy who tried to do me, the guy who turned me into a fucking addict is a cop. He's the reason I don't sleep. He's the reason I'm all the time looking over my shoulder."

"I know."

"You don't know shit."

"I know the guy who's trying to kill you is a cop."

"So you got a snitch who's putting my business in the street. As if I don't have enough to worry about."

Jenn Sanchez was silent. Then she said, "This cop who's after me is a whole different story. You already know this guy. That's the thing."

Ross squeezed the phone with both hands. "What's his name?"

"Why? So you can fuck up some more? He's smarter than you'll ever be. Until a few days ago, I had him thinking I was dead. Then you come along. Now he's after me again."

"What do you mean?"

"You think Emilio committed suicide? Think again. And while you're at it, ask yourself how this cop came to find Emilio. You want an answer, you look in the mirror."

"You're saying *I'm* responsible for Albert's death?"

"You led this guy right to Emilio. Ain't about to let you do that to me, sweet cheeks. Just stay the fuck away, OK? I can take care of myself—"

She hung up.

Seconds later the phone rang again. *Jackie Blue.*

"Man, the bitch run off. She seen a cop car and she take off like they after her. The woman is crazy. I got to get her. Catch you later."

The line went dead.

Ross kicked the door with her heel. *Damn.*

She hung up the phone, feeling defeated and angry. Wanting to break something. *Anything.*

And then she saw it. Sitting on her desk calendar.

A paper frog. The cutest little thing. Folded from a single sheet of yellow paper and small enough to fit in the palm of her hand.

The only way to describe it was *exquisite*.

On its back, in dark blue ink, a single word.

Soon.

20
Overkill

"What's that, a new way to fight crime?"

"This? It was on my desk when I came back from Fargnoli's office."

"A paper frog. Well now, where's mine?"

"Probably still in the pond splashing about."

Harry Earles stood in the doorway of Ross's office and scratched the back of his head with the edge of a file folder. "You look worried. Afraid of catching warts?"

Ross turned the frog around in her hands. "I have a few things on my mind."

Jenn Sanchez. And the cop who's following me so he can find Sanchez and kill her.

She'd checked past issues of newspapers, looking for information on cases worked by Sanchez. Looking for anything that might shed light on Sanchez's problem with other cops. She'd found nothing.

Her next move: Check out Sanchez's personal life. Also look into every arrest Sanchez had ever made.

Every case she'd ever worked. Every cop she'd ever known.

It meant going back to the academy. Start with Sanchez as a rookie, then move on to her years as a detective. Look into her relationships with cops as friends, coworkers, and lovers. It amounted to a full-time investigation, one for which Ross lacked any clearance.

Nor was she likely to get clearance. Her superiors would go by the book. *You're not assigned to investigate Jenn Sanchez. Internal Affairs investigates cops. Any information you have, you turn over to them forthwith. You work with them or you work with us. You choose.*

She had nothing to give IA. Nothing but a report of a conversation overheard by Freddy Palacio, a cop turned informant. And her gut instinct that said Jenn Sanchez was in serious trouble.

Ross placed the paper frog in front of her Rolodex. Froggy was adorable.

Her hand brushed its back. The frog hopped. Ross squealed with delight.

"Harry, did you see that?," she said. "Did you see that? He jumped."

She tapped the frog's back again. It hopped, hit the Rolodex and fell on its side. Ross put a hand to her mouth and looked at Harry in amazement.

"Isn't he great?"

"Takes patience to turn out something like that," Harry said.

"I know. I could never do it."

Ross picked up Froggy for a closer look. Maybe it wasn't meant for her after all. Maybe the cleaning lady had accidentally left Froggy behind. It could have been a gift for one of her kids. And what did *soon* mean? Did it mean *soon* as in "shortly," "promptly," or "in a few seconds"? Or was it an abbreviation of some sort?

Harry leaned against the doorjamb. "You were talking to someone as I came down the hall. Is there a problem?"

Ross swallowed the last of her coffee. Connie and Jackie Blue were the only two people she'd told about Jenn Sanchez. She hadn't mentioned a word to her backup. Why create more problems for herself?

Getting involved with Sanchez meant going after the cop trying to kill her. Which meant making enemies. Going after a brother officer *for any reason* made you a rat. A "cheese eater."

Ross was better off keeping quiet about Sanchez. Especially around cops.

"Might help if you talked about it," Harry said.

Ross leaned back in her chair. "Not this time."

She'd handle Sanchez alone. It would have been nice to bring in Harry; they made a good team. The ghost with his experience and Ross with her instincts. Together they were keepers of the peace and protectors of the public. Not to mention the scourge of evildoers in all five boroughs.

Working without Harry would be awkward; she'd come to rely on him completely. Were it not for her ghost, Ross would be history. Just like the female undercover who'd burned to death two years ago in a crack-house fire. With Harry watching her back, that wasn't going to happen. Harry didn't make mistakes. That's what you wanted from someone who held your life in his hands.

Harry did have one drawback. He was something of an iceberg. Apt to give Ross the cold creeps at times. Always in control. Rarely making an awkward or clumsy gesture.

No exaggeration or overstatement for Harry Earles, known as Duke, after the song "Duke of Earl." Was he a perfectionist or just a tightass? Probably both. Either way, there were times when he could be frosty. Definitely frosty.

She still couldn't get over his fascination with opera. He was the only cop she knew who was into that kind of music. His retirement plans called for moving to Italy in order to be near the great opera houses.

He kept a Christmas tree all year round. His wife liked it.

She liked vodka even more. Like many cop wives, Mrs. Earles had a drinking problem. Harry, however, remained devoted to her.

He and Ross would have their little talks, just the two of them. Like today when they were scheduled to go over her plan for scamming Mercy Howard with a phony photography session. Anytime Ross was working undercover, she could count on Harry paying her special attention. Privately. Away from the rest of the team. She didn't mind. If it helped him to protect her, no problem.

Squeaky clean didn't begin to describe Harry's personal life. He didn't drink, gamble, or use profanity. Which as far as cops were concerned, was enough to have him bronzed and put into a museum. Incredibly enough, Ross had never heard of him cheating on his wife. He was attractive in a Republican kind of way. Wholesome-looking and a snappy, though not very hip, dresser. Ross saw how some women looked at him. If Harry wanted action, or as cops called it, "strange pussy," he could have it easily enough. But apparently he was behaving himself. If he was a player, he'd managed to keep it quiet. He wasn't doing a thing you could pick up on.

He had a favorite word, one he lived by. The word was *PEP,* an acronym for "Planning Equals Perfection."

Plan correctly, he'd said to Ross, and you'll accomplish your goals. Planning eliminated indecisiveness. It gave your life direction. Planning, he insisted, was indispensable.

He could get preachy on the subject, but Ross had to admit he knew what he was talking about. Any plan devised by Harry Earles was money in the bank. Count on things to run smoothly. Also count on Harry to have that smug look whenever he talked to Ross about police work.

The "Harry look," she called it. Head down, hooded eyes, half smile. Harry getting into the game. Like now.

He leaned against the doorjamb, the file under his arm. "You didn't want to tell me about that guy you'd killed, but you did. Made you feel better, didn't it?"

"God, that was ages ago."

"Eighteen months ago to be exact. Around the time we started working together. Not what I would call ancient history, by any means. You didn't want to discuss the shooting. We ended up talking about it anyway."

"Harry, let's face it. You're a silver-tongued devil

and you wear those cute little bow ties. Like the one you have on now."

Harry touched his tie. "It's puce, according to my wife. An ugly word. I say it's brown, but she refuses to budge. She gave it to me for Christmas. Not my color, really, but I didn't want to hurt her feelings. I still say it helps when you talk things out."

Ross shook her head. "Thanks anyway but I'll be fine."

"That guy you shot was bad news. A con man preying on gays. Met them in health clubs and gay bars. Got inside their homes then 'borrowed' stuff. When gays tried to get their property back, he'd beat them to a pulp. Had his victims so intimidated, nobody would file a complaint. Then you come along. You talk a vic into testifying against this guy. One night the hustler pays your vic a visit while you're there. Hustler pulls a knife, you blow him away. Game, set, and match."

Ross said, "After it happened I needed a couple of days to pull myself together. Started out feeling shaky, but that passed. Ended up feeling like every cop does in that situation. I was just glad nothing happened to me."

She picked up the paper frog. "Now I don't think about it at all. The shooting was part of the job. Something that had to be done."

Harry said, "It told me all I needed to know about you."

"How so?"

"It told me you were decisive, that you could function in a crisis. I was impressed. And I have to say my judgment has since been borne out. You're the best undercover I've ever worked with, bar none."

"Really?"

"You're a natural. I've never seen anyone do it better."

"Coming from you that means a lot."

He waggled a forefinger at her. "But don't get complacent. The only people who make mistakes are the ones who know it all."

"Harry's rule: Never get complacent. I haven't forgotten."

"Stick close to me and you just might die of old age. Anyway, let's talk about Mercy Howard. This photography thing sounds promising. It presents you and Lou Angelo with a perfect opportunity to talk 'divorce.' Who's your husband going to be?"

"It can't be you."

The hurt look on his face surprised her. Then he forced a smile. "You cut me to the quick."

"Harry, it's one or the other. You've already introduced yourself to Lou Angelo as my security chief, remember?"

He looked visibly relieved. "You're right. I forgot about that."

"Glenn and Artie are also out. Angelo may have seen them at the fund-raiser. I've spoke to a couple of our detectives. Roy Amado and Jerry Zimmerman. Both say they'll pose as my husband. Zimmerman being Zimmerman, he thinks we should have a trial honeymoon. Wants to make sure we're compatible."

Harry opened his folder. "Sounds like Jerry. Let me know when you pick your spouse. I have to brief him on the case. On the photo session itself, a suggestion. When Lou Angelo asks about your plans for the photographs, give him specifics. Album, artist, et cetera, et cetera. Make him feel happy."

Ross nodded. "I'll work that out with Gloria."

"Now let's talk about your backup while you're at the studio."

Ross held up one hand. "Whoa. I think we're getting into overkill here. I don't need backup just to watch some guy take pictures."

"You never let your guard down. I've told you that many times. You only get one mistake in this game."

"Harry, lighten up, OK? This one doesn't need backup. I'll be fine."

"The Reiner case is major. We either ride to glory on this one or we crawl off into the woods to die. One slipup, *one,* and we're history. In undercover work, you have to be ready for anything. You should know that by now. You're going to be inside, behind closed doors. Possibly a locked door."

"Harry, I know the drill. You've told me often enough. 'Never *ever* put a locked door between you and your backup.' See, I remember. But I'm not going to a crack house. And I won't be on some South Bronx street corner at four in the morning. I've spoken to Gloria. It couldn't be safer. We meet at the photographer's studio and we're surrounded by people. Not a perp in sight. It's cool, Harry. Everything's cool."

Ross shifted uncomfortably in her chair. She appreciated Harry's concern. But there was no need for him to be so protective. Not this time.

She owed Harry. And she had to work with him. The last thing she needed was bad blood between them. But there was no getting around it. Harry was turning into a control freak.

These days he had her feeling as though she were on a leash. Backup at a photography session. Was he serious? It was a waste of manpower. The kind of thing Fargnoli would turn down without comment.

Ross smiled, trying to make a joke of it.

"Harry, when photographers shoot anybody, they usually do it with a camera. I don't know Gloria's guy, but I'm betting there aren't too many drive-bys in his studio."

Harry rubbed the back of his neck. "She uses Paul Beaufils. He's worked for her for years. Works out of his loft in TriBeCa. Specializes in entertainers, musicians mostly, though he's done some work for politicians. He's had two divorces, dates models, and owns a Harley. Loves bikes. Spent eighteen thousand dollars customizing the Harley."

Ross shook her head. "You are unreal. Is this man a detective or what? Tell me something: Is there anything you *don't* know?"

"I know everything about everyone I've ever worked with."

"That's a rather sweeping statement, don't you think?"

"It's true."

Ross thought, you don't know everything about me.

"Boredom," Harry said. "That's the answer."

"I'm sorry. Did I miss something?"

"Boredom. That would have been your answer had I asked the question."

"What is this, The Psychic Hotline? What question are we talking about?"

"You love horses. So why did you leave the mounted patrol?"

Ross bowed her head. "Score one for the ghost."

She looked up. "You're right. I love horses and the

mounted unit became too boring for me. So I transferred out. No regrets."

End of Ross baring her soul. Now it was back to smoke screens, white lies, and unspoken thoughts.

Concealment. That's how she survived on the street. That's how she protected her sister.

She didn't have Harry's experience. But she'd learned this much: You never reveal your secrets. If you didn't wish to be betrayed, keep quiet. *The silent bear no witness against themselves.*

Your secrets could be used to destroy you. No one knew that better than Ross.

Secrets and betrayal. That's what undercover work was about.

"Too boring," Harry said. "Is that all you have to say about it?"

"That's how undercovers are. Always hiding."

"Not hiding. *Pretending.* It's a more fitting word."

Ross went rigid in her chair. *Pretending.*

The word struck a nerve. What the hell did Harry mean by *pretending?*

Rubbing the back of his neck, he stared at the floor. "We'll handle the photo session your way. Just you. No backup."

He lifted his head and gave her the look. Telling Ross he knew more about her than he was letting on.

21
Origins

. . . .

In the darkened basement of his Queens home, Harry
Earles opened a floor safe and removed ten thousand
dollars in cash. The money went into the attaché case
he'd used to bluff his way into Emilio Albert's apartment.

He was in a cramped storage room with a low ceiling, concrete floor, and moistened walls. Garden tools
were kept here, along with old clothes, broken lawn
furniture, and a set of golf clubs he'd used only once.

And of course, the safe.

It was a class E model, fireproof and just about
impossible to crack. He'd made it even tougher to open
by welding a steel plate to the bottom and dropping
the safe into a hole drilled into the floor. Fresh cement
was then packed around the safe and allowed to
harden. Hidden under an old rug, the safe was now
permanently fixed in the ground. A thief trying to pull
it loose would die of old age before the safe moved an
inch.

Harry returned to the living room carrying the

attaché case. Outside it was nearly dark. For Helene this meant the hour for bridge-watching had arrived.

She was in her wheelchair, parked at the front window. Grenada stood nearby, one eye peeled for her husband Levell who was picking her up in his taxi.

Grenada said to Harry, "Mr. Earles, I didn't know you were a church man."

His broad smile was accompanied by a hard stare, the stare apparently going unnoticed. "Well now, are you sure you have the right Mr. Earles?"

"I just heard your momma was a preacher. My momma works for her church too. Over in East New York."

"Really?" Harry Earles seated himself on a couch covered in off-white sailcloth. The attaché case went on the floor near his feet.

"Plays the organ. Knocks herself out every time. Kicking it in the name of the Lord. That's my momma."

It was in Grenada's smiling brown face. The feeling that he and she shared something important. Which is to say they both had mothers who'd given themselves to Jesus.

The last thing he wanted talk about was his mother. What could you say about a right-wing Christian Fundamentalist who divided her time between saving souls, gorging herself on catfish and okra, and beating the crap out of her only child with a curtain rod?

Then again how could he avoid talking to Grenada? Helene was dependent on her. Some degree of courtesy toward the nurse was advisable.

He'd handed his wife over to Grenada's mercy. To keep the peace he'd best show a little mercy himself.

He said, "My mother was a traveling preacher."

Grenada paused in the act of sipping tea.

"Are you serious?" she said.

"Her specialty was putting the fear of God into any-one who crossed her path. You could say this was her way of saying hello. Everything was black or white with her. Nothing in between."

"Sounds like a handful," Geneva said.

"And then some."

"I hear she preached all over—tents, parking lots, school auditoriums."

"Don't forget county fairs and the occasional cow pasture. We worked the South and Southwest. Six months on the road, six months in Florida where we lived."

Helene turned from the window. "Can you imagine Harry, barely a teenager at the time, going into a strange town all by himself and setting up his mother's show. Handing out fliers, contacting the newspapers, booking hotel rooms. He was very organized at an early age, weren't you Harry?"

A nearby bamboo coffee table held a dish of raw pecans. Harry took a couple and shook them in his fist.

"The pressure never stopped," he said. "Especially since my mother didn't tolerate mistakes. My job was to ride point. Go into town before the company arrived, look things over, then report to my mother. She'd take it from there."

Helene said, "Sort of like what you do now."

Harry opened his hand and stared at the cashews.

"I did it all," he said. "Checked to see if there was a rival ministry in town at the same time. Checked to see if the local sheriff was hostile. Checked to see if there were any outstanding judgments against the ministry. Once I gave the all-clear, my mother would come running. The tent would go up, we'd do our show, and take up a collection. Then it was on to the next town."

He popped the cashews into his mouth. "We gave them their money's worth, believe me. Gospel singing, Bible reading, then Mom preaching hellfire and brimstone. She'd knock 'em dead. What struck me were the people who came to hear her. The word for them is *scary.*"

Grenada waved him away. "Child, don't I know it. All them people *testifying.* Standing up and shouting about being born again. Crying and carrying on."

"Scared the daylights out of me."

"That why you didn't become a preacher?"

"My mother tried to bring me into the fold. Didn't work. Just wasn't in me to be a Bible thumper."

"What about your daddy. What did he do?"

Harry looked at his watch. Where in God's name was Levell?

"He preached as well. Not as flamboyant as Mom but he got the job done. Our little traveling circus was his idea. Put the whole thing together himself. A good man. Great singing voice. Big, booming baritone. Got me interested in reading, history mostly, and he introduced me to opera. At one time he wanted to sing opera professionally. Unfortunately, he didn't push himself hard enough."

So he drank himself to death, leaving his wife to run the show, and work Harry until he dropped. Until he left home at seventeen and joined the marines. Going

into another tightly structured world. The only kind
he'd ever known. One without a mother, however.

Harry rubbed the knife scar on the back of his neck.
"I joined the marines and saw the world. When my
hitch ended I came to New York to see Maria Callas
and never left."

Grenada said, "Who's Maria Callas?"

"The greatest singer who ever lived."

The black woman frowned. "What kind of singing
she do?"

"Opera."

"Opera." Grenada said the word as though it were
a foreign country. Then, "Your momma still preaching?"

Harry shook his head. "Not in this world. She was
murdered. Some mental defective out in Oklahoma
jacked her new car. He demanded the keys, and when
she didn't move fast enough, he shot her point-blank in
the face. I was in Tokyo at the time, pulling embassy
duty. I cried when I heard the news."

Grenada said, "You probably loved her more than
you thought you did. Also you never had the chance to
say good-bye."

"Who knows what goes on in a man's mind? Until
then, I'd seen myself as the epitome of silent manliness.
You just never can tell."

On one side, grief. On the other, the hellish life
she'd put him through. A no-brainer. He'd take grief
any day.

"Your mother made you strong," Helene said. "You
may not think so, but she did."

Harry's reply: a tactful grunt.

Another year with his mother and he'd have ended

up walking into McDonald's with an AK-47. She'd been the most demanding woman alive. And thoroughly ungrateful. No matter what he did for her, it hadn't been enough. Just like Magellan and other policewomen he'd worked with.

Grenada said, "Mr. Earles, I can't see you killing nobody for no reason. I mean all those awards you got from the police department. You're the kind of cop this city needs. The kind black people can respect."

Helene said, "He'd have gotten more awards, but everything's so political these days. The department often gives policewomen credit for things he's done. Isn't that right, Harry?"

Harry patted the briefcase. "We don't want Grenada to think I'm against women. I'm not. As the poet says, women are the source of the most lasting joys."

Helene addressed her remarks to Grenada. "He's won the Medal For Valor and any number of citations. He's also won the Police Combat Cross I don't know how many times. That scar on the back of his neck?"

Grenada nodded.

Helene smiled at Harry. "He was 'in the bag' at the time. That's what cops call being in uniform. Harry and his partner Sean responded to a radio run. Family dispute in the Bronx. Right away the Puerto Rican couple stop arguing with each other and go after Harry and Sean. Sean got shot twice in the abdomen, directly below his vest. Harry's dragging him behind a couch when this Puerto Rican woman tries to cut his head off with a machete. Fortunately she only wounds him in the neck. Then she runs into the bathroom with her boyfriend, who's shooting at Harry the whole time. Harry ends up firing ten shots—"

"Eight," Harry said.

"Eight shots through the bathroom door, killing them both. He gets his first Police Combat Cross. Sean Costello gets one as well. Except he gets it posthumously because he died on the operating table."

"Twenty-two years old," Harry said. "A year on the job and he's dead."

Helene said to Geneva, "Harry took it hard. He always looks out for his people, like he did for his mother. Speaking of looking out, Harry, you were saying something about Ross Magellan when you came in. I was a little groggy from the medication and didn't quite get all of it."

He rubbed the back of his neck. The scar always tightened in rainy weather.

"I said the word's on the street. They're going to try and kill her."

Helene said, "My God, you can't let that happen. She's one of yours. Who's after her?"

"Could be anybody. She's made a few enemies."

"Can't you help that woman?" Grenada said.

Harry raised one eyebrow. "I can try. But these days she doesn't always listen to me."

Helene gripped the handles of her wheelchair. "She'd better start listening if she knows what's good for her. Once upon a time Magellan would hang on your every word. Now suddenly *she's* the expert. If she's not careful she'll wind up like—"

She looked out the window. "Grenada, it looks like your husband's here. Give him our best, will you?"

The nurse peered through the window, then waved

at a taxi parked in front of the house. Two quick toots of the horn came back in reply.

When Geneva had gone, Helene said to Harry, "I didn't mean to come down so hard on Ross. You usually have good things to say about her. It's just that I don't like to see you being mistreated. Especially by people you've helped. And speaking of help, it looks as if Ross will need some to stay alive."

"I'll do whatever I can. You know that."

"Any idea when they'll try to kill her?"

"Soon."

22
Change of Heart

Paul Beaufils's photography studio was on Hudson Street in lower Manhattan, in an old paint factory opposite Duane Park. Ross Magellan, in jeans, wraparound shades, and a G&E warm-up jacket, arrived at two in the afternoon.

She carried CDs and press kits for next week's party promoting Gloria Paz's new salsa singer. She also had a business card identifying her as vice-president of G&E.

Window dressing. That's all it was. When it came to Latin music, Ross didn't need props. She could talk anyone into believing she'd been born into the business, that she'd never worked at anything else in her life.

She entered a freight elevator in the paint factory, a squat building erected before the Civil War. Beaufils owned the second floor, giving him five thousand square feet in which to live, work, and play. Play, according to Gloria Paz, sometimes consisted of Beaufils taking models on nude motorbike rides around the loft in the wee hours of the morning.

Ross stepped from the freight elevator and into *party time*. Into an enormous space with exposed brick walls, high ceilings, and a gleaming hardwood floor. Into the sights and sounds of three shoots going on simultaneously. Into a mix of pretty faces, advertising execs, makeup stylists in platform shoes, agents with beepers, wanna-bes with portfolios, and the pounding bass of dance music coming from wall speakers. Ross thought, *Chaos*. A free-for-all with buzz cuts and breast implants.

She looked around for Paul Beaufils. She'd never met the man, but she'd seen him on television newscasts and in newspapers, attending parties, openings, and art shows. And in the tabloids, following a drug bust, his long face shielded by a magazine. One way or another Beaufils managed to call attention to himself. Easy to do when you were a horse-faced twenty-nine-year-old, with dyed-orange hair and a black feather dangling from one ear.

Some of his photographs were displayed on a wall near the elevator. Ross recognized the faces; they were among the biggest names in show business. There were also shots of sports figures, supermodels, and a U.S. Supreme Court justice. According to Gloria Paz, Beaufils had just directed his first music video. He was a celebrity, a somebody. A *face*. Beaufils had arrived.

Did it bother Ross to use Beaufils's celebrity without his knowledge? Not at all. As a cop, you did what you had to do. Given restrictions and limitations placed on police, you couldn't do your job without breaking the law.

Ross gave her name to Beaufils's receptionist, a young black woman sporting a sari, shaven head, and jeweled toe ring. Miss Baldy, clipboard on her bony knees, sat on a high stool near the elevator. Backing her up was a uniformed security guard, a barrel-chested Korean reeking of garlic. Miss Baldy checked off Ross's name, then pointed south, toward what Ross assumed was the G&E shoot.

She headed in that direction. Thinking, *Don't get yourself in a state over Mercy Howard. Lou and Mercy, I cut throats for a living. Nothing personal, it's just business.*

She dropped her sunglasses in the shoulder bag. Sweet, trusting Mercy. How could you not like her? When Ross told her about the record cover deal, Mercy had freaked. She cried, laughed, and hugged Ross until her ribs ached. Suddenly Ross was her new best friend. Even Lou Angelo, who'd been around the block a few times, was grateful to Ross for getting Mercy into show business. Was he serious? Apparently, yes.

Miss Mercy and Big Lou were walking around starry-eyed. And all because of Ross. If the lovebirds were happy, it was her doing.

It would also be her doing when police and FBI appeared at Big Lou's door with arrest warrants, to be followed by fingerprinting, arraignments, preliminary hearings, and the scramble to make bail. Lou and Mercy would then be in the hands of unforgiving strangers, to be used and abused in the name of righteousness.

They would be lied to. Sandbagged and played until they were punch-drunk and unable to see straight. At which point Lou and Mercy would go along with the program. They would do the right thing. They would willingly betray each other and themselves.

As for Ross, she would have destroyed two more lives. And that was the easy part.

The hard part: continuing to justify this to herself.

She found Mercy Howard standing in front of a white backdrop, surrounded by Latin percussion instruments—congas, bongos, timbales. Mercy in a short-sleeved white dress and barefoot, with gold bracelets around her ankles. She clutched a trumpet and a koala bear and looked absolutely virginal. Factory-fresh and straight from the oven. Had Ross been meeting Mercy for the first time, she'd never have taken her for a working girl.

Under pressure Mercy could be cranky and irritable. Lou Angelo put it down to hypoglycemia, low blood sugar. Too many sweets or too much stress and Mercy became testy. Abnormally sensitive. At the moment she was a bundle of nerves, worked up and wired. Ready to fall apart. Ross watched her take a sudden dislike to the dimpled Puerto Rican who was trying to pin her dress, and smack him in the head with the koala bear. He called her a bitch and threatened to stick pins in her ass. Lou Angelo, in a denim suit and black silk tie, stepped in to keep the peace, taking Mercy in his arms and talking her down, apologizing to Gloria and the Puerto Rican on her behalf.

Ross waved to a teary Mercy who meekly waved back. Ross then gave her a thumbs up. Mercy smiled. Ross thought, mercy for Mercy's sake. Can't hurt.

The shoot looked ready to go. Camera, lights, black umbrellas to bounce light onto Mercy. Paul Beaufils was missing. Otherwise everything was in place.

A young Asian male, in tank top and droopy shorts, peered at Mercy through a viewfinder. Ross was starting to get pumped. Then she reminded herself it was all *bogus*. Phony from the get-go. A daydream soon to become Mercy's nightmare.

Lou Angelo left Mercy to give Ross a hug. Ross and the widowed Gloria, a forty-six-year-old Cuban butterball, then exchanged air kisses. Gloria, in red dress, spike heels and Santeria beads, seemed jumpy.

Her face said it all. *End this farce before something goes wrong.*

She'd inherited a small record company from her late husband and built it into a successful business, adding music publishing and talent management. Her acts were Latin musicians on the way up and those on the way down, making it unnecessary to pay out big salaries. She was quick-thinking and kindhearted, with uncontrolled nervous energy. She could also be resentful, suspicious, and mentally cruel.

Gloria's only child, a daughter, was in her last year at the Yale drama school. A younger brother, the one Ross had saved from prison, ran a Chelsea pet shop selling Akitas. Ross got along with Gloria, but the two weren't friends. Gloria owed Ross, and nobody, especially Gloria Paz, liked being obligated.

Tapping Ross's arm, Lou Angelo pointed to Mercy. "Isn't she the most beautiful thing you've ever seen? Takes my breath away just to look at her. She's having the time of her life, this kid. I'm so proud of her. No way am I letting her go back to what she was doing. OK, she's a bit high-strung today, but man does she look good."

Lou Angelo put an arm around Ross's shoulders. "I thank you from the bottom of my heart for this. I mean it."

Gloria Paz tugged at the beads around her neck and looked at the floor.

"Hard not to like Mercy," Ross said to Lou Angelo. "Let's hope this is just the start of good things for her."

Lou Angelo nodded. "Amen." He snapped his fingers. "Espinosa. The guy stealing your records. What's with him?"

Shit.

Ross hadn't mentioned this to Gloria Paz, who now stood behind Lou Angelo, looking confused. Why? Because Ross had flat out forgotten.

Ross said, "We're not pressing charges. The guy worked for us for a long time. I think we can cut him some slack on this one."

"Sounds OK to me," Lou Angelo said. "A little kindness never hurt, they tell me."

Ross smiled. "So they tell me."

Gloria Paz raised her hand to catch Ross's attention. "Lou asked me about the photographs of Mercy. About our plans for them. I told him this was one of your *special* projects."

Putting it on Ross. Leaving her to tell her own lies.

Ross gave Lou Angelo the sincerest of smiles. "We're using it on a G and E all-star album coming out in six months. We do one every two years, always with our best musicians and singers. Every Latin music company does the same thing. It's the equivalent of an all-star game."

Lou Angelo nodded knowingly. "Gotcha. Sounds great. Put me down for a hundred copies. I'm serious. I'll hand them out to friends, clients, to everybody I know."

Gloria Paz linked arms with Angelo. "I like this guy.

Bring me some more of your girlfriends. I'll give them a cover too."

She said to Ross, "Your friend Lou, he's very funny. He told me some wonderful stories. I liked the one about the midget nun."

Lou Angelo said to Ross, "It's an old joke about a guy who gets drunk and goes dancing with a midget nun. That is, he thinks it's a midget nun. Turns out he spent the whole night dancing with a penguin."

Mercy said, "I like that one too."

Angelo jerked his head toward Mercy. "She likes penguins. Don't ask me why. She has penguin books, statues, T-shirts. She thinks they're cute."

Mercy nodded. "Tell Ross about the time we went to the Central Park Zoo to meet this woman who's in trouble and we met her where they keep the penguins—"

Lou Angelo shook his head. One hand went up in an abrupt stop signal.

Mercy Howard quickly brought the koala bear to her mouth. "My God, I forgot. Lou, I'm really sorry. Shit, I can't do nothing right today."

She looked guilty. Suddenly Mercy cried out. Looking over her shoulder, she glared down at the dimpled Puerto Rican male who smiled sweetly. Before Mercy could swing the koala bear, Lou Angelo stepped forward, grabbed her arm and whispered in her ear.

Nodding, she dropped her arm.

Back with Ross, Lou Angelo lowered his voice. "I hope I didn't upset her. I know how important today is."

Ross said, "She'll be OK. You weren't too hard on her."

Lou Angelo's voice dropped even lower. "Some guy's making trouble for a lady. I'm just helping out."

Jenn Sanchez.

"Just what the world needs," Ross said. "Another male who won't take no for an answer."

Lou Angelo held out a pack of cigarettes to Gloria and Ross. Both women declined.

Angelo put a cigarette in his mouth without lighting it. "Quitting's easy. I've done it hundreds of times. The guy after this woman, he's not a husband or a boyfriend. He's a guy she used to work with. Somebody who wanted to get up close and personal. She wasn't interested. The guy's as diabolical as they come. Total psycho."

Gloria frowned. "Can't the police do something?"

Passing the cigarette under his nose, Angelo inhaled the tobacco.

"Police aren't going to do a damn thing. Bastards protect their own."

Gloria's jaw dropped. "This guy you're talking about, he's a cop?"

"Psycho cop." Lou Angelo took a lighter from a jacket pocket. "He makes you worry, this guy."

Gloria crossed herself. "Someone like him, he should burn in hell."

Lou Angelo smiled. "Hell was full, so he came back."

He opened and closed the lighter. "Being a cop means he's protected. This woman, all she can do is hide and hope he doesn't catch up to her. She can put this son of a bitch on death row."

He sighed. "There has to be a way of handling this. I just haven't come up with it."

He looked at Ross. "Speaking of handling things, what about your divorce? I spoke to this judge you nearly met the other night. He's ready anytime you are."

Ross looked at Gloria Paz who'd been clued in about the "divorce problem." *No reason to look surprised this time, girlfriend.*

Ross said to Lou Angelo, "My husband isn't quite as diabolical as your cop, but he's still a problem. I want him out of my life as soon as possible. He's holding out for alimony, our condo, and a new car. He thinks that I'm rich and therefore, I should continue to keep him in the style to which he's become accustomed."

"I know the type," Lou Angelo said. "I think we can work something out. In fact, I know we can. But first we have to take care of the judge, know what I'm saying?"

Ross nodded. "I want this guy out of my life as soon as possible. You just tell me how much."

Angelo lit his cigarette. "It's probably none of my business, but why the big rush? You sound like you're willing to pay anything to get rid of this character."

"Am I ever. Gloria and I are expanding. We're opening an office in Miami."

A wide-eyed Gloria nodded in agreement.

Ross said, "We're taking over a building in Little Havana. And this time we're putting everything under one roof—offices, recording studios, management, publicity. We're even planning a gift shop. T-shirts, sweatshirts, mugs, key chains. And records, of course."

"Sounds great," Angelo said. "So I take it you want your husband gone before this deal is finalized."

An emphatic nod from Ross. "Exactly. I don't want him looking at our expansion and thinking he can squeeze me for more."

"I understand. Well, why don't we talk later about the cost?"

He leaned closer to Ross. "You understand we're talking cash?"

"I understand."

Gotcha.

Ross's pager went off. She checked the number. *Fargnoli.*

What the hell did he want? Didn't he knew she had the hook in Angelo's mouth?

She said it's Connie, excused herself, and walked away. When she was far enough away from the camera, Ross took out her cell phone and called Fargnoli.

"*Hustler* or *Juggs*?" he said. "Which one's it gonna be? Or will you be appearing in both of these fine publications?"

"I'll let my public decide. Meanwhile, Angelo's in. He'll help with the divorce. And he wants cash."

"We're moving then. That's good. Speaking of the judge, I just spoke to Labriola, your favorite federal prosecutor. He's very interested in what you said about Albanians setting up drug deals in Reiner's summer home. He wants to bug the place. Meanwhile, a call just came in for you. Guy claims he's having trouble reaching you directly. Could be the rain or those downtown degenerates you're with. I make him as one of your snitches. Calls himself R. He left a message."

R for Reilly. Jackie Blue's old name.

Ross said, "He's the guy who tipped me about the Albanians. What did he want?"

"He said, and I quote, 'She's willing to meet you.' "

Ross held her breath. *Yes.* She spun around and stared through the southern exposure at the rain clouds. Good things were starting to happen.

Fargnoli said, "You still there?"

"I'm here, Loo. I was just thinking about something."

"R insists the meet go down now. The lady you want to meet is leaving town tonight. Seems somebody is making her very nervous. R says meet him in the same place as last week."

Ross, her heart pounding, nodded. "I understand."

"R and the lady will meet you there."

"Yes." She didn't trust herself to say more.

"Three o'clock," Fargnoli said. "Gives you forty-five minutes. Seems your boy R likes to cut it close. Is this thing so important that you can afford to leave Angelo right now? You tell me."

23
Jackpot

At 2:35 that afternoon, Ross Magellan left a TriBeCa bank, carrying a thousand dollars in cash. An uptown subway took her to Broadway and Ninety-sixth Street. From there she walked three blocks in a heavy downpour to Ninety-fourth Street and Amsterdam Avenue, a Spanish-speaking neighborhood of bodegas, check-cashing locations, and stores selling religious candles. She stopped at a traffic light long enough to touch the .380 in her jacket pocket and look back toward Broadway. She hadn't been followed. She was sure of it.

She crossed the street and entered a small coffee shop. Her watch read five minutes to three.

There was no sign of Jackie Blue or Jenn Sanchez.

The coffee shop was a grease pit—three booths, a counter with frayed stools, and a cracked front window held together by duct tape. The air smelled of burnt food, cigarettes, and disinfectant. There was no air-conditioning. Ross chose a counter stool nearest the front, giving her a view of the street and the entrance.

Jackie Blue was a regular. He came for the pancakes, he told Ross. He did everything but wink and jab Ross in the ribs when he said it.

They both knew he came to the coffee shop to sell product, networking with small-time locals who lacked his wholesale drug connections. Jackie Blue wouldn't know a pancake if it fell from the sky and bit him in the ass. He and Ross had gotten together in this dump a few times, and not once had he ordered pancakes.

She unbuttoned her jacket, considered running a comb through her hair, then decided it wasn't worth the effort. She told herself to think positive. Sanchez was going to show up. Why shouldn't she? Jackie Blue, God's gift to all women, could talk her into it. All he had to do was try.

Thirty minutes. That's all Ross intended to give them. If Jackie Blue and Sanchez hadn't shown by then, Ross was heading back to the office and contacting Frank Beebe about the "divorce" payment to Lou Angelo.

She already had company. With her in the coffee shop were three Dominican males, all in their late teens or early twenties. One was the counterman, a beanpole with a fade haircut, pointed chin, and wearing a spotted white apron. He dried silverware and watched a televised soccer game out of Mexico City.

The remaining two played dominoes in a back booth, slapping the tiles on the table so loud that Ross jumped every time she heard the sound. The oldest had prematurely thinning black hair and wore silver earrings shaped like crucifixes. His friend, younger and broad-shouldered, was bare-chested under a leather vest and wore bracelets made of bent spoons on both wrists. He drank from a brown paper bag, smacking his lips after each swallow. Neither bothered looking at Ross. Strange because Latinos always checked her out.

She was getting a feeling. *They knew she was a cop.*

The skinny counterman looked at Ross.

"Coffee," she said, "no food." Ross would sooner swim in raw sewage than eat here.

The counterman grinned. *"Un café para la bonita.* A coffee for the most beautiful lady in the house."

Ross gave him a half smile. Maybe she wasn't over the hill after all.

Her eyes went to the back booth. Spoons and Crucifix Earrings were whispering to each other. And continuing to ignore Ross.

She watched Spoons take another swig from the paper bag. The drink was probably malt liquor, a street favorite. Homeboys wouldn't be homeboys without it. Young blacks and Latinos drank that stuff by the quart, mixing in sweet wine or blackberry brandy. Ross wanted to barf just thinking about it.

Public drinking was illegal. However, this wasn't the time to call Spoons on it. Arrest him and Ross would have to summon a radio car to take this mutt to the nearest station house. That would create a scene, scaring away Jenn Sanchez.

Ross had taken the thousand dollars from her account as a present for Sanchez. Being on the run wasn't cheap. A thousand dollars wouldn't last long, especially when you had a drug habit. With luck, Sanchez would be grateful enough to name the cop who'd tried to kill her.

Ross looked through the plate-glass window. The rain was pounding the streets, soaking pedestrians, making drivers short-tempered and sending trash floating along gutters. Cops didn't mind bad weather. It kept people indoors and away from each other, reducing street crime. On the other hand bad weather would send some drivers over the edge. Ross had worked traffic as a mounted cop—in torrential rain, blizzards, and hailstorms where the hail was the size of golf balls. She hoped to God she never had to do it again.

Three-fifteen. Maybe Jackie Blue was stuck in traffic. Could be he was parked somewhere pleading with Sanchez to do the right thing. Either way he was turning Ross into a basket case.

She watched the counterman pour steaming coffee into a white mug. He moved at a snail's pace and spilled coffee, which he didn't bother wiping up. Instead, he simply covered the spill with a place mat. He had to be the worst waiter Ross had seen in years. She was about to say forget the coffee when he stopped pouring and looked through the front window.

She followed his glance. *Well, all right.*

A Rolls-Royce Corniche had just double-parked out front, slowing down traffic. Jackie Blue. The Jackman cometh.

Jackie in his latest ride, a car Ross hadn't seen before. But then Jackie Blue was a man of excess. Cars, fur coats, gold jewelry, and women. With Jackie B., too much was never enough.

Ross felt a buzz. Her palms became damp, and her heart was beating way too fast. But the Sanchez thing was coming together. For the moment, nothing else mattered.

She was glad to get away from the Dominicans. Something about these guys just wasn't right.

She placed two singles on the counter, then picked up her umbrella. Jackie Blue's Rolls was as good a place as any to meet. Anywhere but here.

She slid off the counter stool and started toward the door. At once she heard footsteps. Rushing her from the rear. She didn't turn. Instead Ross dropped the umbrella and went for her gun. Her hand was on the grip when she felt her arms pinned to her sides. As she tried to pull free from her attacker, someone else cut the straps on her shoulder bag.

Ross jammed a heel down on his instep. He grunted, but refused to loosen his hold. Instead he lowered his hips, lifted Ross from the ground and swung her around to face the long-legged bogus counterman. Glassy-eyed on speed, the counterman held her bag and a straight razor in his hands. Ross, woozy with fear, could hardly breathe. *God, don't let him slash my face. Please not my face.*

The counterman handed Ross's bag to Crucifix Earrings, then patted her down for weapons. The .380 was discovered immediately. Then Bogus decided to play. He fondled Ross's breasts and felt between her legs, and when he was finished, he pressed the flat of the razor to her cheek and licked her ear.

"You my new meat," he said. "You and me, we're gonna party like it's 1999. Prince does that song. You like Prince?"

Ross was scared shitless. *Where was Jackie Blue?*

She refused to enter into a staring contest with Bogus. Look into his eyes and she'd lose the power to act and think. Ross stared past him, at the kitchen door. She was a cop. She was paid to confront these animals, not submit to them.

She'd been groped and threatened with rape before. It went with the job. The best she could do was put fear on the back burner and hope her luck held.

She went limp in Spoons's iron grip. She had no choice. His spoon bracelets dug into her stomach, cutting off her wind. Her elbows felt ready to crack. Ross was in a jackpot without Harry to back her up. Her worst nightmare had come true.

She willed herself to concentrate. To think only of survival.

The Dominicans knew she was a cop. She hadn't been picked at random.

Harry. She'd never been in a jam like this without him as backup. Not until now.

She watched Crucifix rummage through her bag. When his eyes bulged, she knew he'd found the money. *"Oye! Oye, mira!"*

The counterman yelled back, also in Spanish. "Put the fucking money back, and leave the bag alone."

Ross thought, *He's not running the show.* Bogus and his friends were foot soldiers. Somebody else was calling the shots. Somebody with first dibs on the money.

She moved one elbow, easing her pain slightly. For a smart cop, she'd allowed herself to be easily manipulated. Someone had jerked her around with a single phone call. Someone who knew a lot about Ross. One call and she was dashing through the rain to meet Jackie Blue and Jenn Sanchez.

Sanchez had warned her. *Keep an eye on the cops you're working with. One of them tried to kill me. You know who he is.*

It could be anyone. Fargnoli or one of his detectives.

Someone on the OCCB switchboard or someone at Police Plaza who could pull Ross's file anytime he wanted to. She knew this much: He was a cop, and he'd just handed her over to the Dominicans. Was he afraid she'd expose him? Or was he Judge Reiner's man, assigned to shut down the investigation by taking out Ross, the chief investigator? Maybe the guy who'd given her up to the Dominicans had his own reasons for wanting her dead, reasons Ross couldn't begin to imagine.

She put herself in his place. *A loner. Jenn Sanchez hadn't mentioned anything about his working with other people. A hands-on type of guy. Hadn't he done Emilio Albert himself?*

So why was he associating with these lowlifes who were doomed to wind up facedown in the woods with the back of their heads blown away, their eyes being eaten away by ants? A smart cop didn't hang with losers. The move was totally out of character for this cop. It made no sense to Ross.

Spoons released her. She massaged her elbows, and wished she'd done it right. Backed out of the coffee shop, keeping the Dominicans in front of her. Keeping one hand on her gun.

Too smart, too late.

She began sizing up the Dominicans. The bogus counterman, called Ralphie, was the leader. His two homeboys were illegals, spoke no English, and probably came from San Francisco de Macoris, a hillside colony of shacks in Santo Domingo that served as a breeding ground for New York drug gangs. Two guns on the set, a Beretta tucked in the small of Spoons's back and Ross's .380, now in Crucifix's possession.

She wondered if Ralphie was packing and decided he was, and that's when a bell jingled over the front door announcing a new arrival.

She took a deep breath, filling her lungs. She felt better. Much better. Jackie Blue wasn't a pillar of the church, but right now he was all Ross had.

She turned to face the door and her heart sank. The Rolls Corniche didn't belong to Jackie Blue.

A Dominican couple stood in the entrance. The male, a chubby teen with gold teeth, held a dripping green umbrella. Beside him stood a slim woman, mid-thirties and square-jawed, with a mole between her plucked eyebrows. Her bleached-blond hair was parted in the middle and pulled back in a bun. She exuded a fierce energy and had a strong air of independence. She was Graciella Catala, and Ross had sent her brother, Ricky, to prison.

The two women stared at each other, Ross focusing on Graciella's right earlobe. It was the only way to hold a Dominican woman's ferocious gaze without wavering.

Graciella gave her a gummy grin. "I heard you were going to be here. So I dropped by to say hello."

Ross took a seat at the counter, in front of her coffee mug. "I heard you're going to have visitors soon. Some people from Cali."

If Graciella was upset by the thought of a run-in with the Colombians she'd been ripping off, she didn't show it. But as Ross knew, that's what made her dangerous. Deep down inside, Graciella really and truly didn't care. That's why she was called *La Loca*. "The Crazy Woman."

"You let me worry about Cali," she said. "Where

your cop friends? Don't tell me you're here by yourself. That would be a shame."

Ralphie spoke in Spanish to Spoons, called Paco, and to Crucifix, called Eduardo. "Her own mother don't know she's here."

Ross answered in Spanish, "My mother wouldn't be interested. She's dead. Only the police have to know I'm here, and they do."

Graciella sat at the counter, a ragged stool between herself and Ross. For a brief moment Ross focused on the burning hatred in Graciella's eyes. It was too intimidating. Ross looked away.

"I hear you all by yourself," Graciella said. "That's what I hear. That's why we come. To keep you company."

She tapped the counter with blood-red nails. Her hands were huge, almost as big as a man's. She'd strangled a child with them, then stuffed the body with cocaine, pretending the child was asleep when crossing the border from Mexico to Texas.

Graciella said, "They just turned down my brother's appeal. Now he got to do the full bit. Twenty years."

"He raped a child," Ross said.

"You have any idea what they do to him in prison?"

"The same thing he did to the child, I'd imagine."

Graciella stood up. "Let's go somewhere quiet. You and me and my little baby dolls. I let them play with you for a while. We make a video, and I send it to my brother. I want him to see how you died."

24
Random Variable

Three-fifteen P.M. *Harry Earles, wearing a Boston Red Sox baseball cap, braked behind a city bus on Eighty-ninth Street and Broadway. A heavy rain, the kind southerners describe as a "toad choker," had slowed traffic to a crawl. It had taken him ten minutes to travel two blocks. At this rate he'd never make it in time. He was driving a borrowed cab, a banged-up squad car he'd sold to a high-strung Pakistani who operated a small cab company out of Flushing and who was afraid of his own shadow. The OFF DUTY light was on, and the doors were locked, the only way to prevent citizens from jumping in and demanding that Harry drive them to the suburbs whether he wanted to or not.*

He wore no disguise today. No postman's uniform. No Con Ed photo ID pinned to his shirt. No piss-smelling rags allowing him to pass himself off as one of the homeless, a group he despised for its laziness and self-pity. There'd be no need for assumed personalities and disguises. Not today. This afternoon Harry was an end unto himself. A multitude of one.

The Red Sox cap didn't count as a disguise. It was his homage to Ted Williams, the greatest hitter of modern times, a man who represented the perfection Harry sought in himself. Theodore Samuel Williams whose 1941 batting average of .406 was the highest since Rogers Hornsby's 1924 average of .424. Whose lifetime average for nineteen seasons was .344.

Ghosting or pulling surveillance, Harry preferred getting around in a cab. You couldn't beat it for traveling without attracting attention. A cabbie could come and go, minus questions or raised eyebrows. Join the ethnics sitting behind the wheel of a cab and you instantly turned invisible.

He knew cops who got their jollies driving around in BMWs, Jeeps, and Corvettes confiscated from drug dealers and pimps. Harry failed to see why, unless it was a case of small minds being amused by new toys. A flashy car was an asset to a cop only when he was pretending to be a perp. Face it, the point was to be anonymous, something you couldn't do when tooling around in a customized Lexus with white sidewalls and a horn that played The Godfather theme every thirty seconds. There were surveillance cops who thought otherwise. But then you could lock these clowns in a supermarket overnight and they'd die of starvation.

He rolled down the window. Rain and the June heat had combined to produce a stifling humidity made worse by the tight-fisted Pakistani's refusal to spring for air-conditioning. The Paki was also dragging his *feet on repairing the car radio. Harry's police scanner, sitting on the dashboard, kept him in touch with the outside world.*

He used a handkerchief to wipe perspiration from his forehead and neck. He'd figured everything down to the last detail. Players, time, place. It had all been worked out. What he hadn't reckoned on was the unexpected. A random variable in the form of five inches of rain in less than an hour.

How could one anticipate the unpredictable? By its very nature, the unpredictable was changeable and irregular, beyond being controlled. According to his Bible-thumping mother, there were no accidents or injustices in God's world. Whatever one saw, heard, or felt was simply the will of the Almighty. Harry saw this as simply more of the woman's windy ravings. But then what else did she have to offer mankind?

He couldn't bring himself to believe in a God who produced a world that was nothing more than one eternal, ongoing horror. God was a fabrication, one used by his mother to hustle yokels and keep herself in ranch mink.

He listened to the blaring of car horns. Did these fools really believe that making noise would clear up the problem? Did they expect the heavens to part and God to present them with a clear road, sunshine, and a full tank? The choices people made out of ignorance never ceased to amaze him.

He was looking at his watch when the news came over the scanner. There'd been an accident up ahead. A car had just rear-ended a flower van at Ninety-third

*Street and Broadway, backing up traffic for blocks.
Harry wouldn't be moving anytime soon.*

He made his decision. He left the car, with the scanner inside his raincoat, and ran through the downpour.

When he reached Amsterdam Avenue, he turned left and headed north toward Ninety-fourth Street.

25
Playing for Time

Graciella Catala said, "We see a cop and you say *anything*, I kill you myself. Even if I have to die for it, I kill you."

"The police already know I'm here," Ross said. "I don't have to tell them a damn thing."

She pointed to the street. "Check your car."

Graciella looked over her shoulder. Immediately her face turned red. She hissed like a snake and clenched her fists. She was looking at a squad car that had just pulled up behind the Rolls.

The Dolls saw it too and looked at Graciella. She'd have to call the shots. They worked for her, took orders from her. When you ran with La Loca, you didn't improvise. You obeyed her or you'd wish you had.

Ross put herself in Graciella's place. The cops were an intrusion. An obstacle in the way of her revenge. Graciella had come here to surprise, not be surprised.

Ross felt a tightness in her chest. Her hands were

cool and sweaty. She knew what was going on in the patrol car. The cops wanted the lane cleared. Graciella
could move the Rolls herself or have it towed to a police pound in Brooklyn. Either way the Rolls had to go.

This was a minor traffic beef, nothing more. For
Ross, that wasn't good enough. To survive she'd have
to convince La Loca there *was* more going on.

Graciella lifted a hammy hand and pointed to Ross.
"The cops come in here, you're dead. I kill you no matter what they do to me."

Ross looked at the Dolls. Reasoning with Graciella
was impossible. Ross's only hope was to try and reach
her crew. She spoke to the Dolls in Spanish.

"You guys want to die?" she said. "Because if you
kill me, you're as good as dead."

Graciella said, "My boys do what I tell them."

"Then tell them how much the department hates
cop killers. Tell them what it's like on death row, eating
shit food, and waiting for someone to strap you down,
and stick that needle in your arm. And while you're at
it, tell them not to believe everything they hear. Whoever said I'd come here alone was wrong. Simple as
that."

"Then you die right now. Simple as that."

"This thing is between you and me. Why should
your crew get bagged because you won't see this thing
the right way?"

Graciella squinted at Ross. "What are you saying?"

"I'm making a buy."

"Who from?"

"Jose Ruona. I'm using him to get to his supplier."

"You want Jackie Blue."

"I know my job. Right now, let's talk about you.

Why don't you go outside, move your car, then we'll talk some more? The cops aren't looking for you. They're looking for Ruona."

"Move my car, you say."

"You can go outside or you can wait for the cops to come inside. If that happens, someone might get hurt. Move the car, then we'll talk."

Ralphie said in Spanish, "We should do like she says. Move the car. This way the cops leave. After that, we wait. Ruona shows, we split. He don't, the bitch is lying and we do her then. But not here. Someplace else."

The Dolls nodded in agreement.

Graciella looked at Ralphie. "OK. The registration and license are in my name, so I talk to the cops."

She ordered Ralphie to accompany her. He spoke English. He could also hold the umbrella and keep Graciella dry. Everyone else was to stay put and keep an eye on the lady detective. They weren't to let her out of their sight, not even to go to the bathroom.

Ross watched Graciella and Ralphie leave the coffee shop, Ralphie in a baggy raincoat and Reeboks, holding the green umbrella over Graciella and getting drenched with every step.

Paco and Eduardo took seats at the counter with Ross. Chubby, the teenager with the gold teeth, plopped himself down in a booth nearest the entrance, one hand on his shaven head, the other on the butt of a .22 in his waistband. Any sudden move by Ross would be fatal. The Dolls were jumpy. Reach for a comb and they'd kill her on the spot.

She watched Graciella walk to the patrol car, apparently unconcerned that Ralphie was getting drenched.

At the car, Graciella stopped beside the driver's window and began talking to the cops.

To keep herself occupied, Ross reached for her coffee. She didn't want any coffee, but reaching for it was something to do. She was about to take a sip when she noticed the cup was cracked. A faint lipstick smear was visible on one edge. Ross pushed the cup to one side. If the cup was this grisly, the coffee had to be worse.

She looked through the rain-stained window in time to see Ralphie entering the Rolls. Seconds later, he drove away. The Dolls cheered and exchanged high fives. Why not? Weren't they two up on the NYPD? Ross was their prisoner, and Graciella had gotten over on the cops. It didn't get any cooler than that.

For Ross, watching the cops remain in their car was to be cheated of her last hope. She'd expected them to do something. *Anything*. Instead they'd bought into Graciella's bullshit and were letting Ralphie drive off into the sunset. La Loca hadn't been ticketed, and she hadn't been towed. She was on a roll, while Ross was having the kind of luck she wouldn't wish on a dog.

The patrol car's roof lights began flashing and the siren wailed. Ross thought, *It's about to get worse*. The cops were leaving to respond to a "Ten" code. *Ten-twenty-two—theft in progress. Ten-thirty—violent assault in progress. Ten-thirty-three—police emergency in progress*. That's why they'd let Graciella off the hook.

Ross was alone. Cut off from all help.

She'd been thrown back on herself. If she didn't get lucky soon, she was history.

Graciella entered the coffee shop to the cheers of the Dolls. She'd returned in triumph. With a new timetable.

"Ralphie's driving around the block," she said to Ross. "When he comes back, we leave. We're taking you to New Jersey. My cousin's got a place near Trenton. We make our little video over there."

Ross said, "I don't think you heard me. I'm here to make a buy—"

"Oh, I heard you. I just don't believe you. I think you're lying. I think you're here by yourself. Those cops who just left? Nothing. They were just passing by."

"Look in my bag."

"What for?"

"It's called money. Ask your boy Eduardo. He found it."

Graciella looked to Eduardo for corroboration. He nodded. "*Dinero.*"

Graciella snapped her fingers and pointed to Ross's bag on the counter. Paco handed it to her. The one thousand dollars meant for Sanchez was quickly discovered.

For the second time in minutes Graciella turned red-faced and angry. *More frustration,* Ross thought. Graciella was coldhearted and self-centered, aware of nothing except her own existence. You couldn't argue with someone like that. La Loca was not on this earth to make friends.

The good news: She was frustrated because she now believed Ross was in the coffee shop to buy drugs.

Ross felt a rush. It was time to take charge.

"The money's useless to you," she said to Graciella. "It's marked and the numbers are on file."

Graciella returned the cash to Ross's bag. She did it reluctantly. La Loca wasn't in the habit of giving money back.

Ross watched her toss the bag on the counter. It was a small victory but an important one. It meant Ross had been able to get into Graciella's head, no easy task. The Dominican woman began muttering under her breath, a mixture of Spanish and gibberish, making it impossible for Ross to understand what she was saying.

Ross looked at the Dolls. Forget Graciella for the time being. Instead, she decided to play Graciella's crew and do it in Spanish. Her goal: to drive a wedge between them and La Loca.

She said, "Leave now and you guys just might be alive tomorrow. That is, if Mommy lets you leave."

Never say too much.

Ross waited. Let the words sink in.

Graciella was the first to break the silence. Turning from the window, she glared at Ross.

"Maybe you answer a question for Mommy," she said. "Maybe you tell Mommy why somebody say you were alone when it's not true. Why would anybody want me to come here?"

Improvise.

Ross said, "You ripped off Tulio Gonsalvo. Big mistake."

"Tulio?" Paco nervously fingered his spoon bracelets. "What's that faggot got to do with anything?"

Ross said, "You hit a Bayside stash house last month. Took away a hundred and fifty thousand dollars. That house belonged to Tulio."

Paco shrugged. "So we hit Tulio. Who gives a shit?"

"Having balls is one thing. Using them for brains is another. You can't take off the biggest drug dealer in Cali and expect to get away with it."

Paco looked at Graciella. "We got plans. We ain't worried about Tulio."

Ross said, "Of course you're not. Meanwhile, let me explain what happens to people who mess with Tulio's money. Two years ago he had a run-in with some Communist rebels. They kidnapped his fifteen-year-old brother and told Tulio to come up with fifty million dollars if he wanted to see Little Brother again."

Ross paused. Graciella and the Dolls were listening.

"Tulio refused to pay," she said. "Instead, he called a meeting of the cartel's top drug dealers. He told them if the rebels could touch his family, no one was safe. They had to send a message. They did. They put together an army of killers and psychos and told them to find Tulio's brother. The army went looking. While they were looking, they killed more than five hundred people—relatives, friends, and acquaintances of the rebels. Tulio got his brother back. Didn't cost him a penny."

Graciella said, "I already know the story. So Tulio got his brother back. Good for him."

Ross looked at her rain-soaked jeans. "You ever find out who killed John-John? Maybe you don't want to talk about that. OK, let's talk about this. Tulio wants also his hundred and fifty grand back. And he wants something else."

Be creative.

Ross looked at Graciella. "He wants you."

Graciella shrugged. "He can't have me. I don't like Colombian men. Too smelly."

"I did mention John-John. The guy who got set on fire on a vacant lot in the Bronx. I think that's what Tulio has in mind for you and your boys. Did I mention he's offering a reward for your capture? A hundred grand to anyone who delivers you to a certain travel agency in Jackson Heights. You're looking at a one-way trip south. What did you think would happen when you took Tulio's money? By the way, if I were you I wouldn't trust my crew. They might be tempted by the money Tulio's offering for your head."

Hand on her own throat, Graciella aimed her chin at Ross. The Dolls exchanged quick looks. Plan or no plan, the boys were having second thoughts about going up against Tulio. Ross could feel it.

She pointed a finger at Graciella. "You were scammed. Someone wanted you out in the open. You've been hiding since John-John got clipped. Now you're out and about. A perfect target."

Paco shook his head. "We leave this city *now* and we go back to Santo Domingo."

Graciella smiled her gummy smile at Ross. "I knew we would have problems with Tulio and the others. That's why I had a plan. My plan was to make a lot of money, then go back to Santo Domingo where we're protected. Where Tulio and his friends can't touch us. In my country we don't have to worry about no Colombians, no DEA, no extradition. We were supposed to leave New York next week. So we change. We go tomorrow, maybe the day after. We'll be safe in my country, and you'll be dead. That's right. I kill you before we go."

Ross said, "You're not hearing me. Tulio has you in the open. And I've got backup. You don't have until tomorrow. You're up to your ass in cops and Colombians *right now*."

Ross folded her arms. *Always be sincere whether you mean it or not.*

"Let me give you your choices," she said. "Stay in New York and wind up like John-John. Or head for the airport *now* and hope you make it before Tulio catches you. Kill me and you can forget the airport. When a cop is murdered this city goes into lockdown. Nobody in or out. Airports, busses, trains—nothing moves. That means you're stuck here with both Tulio and thirty-eight thousand cops looking to cap you. Your choice."

Silence.

Ross waited, this time holding Graciella's gaze.

The silence grew stronger. Ross thought, *They're hooked.* She'd made Graciella and her crew distrustful of one another.

She had them thinking. Caught up in their own confusion.

Playing for time. It was the best she could do.

Then, disaster.

The Rolls returned. Ross saw it through the window. The tightness in her chest came back. *She'd lost the game.*

Ralphie blew the horn. Graciella turned toward the street.

Ross dug her nails into her palms. *Stay calm,* she told herself. *Keep it together.*

The silence was broken by the bell over the front door. Ross flinched as though someone had fired a shot next to her ear.

A man stepped into the coffee shop out of the rain.

Ross choked back a scream. She was hallucinating. It couldn't be. She rubbed both eyes with her fingertips and looked again. He was still there, cool green eyes sizing up the coffee shop and everyone in it. Harry. That's who it was. *Harry.*

He stood at the entrance, calm as you please. Frowning slightly, but nothing extreme. Harry wasn't the worrying type. He'd once said to Ross, "*You* worry. I *think.*"

Graciella was shaken. For some reason Harry terrified her. Ross couldn't imagine La Loca being afraid of anybody. But she was definitely scared of Harry.

She backed away from him. Following her lead, the Dolls did the same. Had Graciella and Harry met before? Or did La Loca feel the vibe that said you don't fuck with this cop? Ross had to agree with her. Anybody in a face-off with Harry had to feel jumpy.

Ross looked around for cover. La Loca and Harry had conflicting interests. There'd be no compromise. Not today. Graciella wanted Ross dead, while Harry was pledged to keep her alive. Ross was willing to bet her pension that a shoot-out was going down. She wished it wasn't true, but the facts spoke for themselves.

Harry wore his customary Boston Red Sox baseball cap in honor of his favorite sports hero. Water dripped from the cap's bill and onto his badge now hanging from his neck on a silver chain. The Glock was in his left hand, which was at his side and half hidden behind his thigh. Ross braced herself for gunfire. *How had he managed to find her?*

She seated herself in the last booth. She could see Harry. At the same time she was looking at the backs of Graciella and the Dolls. Ross's plan: Dive under the table at the first shot.

Graciella stopped near the end of the counter. So did the Dolls.

On the small black-and-white TV set near the cash register, the announcer screamed, "Goal!", drawing the word out. The stadium crowd went nuts.

Harry did his cat walk toward the Dominicans, treading softly as though not wanting to wake anyone. He was the center of all eyes, which didn't seem to bother him at all. Two more steps and he stopped. When he spoke, he couldn't have been more polite.

"Weapons on the floor. No sudden moves, please. When you're finished, everyone down, facing the kitchen."

Graciella said to him, "You planned this, didn't you? *You*, Mr. Cop. You come here to kill me. I can feel it."

Ross thought, *She's out of her mind.* Harry kill Graciella? No wonder they called her La Loca. What reason would Harry have for killing this nutcase? As for any planning, the question here is, What was Graciella smoking? Harry wouldn't set Ross up to be murdered. Never happen.

But she couldn't dismiss a nagging thought, namely that this entire episode had been *prearranged*. No other word came to mind. A voice seriously said everything's been calculated to produce this moment, one allowing Harry to dash through the door and play hero. *Not true,* she told herself. No way can it be true. Harry was here, and nothing else mattered.

Sliding a hand into her purse, Graciella fixed her tiny dark eyes on Harry.

"I *know* what happened," she said to him.

She nodded her head rapidly. "I know why you got me here."

Harry smiled at her, and in that instant the two seemed to agree on some unspoken truth and then his arm came up, and he shot Graciella in the forehead. She fell backward and landed on the floor in a sitting position, her back against the counter. A foot twitched, throwing off a worn pump. A silver-plated .22 slipped from her open purse.

Paco dropped into a crouch, a hand pulling at the gun in the small of his back. Ross shouted, "Gun!," a warning to Harry, then dove under the table. She looked up to see Harry shoot Paco in the face. The shot spun the young Dominican around. He landed on the floor in front of Ross, sprinkling her hands with his warm blood.

A terrified Eduardo turned, intending to run into the kitchen. He'd taken one step when Harry shot him in the back of the head. Arms extended in front, the balding Eduardo stumbled forward, then disappeared through a swinging door leading to the kitchen. The door swung back, allowing Ross to see Eduardo lying on the kitchen floor, sneakered feet crossed at the ankles. Then the door swung closed.

Three head shots. Three dead.

Ross climbed off the floor and sat in the booth. Quickly pulling a handful of paper napkins from a dispenser, she rubbed the blood from her hands. Her ears rang, and the smell of gunpowder was sickening.

In the street, a driver put his hand on the horn and kept it there. The sound entered the coffee shop, attacking Ross's ears and nerves. The horn blower was Ralphie. He'd seen what had just happened and was running for his life. He swung left, attempting to drive around a TV repair van blocking his way. There wasn't enough room. Ralphie didn't care. He shattered a headlight on the Rolls, dented the van's rear, and kept going.

Three head shots. Three down.

Ross looked at the floor. One Doll, Chubby, was still alive. He lay sobbing and curled in a ball, brown hands clutching Graciella's lifeless arm.

Harry aimed his gun at Chubby's head. Ross screamed, "Harry!"

Harry let his gun hand fall to his side. Then he pressed the Glock against the teenager's cheek, and as Ross tensed, Harry relieved Chubby of the .22 and a switchblade. Both weapons went on the counter.

Then Harry walked toward Ross.

He was smiling. "Everything's under control. No need to worry. Harry's here and all's well."

26
Three and Counting

"News has reached my ears. I understand you come close to getting yourself neutralized, Detective."

"There's a news blackout. You're not supposed hear anything."

"No news blackout on the street, Officer. Free enterprise running wild out here. You white folks call that hustling. Us black folks call it surviving."

"The shootings. What did you hear?"

Ross was on the phone with Jackie Blue. Eleven-fifteen at night and the phone at her West Side apartment hadn't stopped ringing. Everyone wanted to talk about this afternoon's shootings at the coffee shop. Ross would have preferred to sleep, but the world didn't see it that way. Fargnoli, IAB, her backup team, Ivy Linder, and a couple of former partners. Everyone wanted to talk to Ross, to see if she was all right and if she could shed some light on what happened this afternoon at the EC Coffee Shop owned by one Edgar Chacon. Police wanted to question Mr. Chacon but at the moment were having trouble locating him. Ross wasn't surprised. Gunfire and bodies tended to make people disperse and fan out.

Connie sat on the couch beside Ross, channel surfing for news of the killings. He'd found nothing. To protect Ross, the NYPD and FBI had imposed a news blackout.

Blackouts, however, didn't exist on the street. And Jackie Blue had big ears.

"Two versions of what went down," he said. "One says Graciella got popped 'cause she tried to rob two undercovers when they showed up at EC, looking to buy product from an associate of my acquaintance."

Ross looked at the living-room window. The rain had slowed to a drizzle. June was turning out to be the wettest month the city had had in years.

She said, "Someone claiming to be you left a message at my office, telling me to meet you and Sanchez at the coffee shop. I show, and Graciella nearly takes me out."

"Dig. This is the first time I called you all day. Took me two hours to get through. Your line been busy tonight."

Ross put her bare feet on the coffee table. She'd been on the phone for three hours without a break. In addition to everyone else, the commissioner's office and the police union had called to offer sympathy, condolences, and a warm heart. Ross appreciated the concern, but at the moment she was tired of being pitied.

She said to Jackie Blue, "Let's hear what's behind door number two."

"This version says a pair of undercovers tried to arrest Graciella for murdering one of Tulio's people. Graciella threw down on the law, an act of impulsiveness, since she now grounded for good."

Ross said, "How did you know I was in the coffee shop? Was my name mentioned?"

"Wasn't necessary. Jackie Blue is a thinking man. Your boy Duke left his trademark behind."

"Head shots."

"Indeed. Your boy Duke is a headhunter. Don't mean shit to him you wearing a vest. He just aim for your head. Meanwhile, it is a natural fact that if Duke is on the set with a female cop, that lady got to be you. Now it so happen they put a jacket over the head of a woman when she leave the coffee shop. I say to myself, 'She got to be Detective Magellan.' "

"Was that a lucky guess, or did I leave something behind with my name on it?"

"To protect his woman cop, Duke clipped three Latinos. Ain't but one lady he look out for like that."

"Do yourself a favor. Don't spread that around."

"I'm cool. Oprah wants me, the answer is no. No *Tonight Show,* no *Nightline* for Jackie Blue."

Ross squeezed Connie's hand and winked. Time to rattle Jackie Blue's cage.

She said to the drug dealer, "Speaking of not talking, when do you start talking to me?"

"What's this we doing? Where I come from, you make noise with your mouth, that's talking."

"You know who suckered me into going to the coffee shop. I want him. He's the same person who's after Sanchez."

Jackie Blue's voice was soft. Cunning. "Baby, why

you play your daddy like that? I open my soul to you. If I knew anything, I'd—"

"Jackie, that mack rap's wasted on me. Five minutes after you met Sanchez, you had that cop's name. And you're sticking with your game plan. You're holding back on giving me that name until you can get something for it. Sanchez is a junkie. That means you have the power. She either tells you what you want to know, or she gets none of your world-renowned pharmaceuticals. You're holding back on me, Jackie. Like I said, when you need a favor, you'll trade. Slick, let me give you some advice. Looking out for number one *sometimes* gets you what you want. Most of the time it gets you what you deserve."

Ross listened to Jackie's breathing. She'd nailed him, and they both knew it.

Which didn't mean he'd stop trying to get over on her. Old habits died hard.

"Baby, you know I'd never play you cheap," he said.

"I told my lieutenant you had nothing to do with the shootings. I said someone had used your name to set me up. Right now the police don't have a beef with you. That could change."

"I hear you."

He turned conciliatory. "Look, I appreciate you not putting the cops on me. I did call to see if you were all right. Other thing is, I wanted to know if everything's cool between us. I didn't want you to think I had anything to do with this."

"It's cool, Jackie. But you still have to do the right thing."

"Forty-eight hours, then Jackie come through. You

can go to the bank with that. Just give me two days."

"The D.A. wants to talk to me. When that happens, your name will come up. Given your line of work, I'd say the D.A. will try to connect you with Graciella. I'll try to keep you out of it."

"Man, don't put me anywhere near that bitch. I'd sooner pick shit out of a dog's ass with a toothpick than do business with her. Stealing from Colombians. The hell was she thinking?"

"She was thinking she could get away with it," Ross said. "The way you keep thinking you can get over on me."

"One of them little boys who follow Graciella around, I hear he still alive."

Ross stared at the television screen. A fat-faced black sportscaster was describing a Yankee loss to Milwaukee in the bottom of the ninth. The last of Graciella's little boys was a chubby, gold-toothed illegal named Israel Novato. At the moment he was being held incommunicado, away from family, friends, lawyers, and the press. Away from anyone who might want to ask him about the female undercover who'd been in the EC Coffee Shop.

He was being shifted from precinct to precinct, at night and in unmarked vans. Moving a perp around gave cops time to obtain warrants, plant wires, protect witnesses, and make additional arrests. It also protected undercovers. Lawyers protested, but there was little they could do about it. All cops had to say is, "It's out of my control."

The paperwork got lost. Your guy's refusing to be fingerprinted. The car taking your guy to the arraignment broke down. The feds are involved, which means taking your guy to the nearest federal court. Unfortunately, this being the weekend, that particular federal court is closed.

Ross said, "Graciella's boy is not your problem. Focus on the cop who's after Sanchez. You're on his list. You can lead him to Sanchez, and he knows it."

"Man, I should never have listened to Angelo. He say I *got* to help him hide the bitch. Dig, ain't but two things I *got* to do and that's stay black and die. I figured Angelo got Judge Reiner in his pocket and if I ever get jammed, maybe Angelo put in a good word for me."

Ross said, "Lou Angelo's jammed up himself. He can go down with Reiner or get killed because of Sanchez."

"This shit's getting too intense for me," Jackie Blue said. "Especially with a crazy cop zeroing in on my ass."

"Help me get him before he gets you."

The drug dealer exhaled.

Then, "You know Manhattan less crowded now that we missing three citizens of the Latino persuasion. The Duke out there doing his thang. Got him a double-matched set. Three men, three women. Watch out, babe, your boy don't make it four."

He hung up.

Double-matched set. What was Jackie Blue trying to say? If he was trying to make a point, it was lost on Ross.

She told Connie about the phone conversation with Jackie Blue.

"You tell *me* what matched set means," Connie said.

Ross sipped brandy. "A warning. Like don't get caught in the cross fire when Harry's shooting at some perp."

Connie aimed the remote at the television set, switching it off.

"Double-matched set," he said. "Three men, three women."

"That's what I thought."

"But today Harry bagged only two males and one female. Either Jackie Blue can't count, or Harry's killed more people than he's let on."

Ross waved him away.

"I've had a hard day," she said. "It's also been a long one. So it's possible I've missed fragments of conversations here and there. I do know Harry saved my life. I wouldn't be here if it wasn't for him."

"You helped yourself. You delayed Graciella. Kept her there long enough for the cavalry to arrive. Timing's everything. Now you take Harry. He could have been anywhere—Manhattan, Queens, Brooklyn. Instead, he turns up on Amsterdam Avenue just when you need him the most."

Ross sipped her brandy, then said, "He was actually working on the Reiner investigation. He'd gotten a tip from a cop at the Two-O, a sergeant who sells him old squad cars. The precinct's been getting complaints from a woman who's having trouble with her ex. It just so happens that this ex is an Albanian with a criminal record."

"This ex. He's not connected to Judge Reiner by any chance?"

"That's what Harry wanted to know. He came up with something. Eighteen months ago Reiner threw out a drug case involving this ex. Makes this particular Albanian a man who has friends in high places."

Connie nodded. "It's looking good."

"The wife and this guy are divorced, but he refuses to let go. Shows up at her place uninvited. Kicks holes in the front door. Threatens her boyfriends. Follows her everywhere. Classic stalker. She's filed a number of complaints against him."

"Has she gotten an order of protection?"

Ross nodded. "She has. The guy ignores it. Harry felt the wife might tell us something we could use against Reiner."

"Makes sense," Connie said. "Where does she live?"

"Ninety-eighth and Amsterdam. Four blocks from the coffee shop."

"Convenient."

"You don't hear me complaining."

Connie turned the remote around in his hands. "A four-block walk and Harry's a hero."

"What are you trying to say?"

"Harry leaves this woman's apartment and he can't find a cab because it's raining. He starts walking."

"Past the coffee shop," Ross says. "Sees me with Graciella and her boys. Knows Graciella has a beef with me for sending her brother upstate. Knows she recently put one of her boys on me."

Connie chuckled. "The late John-John who was going to be toast one way or another."

"Right away Harry knows something's wrong."

"So he comes into the coffee shop with his gun drawn. Didn't take him long to figure out that Gracie was up to no good."

Connie rose from the couch, walked to the television set, and placed the remote on top of the cable box.

"That frog someone left on your desk," he said. "The one with *soon* written on the back. You have it?"

"Not here. It's at the office, on my desk. Why?"

"Froggy was a message. Someone was putting you on alert."

"A warning maybe."

Connie shook his head. "No. Just an alert. You didn't get much in the way of details, which is what you'd have received with a warning. Someone knew Gracie would try to kill you."

"I agree. The question is who."

"Graciella accused Harry of planning to kill her, right?"

Ross closed one eye and nodded. "Graciella was nuts. You can't take anything she said seriously."

"These days we think of them as 'misunderstood.' "

"She was a psycho-loony and you know it."

Connnie took the copy of *TV Guide* from the television set.

"OK, she was crazy," he said. "Now let's talk about the guy who tricked you into meeting Gracie. He's tried to ice Sanchez. He's in and out of your place like he lives here. He knows your cases and your informants. You can assume he's aware you're after Judge Reiner, something the judge would give his left nut to know. He knows everything there is to know about you. What we have here is a cop who's a stalker. Which means our guy knows all the tricks."

Connie flipped through the pages of the *TV Guide*. "He's one slick dude. Very, very good at what he does. He proved that when he saved your life today."

Ross started to speak, then stopped. "Wait a minute. Is that some kind of joke? Because if it is, I don't find it very funny."

"It's no joke and neither is this."

He returned to the couch and handed Ross a CD. She said, "Did you buy that?"

"No. I know your taste in music and this isn't it. I didn't buy it and neither did you. I found it just now."

He pointed to the television set. "Over there under your *TV Guide*."

Ross looked at what Connie had just given her. It was a CD of *Tosca*, Harry's favorite opera.

27
Imposed Penalty

At sundown Harry Earles, wearing a hooded poncho and dark glasses, entered a rundown hotel on the Van Wyck Expressway in Queens. The rain had stopped, leaving behind moist air and a blackened sky. Harry lowered his head, attempting to hide his face, which turned out to be unnecessary.

Behind the front desk a young Haitian male continued reading the *New York Post*. He remained focused on his horoscope as Harry stepped into a waiting self-service elevator. The staff at this hotel—Harry had done undercover narcotics work here—wasn't exactly top drawer. But then the hotel was a sinkhole, a home to sleazeballs, deadbeats, and others who knew they were going under.

He left the elevator on the third floor, choosing to stand in the empty corridor rather than seek a room number. Reaching under his poncho, he pulled out a pair of steel balls, each the size of a plum. They were hollow inside and contained sounding plates that chimed whenever the balls moved.

Placing the balls in the palm of his left hand, he rotated them first clockwise then counterclockwise. He bent and stretched each finger in sequence, causing the balls to circle each other. He kept the joints of the hand in motion, allowing the forearm muscles to contract and relax. With each movement, the balls sounded like miniature church bells, a sound Harry found quite pleasant.

After a couple of minutes he switched the balls to his right hand, following the same rotation sequence—clockwise then counterclockwise. He was still rotating the balls as he walked to the middle of the corridor. When he reached the room facing the fire exit, he used one of the steel balls to knock on the door. He knocked twice, waited several seconds, then knocked twice more.

He heard two men inside talking in Spanish. The talking stopped when he knocked. He shook his head. Not good.

He was scheduled to meet one man, not two. Two men meant Harry was in for a surprise, and he didn't like surprises.

He rotated the balls as he waited, fingers moving with a magician's dexterity. The door was finally opened by someone who kept out of sight.

Harry stepped into a small room whose single window overlooked the Van Wyck Expressway, now clogged by rain-slowed traffic. There was barely room for an unmade bed, floor lamp, and dresser. A television set announced the start of a Spanish variety show entitled *Merengue y Mas*. A tiny night table held an empty wine bottle, an overflowing ashtray, and a .45 automatic. The air smelled of farts, fast foods, and marijuana.

The door closed behind Harry, who turned to see a potbellied man in shorts holding a sawed-off shotgun by the barrel. The man was Hilton Prigo, a beefy Dominican albino in his mid-thirties, with the pink skin and white hair of a rabbit. His bare chest and arms were covered with tattoos of crosses, coiled snakes, and naked women. He should have been alone. He wasn't.

Seated on the bed was a young Dominican male, slim and dark, with an extremely large forehead and a charming smile. He wore a lime green jumpsuit and blue sneakers and had his dark hair combed forward in bangs. His left hand, hidden under a pillow, rested on the bed. Harry was certain the pillow hid a gun.

He'd never met the young guy, but he did know him by reputation. Which is to say he'd heard about him from cops who'd sent him away. The guy was Israel Valencia, Izzy V, and until last month he'd been inside for manslaughter. Prior to his arrest Izzy had been running a crew of homeless men selling crack, weed, and assorted pharmaceuticals in Manhattan's men's shelters.

One employee had gone into business for himself, using half for personal pleasure and selling half for personal gain. Izzy reacted by force-feeding the man rat poison, then crushing his skull with a dumbbell. For his enthusiastic application of managerial skills, Izzy got eight to fifteen in Attica.

As for Hilton Prigo, he too "had his ways," as Harry's mother use to say. He was underhanded and sadistic, a chronic worrier who was both indecisive and self-deceiving. He'd made his bones while doing time for car theft in Puerto Rico, where he'd chopped an informant into bits, then flushed the bits down the toilet. The skull was wrapped in a pillow case and smashed against a cell wall, with the fragments also ending up in the crapper.

Prigo was called *El Conejo*, "the Rabbit," which seemed fitting for an albino with buckteeth and a nervous tic. Like most criminals in Harry's experience, Prigo was dedicated to doing what he wanted to do. To expect otherwise was to be disappointed. Prigo had yet to disappoint Harry. But then Harry was the one man Prigo feared.

Harry rotated the steels balls in his left hand. Izzy V didn't belong here. Harry had scheduled a private meeting with Prigo who'd apparently taken it upon himself to invite a third party. Clearly a mistake on Prigo's part.

Harry spoke to Prigo as if Izzy weren't in the room. "What's he doing here? This meeting isn't open to the general public."

Izzy never lost his smile. "The big bad detective. You smoke a crazy woman and some punks and I'm suppose to be impressed."

Harry rubbed the scar on the back of his neck. Like most ex-cons, Izzy seemed to feel that prison had made him wiser and stronger than the rest of humanity. He also possessed the contempt for cops all too common among today's criminals. Would Izzy survive his ignorance? Probably not. As Harry's mother use to say, "Fools outnumber the rest of us," adding, " 'twas ever thus."

Izzy, his hand still under the pillow, said, "We're talking business here. Me and my friend. I go when we finish, not before."

Prigo's nervous tic was more pronounced. He knew Harry better than Izzy did.

"You go," Prigo said to Izzy. "We talk later."

Izzy shook his head. "For eight years people been telling me what to do. Them days are gone. We finish, then I go."

Harry removed his sunglasses. Then he pulled back his hood and looked at Izzy for the first time. Izzy cocked his head to one side and held Harry's gaze. *Just like a prison yard,* Harry thought. *Don't let 'em stare you down.* Except Izzy wasn't in prison anymore. He was outside where the rules were different. For one thing, Harry usually got his way.

He took a handkerchief from his pocket, knotted one of the steel balls into one corner and smiled at Izzy.

Harry said, "Welcome to the free world," and swung the handkerchief like a blackjack, cracking Izzy across the shins. Once, twice. Moving faster than anyone Izzy had ever faced. Screaming, Izzy bent over and grabbed his pained legs.

Grabbing Izzy's bangs, Harry pulled him to the floor. Then he reached under the pillow.

Well, now. Izzy was packing a five-shot Taurus .38. Not the most powerful piece around.

Harry said, "Is this the best you can do? Or is it against your religion to carry excessive firepower?"

Izzy lay on the floor, rubbing his shins and giving Harry the hard eye. *Still feisty, our Izzy.*

Harry tucked the Taurus in his belt. Then, almost as an afterthought, he kicked Izzy in the head.

Izzy make a soft noise that sounded like *eeeeee* and went rigid.

"Take off your clothes," Harry said.

A glassy-eyed Izzy looked up at him with defiance. Then he shook his head. He spoke through his teeth, "Fuck you."

"Allow me to rephrase that," Harry said, and kicked Izzy in the head again.

Grunting loudly, Izzy quickly covered his nose with both hands and rolled over on his side. Blood trickled from between his fingers.

Harry looked at an ashen-faced Prigo. "Undress him and don't take all day doing it."

Minutes later a naked Izzy, his face swollen and bleeding, stood on his feet, clinging to the dresser for support. The cockiness was gone. He wasn't staring at Harry anymore but at the floor.

Harry said, *"Now* you can leave. And if I see you in the hall or anywhere near the hotel, I'll kill you."

Izzy looked at his clothes now in a pile at his feet.

"Everything stays here," Harry said. "Hilton, give him a dollar. One dollar, no more."

The albino did as ordered.

Harry said to Izzy, "You have ten seconds to get out of my sight."

He looked at his watch. "Starting now."

Alone with Prigo, Harry seated himself on a folding chair and resumed his one-handed rotation of the steel balls. Neither man spoke for a long time.

Finally Harry pointed toward the door. "You want to explain that?"

Prigo cleared his throat. "He's going to be one of

my lieutenants. I'm putting together my organization—"

"Let me stop you right there. You are not in the drug business. Not yet. You're in the drug business when I say so and not before. Is that clear?"

"I understand."

"I sincerely hope so, for your sake. Truth is, good advice is useless because no one follows it. Which is why I didn't waste time talking to your friend. Now to business. I'm here to collect my money. I'm also here to deal with the problem caused by Denny Rinko. What I didn't come here to do is to watch you build an empire."

"I understand."

"You keep saying that. I have my doubts. Meanwhile let us proceed."

He saw Prigo looking at the steel balls.

"Chinese medicine," Harry said. "It's called *Jingluo*. Keeps the blood and vital energy circulating throughout the body. Prevents disease, aids your memory, prolongs your life. And speaking of prolonging one's life, you do have my money?"

"I'll get it."

"That would be appreciated."

Prigo crouched beside the bed. His boxer shorts were low on his hips, exposing the crack of his butt and making him look like a cartoonist's idea of a plumber.

Using the tip of his shoe, Harry pushed a condom wrapper away from his chair. When he wasn't building an empire, Prigo was fornicating his stupid life away. Being ugly as sin meant paying for his pleasures. His taste in women ran to Asian whores with boyish figures, cropped hair, and small breasts, a preference Harry saw as being that of a closet homosexual.

"I see you've been entertaining," Harry said.

Prigo pulled a worn brown suitcase from under the bed and placed it on top of the sheets. "I got my needs, you know? Ain't much else to do, waiting around here for you to call."

"Did Izzy or those Asian dwarves you're partial to see this case?"

Prigo shook his head. "No way. I swear on my mother's grave nobody saw nothing."

Reaching under his poncho, Harry pulled out a white envelope and tossed it to Prigo.

The albino looked in the envelope and smiled, an ugly sight.

Harry said, "Ten grand. The money I promised for getting Graciella to the coffee shop."

He could have punished Prigo, who was no rocket scientist and basically had the IQ of a claw hammer. But there were times when violence was counterproductive. This was one of them. Yes, Prigo was a pinhead. Lord knows they didn't come any dumber. But Harry needed him. Under the circumstances the best move was to crunch Izzy and hope Prigo got the message.

Prigo fingered the bills in the envelope. "Glad everything worked out with Graciella. Crazy bitch. She was bound to get snuffed."

Harry said, "Couldn't have done it without you. It was better she hear about Magellan from someone like you instead of me. Someone on her social level, so to speak. My approaching her wouldn't have worked."

Prigo looked at him with admiration. "You popped her just like that. Never once hesitated."

Harry held up a finger. "Self-defense, remember?"

"Self-defense."

Prigo put the envelope in the top dresser drawer. Earles was one crazy bastard and you never asked a cop like that why he killed somebody. His answer might not be what you wanted to hear. Wasting Graciella was Earles's private business. Prigo didn't know why the guy wanted to clip Graciella, but you could bet it had to do with that female detective. The one Earles had *rescued* from Graciella. Earles never spoke about her, and Prigo wasn't going to push the point. Mess with Earles and the man would fuck your life.

Harry said, "Let's have a look at my money."

Prigo thumbed open the suitcase locks. The case was full of hundred- and fifty-dollar bills.

"Three million," Prigo said. "Count it."

Harry grinned. "I trust you."

A lie. If so much as a nickel was missing, Prigo would wish he'd never been born.

Harry said, "Any more from Denny?"

Prigo shook his head. "Not since I last spoke to you. He refuses to give me all the merchandise. I can't sell what I don't have."

A vein throbbed on Harry's forehead. "Makes sense. And he wants more money."

"He wants to be paid. He says after the chances he took, you got to do the right thing. He wants double."

Harry pulled a raw cashew from under his poncho and bit it in half. *Double.* A million-dollar payday for that little twerp. Four times what Harry was paying Prigo. Not that Prigo knew what Denny was getting, but still.

Harry *had* planned to kill Denny. Scheming little

shit that he was, Denny had that figured by now. Look for him to be on full alert. Killing him wouldn't be easy. But never fear. Harry would find a way.

Prigo sat on the bed. "He say don't call him unless you're serious. He say he's not into bargains and he ain't running no low inventory sale. You don't give him what he wants, he keeps the shit for himself. Or he finds another buyer. He's waiting to hear from you. You got his beeper number. One meeting. You show up with the money, he shows up with the stuff. And he picks the place."

"Never trust thine enemy: for as iron rusteth, so is his wickedness. Though he humble himself and go crouching, yet take good heed and beware of him."

Prigo squinted at Harry. "What's that you just said?"

"Ecclesiastes. Chapter twelve, verses ten and eleven. So Denny wants double. I vote for two behind the ear."

"I'm down with that."

Harry leaned back in his chair. "The little putz thinks I'll do him like I did Graciella and her friends."

"How'd he hear about that? Ain't nothing on TV or in the papers."

"Denny works part-time at police headquarters, remember?"

"Right. So how you going to take him out?"

Harry shook his head. "Not me. *We.*"

"We?"

"Shoulder to shoulder on this one, *mi amigo.* I set him up, you take him down. You get another fifty thousand for your trouble."

Prigo grinned, "Hey now."

Harry stood up and stretched his arms. "One week.

That's all I need. By then it'll all be over. The Denny problem will be solved, I'll have made my deals, and a happy retirement will be in my immediate future."

"Denny's a punk. He knows about computers, so he thinks that means he knows everything. I can't wait to see his face when we bag him."

Harry looked at his watch. He had to get home so Grenada could leave.

He shifted the steel balls to his left hand. "We can't kill Denny until we have the merchandise. Remember that."

"I will."

Harry closed the suitcase, grabbed the handle, and walked to the door. At the door he turned and smiled at Prigo.

"Be well, do good work, and keep in touch. Oh, and be careful. Someone spotted a naked man around here. Don't let him catch you bending over."

28
Bad Hair Day

The beauty salon on Broadway and Sixty-fourth Street faced the plaza fountain at the Lincoln Center for the Performing Arts. Ross Magellan, in cocktail dress and heels, arrived late in the afternoon to have her hair colored.

Ross used her cell phone to call Chessy while David, a sharp-nosed forty-year-old Australian, added auburn highlights to her hair. The highlights were Chessy's suggestion. "Makes you look way cool," she told Ross. Chessy had been right. On the street and in the music business you had to look "way cool."

The highlights also hid the gray Ross had since she'd gone undercover to nail a male nurse stealing computers from a hospital and carrying them out in a garbage bag. She'd cornered him in a hospital stairwell. Before she could get out of the way, he stabbed her with what he said was an AIDS-tainted needle.

While the needle turned out to be filled with water, Ross still felt the need for an AIDS test. When it came back negative, she cried. The experience left her with gray hairs and a resolve to shoot the next perp who attacked her with a needle.

Closing the cell phone, she took out her notebook and began writing. As David combed in the color, Ross wrote about Harry. Not the Harry she'd known for the past two years, but the Harry of the past forty-eight hours. She underlined his name each time as though warning herself to be on guard.

Harry. Think the unthinkable.

"We're getting grayer," David said.

"Don't remind me."

"A friend in the film business told me about Grace Kelly. Apparently Miss Kelly started out with a fifteen-minute makeup call. Then it began getting longer. A half hour, forty-five minutes. Then it was an hour and a half, and finally when it became two hours, Miss Kelly decided it was time to leave the business. She found herself a frog who was a prince and moved to France."

"David, she went to Monaco, not France, and I don't think the people in Monaco are French."

"Can't say as I blame them. Who wants to live in a country where the money falls apart and you can't tear the toilet paper? You're dressed for success, I see. Going dancing with the Greek tonight?"

Ross looked up from her notebook. "That's why I'm here."

David ran his comb under the tap. "How is Chessy, by the way?"

"OK."

As OK as a teenager could be in a funny factory.

David said, "Still wearing her hair long?"

"Long enough to sit on."

"Have her come in and see me. I'll treat her like a queen. We queens take care of our own."

"Thanks. Maybe after I wrap this case."

"Not that I'm prying any more than usual, but you are looking rather solemn."

Ross tapped her notebook with her pen. "What do you do when someone you've been betrayed by is someone you trust?"

Irony of ironies. Harry was doing unto Ross as Ross did unto others.

David stopped combing. "You're the police person. You tell me. But I offer this for your consideration. A certain Irishman of my acquaintance once held my heart in his hands, but that was long ago and far away. He owns a bunch of illegal casinos in Manhattan and Queens. Employs Irish tough guys to keep out the riffraff. Illegals, ex-cons, IRA goons. Some might call *them* the riffraff. Anyway, my Irishman hired a former rugby player to manage a couple of these casinos, paying him a fairly decent salary. I suspected the two shared a certain closeness, but I couldn't prove a thing."

He shrugged his thin shoulders. "To continue. The rugby player's job was to collect the money, thereby keeping it from the hands of thieves, cops, and tax collectors. Last week he collected over a hundred thousand dollars. I'm talking serious simoleans. Well, what did our handsome collector do? He disappeared. Vanished in a puff of smoke. No one's seen hide nor hair of him since. My Irishman feels very betrayed, which is why I suspect his relationship with Mr. Rugby was more personal than professional. What do you do when you're let down by the light of your life? You survive. That's all you can do."

Ross said, "What if the person who betrayed you is dangerous? What if he can hurt you. Seriously hurt you."

"My Irishman has people who can deal with Mr. Rugby. And sooner or later, I suspect they will. Meanwhile, I told my Irishman you pay for every piece of ass you get. He didn't appreciate that."

"Anyone ever tell you you're a smooth talker?"

"This person you once trusted, is he capable of killing people? My Irishman is. He once told me—"

Ross's phone rang. She brought it to her ear and said, "Detective Magellan."

A male voice said, "Three people shot to death in front of her, and her response is to go to the hairdresser. You're a cool one, I'll grant you that."

Harry.

Ross closed her eyes.

"Magellan, you still there?"

"I'm here, Harry."

"Two days and not a word from you. What gives? We're still working Judge Reiner, correct?"

"You're supposed to be home recovering from posttraumatic stress."

"Really? Must remember that in case I'm asked why I took time off. I did need to catch up on some sleep. Now seemed as good a time as any. Post-traumatic stress. Any chance I could get on *Oprah* or *Rikki Lake*? Might be fun having a tearful breakdown on camera. On the other hand, I can't see getting wet-eyed and heartbroken over having to do Graciella and two of her loonies. The department, IAB, and the grand jury don't appear too concerned either. I understand Lou Angelo took the bait."

Ross looked at her notebook. "Noon today. I made the first payment on my 'divorce.' Five grand. Angelo wants thirty."

"Of which Judge Reiner will see a buck and a quarter if he's lucky. Where did it go down?"

"At the East Side apartment."

"Without me," Harry said.

Ross thinking, *We'll work together again when hell freezes over.*

She said, "Labriola's in a hurry. You know that. He wanted a nut on Angelo as soon as possible, and he wasn't about to wait. We had no choice. We had to go ahead without you."

Earlier this afternoon. Ross serving lobster salad, dark bread, and red wine to Lou Angelo and Mercy Howard on the terrace of the East Eighty-first Street duplex, the undercover crib. No cooking for Ross; she'd ordered in from a York Avenue deli, adding a good Margaux, French cognac, and Italian pastries, all at the FBI's expense. Special Agent Frank Beebe the Bear, himself, hid in the bedroom with a camcorder, filming Ross handing over 5K in marked hundreds to Angelo. In exchange, Big Lou promised to speed up Ross's "divorce" from Detective Jerry Zimmerman, whose photograph was on prominent display throughout the apartment.

Handsome Jerry's presence lent authenticity to the scam. He was, after all, the so-called owner of the apartment or would be when the divorce was final.

A second witness, Glenn Ford in his role as chauffeur, sat at the bar in the sunken living room, drinking tomato juice and reading Black Tail, *his favorite black*

*skin magazine. Ford hearing about the payoff through
an earpiece wired to a mike in a vase of flowers on the
terrace. Hearing Angelo admit that the money handed
him by Ross would be going into Reiner's campaign
war chest for surrogate judge.* "A formality," *said Big
Lou. Trust him, it was all legal.*

*Mercy Howard, who'd tagged along, couldn't stop
raving about the fun she'd had shooting the record
cover. And how much she was looking forward to
shopping for an outfit to wear at the party honoring
Gloria's new salsa singer.*

"Here's a thought," Harry said. "We know Angelo's
skimming. That's a given. I bet he gives his girlfriend
cash to buy her new outfit. She doesn't have plastic.
What do you bet Angelo gives her some of the marked
bills you passed him? He does that, we own him. Now
and forever, he belongs to us."

"I'm ahead of you," Ross said. "Tomorrow I'm taking Mercy to a wholesale fashion outlet recommended
by Gloria. They sell designer stuff at a discount. If
Mercy pays in cash, I'll retrieve the bills."

"Well, now. You are out in front on this one."

"For once."

*A lie. Ross hadn't thought of going after the marked
bills so soon. Not until Harry mentioned it. And then
she'd felt a strong urge to get the better of him. Any
way possible.*

Harry said, "While we're on the subject, there are
things you're not telling me."

"Come on. You know as much about this case as I
do."

"Do I now? Well, answer me this. Since when did
you start checking up on me?"

"I don't understand."

"You were at the Two-O today. You wanted to know whether or not I'd made contact with the ex-wife of a certain Armenian thug."

"Harry, I—"

"Yes or no."

"Yes."

Harry exhaled. "You're checking up on *me*. When did that become a part of your schedule? Was it before or after I saved your life?"

Ross had no answer. Or rather she had no answer she could give Harry without triggering a reaction.

He said, "So now you've taken it upon yourself to verify anything I tell you about our cases. Harry's now some kind of dope fiend–informant whose every word has to be verified. Since when?"

Ross thinking, Since I caught you lying to me. You said you'd approached the coffee shop from Ninety-eighth and Amsterdam. A lie. You said you'd been to see the Armenian's wife. A lie. You said your showing up at the coffee shop was a coincidence. A lie.

The truth: You set me up. You invited Graciella to kill me so that you could kill her. You left a recording of Tosca in my apartment. You've been following me for days, and I'm too frightened to ask why.

Harry said, "After all I've done for you, this is hard to take. I've been there for you anytime I had to be. Right or wrong."

"I can't argue with that, Harry."

He whistled tunelessly down the phone. Then, "Seems the more I do for you, the more ungrateful you are. I put myself on the line and you react by running off to Pavlides. He didn't deliver you from the fire. I did. In the past two days you could have found the time to call me. Just to say hello if nothing else. I see something wrong here. Something seriously wrong."

Ross shivered. She looked up to see a worried-looking David staring at her.

"Pavlides won't always be there," Harry said.

Ross leaned forward. The conversation was taking a strange turn. One she didn't like.

"Harry, what's Connie got to do with any of this?"

"You couldn't do your job without me. Whether you admit it or not, that's the truth."

"I asked you a question. What's Connie got to do with our working together?"

"Gratitude isn't one of your strong suits. I suppose you have other things on your mind. Such as dancing the night away with Pavlides."

Stepping from the chair, Ross took one step forward and looked through the front window. She developed a splitting headache without warning. She closed her eyes to shut out the pain. To shut out Harry.

"Where are you?" she said.

He could see her every move. She knew it.

Harry said, "Tell Auntie not to put too much red in your hair. You're an undercover cop, not Lucille Ball."

29
Journal Entry

Harry Earles left his Queens home at midnight and walked to the cab parked in his driveway. A star-filled sky promised a night without rain. Something to look forward to.

In the front seat, he unlocked the glove compartment and removed his journal. He sometimes made entries at night, in the privacy of the cab. It was a time when he was truly in a world of his own.

He wrote by flashlight, listing the latest items he'd taken from Magellan. Nothing of great value. Just a single earring and a cracked comb. Pathetic as the world went but full of meaning for him.

In the past few weeks he'd removed several articles from her apartment and office. As always, he avoided anything valuable or large, limiting himself to things she wouldn't miss. Stuff she didn't use or would assume she'd simply misplaced. All under lock and key in his bedroom and neatly displayed on a teakwood table. A shrine of sorts.

Among the items were a video of Magellan's wedding, a silver ring, a folded washcloth, a brassiere, an old address book, and one of Magellan's favorite Latin music CDs. With a laptop and help from Denny Rinko, he'd compiled a world of information on Magellan, building a pretty good database mostly from public records. He knew it all, from her medical and professional history down to the number of the hotel room where she'd spent her honeymoon. He even knew the weddings, birthdays, and personal history of her relatives. Magellan may have been a profound mystery to the rest of her colleagues but not to Harry.

His prized possession was a framed color photograph of Magellan taken the day she'd graduated the academy. Magellan, young and radiant in her uniform, looking upbeat and hopeful, at the time believing more than she doubted. Today, as he did every morning, Harry had placed a rose in front of the picture.

He looked in the rearview mirror. The phone conversation he'd had with Magellan today was a reminder that love and hate were inseparable, that both were two sides of the same coin. He sometimes thought they were the same thing seen from different angles. Just hours ago he'd saved her life. But instead of being with him, she was off dancing with Pavlides. Magellan had the ingratitude of a spoiled child, and Harry was starting to resent it.

What right did she have to check up on him? To go behind his back in an attempt to discredit him or prove he was lying?

He turned a page in his journal. Difficult as it was, he now had to consider the possibility that Magellan could disappoint him as the others had done. He disliked thinking that way, but facts were facts.

The *others*. Their treachery had been too much for him to bear. In the end, his only peace had been to kill them. He hoped it wouldn't come to that with Magellan.

He opened a pack of raw cashews. Once you stopped loving a woman, it was amazing how despicable and trivial she became. At the same time, hating a woman gave him a wild and uncontrollable energy, a pleasure in itself. His hatred had become the religion his mother had been unable to instill in him. Hate made him feel alive.

He turned to the front of the journal, to a three-year-old entry on Celia Cuevas aka "CeeCee." She'd been the first, a young, lovely Latina and one of the smartest undercovers he'd ever worked with. A single mother and cute as a button in her uniform. His stint training her for undercover work had been a happy time for the both of them. They'd started with low-level narcotics work, buy-and-bust in crack houses and on street corners. Nickel and dime stuff. But CeeCee had the talent. Before long she was working Organized Crime, Wall Street white-collar types and city councilmen with sticky fingers and a severe overdraft. Under Harry's guidance, CeeCee became a star.

He'd kept her alive, as he'd done with Magellan. Taught them how to mess with a perp's mind and break his heart. Both women were born liars, making them star material. Harry gave the edge to Magellan who lied so convincingly that on occasion even he was taken in by her con.

Both women knew how to play the game of gender

politics in the NYPD, no small feat in a bigoted, chauvinistic military organization. Again, Harry had to give the nod to Magellan who'd gotten her gold shield through her political smarts.

But as smart as CeeCee was, there would be no happy ending for her and Harry. She didn't love him. Wouldn't love him. Worse, she was incapable of gratitude. Anything Harry did for her, CeeCee took as her due. She became far too wrapped up in herself to suit Harry. In the end he'd had no choice. He'd taken measures, punishing CeeCee for her thanklessness.

Journal entry/ CeeCee. Her corpse is on fire. The body stiffens, blackening as it turns rigid, tensing as though caught by surprise. Attacked by orange flames, the body contracts faster, shriveling and becoming smaller, disappearing within itself by inches. And then the flames burn brighter, devouring the hands and lifting the feet, drawing them inward. There is a stench. Sickening. More foul than one could imagine. Then a change. The odor becomes bearable. Familiar. An odd truth: When burning, at some point the human body smells exactly like barbecuing meat. Strange.

Body parts fall off. Fingers, hands, feet. A point to remember for the future, since these items might leave incriminating evidence. Note: The odor of gasoline partially hides the overall smell but not completely. The head falls last, breaking from the body to roll off to one side like a rock going downhill. Fact: The body sizzles in its own fat, an unpleasant sound. Worse, con-

tinued burning causes the body to swell and explode. Burning to death is an ugly business.

Harry brought the journal to his face. He'd sprinkled CeeCee's perfume on her entry pages. They'd shared some good times. Even killing her had given him pleasure.

He closed his eyes in thought. Would killing Magellan also be pleasant to remember? Who knew about destiny? In any case she'd raised hopes in him that must be fulfilled.

He closed the journal and slipped it into a jacket pocket. He'd attached his dreams to Magellan and had no intention of letting her disappoint him.

Switching on the ignition, he backed out of the driveway. Helene had taken a sedative and would be out for hours.

He headed toward Manhattan and Magellan. Keeping watch over her was the most important proof of his love.

30
A Night Out

Café Con Alma on Bleecker Street in the Village still had the tin ceilings, revolving fans, and a big wooden bar from its days as a popular 1920s speakeasy. Ross liked the club because it attracted an older dance crowd, with little interest in drugs and guns.

Something else: Con Alma had Benny B, one of the best deejays in the city and a friend of Ross's. Crowds followed Benny B from club to club, drawn by his mix of salsa with old bands like Machito, Noro Morales, Mario Bauza, and the greatest of them all, Tito Puente.

Tonight Benny B started with twenty minutes of Puente's early hits, dedicating the set to his good friend Ross Marino and kicking it off with two of her favorites, "Albaniquito" and "Mambo Diablo." She danced with a ferocious skill, acting out her fears and anger. Couples stepped back to watch her and Connie, but most eyes were on Ross. The set ended with Ross being applauded as she collapsed in Connie's arms.

Back at their table they held hands and listened to Tito Rodriguez's achingly beautiful ballad, "Mio."

"Maybe you should stay at my place tonight," Connie said. "You need to relax."

"I'm sorry. I was a little wild out there just now. Your place sounds fine. Harry is *scary*. I have nightmares about waking up and finding him standing at the foot of my bed, giving me that goony grin of his. All of a sudden everything about him is creepy, from those nuts he's always eating to those steel balls he plays with."

"I think Harry's losing it."

"Harry? No way. The man's got ice water in his veins. The day he comes unglued is the day hell freezes over twice."

Connie sipped a scotch. "That call to the beauty salon this afternoon says he's walking the edge. He did everything but admit to stalking you. I say the job's getting to him. He wouldn't be the first cop to snap."

"I can't work with him anymore. Fargnoli will have to find me another ghost."

Connie tapped his drink glass with a plastic stirrer. "Harry's a cop, and cops know all the tricks."

"What are you saying?"

"It means he knows how to cover his tracks. Breaking and entering. Pulling your records. Following you without being seen. He can do it all. He can also count on other cops to protect him. Even if he's doing wrong, they won't rat him out. I'm saying when you talk to Fargnoli, you're not going to have any hard evidence pointing to Harry's guilt."

"I have to try. Harry's not normal. And yes, I know

all about the Blue Wall of Silence. I've been a part of it at times."

Connie looked into his glass. "So I don't have to explain to you how the system works. It works against a cop who's going after another cop. Anytime you do that, you stand alone. I don't think it'll ever change. Harry will have cops covering for him, lying for him, even going after you if it comes to that. And he won't be the bad guy. You will. Why? Because you're bringing a complaint against another cop. Be careful what you tell Fargnoli. It could come back to haunt you."

Ross said, "I went through this when a friend of mine was raped by her sergeant."

"Sergeant Poontang. You told me. Look, you could have pictures of Harry cutting the pope's throat and you'll still find cops who won't believe he's guilty."

"Harry's not just guilty. He's dangerous. He doesn't belong on the force."

"He's a hero with awards and commendations up the wazoo. Pointing the finger at him is not going to make him a stalker. Not to people who see him as a hero. What's more, you're bad-mouthing a guy who's your backup. Who's saved your life more times than the mayor has comb-overs."

Ross reached for her drink. "Maybe I'll have more credibility if Harry invites me to a coffee shop and blows my brains out."

Connie took her hand. "I'm not trying to scare you. I just want you to know there're no easy answers with a stalker."

"Especially if he's a cop."

"You got that right. A cop stalking a cop. One for the books."

Ross said, "Does your company get many stalker cases?"

"We get our share. We're usually called in when cops are too busy. I've seen cases involving women as young as twelve. The biggest problems come from stalkers in the workplace."

"Why's that?"

"The stalker knows where you'll be. He knows exactly where to find you. Going to work leaves you exposed."

He looked at the tin ceiling. "I hope I'm wrong, but it looks as if Harry's following a classic stalker pattern."

"Which is?"

"He's isolating you. That's what his bad-mouthing me is all about. He killed Graciella to win your gratitude. And with Harry, gratitude means being grateful to him and nobody else. That's how stalkers operate. They cut their victims off from everybody—family, friends, everybody. Isolating you is easy. You're already dependent on Harry."

Ross made circles on the table with her drink glass. "I've heard about women being stalked. Never thought it would happen to me."

She looked at Connie. "Harry wants to control my life. On the job and off. Who I see, where I go, how I dress. Everything has to meet with his approval."

"It's about power and control," Connie said. "To get it, you intimidate the victim any way you can."

Ross threw up her hands in frustration. "So I'm alone. Is that what you're telling me?"

"Look at me," Connie said. "Go on, look at me." She did.

Connie said, "When Harry comes after you, he

comes after me. I'm not standing by while he does his psycho thing. Straight up, he hurts you, I hurt him."

Ross squeezed his hand.

"I think you should talk to Fargnoli," Connie said. "He'll listen. Play it by ear. Feel him out."

"I want him to do more than listen. I want another ghost."

"What reason will you give for not wanting to work with Harry?"

"I don't know. But I'll think of something."

Connie thought for a while. Then, "All I can come up with is stuff you can't tell Fargnoli. You can't tell him Harry's breaking into your apartment, that he's stalking you. It's Harry's word against yours. If you say he lied about his whereabouts before he shot Graciella, again that's he said, she said, and it'll go nowhere. Fargnoli will never believe Harry deliberately executed Graciella so he could get next to you. I mean it's bizarro mundo time."

"Don't forget the paper frog," Ross said. "Who's going to believe me when I say Harry's communicating with me through a paper frog?"

Connie laughed. "Couple of gypsies, maybe. I just thought of something. You've given a sworn statement that Harry saved your life at the coffee shop. Withdraw it now and you'll tear the squad apart, not to mention painting yourself as some kind of nutcase."

"Bottom line."

"Find the smoking gun. Nail Harry with something so strong, Fargnoli's got to believe you."

"I need another drink." Ross held up her glass and caught the eye of an elfin Puerto Rican waiter with a neatly trimmed beard.

She looked at Connie. "A week ago Harry was my hero. Now I know stuff that could send him to prison."

"You mean there's more?"

Ross shook the ice cubes in her empty drink glass. "Nothing you don't already know. But I'm now getting a clearer picture. Jenn Sanchez said a cop tried to kill her. She also said this same cop airmailed Emilio Albert and his pit bull from an eighth-floor window. It's a given this cop lured me to the coffee shop so Graciella could have her fun with me."

She pushed the empty glass away. "Sanchez warned me. She said I was working with the cop who'd tried to kill her. I didn't want to believe it. At one point, I thought Frank Beebe might be the bad guy. Not anymore. It all points to Harry."

"Graciella's pointing at him from the grave," Connie said.

"What about John-John? I think Graciella sicced him on me. Unfortunately for John-John, he ran into Harry. My *protector*. John-John got what Graciella got, plus a few extras like handcuffs and being burned alive."

"What happened when you called the Two-O and asked about Harry and the Armenian's ex-wife?"

Ross watched the Puerto Rican waiter place her new drink on the table, then leave.

"I inquired in a roundabout way," she said. "I identified myself and said Harry was ghosting for me, that he'd left a radio in a taxi he'd been using for surveillance. Seems Harry abandoned a cab on Broadway in order to come rescue me. Local cops cut him some slack and didn't impound it."

Connie said, "Cops caring for cops. Just thinking about it gives me a glow."

"I didn't tell the Two-O Harry was lying. Meanwhile, I still can't figure out how he did it. How he set me up with Graciella."

"You talked your way into staying alive. Remember that."

"Harry never spoke to Graciella directly. She'd have mentioned it if he had."

"Meaning?"

"There's another player. Harry used someone to talk to Graciella. He'd never have approached her directly. Whoever he used was somebody she'd listen to."

"Some drug-dealing scumbag probably. How about your friend Jackie Blue?"

Ross shook her head. "I did say his name was used to lure me to the coffee shop. But he never made the call. Don't forget: Graciella was ripping off dealers, and Jackie Blue was probably on her list. Sooner or later, she'd have robbed him blind. And why work with Graciella when the Colombians are looking to whack her. Jackie Blue isn't stupid. Besides, with me dead he loses a friend at court. No, Harry used someone else to approach Crazy Grace."

"Any ideas?"

Ross sipped her drink. "I figure it's someone who's too frightened to say no to Harry. I also think Harry's sold me out to the feds. Labriola needs to make the Reiner case. If he can dump me and grab the credit for himself, he will."

"What's Harry get for selling you out?"

"A job with the Justice Department. Immunity for

something he's done. A finder's fee maybe. What I can't figure out is why Harry's after Jenn Sanchez."

"Ask her."

Ross grabbed Connie's arm. "My God," she whispered.

She pointed to the far edge of the dance floor.

Connie looked in that direction.

Watching them from behind a fake palm tree was Harry Earles.

31
Laying the Groundwork

Harry Earles and Frank Beebe met for lunch on the terrace of Central Park's Boat House Café. A threat of rain had emptied the terrace. Except for pigeons perched on the stone railing, the two men were alone.

Harry dropped a few white cashews into a tossed green salad, then added vinaigrette dressing.

"The nuts give it pizzazz," he said.

Beebe bit into a bacon-cheeseburger. He chewed methodically, swallowed, then used a pinky finger to pick food from between his teeth.

"Pizzazz," he said. "One of those big-city buzzwords. Damned if I know what it means. Damned if I care."

"It means 'sparkle,' 'verve,' 'panache.' "

"Forget I mentioned it. You just continue putting nuts on your greens. I could be wrong, but I think it's possible to get the same effect with gravy. Meanwhile, I'll stick with red meat and crispy bacon."

"Interesting nut, the cashew. Comes from a tree belonging to the same family as poison ivy, poison oak, pistachio, and mango."

Beebe said, "No shit." The FBI agent ate french fries with his fingers, dipping each one into a saucer containing a mixture of ketchup, mayonnaise, and chopped pickles.

"The cashew tree grows as high as forty feet," Harry said. "An oil found in the nut is also used for plastic and varnish."

Beebe pointed to Harry's salad with a greasy forefinger. "So now your little salad is slicked down with varnish and wrapped in plastic. Glad we got that settled. Want to tell me why I'm sitting across from you, waiting for it to rain on my new shoes?"

"You and Labriola wanted to be kept informed. You wanted to be notified if Magellan was holding back anything."

"She is an actable lady. Or so I've been led to believe."

"Actable?"

"Lively," Beebe said. "Spry. Don't you people up here speak English? Anyway, you were saying something about Miss Magellan holding back."

"She's going shopping with Mercy Howard, the point being to catch Miss Howard with some of your marked money."

Beebe licked his fingers. "That Magellan. I'd eat a mile of her shit just to see where it came from."

Harry kept his face expressionless. "I've always said that without poets there'd be no civilization, no humanity." He tapped his chin with a forefinger. "You're dripping."

Beebe picked up a paper napkin and dabbed near his lower lip. "Tell me about Miss Magellan."

"I found a woman who can help us on the Reiner case. Name's Marisa Durres. She's Albanian and lives here in Manhattan on the West Side. Her ex-husband, one Enver Durres, also Albanian, runs with an Albanian crew working out of the Bronx. They're into everything from robbing banks to drug dealing. Mr. Durres is the point of interest here. I learned about him from a contact at the Twentieth Precinct."

"Exactly how did Mr. Durres come to the attention of your friends at the Two-O?"

"He's harassing his ex-wife. She's filed complaints, taken out an order of protection, and even had coworkers walk her home. Mr. Durres has her terrified."

Beebe drained half of a cherry Coke before saying, "I take it there's a connection between Mr. Durres and Judge Reiner?"

"Two appearances in front of Reiner. Walked both times."

"And Mrs. Durres? How much does she know about her husband's activities?"

"She's been taken away from me so I'm in no position to say."

Beebe paused with his hand hovering over his french fries. "What does that mean exactly?"

"It means Magellan went behind my back. It means she conned my lieutenant into believing it would be best if Mrs. Durres worked with a woman. These days the department's very sensitive to the feminist issue. Bottom line: My informant, Mrs. Durres, was taken away from me and handed to Magellan."

Beebe put down his cheeseburger and leaned back in his chair.

"Got you too," he said. "Goddam political correctness is enough to make a preacher lay his Bible down. The bureau skunked me last week. I got passed over in favor of some *African-American*. Politics. This spook's got his own antiterrorist squad, which puts him on the fast track to promotion. Me, I got diddley. Fifteen years I'm busting my bloomers for the bureau and what do I have to show for it? Got my nose pressed to the glass, is what I got. Anyway you slice it, that means you're outside looking in."

He stared at Harry out of the corner of his eye. "Boy, you got yourself one pussy-whipped lieutenant is all I can say. Taking away your informant and handing her to a lady cop who got no more sense than to get herself surrounded by a bunch of wild-eyed greasers."

Harry said, "She went to the coffee shop without Fargnoli's permission. And without backup."

"You're shitting me. And she's supposed to be a good cop?"

"She's alive because I was in the area. I wanted to personally tell Mrs. Durres we wouldn't be working together anymore. She took it hard. She's met Detective Magellan and doesn't want to work with her. Finds her too pushy, too aggressive. Too masculine."

Beebe smiled. "Well, bless my little cotton socks. If that don't beat all. Too masculine."

"Unfortunately for Mrs. Durres, Fargnoli's playing hardball. He's told her to work with Magellan or forget about receiving police protection in the matter of her lunatic husband. It's not the first time Magellan's taken away my informants. And Fargnoli lets her get away with it."

Beebe said, "So Magellan is just one more New York hype. She's getting over by stealing informants and taking credit for your work."

Harry poked at his salad. "The department wants women to succeed. It *needs* them to succeed if it wants to continue receiving federal funding. A female presence also keeps civil-rights investigators away. Magellan's got a great reputation, and not all of it's hype. Some, but not all. Has she spoken to you about Marisa Durres?"

"Hell, no."

Harry threw up his hands. "That's what I mean. She's holding back. A case this big, she makes it, she writes her own ticket. Her goal is to make detective first grade. In the whole department I think only fifty cops hold that rank. If there's three women who hold it, I'd be surprised."

Beebe resumed eating his french fries. "So you've been propping her up all these years. How come you didn't request a transfer so's you can work on your own or with a male cop?"

"I did."

"And?"

"Got turned down. It's in the department's interest to have successful female cops. Someone they can showcase. Anything's better than being picked apart by women's groups and the media. The plan is to push Magellan front and center, thereby keeping the wolves at bay."

"And someone's got to prop her up. I take it that's you."

Harry smiled, allowing Beebe to write his own script.

Leaning across the table, the FBI agent lowered his voice. "Wasn't too long ago, the bureau had some trouble with black agents. Spooks were yelling about discrimination and not getting promoted, and I'm telling you it was bogus from the get-go. Cost the bureau a bundle to put this thing behind them. Meanwhile, black agents are getting promoted beyond their skills if you ask me. Anything to keep the peace, right?"

"Amen."

Beebe sat back in his chair. "*Empowerment*. That's the big word these days. You got black agents who can't even pronounce the word, let alone spell it. All they know is, if they yell loud enough somebody listens. Squeaky wheel gets the oil, right?"

Harry said, "Couldn't agree more. Anyway, you now know why you haven't heard anything about Marisa Durres. Magellan wants this one for herself. You'll learn what she wants you to learn."

Beebe opened the remains of his cheeseburger, picked up a piece of bacon and popped it in his mouth.

"So the department's covering its ass by using you to keep Magellan happy."

"That's why I'm thinking of switching to the bureau when this case is over."

"I promised I'd put in a word for you, and I'll keep that promise. We got some NYPD detectives assigned to our antiterrorist squad. Happened after the World Trade Center bombing in Ninety-three. You had us and the NYPD going to war against each other. The bombing happened on your turf, so your people thought they should be running the show. We thought we should be calling the shots because terrorism is a federal offense. Ended up with some of your gold shields being assigned to the FBI on a permanent basis. They report back to the NYPD, but they work under us. They get their police salary, plus a police bonus. On top of which they get five figures a year from the FBI. Sound good?"

Harry smiled. "Very appealing."

"Do your twenty for the department then retire with a federal pension. Which I can tell you pays more than your police pension."

"You've got my attention."

"You just keep feeding me goodies on Miss Magellan and I'll make your fondest dreams come true."

Harry smiled in agreement. Bear Beebe, he of the corduroy suits and brown boots, was temperamental and insensitive, ruthless about what he wanted, and willing to sacrifice anyone to get ahead. Get him worked up enough, he'd kick his grandmother in the head and never feel a pang of guilt. For that reason Harry didn't trust Beebe as far as could throw him. Beebe would promise Harry anything so long as it meant getting information on Magellan.

Beebe tossed bits of his hamburger bun at the pigeons on the railing. "You ever think about getting Magellan pushed off this case and taking it over yourself?"

"Every day. Then I hear the department appreciates what I'm doing for her. At the same time, I hear what could happen to me if I don't play ball."

"Don't look like you're going to be the big dog in the meathouse on this one."

"Magellan's got the informants," Harry said. "Plus

she's close to a woman named Jennifer Sanchez. Sanchez used to be a cop. Now she's a junkie and no longer on the force."

Beebe looked at him in a vaguely curious way. "How's this Sanchez figure in my life?"

Harry put down his knife and fork, then touched a napkin to the corners of his mouth. He stared at the Central Park lake where ducks and geese rode the choppy water with calm grace.

He said, "A year ago Sanchez and the detective who was her partner took down a known drug dealer. Instead of booking him, they sold the dealer to a rival drug mob for a lot of money. Needless to say, the dealer died that very night in messy fashion."

"Why is this interesting to me?"

"What if I told you Sanchez tried to blackmail a certain VIP who ordered that murder. She went behind her partner's back, approached this VIP, and asked for a substantial sum of money. The person refused and instead ordered her execution. That's why Sanchez is on the run."

Harry took out his notebook, wrote down a name, then tore out the page and folded it in half. After a few seconds he pushed the paper across the table to Beebe.

Harry said, "The intended blackmail victim. Present at the drug dealer's murder, which I should note occurred at his home. Not exactly in accordance with the accepted principles of right and wrong."

Beebe frowned, connecting his bushy eyebrows across the top of his nose. He didn't speak for a long time.

Finally the agent said, "Partner, this case we're working on just got a whole lot bigger. And I'll tell you just how big. It'll make your teeth white, your skin tight, and childbirth a pleasure."

"I'd hold off telling Labriola if I were you. Let's get something more concrete before bringing him into the picture."

"Agreed. I don't want to mess this one up. We'll go slow. Just you and me, partner. You and me."

Harry picked a cashew out of his salad and ate it. "Now you can understand why Magellan won't show her cards. Why she's keeping Sanchez and even Marisa Durres to herself. Sanchez is a stepping stone to bigger things. Like that name you're holding in your hand."

Beebe flopped back in his chair. "Don't that just tear the plank off the house. Thank you, Detective Earles, until you're better paid. This is something. I owe you big-time for this one."

"I'll stick close to Magellan. When she turns up Sanchez, we step in."

Beebe held up the folded piece of paper. "Our friend here would have Sanchez killed faster than you can pluck a chicken. Assuming you are correct in your assessment of his actions that dark and stormy night."

"I am."

Beebe threw both fists in the air. "Partner, this puts us in the expensive seats. We take Sanchez away from Magellan, sit her down in front of a tape recorder, and we are home free. Any idea who this detective is, the one who worked with Sanchez?"

Harry grinned. "If I tell you, I might have to kill you."

Beebe said, partner, you are something else, and laughed loud enough to send pigeons flying from the railing.

32
Missing Information

Ross Magellan, carrying a bottle of club soda and a large brown envelope, entered the lobby of the Greenwich Village OCCB building at 10:00 P.M.

She waved to the night security guard, a chubby, fortyish black woman who worked weekends as a blues singer. The guard, seated behind a metal desk, looked up from a Danielle Steel paperback and gave Ross a smile, an upward curving of the corners of her very wide mouth. Ross returned the smile and said she'd returned to pick up a report she'd left behind.

She walked past the guard without signing in. Lying came so naturally to Ross that she didn't think of herself as having scammed the guard.

She was here to examine Harry's past cases. Signing in would have been a mistake. Harry would have wanted to know why was she keeping such late hours. So would Fargnoli. Let the word get out that she was looking to bring down a cop and Ross would be crucified.

She hadn't lied to the security guard. She'd simply hidden the truth from her.

In her office, she locked the door and jammed a chair under the knob. The building was empty and the cleaning lady wasn't due for another hour. As far as Ross knew, she was alone on the floor.

But there was Harry. Always Harry. Appearing everywhere and anywhere. Harry who was persistent and clever and possessive of what he believed belonged to him. A law unto himself. He was all of this and more, and Ross had trusted him with her life. Not anymore.

She switched on her computer, then drank some club soda from the bottle. The carbonation helped ease her queasy stomach. And the headaches. They were back with a vengeance. First time since her marriage.

Harry.

Earlier she'd gone to the Forty-second Street public library, the first step into checking out his back cases. It meant digging through five years of newspaper back issues, but eventually she'd found what she wanted. She read each story twice, seeing a pattern emerge. Based on Harry's lies, information from Sanchez and Jackie Blue, and on what Ross now suspected, her instincts and experience allowed only one conclusion.

Harry Earles was a multiple murderer.

His victims: the female undercovers he'd been entrusted to protect.

He was careful and precise. A whiz at covering his tracks. Ross hadn't expected to come up with a smoking gun. Harry was much too clever for that. At best she'd hoped to stumble across something Harry might have overlooked.

She had.

He'd overlooked the press.

Ross sipped more club soda. Worrying about Harry was harmful to her health. At this rate she'd be back smoking in no time. Seeing him at Café Con Alma not only killed her appetite but made it impossible for her to sleep. She'd lain awake until dawn in Connie's apartment, wondering why Harry had allowed them to see him.

Harry was the best ghost on the planet. If he didn't want you to see him, you didn't.

Last night, for whatever reason, he'd wanted to be seen. He stood at the edge of the club's dance floor, smiling. Waiting to swoop down and pounce. When Connie rushed him, Harry disappeared in a fraction of a second. It was as though he'd dropped through a trapdoor, passing out of sight or even existence.

She looked at her computer. Like so many OCCB computers, hers was obsolete and slow as hell. She'd considered sneaking into Harry's office and hacking his computer. He had to be keeping personal stuff there. In the end, Ross decided against it. Too risky.

For one thing, she wasn't a hacker. Working her own computer was hard enough. Then she'd have to dig out Harry's password, which he changed weekly. No one, not even Fargnoli, knew what it was. Better to stay out of Harry's office for now.

She waited for her files to be loaded, killing time by moving the cursor back and forth across the screen. She'd spent a lot of time today kissing Harry's ass. At least it seemed that way to her.

In separate interviews the commissioner's office, IAB, and Fargnoli had questioned her on the Graciella shooting. Being aware of departmental politics, she knew better than to make waves. Hero cops were important to the department's image. Since Harry was now a hero, Ross knew better than to bad-mouth him. Do that and she could actively start looking for more suitable employment. So she kept her answers to a minimum, letting the dick club run the show.

Tonight, however, she was striking back at the man who treated her as though she were his creation. As though she had no life of her own.

She looked at the brown envelope lying on her desk. The newspaper articles it contained were enough to convince Ross that Harry was a murderer. Convincing others, however, wasn't going to be easy. Without hard evidence and witnesses, a trial—criminal or departmental—was a long shot. Wiping the smirk off Harry's face wasn't going to be easy.

Was he good, lucky, or both?

The phone rang. Ross flinched and threw up her hands.

Don't let it be him.

Slowly bringing the receiver to her ear, she took a deep breath and waited.

"Ross? It's Connie."

She exhaled. "I thought you were *him*."

"Not today. Speaking of *him*, I never saw a guy disappear so fast in all my life as he did last night. One minute he's eyeballing us from the other side of the dance floor. The next minute he's gone. What did he say when you saw him today?"

"He didn't come in. He's still on leave, recovering from the 'trauma' connected with killing Graciella and her friends."

"The bastard's not so traumatized that he can't go

wandering around at night. I'm still at the convention center. Should finish up in about twenty minutes. I'll phone from the car and meet you in front of your building. Any sign of your friendly ghost?"

"You only see him if he wants you to see him. That's why I can't figure out last night."

Connie chuckled. "The man's showing off. Wants us both to know he's not afraid of me. He's saying he can do whatever he wants and I can't stop him. Harry's styling in his own sweet way."

Ross nodded. "That's Harry. Got to maintain his power no matter what."

"You come up with anything on him?"

Ross watched a directory appear on her computer screen.

"Yes," she said. "Public library. The same day I talked to Emilio Albert, I went to the library in Queens to look up Sanchez in the back issues of the local papers. I came up empty. I didn't know it at the time, but I should have been checking on Harry. That's what I did today."

"And?"

"His past cases make interesting reading."

She pulled the brown envelope toward her. "I have photocopies of newspaper articles I want you to see. It's all there. Harry's need to control women. The reason his career never took off. And the reason Jackie Blue warned me to avoid becoming female victim number four."

"I get the feeling your boy Jackie's not telling us everything."

"He will when he wants something from me."

"Four dead men, four dead women. I still don't see where Jackie boy's going with that. If he's right,

Harry's got eight bodies on him. So where are they?"

Ross reached into the brown envelope. "You asked about bodies. Start with the dead undercovers. I think I'm on his list. If not, I soon will be."

"Whoa. You lost me. Harry's killing undercovers? Since when?"

"He started five years ago. And he's getting away with it."

"Nobody kills cops and gets away with it. Not even Harry."

"The pattern's there. It's just that no one's picked up on it."

"Like you, I think he's wacky. The way he smoked Graciella is enough to condemn him in my book. But cops? If he killed them, he did it with the world looking on. You telling me nobody noticed anything?"

"I'm not crazy. And I'm not making this up."

"I didn't say you were. But admit it: You've set the bar pretty high on this one. You're telling me Harry Earles is killing cops he's suppose to protect and nobody's caught on. That is what you're saying."

"You have to know Harry," Ross said. "He's smart and he's lucky. Maybe he's got something else going for him. Something we don't know about. That's why I'm here."

Connie said, "He must think he's David-fucking-Copperfield with that disappearing act. Anyway, I'm just about finished here. Just have to lock up the dolls and escort our Japanese friend back to his hotel. After that—"

"Connie, you've got to believe me. Even if I come up with nothing tonight, there's enough in the papers to point the finger at that son of a bitch. Two female undercovers Harry ghosted for are dead. Another, Jenn Sanchez, was supposed to die, but she got lucky. That makes three."

"And you make four. Let's say I buy that. That still leaves four males. A double-matched set, Jackie Blue said. Four men, four women. All killed by Harry."

Ross said, "Four males? How about Emilio Albert, John-John and—"

Connie's voice dropped to a whisper. "And the two guys in the coffee shop."

"Back to the women. Harry ghosted for Sanchez."

"He what?"

"Only one paper mentioned it, and they buried the story. Harry never let on he knew Sanchez, but let's put that aside for now. According to press reports, an Albanian drug dealer was found beside the Henry Hudson Parkway with his throat cut. There were rumors he'd been arrested by a cop who then sold him to a rival gang. Nothing was ever proven, and the rumors died. A number of cops were interviewed, among them Harry and Jennifer Sanchez, both of whom had been investigating the deceased."

Connie said, "What's that tell you?"

"It tells me Harry could have arrested the dealer and made a bundle by turning him over to some people who wanted him dead."

"Business is business."

"Sanchez said the cop who tried to kill her now works with me. I make Harry to be that cop. Nobody else on my team has ever worked with Sanchez. Only Harry."

"What about the dead undercovers? How did Harry kill them and get away with it?"

"He's good, remember? And he always had an alibi. When one undercover died of a drug OD, Harry was home sick. When another was chained to a radiator in a crack house and burned to death, Harry was miles away at a police sergeants' convention. Jenn Sanchez supposedly tried suicide by locking herself in her car and inhaling carbon monoxide. She's still alive, but she's a junkie. I'm betting when she allegedly tried to end it all, Harry was surrounded by people who'll swear he never left their sight."

"No offense but could you be, let's say, reaching?"

She shook her head. "I know Harry, and I know how he works. The press reports dead women made mistakes. In other words, they didn't do what Harry the control freak told them to do. Supposedly the one who died in a crack-house fire broke one of the first rules of undercover work. She went behind a locked door. You know how many times Harry's warned me about that?"

"I'd say, a lot."

"Another undercover supposedly fell in love with a perp and ODed when he dumped her. The only source quoted on this, by the way, is Harry. Again, you have a female cop who violated proper police procedure. Didn't follow Daddy's instructions. Sanchez? Apparently the pressures of undercover work became too much. So she tried to kill herself."

Connie said, "How did Harry learn Sanchez was still alive?"

"Probably followed me. Who the hell knows? Just a minute."

"What is it?"

"I'm having trouble accessing Harry's old cases. Not all of them. Just the ones that—"

"Just the ones that what?"

"Let me try again."

She typed another command. "Connie, I've got a feel for this one. Harry's a murderer. I know he is."

"If you're right, you got problems. Harry will come for you."

"He's doing that now. By the way, his problems with women didn't start with female cops."

"Don't tell me. When he was a kid, Mom made him wear her garter belt."

Ross smiled. "Go back, six, seven years. A female informant named Paula Pereira. Used to work for Andre Dushenko, big-time criminal lawyer."

"I remember Andre. Loved fur coats. Owned an apartment just for his furs, nothing else. A big money man for Italian and Russian mobs. He's doing a federal bit somewhere."

"Twenty to life in Atlanta, thanks to his former secretary, one Paula Pereira. The two were having an affair. When he wouldn't leave his wife, Paula ratted him out to Harry."

"Pussy will get you every time."

Ross said, "Thank you for your insights. Anyway the point is this: Ninety percent of all cases are made by a snitch. A cop's only as good as his informants."

"The secret of my success. And yours."

"Paula Pereira's a great reader, and Harry's wife use to be a librarian which is how they met. Harry's wife brought him into the picture, and suddenly he's getting this great information on Dushenko and the money laundering Dushenko's doing for the Italians and the Russians. He was handling hundreds of millions of dollars through companies he'd set up in the Bahamas, Ireland,

Panama, and God knows where. Pereira was the answer to Harry's prayer. This case was going to be the biggest of his career. Then someone dropped the hammer."

"You've been talking to Ivy Linder, I see."

"Her and a few cops who worked with Harry. All say the same thing. The brass took Paula away from Harry. Took away the woman who was the biggest informant of his career. Harry didn't like it."

"No shit. In his place I wouldn't like it either. That case was a monster. It would have made Harry a star. He got fucked."

"Police work is about politics. Which means you need friends to get ahead. Harry just didn't have the juice. Not on the Dushenko case. Someone else did, and he pulled strings to get Harry's informant. The guy who screwed Harry now works in the commissioner's office and gets driven around in a limousine by a second-grade detective."

Connie said, "It took a combined state and federal task force to make all the arrests in that case. They busted wiseguys, Russians, some dork from the city council, and the head of a big Jewish charity, who was laundering money through his synagogue. I know two cops who made first grade out of it."

"Harry wasn't one of them. He got zilch. *Nada.* At the same time his wife had a car accident and ended up in a wheelchair for life."

"Poor bastard."

Ross said, "When the accident happened, Harry was downtown at headquarters fighting to hold on to his snitch."

"If he'd succeeded, his life might have been different."

"It's possible," Ross said. "I'm sure that's how Harry saw it. The impression I get is that he never wants to lose a valuable contact again. Especially if that contact's a woman. So if he finds a female undercover who can help his career, he gets a death grip on her. I know this from personal experience. Just as I know things can turn ugly if he thinks he's losing you or you show yourself to be too independent."

Connie said, "Sounds like a classic sociopath to me. Very controlling. Manipulative yet always the victim. Nothing is ever his fault. No matter what happens, he's the injured, abused person. Five years and nobody's noticed what this loony tune is up to."

"I have," Ross said. "The three female undercovers he's gone after have something in common. All were Latinas. Celia Cuevas, Raymunda Montano, Jenn Sanchez. Harry ghosted for all of them. Two are dead, and one's working on dying young."

"Jesus."

"Each was tall, dark. Early thirties."

Connie said, "Like you."

"I know."

Neither spoke for a few seconds.

Then Ross said, "Connie, I'm having a problem with Harry's files. I can't access certain information."

"What are you talking about?"

Ross said the information on Harry and the cases he'd worked with Cruz, Montano and Sanchez was no longer available. Apparently someone had pulled it from the database.

33
Showtime

Harry Earles, carrying a gym bag in one hand, left the Ukrainian restaurant on St. Marks Place at 10:30 P.M.

Next to the restaurant was a shop offering the most frightening leather goods he'd ever seen. Turning his back to the store, he unfolded a cell phone and brought it to his ear.

"I'm here, Denny. Now what?"

"You don't look happy, my man. All these freaks bugging you?"

"The East Village has always been too vibrant for my taste. Pierced tongues and nipple rings make me want to eject part or all of the contents of my stomach. Can we conclude our business now?"

Harry held up the gym bag. "I don't know if you can see this, but I have your money. It's yours when I get the rest of the tapes."

"I see you, my man. And right now, this is close enough. People in the coffee shop got close to you, and look where they are now. Wasn't the first time you iced somebody. Now ask me how I know."

"Something to do with those wiretaps you refused to hand over to me."

"You ain't as dumb as you look. Before I forget, you lied to me, which I ain't too happy about. You said they'd never suspect I copped them wiretaps. Guess who's the first one the cops come looking for. I just got to believe you had something to do with that, you being a sneaky fuck and all. Yeah, I know about you, dude. That's why I'm being very, very careful. Hey, you mentioned nipple rings. Check this out. Last year I had my cock pierced. I got this cute little gold ring right through Mr. Happy's head. Increases your sensitivity, know what I'm saying? Gives you a dynamite orgasm."

"Business, Denny. Business."

"Downside is the pain. That ring? When it first goes in, you ain't never felt pain like that in your life. It's like pissing broken glass. You stretch, move a muscle and that ring, man, it yanks on your foreskin like a fishhook. Hurts, man. Actually I had the combo platter. I figured I might as well get everything done at the same time, know what I'm saying? What the hell, go for it, right?"

"Denny, I'm getting tired standing out here."

"Combo platter means you get it all. One price to have my dick pierced, enlarged, and thickened at the same time. Doctor takes skin from my ass and shoves it in my johnson. I needed five months to recuperate. Five months gripping the pipes while I peed. But I got me a brand-new one-eyed wonder worm. My operation turned out OK, but some guys, they have it and nothing goes right. I mean you mess up a dude's tally-whacker and he's really going to be annoyed. Six grand it cost me. Six fucking K. The whole time I couldn't do nothing. Not even beat my meat. Hey, you know the difference between fish and meat? You beat your fish, it dies."

Harry stared at the moon. There was a ring around it. More rain on the way. Not good for his neck. Not good at all.

He said, "Do you want this money or don't you?"

Denny laughed. "Chill. If you're not careful, you'll swallow your little bow tie. I just want to make sure you're alone."

"You should know that by now. You've watched me spend the past two hours sitting in a dump of a restaurant, smelling stuffed cabbage, and watching Russian waiters spill potato soup on bald-headed old man with steel teeth. This is not my favorite way to kill time."

"Better to kill time than to kill me. Denny don't dig getting shot in the head."

Harry watched a cadaverous-looking black panhandler pick through a wire trash basket, retrieve the remains of a discarded hamburger, and begin eating it.

Harry said, "If you're referring to Graciella, she and her friends were about to kill an undercover police officer."

"Funny thing about that. Cops say you're a hero. Me, I know better."

"And what do you know, Denny?"

"I know you got the hots for Detective Magellan. And I know you are one conniving cocksucker. There's got to be more to this than what you're letting on."

"Cock sucker. Is that one word or two?"

"Cool. I like that. See, I know how you think. You like to pull strings. You like to finagle. Can't help yourself. It's just the way you are. I figure you smoked Graciella what's-her-face for a reason. Her and her amigos. What it is, I don't know. Maybe you wanted to get closer to Magellan. Tell you this much: It made me nervous, that's for sure. I need to know you didn't bring nobody with you."

Harry tightened his grip on the gym bag. What he wouldn't give right now to be jamming both thumbs into Denny's eyes. The little bastard had him jumping through hoops. Two hours in a smelly Ukrainian restaurant, watching fat Russians stuff their faces with kielbasa. Denny was going to pay for that.

As for Harry being alone, he wasn't. Hilton Prigo was at the end of the block. Sitting behind the wheel of one of Harry's renovated cabs. Awaiting the signal to go forth and kill Denny Rinko.

A blue-and-white cruised by. Harry turned his head. Not that he'd be recognized by cops in this light, but why take chances? He was supposed to be home, recovering from shooting-induced trauma. Not out and about and killing citizens.

With the squad car gone, Harry let his eyes roam the street. He was surrounded by weirdos, panhandlers, and tourists, all looking for God knows what. Freakazoids like Denny didn't exactly stand out in this crowd. He could be standing ten feet away and Harry wouldn't see him. Denny was right about one thing. Harry had killed Graciella with the idea of achieving more than a net social gain. He wanted Magellan to be grateful. Grateful enough to deliver Jenn Sanchez to him.

But instead of showing gratitude, Magellan had turned hostile. Cold. Now, she was even digging into his past cases. She was trying to hurt Harry, and he couldn't have that.

Denny said, "I'm enjoying this, watching you squirm. I can see you, and you can't see me, and there ain't shit you can do about it."

"Thank you for pointing that out to me. Now—"

"Don't rush it. This is like foreplay. You know, stroke before you poke. The licking before the pricking. Of course, you don't have to do that with farm animals. Am I right?"

He laughed in Harry's ear. "OK, OK. So let's get it on. Start walking toward Second Avenue. Stay on this side of the street. Just before you get to the corner, you'll see a bar. A real dump. Go in and take a table near the crapper. Now put your phone away and no more calls. You talk to anybody and I am gone and so are your tapes. You got two minutes."

Denny hung up.

Harry folded his phone. But not before pressing the Redial button, the signal telling Prigo to move in.

Time for a stroll. Harry walked past sidewalk vendors, blond German tourists, runaways with fuchsia hair, and muscular young black males in tank tops and homeboy wallets on a chain. He didn't rush. Prigo had to be able to see him.

The bar was called Dup's. It appeared to have been a dancehall at some point, probably Polish or Ukrainian, given the neighborhood. Now it was a long, dark room with a low ceiling, wooden floor, and a mirrored wall that hadn't been washed in years. A jukebox offered soul music from the sixties and seventies. The place was half full, mostly with beer-drinking students trying to talk over one another, each attempting to raise the moral consciousness of the world without having first raised his or her own.

Harry found an empty table near what appeared to be a communal rest room. He shook his head disapprovingly. The idea of men and women sharing a public toilet offended him. Moral and ethical standards had gone to hell, and it was shameful. Nothing less than shameful.

Denny showed up almost immediately, coming through the front door seconds after Harry. He'd changed his appearance. He was now clean-shaven. No more mustache and wispy goatee. He'd even shaved his head. He wore a black canvas backpack and carried a shopping bag.

Part of the old Denny remained, however. He was wearing a dirty T-shirt, torn jeans, and unlaced Timberland boots. A plaid flannel shirt was tied around his thin waist. His personal hygiene remained suspect—he smelled like a bike messenger, and his teeth were still rotting.

He sat across the table from Harry. The backpack and shopping bag went on the wooden floor.

"Well, here we are," Denny said. "I thought somewhere public might be best. This way I don't have to worry too much."

Harry peered down into the shopping bag. He saw what appeared to be dozens of audiotapes.

"I take it they're all there," he said.

Denny Rinko held out his hand. "May I?"

Harry gave him the gym bag. Denny unzipped it and looked inside. "I take it all my money's here."

Harry said, "Count it." He'd shortchanged Denny. Given him three hundred grand instead of half a million. And Denny wouldn't be keeping that for long. Not if Hilton Prigo followed orders.

Harry was gambling that Denny wouldn't count the money in the bar. Denny was afraid of Harry. He'd want to be on his way as soon as possible. Therefore, he wouldn't hang around to tally his cash. He'd leave the bar in a cloud of dust. Once outside, he would become just one more crime statistic. Hilton Prigo, in a cab provided by Harry, was waiting to kill Denny. Send the little twerp to a better world after first relieving him of the money. A simple plan. What could possibly go wrong?

Denny said, "I didn't like how you pushed me around the other night. Digging your fingers in my throat. I don't trust you, so I took precautions."

"Precautions," Harry said. "And what might they be?"

Their attention was drawn to the jukebox where three women, white females in their late teens, suddenly stopped dancing with each other and hurried toward the rest room. One, a redhead, appeared ready to throw up, a situation viewed with repugnance by Harry. She'd covered her face with a handkerchief. As she passed him, Harry leaned away in self-protection.

Denny said to Harry, "I got to watch my ass around you. So I'm covered, dude. Denny is definitely covered."

Harry looked at the shopping bag, then at Denny. He thought for a while, then nodded.

"You're holding out on me," he said. "You still haven't given me all the tapes, have you?"

"Put it this way, kill me now and you're fucked. You got nearly everything, but you're right—you ain't got it all. It's up to you whether I walk out of here in one piece or not. By the way, your name's mentioned on one of them tapes. Did you know that?"

"Really? In what context, if you don't mind my asking?"

Denny grinned. "Listen, then you tell me. I'll say this much: At one point they wanted to investigate your ass regarding the death of a female cop. Lucky for you the evidence wasn't there. You got to hear this tape. Fucking unreal. Mentions somebody else's name along with yours. Somebody very important. Old friend of yours."

Denny stood up, gym bag in one hand and backpack in the other.

"Got to take a whiz," he said. "I come back, we'll talk some more."

Harry pointed to the gym bag. "Sure you wouldn't want to entrust that to my care while you're gone?"

Denny grabbed his crotch. "Entrust this."

Harry said, "Cynical, Denny. Very cynical."

He watched Denny enter the rest room. As the door closed behind him, Denny could be heard saying, "Ladies, how's it hanging? Anyone here ever mix Ex-Lax with Spanish fly? Makes you hot to trot."

One of the women said something Harry couldn't hear. Everyone in the rest room laughed, Denny included.

Harry took out his cell phone, pressed Redial, then brought the phone to his ear.

"Just listen," he said. "Don't speak. Do not kill Rinko. I repeat, you're not to kill him. He didn't bring all the tapes. He's still holding back. That moron thinks he's endowed with brains. When he shows, throw him into the cab. I'll join you. We'll see how clever he is after I've applied a straight razor to his reconstructed johnson."

Closing the phone, he returned it to his jacket pocket just as the three girls stepped from the rest room. The redhead still held a handkerchief to her face. And still required her companions to prop her up. Harry thought, *Why drink if you can't handle it?* He decided it was typical of today's young people and their lack of shame.

After watching the women leave, he turned his attention to the rest room. *Come out, come out wherever you are.* If Denny didn't make an appearance soon, Harry was going in and dragging him out by the tonsils. They had to talk. Harry wanted all of the tapes, and he wanted them tonight. And if he had to skin Denny alive to get them, so be it.

Suddenly he bowed his head. *No,* he thought. *No, no, no.*

Pulling out his phone, he pressed Redial.

When he heard Hilton Prigo's voice, Harry said, "He's outside. Probably going past you right now."

"No. I see nobody looks like the picture you gave me. Some women come out and get in a cab. Some other women go in with some men. Don't worry, I ain't gonna miss your boy."

Harry rose from the table. "We've missed him. Stay put. I'll call you right back."

He entered the rest room. A chubby blonde with a protruding lower lip atop a protruding chin stood in front of a dirty mirror, applying hair spray to wispy bangs. She paused just long enough to look at Harry's reflection, then returned to spraying her bangs.

Harry said, "Where'd he go?"

"Where'd who go?"

"Denny Rinko. He followed you and your friends in here. He just left disguised as a woman."

"I think you'd better leave. Now."

Harry started toward her.

She continued grooming her hair, never taking her eyes from the mirror. Harry noticed that she wasn't afraid of him. On the contrary, she appeared to be enjoying the confrontation.

"Stop right there," she said.

Something in her voice made Harry follow orders.

"I know all about you," she said. "You're a cop, and you just shot three people. You're also in possession of material stolen from police headquarters so you can't afford to attract attention. Too much going on in your stupid life."

Harry froze, a hand on his bow tie. Unbelievable. Harry Earles faked out of his shorts by schoolgirls and a little shit with rotting teeth and a craving for teenyboppers. Harry Earles, standing around in a disgustingly dirty urinal and taking orders from some bitch with lacquered hair.

The blonde looked at her watch. "You got ten seconds to move your ass." She hooked a thumb toward the door. "That way."

Harry saw the backpack on the floor. Beside it, Denny's torn jeans, T-shirt, and plaid shirt.

Harry said, "Tell me where he's gone or you'll wish you had."

The blonde screamed. And kept screaming while continuing to work on her bangs.

A startled Harry backed away.

34
First Blood

Lieutenant Carlo Fargnoli was waiting for Ross Magellan in the doorway of his office, looking long-faced and troubled. "We have to talk."

"Thanks for seeing me, Loo."

Ross looked at her watch. Seven-thirty A.M. Getting up this early usually meant a major bust was about to go down. Or that an intense manhunt for a cop killer was in progress.

Not this morning. This was personal. Ross wanted to talk to Fargnoli about Harry and do it without witnesses. She wanted Harry replaced as her ghost. And she wanted him investigated for murder.

Were this conversation to be overheard, Ross would be finished as a cop. She'd be labeled a rat, a cheese eater. Her career would be in the toilet.

The entire precinct would declare war on Ross. Her tires would be slashed, her locker trashed, her personnel records tampered with. No cop would work with her because no cop would trust her. On the street, she'd find herself without backup; her call for assistance, no matter how great the danger, would be ignored. There'd be nowhere to hide. A transfer wouldn't help. Anywhere Ross went, she'd be the woman who tried to get a brother officer kicked off the job.

That's why she and Fargnoli had to talk privately.

Fargnoli closed the door and pointed to a chair in front of his desk. That's when Ross realized that Fargnoli wanted to talk, not listen. He had something to say to Ross. Her gut feeling said she wasn't going to like it.

He sat behind his desk, rubbed his eyes, then reached for his coffee. For several seconds he simply gripped the cup, eyeing it as though waiting for something to jump out.

"I've just spoken with Harry," he said.

Ross felt a slight dizziness. She closed her eyes until it passed.

Fargnoli pulled the coffee toward him. "You're a good cop, but good cops have problems too. Especially undercovers. This job puts you on the edge of a razor twenty-four/seven. No way you can be normal."

"Is that what you and Harry talked about, the amount of stress connected with my job?"

"He says you've talked about killing yourself."

Ross looked away. "He's lying."

Harry was going to pay for this.

Fargnoli leaned back in his chair. "Undercovers keep things to themselves. We all know that. But according to Harry, you go too far. He thinks you're too secretive."

"I've been doing my job, Loo, and you know it."

"Ross, I don't have a problem with you. But I've got to be up-front. This business with Graciella."

"What about it?"

"You ended up in a jackpot and nobody covering your back. How the hell do you think I feel? I got asked questions. Hard questions. Like, Do I take care of my people or what? I don't like those kind of questions. No fucking way do I like it."

"Loo, I—"

"Harry says you disobeyed a direct order."

Ross said, "I *what?*"

"He says you were told not to go to the coffee shop alone. You ignored him and went anyway."

Ross thought, *Just like the other undercovers. Harry's saying I disobeyed Daddy. Bad girl. Bad, bad.*

Fargnoli said, "You're a star, I grant you that. But Harry's your sergeant. He runs the team. As difficult as it may be for you to accept this, he *is* the man in charge. So I'm asking: Did you go off on your own or not?"

Ross threw up her hands in frustration. First blood went to Harry, a master at staying one step ahead of his enemies. In a preemptive strike he'd gotten to Fargnoli first, painting a picture of Ross as a headcase on the verge of a breakdown. A glory hound who'd ignored proper police procedure and nearly gotten herself killed. Industrial-strength bullshit is all it was. But the fact remained that Harry had beat her to the punch. A smart move, since it put Ross on the defensive instead of allowing her to attack.

And Harry was attacking Harry-style. He was *gaslighting* her.

"I told you what happened," Ross said. "You

passed on a message to me from an informant who I then went to meet. Since when do I need backup for that? As it turned out, I'd been set up."

"By who?"

Harry.

Ross said, "By someone who knew Graciella wanted to kill me. By some slick bastard who arranged for me and Graciella to be in the same place at the same time."

"Anyone we know?"

Harry.

"I'm working on it," Ross said.

Fargnoli tapped the edge of his coffee cup with a letter opener. "Keep me informed."

"Of course."

"Harry mentioned your family history. He thinks some of the pressure you're under could be coming from that."

Ross leaned forward in her chair. "Tell Harry to keep his fucking nose out of my personal life."

Fargnoli put up a hand in a stop signal. "You're freaking out over nothing."

"Nothing? The bastard's gaslighting me and you're saying it's *nothing?*"

"Look, he likes you. He likes you a lot, as a matter of fact. He feels the two of you make a great team. No argument there. Together you guys make it happen. We're this close to nailing Lou Angelo. We turn him, we got Reiner. Harry says you're playing Angelo like a champ."

"But—"

"But nothing. You brought Reiner to us. Even Harry admits that. At the same time, he felt he had to pass on what other cops are saying about you."

Ross opened and clenched her fists. "Which is?"

"He says some of the guys are calling you an opportunist."

"A *what?*"

"Now this is Harry talking. He says, you're getting a reputation as someone who'll use any situation to advance herself."

Ross watched Fargnoli carefully. "You believe that?"

"Harry's one of my officers, and he's been on the job a long time. Until I know different, he has my respect. I have to listen to him. Especially when it comes to anything affecting the performance of officers under my command. He says your reputation as a star makes cops reluctant to knock you."

Ross said, "My *reputation* hasn't stopped Harry from trashing me."

"He also says some cops see you as a pathological liar. He says it never bothered him until now."

"Now?"

"He says you're bad-mouthing him. That you're claiming he puts undercovers in situations where they can be killed. You did go to the coffee shop on your own. Does this mean you question Harry's judgment?"

Ross looked through the window at Christopher Park. Connie was right. Harry was isolating her, leaving her angry and afraid. Very afraid.

Fargnoli threw up his hands. "Look, maybe it's my fault. You make us all look good, the way you work. The more I push you, the better we look. On the other hand, maybe it's something else. Like a communications problem between you and Harry."

He placed both hands around his coffee cup. "I

don't think you're a headcase. If I did, your ass would be out of here in a heartbeat, women's lib or no women's lib. Could be what Harry's hearing is so much crapola. We both know there are cops who don't want women on the job."

Ross said, "I run into them once in a while."

"Woman like you comes along and outshines a male officer, it ticks these guys off."

"I think we're talking about dumb cops. The ones who're so stupid, they stay up all night studying for a urine test. Meanwhile, they keep drawing a paycheck."

"Look, I know this stuff goes on. I've done my share. But not where you're concerned. Nobody can knock you to my face."

Ross turned from the window. "Harry did."

"He's saying what we all know. Which is you've been working nonstop for months. Even you will admit that."

Fargnoli ran a hand through his gray crew cut. "You look tired. If that's sexual harrassment or whatever they call it, you can fucking sue me."

"Don't be ridiculous."

"Never knew an undercover who wasn't paranoid. And with good reason. Cops getting killed left and right and all you hear is, we're being paid to get killed. I say we're not. But try telling that to a citizen who's unhappy about paying his taxes. Anyway, I've got something important for you and Harry to do. Finish it, then take a couple of weeks off. This one's big. As big as anything you two ever took on."

Ross said, "Before we get into additional assignments, I'd like to say something. I want another ghost. Starting now. Anyone but Harry."

"No can do," Fargnoli said. "Not on this new assignment. And not on the Judge Reiner case. We could maybe work something out in the future. For now the brass wants you two working together. This new thing is primo. You'll see why. You guys got a good thing going. And nobody wants to break up a winning team."

"Excuse me, but what could be more important than nailing Judge Reiner?"

Fargnoli stood up. "Harry's next door."

Ross looked away from Fargnoli. She felt sick to her stomach.

"I'm leaving you two alone," Fargnoli said. "Work out your differences and don't take too long doing it. I come back, we'll talk about the new assignment. I know you usually work just one undercover job at a time but this is an exception. Couple days and you should have it wrapped up. If you're wondering who dropped this assignment on you, try downtown. The commissioner's office."

He opened the door to the reception area and said, Harry, get in here.

35
Allow Me to Refresh Your Memory

"I don't care what the assignment is. I don't give a shit what the department says. I'm never working with you again."

"Never say never."

A smiling Harry sat on the edge of Fargnoli's desk. "You'll love this assignment. I know I will."

He knows something, Ross thought. *And he's dying to tell me.*

She decided to keep quiet and listen. Treat Harry as she would a perp. Watch and wait.

Harry said, "You told your boyfriend I'm stalking you, didn't you?"

Ross said nothing.

"Not true," Harry said. "Nor was I ever in your apartment. You've been working hard, and you're starting to lose it. I suppose you blame me for that. Fine. I understand. Fargnoli's right, though. Some time off might do you good. Think about getting out of

Manhattan for a while. Spend some time at the house with Helene and me."

Ross rolled her eyes toward the ceiling.

"Well, how about this?" Harry said. "I'm retiring to Italy. First of the year. Remember my saying I'd like to be near the great opera houses? Well, it's going to happen. You and I could go over first. Get the house ready for Helene."

Ross finally spoke. "You're out of your fucking mind."

Harry's green eyes bore into her. "You mean a lot to me. Professionally, you understand. Since working with you my career's taken a quantum leap. Now it's about to improve even more."

Ross said, "Professionally or otherwise, I'm not interested in anything you have to offer. We're through as a team. I don't want you watching my back. Not anymore. I know all about you."

"Really? And what do you know?"

"I know about the others," Ross said.

Harry folded his arms across his chest. "The others? What are we talking about here?"

"The undercovers you were suppose to protect and didn't. Want me to go on?"

"Let's see if I have this right. You're blaming me for cops who commit suicide. Or who, because of their own negligence and lack of professionalism, wind up suffering grievously. These are incidents over which I have no control, believe it or not. You're upset, but I really don't think you should go down that road. Accusing your partner, I mean. You'll have problems, believe you me. There isn't a cop in this house who won't think you're losing your mind. I'd forget the 'homicidal Harry' theory if I were you."

"Forget that you've killed two cops and God knows who else? I don't think so."

"My, we have been busy, haven't we? Phone calls to my former partners, accessing computer records, and checking through old newspapers. You've even presented your oddball theories to the widow Linder who's much too old to be poking her nose into nooks and crannies. Then again, how does one break the habits of a lifetime?"

Harry held up a forefinger. "Now Pavlides I can understand. Love makes him trail around behind you. But people like Mrs. Linder should know better. Then again, I suppose I should feel flattered. All this attention for little old me."

"We're finished, Harry. I've seen what happens to women who turn their back on you."

"You've heard me speak about the power of secret knowledge. It does have its value. Indeed, it does. Allow me to refresh your memory."

He popped a raw cashew in his mouth and stared at the windowsill, which was now a bright orange under the morning sun. His voice was soft. Soothing.

"Ross Magellan. Real name: Rosalinda Iris Secora Moniz. One of two daughters born to a well-to-do Cuban-American family. Father owned a popular Long Island seafood restaurant with a yearly gross in the millions. Both parents now deceased. Closest living relative: a sister, Francesca, nicknamed Chessy. Mother killed during Palm Beach vacation. Died when struck by car driven by an eighty-seven-year-old woman who'd died of a heart attack while at the wheel.

Mother dragged one hundred yards after the woman's car went out of control and mounted the pavement. Father's death will take some explaining but we'll get around to that shortly.

"Chessy is currently tucked away in a Long Island mental hospital. Which brings us to Daddy and what the world knows as his suicide. His alleged suicide, I should say. It appears he molested Chessy, then crushed by guilt, shot himself. That's the official version.

"Now here's how Harry sees it. Harry thinks Chessy shot Daddy, and Rosalinda covered it up so Sister wouldn't go to prison. This way Chessy gets to enjoy a comfortable life with cable TV, birds on the windowsill, and nurses who wash beneath their fingernails. Chessy, bless her, gets frequent visits from her big sister, Rosalinda, who takes her riding in the woods. I understand Chessy could get released soon. Perhaps as soon as next year. Won't happen if she gets hit with a murder charge. Could send little Chessy over the edge and round the bend.

"Harry also thinks Rosalinda Moniz changed her name to cut herself off from her incestuous degenerate of a father. That's why she's Ross Magellan. Note the Ross instead of Roz. A clean break while maintaining the same initials. Now that's using our police training. Anyway, let's talk about Chessy. Harry thinks if Rosalinda doesn't stop poking around Harry's life, Harry will see to it that little sister stands trial for murder.

"And while we're on the subject of murder, let's touch upon Ross's late, unlamented husband Alan. Now there was a piece of work. Handsome, smooth-talking, and a good dancer. Loved to tango, our Alan. He did have this one little flaw. He was addicted to gambling and managed to lose some twenty million dollars—a good chunk of it, other people's money.

"Doesn't say much for our banking system that a man with his credit rating was still able to get huge loans. He used personal bankruptcies, numerous aliases, bogus corporations, borrowing from friends—all in an unending quest to scrape up a buck. The consummate con artist. Managed to talk you into giving him a hundred thousand dollars to 'invest.' You're not still waiting for that money to be returned, are you?

"Someone should have warned Alan. Those southern boys play rough. Especially when they catch you cheating at cards. What did they use on him, a shotgun? Wasn't so good-looking after they finished, was he? Well, such is life.

"Anyway, Alan's gone. And your parents are dead. Which leaves only Chessy as immediate family. Think she'd hold up if she was put on trial for murder? You do know there is no statute of limitations on murder? They can come after you at any time. Twenty, thirty years after the crime. Something to think about."

Harry slid off Fargnoli's desk. "I want this assignment. It'll make up for a lot of the hard times. And you, Detective Magellan, are going to work on it with me."

Fargnoli reentered the room.

Harry mouthed the words to Ross, *Your call*.

Fargnoli walked behind his desk. But he didn't sit down. Not right away. Instead he looked at Harry for long seconds.

Finally he said, "Everything copacetic here?"

Harry grinned. "Misconceptions all cleared up. Time to put on a happy face."

Fargnoli looked at Ross.

Head down, she nodded.

Fargnoli permitted himself a smile. "Is this a great country or what? OK, people, listen up."

Still standing, he opened a folder on his desk. "You keep this one quiet, and I do mean quiet. You don't talk in your sleep, you don't talk to the trees, you don't talk to nobody. This comes from downtown. That's the commissioner's office in case you've forgotten."

Fargnoli sat down. "Some wiretaps have been stolen from headquarters. We're talking political dynamite here. Dynamite means illegal. These taps are illegal because we, the NYPD, made them when we shouldn't have. Allow me to explain."

He tapped the folder in front of him. "This describes the problem with which we are now faced. When I finish, my orders are to burn every scrap of paper in this folder, then flush the ashes down the toilet. As far as you two are concerned, nothing goes on paper. Nothing from me to you. Nothing from you to me. We never had this little talk."

He leaned back in his chair, hands behind his head. "Two people have been murdered because of these taps. That's two people in less than twenty-four hours. You don't need to be a rocket scientist to figure out that more are going to die if we don't get those taps back and soon. I mean like yesterday."

He looked at the ceiling. "Why me, oh Lord?"

He eyed Ross and Harry. "You two don't come through on this and we are looking at a shit storm of unwelcome attention, starting with the media and ending up with downtown. Some of the stolen stuff is legal. It's the illegal stuff that has downtown all hot and bothered. Let me say that we had court orders before we made the taps. We followed procedure. When necessary, we had the court orders renewed. Where did we go wrong? *Minimization*. That's where we fucking went wrong. It got ignored, and now the department's got its tit in the wringer. That's where you two come in."

Ross started to reach for her notebook, then remembered. Nothing on paper.

"Minimization" meant if you were bugging a suspect's conversation and heard things with no bearing on your case, you turned the wiretap off. And you did it immediately. Recording anything unrelated to a court-ordered investigation was illegal. If it wasn't sanctioned by the court, you had no business listening in. Illegal wiretapping compromised an entire investigation. It also gave judges, the media, and the civil-liberties crowd an excuse to go cop bashing.

Ross reached for a stick of gum. Shit storm was right.

Fargnoli said, "I mentioned that two people got whacked. Both were informants. Somebody got their names from the taps, then paid them a visit. There's also been talk of blackmail. Ain't our business if a guy's gay or a wife's fooling around or some city council member's got a numbered account in the Bahamas. We didn't have a court order to tape those conversations. Such information is therefore useless. But it's not useless to whoever stole these wiretaps. He or she is sitting on a gold mine."

He ran a hand through his graying crew cut. "You two get that shit back or we're all dead. And you get it back before politicians, judges, and the very liberal media know it exists."

He looked at Harry. "I'd like a word with Ross."

Ross watched Harry walk toward reception. She could tell, by the smirk on his face, he knew what was coming.

A headache began worming its way through her brain.

When the door closed behind Harry, Fargnoli said, "Connie Pavlides is a suspect in the theft of these wiretaps."

Ross brought folded hands to her mouth. "Is this some kind of joke?"

"I wish it was. The department wants you to go after him. Treat this like any other undercover assignment. You know the drill. I feel funny saying this, but I got no choice. You're to gain Connie's trust, then do what you gotta do."

Do what you gotta do. Betray Connie.

Ross shook her head. "No way. Get somebody else. I'm not stabbing Connie in the back. You've no right to put me in that position."

"You put yourself in that position the day you became a cop. And I'll pretend I didn't hear what you just said. Because if I did, I'd have to ask for your badge. The department isn't a democracy. It's a military organization, and that means a chain of command. You do as you're told or you find other work. There's no in-between. And it's not about being a man or a woman. It's about being a cop and taking orders. You're a good cop, which means I don't expect no bullshit from you. The people who've handed down this assignment feel the same way."

He placed both palms down on the desk. "You took an oath. You either keep it or you don't. Are we doing the right thing asking you to investigate your boyfriend behind his back? No, we're not. But don't look for pity, because frankly, the NYPD and one billion Chinese both don't give a shit. There's VIP asses on the line here. Headquarters is looking out for number one, which means they ain't looking out for you."

He softened his voice. "It could be worse. You could turn in your badge, somebody else gets the assignment, and it really goes bad for Connie. This way maybe you can do him some good. I don't know how. I'm just throwing this at you."

You live by the sword, you die by the sword.

Ross struggled to find her voice. "How, I mean, what, ties Connie to these wiretaps?"

"The chief suspect is a computer geek from Connie's security company. Citizen name of Denny Rinko. The feeling is, Connie put him up to it."

Ross closed her eyes. Harry had known Connie was jammed up and that she'd have to go after him.

What she really wanted to know was, had Harry set Connie up?

36
Holding Back

In the living room of his Brooklyn Heights apartment, overlooking the Brooklyn Bridge, Connie Pavlides walked toward Ross, carrying a black plastic garbage bag.

"So they've still got you with Harry," he said. He seemed distracted. Troubled.

"What's wrong?" Ross said.

He sat beside her on the couch and tossed the bag on the floor.

"Nothing I can't handle," he said. He patted her knee. "Sorry it turned out bad for you. I know how badly you want to dump the guy."

"The department's in a bind over those missing wiretaps. At the moment, my wishes don't count. What counts is getting those wiretaps back as soon as possible. They think Harry and I can do it. So I'm stuck with him. At least for now."

They'd ordered in tonight. Chinese with two bottles of Merlot. As things turned out, neither Ross nor Connie had had an appetite. She finished most of an egg roll, a few bean sprouts, and picked at the fried rice. Connie didn't do much better.

At first she suspected he knew she was investigating him. But as time passed and he said nothing about the wiretaps, Ross decided something else was bothering him.

She poured herself a glass of wine. She'd told Connie about this morning's meeting with Fargnoli. About the stolen wiretaps and Harry's threat to have Chessy tried for murder unless Ross continued working with him.

What had she held back?

She hadn't told Connie he was a suspect in the theft. And she didn't say she'd been assigned to investigate him. How long could she withhold information from him? She didn't know. She only knew she didn't want to lose him.

Connie picked up a sparerib. "Strange they should dump this assignment on you guys. You've already got one major investigation. If going after the chief judge of New York narcotics isn't major, what is?"

Using chopsticks, Ross helped herself to some snow peas. Connie was a good cop. Too good not to notice the obvious.

"Harry and I work OC," she said. "Colombians, Russians, Chinese, Italians. People under investigation and who have major court cases pending. People interested in locating informants and witnesses who can put them away. They'd pay a fortune to hear those wiretaps."

Connie said, "Whoever stole them is an instant millionaire."

"Money that big always leaves a trail. Follow it and who knows where it'll lead?"

Connie bit into the rib. "So how do you intend to handle Harry?"

"I can't have him hurting Chessy, that's for sure. If her case is reopened, she could go to prison. She'd never survive."

Connie said, "The man just can't stop conspiring. Next time you two get together maybe your gun can go off."

"Chessy belongs in a hospital. But try telling that to a jury."

"You know what they say about the trial system. Your fate's in the hands of twelve people who are too dumb to get out of jury duty."

"Don't I know it."

She put down her chopsticks. "Your turn."

"My turn?"

"The garbage bag. What's that all about?"

Connie dropped the sparerib on a paper plate, then wiped his fingers on a damp napkin. Reaching in the garbage bag, he removed two videocassettes and placed them in Ross's lap.

He said, "If you plan on throwing up, turn your head."

Ross picked up one cassette. "Oh my God."

Connie reached into the bag again. "It gets worse."

Ross was holding a kiddy-porn video. Beside her, Connie removed similar porn items from the plastic bag—more videos, magazines, newsletters, lists of man/boy love organizations, lists of Web sites devoted to pedophiles. There were also photographs of adults having sex with children.

Ross held up her hands and looked away. "I think I am going to be sick. Where did you get this stuff?"

"Look closer. My name's on some of the items."

"What are you talking about?"

"I've been put on mailing lists, computer bulletin boards, and personals, all of it dealing with kiddy porn. I've got a dozen subscriptions in my name to porn newspapers, porn book clubs, you name it. I never signed up for any of this shit. I wouldn't touch it with a ten-foot pole."

"Who would do this to you?"

"My guess is Denny Rinko. He has a beef with me, and he has access to my computer. I did ruin the guy's love life, remember?"

Ross took his hand. "How did they react at work?"

"Let's just say I got asked a few questions. Tom, my boss, he's cool. We've known each other fifteen years. He knows I'm not into this. But word's reached some of the clients. And their wives. I've been taken off a couple of assignments. Supposedly it's temporary, but you know how that works. I told Tom I'd prefer a leave of absence so I can look into this thing myself. He said no problem. He's keeping me on full salary, at least for now. If I need anything I'm to come to him."

He reached for his glass of wine. "In my business, you lose your reputation, you can pack it in. Some people will back me. Others will swear they knew I was into little boys from day one. I've got to find Denny Rinko. When I do, we're going to get busy. He's got something to tell me."

"Could there be more to this than Denny's revenge?"

"Who knows? I know it was set up to destroy me, and I don't see Denny being that sophisticated. I'll find him. Believe me, I'll find him. And when I do he *will* tell all."

Ross shook her head in frustration. "Connie, this is overkill. If there's someone else involved, he's one sick bastard."

"I've done some checking. A video company, a newspaper, and a Web site all said the same thing. My name and address came to them by computer. The most interesting thing? All subscriptions and listings started at the same time. This shit was well planned."

"If there's anything I can do, let me know."

"I've gone to the East Village looking for Denny. He hasn't been home in two days. I've checked clubs, bars, Internet cafés, chess clubs. Nothing. No one's seen him. Did come up with one thing. I'm not the only one looking for him. Someone else, an albino, a big guy with pink eyes, he's also asking about Denny."

"Albino? Pink eyes? What's that all about?"

"I have no idea." Connie snapped his fingers. "You might want to talk to Denny about those missing wiretaps. He worked at police headquarters several hours a week. For him, ripping off the department would have been easy. I have to wonder if his playing hard to get hasn't got something to do with those missing taps."

"What would he do with them?" Ross said. "Whoever took them knew their value. Frankly, Denny doesn't strike me as being connected."

"He isn't. If he did take them he's turned them over to someone else."

"The question is who."

"A master criminal he's not. Denny's just a nerd with a taste for jailbait."

Connie put his arm around Ross. "I'm sorry to bring you my problems when you've got your own. I wish I could help you with Harry, but at the moment I'm jammed up. Denny—"

Ross pressed her fingertips against his lips. "Nail Denny, and don't worry about me. I'll be fine."

"I wouldn't underestimate Harry. He has friends in the department."

"I know."

"Suggestion," Connie said. "Reach out for Jackie Blue. Tell him you want to hook up with Sanchez as soon as possible. Remind Sanchez that what happened to Graciella can happen to her. You might also want to check Jackie Blue about those missing wiretaps."

Ross nodded. "Will do."

"Would Jackie Blue admit to being one of the buyers?"

"Jackie's mine. I own the guy. Harry's the problem. If I go to meet Sanchez, chances are he'll follow me."

"Create a diversion," Connie said. "Send Harry off on a wild-goose chase, then check out Sanchez."

Ross nodded in agreement. "I like it. But Harry's nobody's fool. He's quick. He'd see through a scam in no time."

"Don't underestimate yourself. You're the one working the perp, not Harry. You're every bit as smart as he is. Maybe smarter."

He drew Ross close, kissed her hair, and whispered. "He can't beat you. Not when you play your game. Do what you do best. Outthink the bastard."

Ross clung to him with all her strength.

She'd never felt so shitty in all her life.

37
Can't Come In Today

At eight-thirty in the morning Harry Earles walked downstairs to the basement of his Queens home, opened his floor safe, and took out an unregistered .22 he'd confiscated from a subway-turnstile jumper. The gun went into the pocket of his robe.

Then he used his cell phone to call Hilton Prigo.

"How are we doing on Denny?" Harry said.

"I think I come up with something."

"Let's hear it."

"He's still here in the East Village. He ain't left."

Harry wasn't surprised. Fugitives always returned to their old haunts. To family and friends. It was human to want to find familiar things in a familiar place.

"Anything else?" Harry said.

"Bouncer at a club on Avenue A, he say he sold Rinko some Special K and Ecstasy. He say Rinko leave the club at three this morning with a young white girl."

"A runaway. If she's over twelve, I'll be surprised. Go on."

"Second person who seen him is an old lady who hangs out in Tompkins Square Park. She seen Rinko and this girl yesterday afternoon. They was in the park eating pizza and drinking beer. The old lady say Rinko give her a beer."

"Hilton, I want that little toad and I want the rest of those wiretaps. He's in the East Village. Stay on him. Sooner or later he'll make a mistake."

Harry looked at his watch. "Check in with me every two hours. You have my beeper number. Get down to the East Village, and stay there until I tell you to leave."

"Where will you be?"

Harry placed a hand on the .22. "I've got some business to take care of. I'll join you later this afternoon. Then we'll see what can be done about locating our town's newest cross-dresser. I also plan to devote time to Detective Magellan. If I'm right, she'll speed up the search for Jenn Sanchez."

"Why?"

"To get back at me for having finessed her into investigating her boyfriend. It's not the sort of thing a woman like her forgets. I figure she'll reach out for Jackie Blue. I plan to watch him and let matters take their course."

Hilton Prigo said, "Jackie Blue. I want to put a bullet in his head so bad, I can taste it.

"All in good time. First, he has to lead me to Sanchez. I'll be here for the next hour or so, until the nurse arrives. Call me if you've got anything. If you find Rinko, don't kill him. Just sit on him until I get there. I want those wiretaps he's got. My guess is he's listened to them and he's heard something he thinks is worth money."

He's heard something about Harry.

Prigo said, "Sounds like a greedy little punk to me."

"Not to worry. His days are numbered."

Harry folded his phone. He'd played Denny cheap, allowing the little weasel to get the better of him. A mistake Harry was now about to rectify.

He closed the floor safe. He'd estimated his share of the wiretaps would be fifty million dollars. So far it appeared he'd been correct. Those interested in buying were coming from far and near. Face it, an enterprising drug dealer had no choice but to buy. If he didn't buy, his competitor would. Harry couldn't lose.

Well, he could if he himself had been bugged. And if Denny, he of the bright red wig, had it all on tape.

Harry went upstairs to the kitchen where he had coffee and juice. Helene was still asleep in the living room. Grenada was due in less than an hour. Helene could sleep until then.

He looked around the kitchen. Some renovations were in order. Such as a new screen door, new linoleum on the floor, and a new garbage disposal. The outside needed work as well. The garage roof had a leak, the patio required new tiles, and the barbecue pit needed cleaning. He'd get around to all of it in time. Harry wasn't one for having strangers in the house. Which is why he'd become a pretty good handyman if he had to say so himself. Lately, however, Magellan had taken up a lot of his time, preventing him from even looking at a hammer, let alone pick it up. No regrets. He'd wanted to be with her. *Thou source of all my bliss and all my woe.*

He poured more coffee. He had a strong longing for Magellan as a woman. The dark hair, the seductive eyes, the graceful way of walking that Latinas and only Latinas seemed to have. On occasion, her mere presence had the effect of a drug on him.

And there was her practical value. She was going to lead Harry to Sanchez. He snapped his fingers, a reminder to do something about Marisa Durres, the lady who was still being knocked about by an Albanian thug she'd once had the misfortune to marry. Harry intended to visit Mrs. Durres and convince her to retract her story. To admit she'd been mistaken when she'd told Magellan she'd never met Harry. After all, it was a woman's prerogative to change her mind.

He lifted his coffee in a toast. *To wiretaps, the greatest thing since the Delete key on computers.* Want to nail a perp? There was no better way to do it than with wiretaps. Whisper *taps* in his ear and a perp would admit his guilt on the spot. There was something decisive and absolute about wiretaps. Not to mention ironic, since a perp was hanging himself with his own words.

Harry didn't need to be reminded of the importance of wiretaps. Cops couldn't buy up in drug organizations anymore. Gone were the days when a Magellan could buy a few ounces of Bolivian marching powder on her way to a multimillion-dollar bust. Eighty percent of all traffickers were now based outside the United States. They did business out of their native lands—Colombia, Mexico, Russia, China, Bolivia, and God knows where. Needless to say, this put them out of the reach of most American undercover operations. Which is why you needed wiretaps, legal or otherwise.

Harry didn't expect the civil-liberties crowd to understand this. The minute word of those illegal taps got out, the NYPD would have a holy mess on its hands. As usual, whatever made the world a better place for liberals made it more dangerous for cops.

His phone rang.

It was Grenada, and she was very upset.

"I'm very sorry, Mr. Earles," she said, "but I can't come to work today."

"What's wrong? Why are you crying?"

"It's Levell. The police are holding him. I'm trying to get him out. He can't stand being cooped up no more, Mr. Earles. Prison just about killed him."

"Grenada, slow down. What did Levell do?"

"I don't know. Police tell me probable cause but that can mean anything. He's black and he's been in prison and that's all they need. I'm meeting with a lawyer to see what we can do."

"Grenada, come here and let me take care of Levell. Someone has to stay with Helene. I can't leave her alone."

"Mr. Earles, you know how I feel about Levell. I can't come anywhere while he's in jail. I got to get him out."

38
Church Meeting

Jackie Blue was waiting for Ross Magellan in a back pew of a Harlem church, looking worried and unhappy.

"Got a problem," he said. "Appreciate you helping me out."

"Excuse me, but we're here to discuss *my* problem, not yours."

Jackie Blue used a thumb to stroke a diamond ring on his pinky finger.

"I need somebody taken off the set," he said. "Dig, I want you to convince this fool that he got no business hanging around New York. Especially when he making it his business to take over my business."

Ross slipped into the pew beside the drug dealer. "You promised me Sanchez. No more games, Jackie. She shows or I'm gone."

Jackie Blue had picked the time and the place. Twelve noon in Harlem. An empty Baptist church on

West 116th Street, not far from the Malcolm Shabazz Mosque, named for the murdered Malcolm X.

In the pew behind Jackie and watching his back was Big Mac. For reasons of space, the 410-pound bodyguard was forced to sit on the wooden bench with one mammoth leg in the aisle.

Ross looked over her shoulder. Two black males guarded the entrance from inside. She counted six guarding the outside. As far as Ross knew, she and Jackie Blue were alone in the church. Which was just as well because from the looks of things, Jackie Blue was under siege. And people under siege rarely looked forward to having company.

Ross said, "If you got me here to take part in some turf war, you've wasted your time and mine. I'm not buying into it."

"Just hear me out."

Ross rose from the pew. "Goodbye, Jackie."

Big Mac stepped forward, blocking her path.

Ross never raised her voice. She spoke softly, and kept her eyes on bodyguard.

"You have eight years left on your parole," she said. "If you don't get out of my way, I'll have your parole revoked. I can do it with a phone call. No trial, no hearing, no bail. You'll be upstate in time for dinner, and you'll do the full bit. I'll throw in charges of attacking a police officer, carrying a concealed weapon, and associating with known felons. That's a dime on top of the eight. Eighteen years if you're counting."

An agitated Jackie Blue rose from the pew. "Nigger, are you out of your mind? Get your funky ass out of her face. *Now.*"

Big Mac quickly moved to one side.

Jackie Blue said to Ross, "I apologize. The man don't mean no disrespect. But he *is* stupid. So stupid he sneak on a bus then pay to get off."

He jerked his head toward the choir. "Check it out."

Ross looked up. Interesting. Three people—two males and a female—stood behind the choir railing. The males were muscular young blacks who sported dark glasses and shaven heads. The lone female was a thin Latina who despite the humid weather wore a team jacket as though in need of protection from cold weather. Ross couldn't ID her from this distance, and in any case, trying to do so was a waste of time. The woman could have been Jenn Sanchez or Queen Elizabeth. Jackie Blue wouldn't be the first informant to try to con Ross.

Ross said, "Tell her to come down."

Jackie Blue beckoned to the trio, then turned his attention to Ross.

"We ain't got Duke with us today," he said. "That *is* what you said."

"He's occupied at the moment. Anyway, he's not your dedicated churchgoer."

"I know what happened at that coffee shop. Anytime he come on the set, people up and die."

"Not today."

The drug dealer grinned. "I swear before God and two white men, you almost got me believing you. Damn, I *do* believe you. Girl, you got it going on."

Jackie Blue resumed his seat in the pew. "I need your help in dealing with some punk-ass wanna-be out to take over my business."

"I'm listening. Which is not the same as getting involved."

"I understand. Two years ago I bought a street corner in Washington Heights from a Dominican name of Hilton Prigo. Son of a bitch is an albino. Pink eyes, white hair. Like something out of Tom and Jerry."

Ross said, "You said he's an albino?"

"That's right. You know Hilton Prigo?"

"Not personally. But I do know he used to sell product, as you call it, until he dropped out of sight. This is the second time in twenty-four hours someone's mentioned him to me."

"Like I said, I buy this corner from Prigo. Serious money. Lots and lots of ducats."

Ross listened to footsteps descending the choir's wooden staircase. She wasn't about to get excited at this point. Not until she'd seen the woman face to face and talked to her. As for Jackie Blue, the price he'd paid for Hilton Prigo's corner was an open secret. A million, two hundred thousand in cash. A small price to pay for being allowed to do business in a choice location without having to go to war.

"The punk took my money," Jackie Blue said. "Then he retired to Santo Domingo to eat fried bananas and pump them skinny little Chinese women he like so much. Started going broke down there. Hurricane trashed his property. Then a sugarcane business he had in Cuba didn't work out. Ended up with one of them Chinese women running off to Brazil with over two hundred thousand dollars of Prigo's cash. Tell me if that ain't one expensive piece of tail."

Jackie Blue put one arm on the back of the pew.

"Last week Prigo shows up in New York. Comes to me and says he wants his corner back. Just like that. He wants me to give him what is mine."

Ross said, "Did he make you an offer?"

"Definitely. Told me to give it up or get bagged. I give it to him free or he kill me."

Ross heard footsteps on the church's stone floor but refused to turn around. "Go on."

"Nigger took the hard line," Jackie Blue said. "He want it all. Want to keep what I paid him *and* take back the corner. Ain't that a bitch?"

"What did you tell him?"

"I told him I'd think about it. Wanted to buy me some time 'cause I don't plan to give him shit. Wanted to see who he with. Where his strength come from. Also, we start gang-banging and somebody get hurt. Gunfire is a negative thing on account of dead people do not put money in your pocket, know what I'm saying? Still, I can't hand over the corner and have my people respect me. I let Prigo bitch my ass, I'm through. Can't show my face on the street again."

"So what do you want me to do?"

Jackie Blue took a deep breath. "I want you to retire Prigo before he get started. Put that albino out of the pharmaceutical trade. Nothing extreme. I'm thinking along the lines of a major felony. Something guaranteed to send his raggedy-ass upstate for twenty years."

He stared at the vaulted ceiling. "We arrange for him to buy something. Then we drop the hammer on his big old pink head."

"We?"

"Yeah. You and me."

Ross folded her arms across her chest. "What's in it

for me? I see you staying in business. But where's mine? And I don't mean that woman you claim is Sanchez. I want more."

"The lady wants more. Well, Jackie Blue got that covered. Dig, why you think Hilton sell me his corner in the first place? The man left New York because he was distressed. Took early retirement in order to keep on breathing. He saw your boy Duke kill an under-cover cop. Saw him burn the woman alive."

In an attempt to conceal her excitement, Ross cov-ered her mouth with one hand.

An eyewitness who could ID Harry for killing an undercover. You couldn't beat that with a stick.

Jackie Blue said, "Prigo's in this crack house, party-ing with a Chinese whore. She was tricking there to support her habit. He see Duke sneak in carrying this woman. Saw him cuff her to a radiator while she still alive and torch her. Prigo is ugly. I mean we *know* the man is ugly. But his brain ain't gone. He know he seen too much. So he decided to move to where people ain't setting fire to each other. You wondering where I got this from, your boy Duke told Sanchez and Sanchez told me."

"What happened to the woman Prigo was with?"

"Ended up like a lot of crack whores. Bitch died of AIDS. People say they got TB when they know damn well they got AIDS."

Ross thought, *Something's wrong with this picture.* If you can nail Harry Earles for killing a cop, you leave town and you don't come back. Not ever.

"Why did Prigo return to New York?" she said.

"Duke sent for him."

"He *what?*"

"The man sent for Prigo. Offered him a job and Prigo took it."

"Slow down," Ross said. "You're saying Harry killed a cop in front of a witness. Then he offers this witness a job, which the witness accepts. I think you've been smoking too much incense."

Jackie smiled. "First rule is you never use the product. Sell it but don't smell it. Listen up. Prigo took the job 'cause he got paid. And 'cause your boy Duke let him live. Some people might consider that a good deal."

"What kind of job we talking about?"

"Duke lately come into some wiretaps belonging to the police department."

The expression on Ross's face never changed. "Go on."

"Suppose to be some good shit on them taps. You learn who's a witness against you and where they at. You learn if you got an informant on your payroll and how the law gonna try you when you end up in court at the defense table, holding a Bible and trying to look like you ain't done shit. Duke ain't giving anything away. He's asking serious money for these taps."

Ross looked at the altar. Harry had stolen the illegal wiretaps with Denny Rinko's help. He'd placed Hilton Prigo in charge of sales. And he'd put the blame on Connie. Son of a bitch.

Closing her eyes, Ross bowed her head as though she'd just received a divine solution to a difficult problem. She had Harry by the balls. All she had to do is make the right moves and he would go down for sure. He'd wanted Ross to go after the wiretaps and in the process arrest Connie for the theft. Well, it wasn't going to happen. Ross was going after Harry for stealing the taps. This time cops, the brass in particular, would back her all the way. The Blue Wall of Silence wouldn't protect Harry. Not with so many police careers on the line.

Ross would need corroboration. Denny Rinko or Hilton Prigo would have to give up Harry.

Whom did Ross prefer as a snitch? No contest. It was Hilton Prigo all the way.

Prigo had been on the set and watched as Harry burned Celia Cuevas alive. Get him to talk and you'd have Harry for murder. The best approach was to charge Prigo with aiding and abetting. With being an accessory. Why not? He'd done nothing to stop the murder. Also, by not coming forward, he'd concealed evidence of a crime. Not just any crime, but a cop killing. Now he was involved in the theft and sale of police property. He could go away until he was an old man.

Or he could be smart and rat out Harry. Admit that Harry had killed Celia Cuevas. Admit that Harry, not Connie, had stolen the wiretaps.

Ross heard Jackie Blue's voice, but she was thinking about something else. Harry's files showed no connection to Celia Cuevas or any of the other undercovers, including Sanchez. You'd think he'd spent his entire career without even ghosting for a single female undercover.

Ross gripped the pew in front of her. Harry was being protected.

Protected by someone with enough juice to remove entire case files.

Jackie Blue said to Ross, "Check it out. The lady in the aisle next to you is Detective Sanchez."

Jenn Sanchez was a tall Latina with a long face, sad brown eyes, and dark hair tied in a ponytail. She wore beige slacks, an Islanders hockey jacket, and green platform shoes with silver buckles. Drugs had taken their toll on her looks. Her skin was blotchy, and her eyes were baggy. There was a cut on her forehead and sores at one corner of her mouth. Despite the humid weather, she shivered inside her warm up jacket. She also continually scratched her hands and arms. The itch came from the quinine used to cut heroin.

A yawning Sanchez took the pew in front of Ross.

Ross said, "Detective Sanchez, I'm Detective Magellan. I've been trying to get together with you—"

Sanchez spoke with a junkie's slur. "I'm not a detective anymore. Don't know what the hell I am. But I damn sure ain't a cop." She sounded regretful.

She studied Ross before saying, "You nearly went down the other day because of Graciella. I should say because of Harry because he set you up. Gave him a chance to come to the rescue. He wants you to be grateful to him. Wants you to rely on Harry and nobody else."

She pointed to the muscular blacks who'd escorted her from the choir. "The brothers dragged me from my crib and insisted I accompany them. Said they were taking me to church. I thought they were kidding."

Ross looked at Jackie Blue. "You can stay. You've heard it all anyway." She pointed to Big Mac and the others. "They can wait by the door."

Jackie Blue lifted a hand. Seconds later he was alone with Ross and Sanchez.

Ross said to Sanchez, "You and Lou Angelo. What's with that?"

"We used to score dope together from Emilio Albert. Lou's a sweetheart. We got to talking at the restaurant where Emilio worked, and he took a liking to me. Strictly platonic. If you know Lou, you know he's into brown sugar. He also likes helping ladies in distress. When I'm low on money or need a place to crash, he's there for me. You're going to send him to prison, aren't you?"

"I can't talk about that."

Sanchez said, "Right now, he's the one good thing in my life. Is there a way you can cut the guy some slack?"

"I can't comment on an open investigation. You know that."

"Nothing's changed. We get them to trust us, then we trash their lives. That's one thing I don't miss about the job. It's a shit way to make a living, in case you haven't noticed. What makes you think I won't warn Lou you're after him?"

Ross said, "Big mistake. I'll arrest Angelo whether you warn him or not. Meanwhile, you go on the NYPD and FBI shit list. You also go on my personal shit list. As Jackie Blue will tell you, that's not a good place to be."

"I hear that," Jackie Blue said.

"Use your head," Ross said. "Harry's looking to kill you. You need all the friends you can get. You'll also need friends when Lou Angelo goes down. I should point out another consequence of talking too much. I could tell Angelo you helped me set him up. Stay cool and just watch the play."

Sanchez nodded. "You're good. Real good. You don't give a shit about anybody, and you'll do whatever it takes. You're right. I don't want to be on your shit list."

Ross removed an envelope from her shoulder bag and handed it to Sanchez.

The former detective looked inside and saw the money.

"A thousand dollars," Ross said. She looked at Jackie Blue. "Make sure nobody takes it from her. I'm holding you responsible."

Jackie Blue said, "Big Mac will see that she gets home safely and don't drop nothing on the way."

Sanchez fingered the cash. "What's this for?"

"Anything you want. I'd say spend it on food, but we both know that's not going to happen. It could, but I don't think it will."

Sanchez's smile was twisted. "Is this where I get a lecture on the evils of drugs? We're certainly in the right place for it."

"Good advice is useless," Ross said. "No one takes it, so why bother giving it?"

Sanchez grinned, showing missing top teeth. "My father use to say people only ask for advice when they already know the answer and wish they didn't."

"He was right."

Sanchez held up the envelope. "Thanks. I can use it. So you want to talk about Harry?"

"Yes. Except for a few loose ends here and there, I think I have most of it."

"You probably don't. But keep talking."

"He's killed at least two female undercovers. And he's tried to kill you. All three of you fit the same professional and physical profile. Young Latina cops who worked undercover and had Harry ghosting for them."

"A fourth undercover also fits those profiles."

Ross said, "If you mean do I know I'm a target, the answer is yes. You were one of the first to tell me that, remember?"

Sanchez's eyes gleamed in the dim church light. "Honey, you're in his book. Everything you ever did, said, or thought. You get a chance, check your apartment, and your office. You're missing stuff."

"What kind of stuff?"

"Clothing, jewerly, a shoe, CDs. Personal shit. Harry stole it, but he's smart. Never takes big things and never takes too much. This way you don't miss it."

"What's he do with these items?"

"Makes a shrine dedicated to you." A sniffling Sanchez wiped her nose with the back of her hand. "Keeps it in his room, which is locked most of the time. Your high-school yearbook, birth certificate, wedding license if you're married. All there. Along with videos of Christmas parties you and your relatives had. Weird stuff. Combs public records to compile your family tree. Even writes down the weddings, birthdays, and addresses of your relatives. Puts it on computer disks or in his journal."

Ross nodded. "I take it you've been to his home."

"Harry never liked me using. He's a puritan. Hates drugs like the plague. But I was using before we started working together and wasn't going to quit for him. Working undercover puts you around drugs all the time. Drugs, money, and people who do exactly as they please. My kind of people. It gets harder and harder *not* to use when you're in that scene. Understand what I'm saying?"

"I do."

"At first I started using just to blend in. Then I got to like it. Pretty soon I got so I couldn't do the job without it. I also needed it to get me through the night. Fucking nights were the worse. Lying in bed unable to sleep. Thinking about how close I come to getting killed, getting raped. To having some crazy Mexicans take me out in the country and literally skin me alive. Shit, I needed something."

"Harry—"

"Give him credit. He did his best to get me off the stuff. But I did what every addict does. I lied. Said I would stop. I didn't. Said I was in rehab when I was shooting up between my toes and under my pubic hairs so the tracks wouldn't show. One night we were in the car and I got sick. Throwing up, passing out. Harry's house was closest, so we went there. His wife's crippled, and when he went to take care of her, I started exploring."

Ross touched Sanchez's arm. "And that's when you saw your shrine."

"I couldn't stay in the house another minute after that. Ran out, grabbed a cab, and left him standing in the street in his bathrobe."

Ross said, "Tell me about the drug dealer you and Harry arrested, then handed over to be killed."

Sanchez smiled. "A real pro. Does her homework. Yeah, we sold that maggot. I needed money for dope, so I did things with Harry I'm not proud of. Guy we sold was Viktor Ramiz. Ran with some Albanians out of the Bronx. They learned he was ratting them out to the FBI, so they took steps."

Jackie Blue said, "That's the guy I told you about. The one they burned with them high-tech rods. Fried him until he looked like bacon."

Sanchez picked up a hymnbook. "Speaking of mistakes, I made one in connection with this deal. All but got me killed. I decided to earn a little extra money, you might say. Not too smart, since it's put me in my present predicament."

Ross said, "You tried blackmail."

Sanchez looked at her. "You're living up to your reputation. What tipped you?"

"Couple things. Extra money. Ramiz killing. You obviously tried squeezing somebody involved in the Ramiz hit. I can tell you that blackmailing Harry isn't smart."

Sanchez held her thumb and forefinger almost touching. "Missed it by that much."

"Missed what?"

"Harry wants me dead. That's personal. Now his friend, that's something different."

"Friend?"

"Ended up in a car, needle in my arm, and inhaling carbon monoxide. Harry, he gave me a hot shot—heroin and rat poison. It was meant to look like suicide. Harry's specialty. Not the first time he's tried that, believe me. I should be dead. Wasn't my time, I guess. I always suspected he'd try to kill me. Pissed him off when I refused to go to Italy—"

"With him and his wife," Ross said.

"You know. Anyway, working with him was one thing. But I said I'd swallow my gun before I let him touch me. Then and there I knew he'd try to ice me. Only a question of when. Then I go and give him a second reason for snuffing me."

"You tried to blackmail his friend."

Sanchez had gone after Harry's protector.

"A girl has to eat," Sanchez said.

"A name," Ross said. "I need a name."

Sanchez's eyes were slits. She was nodding out.

She began to sing. "He knows when you've been bad or good so be good for goodness sake."

She waggled a finger at Ross. "He knows every move you make. He's known all along."

"Harry?"

Sanchez giggled. "No. Santa Claus. They've been working together for a long time. I didn't know until Ramiz—"

She slumped down in the pew.

Jackie Blue leaned forward. "She's out cold."

"No, no, no," Sanchez said. "Not yet."

Ross looked at Jackie Blue. "You know who she's talking about?"

The dealer shook his head. "First time I heard about this guy, whoever he is."

Sanchez said, "Magellan, Harry's gonna move on you."

"I know."

"He nailed Celia Cuevas, Raymunda Montano. Nearly got me. Sure he didn't follow you here?"

"I'm sure."

"You got chops, girlfriend. I give you that. So, we got the pupil versus the teacher."

"I'm not looking forward to it. The guy knows all my tricks. I have to come up with something he hasn't seen or I'm dead."

Sanchez said, "Not that way, girlfriend. Not with this crowd."

"What do you mean?"

Sanchez tried to sit up. She failed. "I need sleep. Want to be safe from Harry? Here's the word."

"I'm listening."

Sanchez said, your only chance is to kill Harry and his little friend at the same time. Go for two. Was Ross down for that?

40
Sending a Message

Harry Earles entered Central Park just as church clocks began striking noon. Oblivious to the rain, he walked past empty benches and vacant soccer fields until he came to the wilderness called the Ramble, a dense woods of tulip trees, streams, and intricate paths.

Turning right onto a meandering footpath, he followed it several yards to a clearing where Frank Beebe, in a gray Stetson and brown belted raincoat, waited under a gingko tree.

The FBI agent looked up at a charcoal-gray sky. "The hell's this rain gonna stop? City's wet as a frosted frog. It's making me tense. I don't know whether to shit or go blind."

Harry lifted his umbrella to better see Beebe's face. Rain or shine, the FBI agent didn't care for New York, a city he described as a pitiful concoction of cement and asphalt, which was only fucking up the landscape.

Harry said, "Rain is simply nature weeping from gladness."

"I'm weeping, but it ain't got shit to do with gladness. Yours truly is weeping 'cause he's standing in mud up to his pecker. Hell's this place called again?"

"The Ramble. Prettiest part of Central Park. It's not usually this deserted. Bird-watchers come here during the day. At night, it's a gay pickup spot."

Beebe pointed to used condoms lying at the base of the ginko tree. "They say if you go into heat, package your meat. Me, I like riding bareback. I take my love without the glove."

He eyed Harry. "You're looking weary. Been staying out after curfew?"

"Credit Magellan for that," Harry said. "She kept me busy yesterday."

"So you said. She had your nurse's husband arrested or something."

"Magellan's way of making sure I didn't follow her. Probably because she was meeting Sanchez."

Beebe said, "Clever little gal you got there."

"Too clever sometimes. She managed to jeopardize my wife's health. I had to spend the entire day at home with a phone glued to my ear."

"How'd that come about?"

"I had to find a replacement for my regular nurse who preferred getting her husband out of jail as opposed to caring for my wife."

Beebe nodded. "Now that's sad enough to bring a tear to a glass eye. I'd say Magellan knows you're bird-dogging her. So much for the element of surprise."

"I dislike the idea of Magellan exercising power

over me. And I intend to let her know how much I dislike it."

"I'm sure you will. Lordy is that woman quick. And good-looking. If I was on death row, I'd want her for my last meal."

Beebe removed a cigar case from inside his coat. A quick look at the sky and he shook his head.

"Man can't enjoy an illegal Cuban cigar in this town," he said. The case went back inside his coat. "How did Magellan get the husband off the street?"

"He drives a cab. Magellan had a patrol car stop him on suspicion of transporting drugs. I worked the phone until my ears ached. I couldn't leave my wife alone and Magellan knew it."

Beebe said, "I can see where that would rattle your slats, you being a proud man and all. I'd say you underestimated your lady friend."

Harry tightened his grip on the umbrella. "She's the little fly who can't be swatted. Yes, she's quick. And resourceful. She could probably follow *you* and you'd never know it."

Beebe shook his head. "No woman's that good, I don't care what the hype says. I made sure I wasn't tailed here. Look around. It's you and me and a ton of wet leaves. Even your so-called homeless got the good sense to stay indoors. You said Magellan thinks we're working together behind her back. How'd she come to this opinion?"

"We got careless or she got lucky. In any case, that's what she's telling Fargnoli. He thinks she's imagining things. He can't conceive of his cops hooking up with the FBI behind his back."

"Don't wake the man. Let him sleep a little longer."

"That's not the end of it. Magellan is having me tailed."

Beebe chuckled deep in his throat. "Is she now? Her lieutenant thinks she's one rib short of a barbecue. So how's she managing to keep tabs on you without his help?"

"She's recruited her friend Connie Pavlides. She can't come after me officially. So she's doing it unofficially."

Beebe said, "A supreme love. That's as good a motive as any. I should point out we're all on the same case. If you and I meet in private to discuss certain aspects of that case, shouldn't be any skin off her nose."

Harry scratched his nose. "As I noted at our last meeting, there's more to this case as you know. More than Magellan is letting on."

"Hmm. Point taken. At the moment I do believe we're alone. Does that mean anybody coming by is gonna think we're queer? Which brings up the question, What's better, to be born a nigger or a fag?"

"Haven't thought about it much."

Beebe laughed. "A nigger. That way you don't have to tell your folks."

Harry tugged on the bill of his baseball cap. "If you say so."

"You said there was something else you wanted to talk about. Besides Magellan, that is. Something that could only be discussed in person."

"So I did. I don't like Magellan playing around with my wife's health. So I've decided to send her a message. Part of the message will be delivered by her sister."

"The one Magellan's got tucked away in some acorn academy out on Long Island?"

"The very same. The other part is to be delivered by you."

Beebe placed a hand on his chest. "Me? What the hell can I tell her?"

Harry said, "Uh-oh. We've got company. By the tree. Near the broken bench."

As the FBI agent turned in that direction, Harry pulled out the .22 and shot him in the back of the head.

41
In the Wind

Ross Magellan walked into Lieutenant Fargnoli's office that afternoon carrying three thousand dollars in a Ziploc bag. She placed the bag on Fargnoli's desk, then sat in a chair near the window. She wanted to feel the sun, which was shining for the first time in days.

Fargnoli sat at his desk, flipping through *Spring 3100*, the NYPD's official magazine. He looked tired and overworked. But then, so were most of the cops in his squad. A rise in immigration had increased the presence of imported organized crime in the city. OCCB had its hands full dealing with mobs who couldn't find their way around a subway but knew how to scam banks, insurance companies, and Medicare.

Any rosy-eyed view of immigrants once held by Ross was long gone. Too many immigrants were the worst kind of people who'd come to America for the worst kind of reasons.

Fargnoli pointed to the Ziploc bag.

"Call it a souvenir," Ross said. "I went shopping this morning with Mercy Howard. She used the money in that bag to buy a new dress. All of the bills are marked."

Fargnoli said, "The same money you gave Lou Angelo two days ago?"

"The same. Second payment on my so-called divorce."

"So you were right. Angelo *is* Reiner's bagman. And he *is* ripping Reiner off."

"Takes his cut before the judge sees a dime. Mercy and I picked out a lovely dress, by the way."

Fargnoli took his feet off the desk. "You wouldn't happen to know where Connie is right now?"

Ross raised both eyebrows. Had she heard right?

She said, "Excuse me, but I just gave you the guy we need to bring down Reiner. I thought this was a major case. What's Connie got to do with Angelo?"

"Far as I know, nothing. This is about Connie and Frank Beebe. Beebe's been found shot to death in Central Park. The FBI considers Connie a suspect. They'd like to talk to him. Right now he seems to be in the wind."

Ross rose from her chair and walked to the window where she stared at the sun. A long time passed before she spoke.

"Connie's not running away from anybody," she said. "When was Beebe killed?"

"Yesterday between noon and two. Any idea where Connie was at the time?"

Looking for Denny Rinko, the guy who stole the department's illegal wiretaps. The creep who followed Harry's instructions and framed Connie with kiddy porn.

Ross turned to face Fargnoli. She was shaky and her heart was in her mouth, and she knew she'd have to choose her words carefully. Connie was going after Denny Rinko. Meaning he was also going after Harry.

Harry didn't work alone. He had a friend who could make case files disappear. Was that friend Fargnoli? Sanchez could have IDed Harry's friend, but she'd passed out in church, the name hidden somewhere in her smack-fried brain. Jackie Blue claimed this was the first he'd heard of Harry's protector. But he'd stay on it. If he came up with anything, Ross would be the first to know.

He knows when you've been bad or good, so be good for goodness sake.

Fargnoli was familiar with Ross's cases. He'd also forced her to continue working with Harry against her wishes. Had he covered up the murder of two undercovers and the attempted murder of a third?

Watch your words.

Ross said, "How did Connie come to be a suspect?"

"His business card was found in Beebe's wallet."

"Is this a joke? Beebe could have gotten that card anywhere. *I* could have given it to him."

"Did you?"

Ross didn't answer.

Fargnoli said, "I didn't think so. For your information, somebody phoned the feebs and said Connie was trying to do a deal with Beebe regarding certain missing data."

"An anonymous caller," Ross said.

"Aren't they all?"

"I suppose 'missing data' means Connie was trying to sell Beebe the stolen wiretaps."

Fargnoli shrugged. "The feebs didn't mention wire-taps. My guess is they haven't a clue. Does Connie have the tapes?"

"No, he doesn't."

"You'd tell me if he did, right?"

Ross folded her arms across her chest. "Isn't that what I'm being paid to do? Rat out Connie?"

Fargnoli shook his head. "Look, if you want to help the guy, have him come in. ASAP. The feebs are looking to blow him away. Beebe's friends in the Bureau don't like the idea of their guy catching one behind the ear. I'll help Connie in any way I can."

"The way you're helping him now? You forced me to spy on him. Now you're asking me to hand him over to the FBI."

"I kept the feebs off your back. Labriola wanted to lean on you to learn Connie's whereabouts. Understand something: A murdered agent is serious business with these people. I told Labriola if he comes after you, he comes after the department. He'd also be putting the Reiner investigation on every newscast in town. I said you haven't been charged with a crime, so where does he get off interrogating you. I also pointed out that Connie is innocent until proven guilty."

"I suppose I should be grateful."

"You should be listening," Fargnoli said. "The feebs are gunning for Connie. I'd take that literally if I were you."

"Where does he go to turn himself in?" Ross said. "Because I don't think it matters. He's screwed no matter what he does. He stays on the street, he's shot. He gives himself up to the department or to the Salvation Army and he's still screwed. The feds will claim jurisdiction because Beebe was a federal agent and they'll get their way. They'll crucify Connie and apologize later. They have the power of the federal government and all the money in the Treasury behind them, and they rule the world. Ask them and they'll tell you."

Fargnoli scratched the tip of his nose. "Can we talk about the wiretaps?"

Ross said, "Whatever you say, *Lieutenant.*"

"Ross, don't make this any harder for me than it already is."

"The lieutenant wants to talk about something else. OK, let's talk about the wiretaps. I understand the Montalvo brothers are saying the taps gave them the witness who put their father away."

Fargnoli nodded. "That witness would be the late Javier Trujillo, or 'Little Javy,' as he was known. Former accountant for the drug-dealing Montalvos. Connecticut state troopers found his body yesterday in the woods outside New Haven. A gradual process of discovery, you might say. A leg here, an arm there. Took a few hours but eventually they found all of Little Javy. Threw the pieces into plastic bags. The Little Javy puzzle pack. A game for the whole family."

"The three Montalvos," Ross said. "Even with Daddy in the joint, his two sons are still on the street doing business."

"Daddy Raphael's doing all day in Lewisburg."

"I remember. When the judge gave him life his brothers went postal. They had to be cleared from the courtroom. Life in a federal prison means life without parole. That's when the brothers vowed to take care of Little Javy."

Fargnoli said, "Right after the trial Little Javy and

his wife take off for Aruba. Six months later he's missing the Big Apple—the clubs, the women, the hockey games. He sneaks back into the city. Changes his name. Finds another lady. Gets another job. This time he's cooking the books for some Indian doctor who's running a medical scam in the Bronx. That's how he ended up on one of those illegal taps. What else you got for me?"

Are you covering up Harry's crimes?

Ross said, "You mean have I squeezed anything out of Connie regarding the wiretaps? Yes, as a matter of fact."

Strike first. It worked for Harry.

Fargnoli folded his hands on his desk and waited.

"I've got a name," Ross said. "Denny Rinko. He's a computer techie at Connie's security firm. Denny also worked part-time at police headquarters. There's his opportunity."

Fargnoli said, "The department's aware of Mr. Rinko and would like to sit down with him at his earliest convenience. I see opportunity here, but I don't see motive. What connects Mr. Rinko to a pair of maggots like the Montalvos?"

"The person who gave Rinko his orders."

Like Harry. Or you.

Ross said, "Whoever Denny's with knows about the wiretaps. Knows how and why they came to be made. Knows where the department kept them and what they're worth on the open market. I make that someone out to be a cop."

"Sounds good," Fargnoli said. "I meant what I just said about helping Connie. Not only for his sake, but for yours."

Ross's beeper went off.

The callback number was new to her. Which meant it could be anyone. Maybe Jackie Blue was calling to say that Sanchez wanted to talk. Or another informant could be checking in with something he hoped would keep him out of prison. It could have been Chessy, out on a pizza run with her bud Fingers, the two calling from Long Island to chat about nothing at all.

Ross dialed the number on her cell phone.

Connie answered.

Ross turned her back to Fargnoli, walked across the room, and sat on the couch.

"I'm here," she said. "I'm in Lieutenant Fargnoli's office. Where are you?"

"I'm in some Avenue C rat hole, which is passing itself off as a storefront. And I've got Denny."

"Great." *No names,* Ross told herself. And keep the conversation short. Better yet, cut it off.

"I can't talk now," she said. "I'll call you back."

"What's wrong?"

"I'm with the lieutenant. I'll call you back."

"Before you go, listen to this. I know how Denny's mind works. There's a store down here that buys and sells used software. Denny uses it as a mailing address in return for fixing the owner's computer."

"Great. We'll talk about it later."

"You need to hear this. Denny says he stole the tapes but that it was Harry's idea. According to Denny, one tape is dynamite. It ties Harry to the murder of an Albanian drug dealer. A murder he committed to protect a big-time player."

Ross looked across the room. Fargnoli had gone

back to flipping the pages of *Spring 3100*. At least it looked that way.

"Another thing," Connie said. "Denny claims Harry and Hilton Prigo are trying to kill him. They want to stop him from talking to anybody. He says he's tired of running. If you guarantee him protection, he—"

Connie stopped abruptly. Then, "Shit. We got trouble."

Silence.

Then Connie said, "Jesus. Denny hit the floor. Down. *Down!*"

Ross said, "Connie, what's going on?"

She heard *pop-pop-pop*.

Gunfire.

And then the line went dead.

Harry Earles entered the spacious lobby of the Oakes
Institute on Long Island, wearing starched hospital
whites. His name tag read GENESIS, a joke that would
have frosted mom's socks had she been alive.

Most of the institute's patients had retired for the
night. A handful remained in the lobby watching the
late-night news on television in the company of bored-
looking attendants. A dwarfish gray-haired woman sat
alone beneath a mural of sailboats cruising Long Island Sound. She smiled at Harry who waved without
stopping.

He'd never seen the old crock in his life. So why
wave? Because being kind was no problem so long as
he didn't have to stop to do it.

He stepped onto a winding marble staircase leading
to the second floor. The stairway, the ivy-covered walls
outside, and the white columns flanking the building's
entrance were straight out of *Gone With the Wind*,
which happened to be Helene's favorite movie. The

only thing lacking, Harry thought, was a white elite sitting around on the veranda while being waited on hand and foot by oppressed black slaves.

Oakes Institute was a mental hospital for the wacky rich, those affluent citizens with enough money to avoid being imprisoned for their wickedness. Magellan had chosen the perfect place to stash her sister who'd killed their sexually abusive father rather than continue submitting to his bestial desires. In Magellan's opinion, Sis had done nothing wrong, and since Magellan had the bucks, her opinion was accepted.

Harry reached in the pocket of his attendant's coat and fingered a bone-handled straight razor. When he finished with Chessy, Little Sister would be so ugly, she'd have to sneak up on her mirror. Magellan had it coming. She must learn that if you decided to play the game, be prepared to play for keeps. She'd used Helene's nurse to outwit Harry, an insult he couldn't possibly let slide.

In any battle of wits between Harry and Magellan, she was overmatched. He was the teacher, and she was the pupil. She could accept this or not.

Accept it and she could benefit from his experience. If not, there'd be a price to pay.

At the top of the staircase he popped a raw cashew in his mouth. Fate, the power that predetermined events, appeared to be on his side. Witness the fate of Hilton Prigo. Earlier today the albino had caught up with Denny Rinko, only to find himself trading shots with Connie Pavlides. A seriously wounded Pavlides had managed to kill Prigo, thereby sparing Harry the trouble of eliminating him. Harry believed in giving thought to the future, and he'd seen no future in allowing Prigo to live much longer. Not with what the albino knew about him.

Prigo's death, however, was a mixed blessing. On one hand, Harry no longer had to pay him or consider the possibility of betrayal at some point. But then there was Pavlides. He could succumb to his wounds, thereby depriving Harry of the satisfaction of seeing him publicly condemned as a pedophile. A dead Pavlides would also have to be eliminated as a suspect in Frank Beebe's murder.

Harry gave the matter some thought, and in the end decided he had actually come out ahead. In fact, fate had given him a small bonus. Pavlides's near-fatal confrontation with Prigo was the diversion Harry needed. One that would keep Magellan grieving at Pavlides's bedside while Harry attacked her weak spot, which was none other than Little Sister herself.

He squeezed the clipboard under his arm. The "old Marine trick," he called it. He'd learned it in basic training. Carry a clipboard and you could stroll the base unmolested by sergeants looking for "volunteers" to clean toilet bowls with a toothbrush. With a clipboard you were a man on a mission, someone already spoken for.

He stopped on the second-floor landing and removed a pen from a pocket protector. Slowly and in a small, neat script, he wrote his name on a blank sheet of paper atop the clipboard. Doing his best to look busy. At the same time, he checked out the corridor in front of him.

Empty.

Chessy's room was at the end of the hallway, opposite a fire exit. Apparently she needed a lot of sleep; she rarely stayed up past ten. And she would be alone. The girl who shared the room was at the home of her father, one of Long Island's wealthiest car dealers. She'd be there until next week.

Harry returned the pen to his pocket protector and headed toward Chessy. Security at Oakes Institute was a joke. Two rent-a-cops armed with flashlights and radios patrolled the grounds. Internal security was equally lax; a single rent-a-cop with a radio patrolled the building's three floors. He worked a night shift, midnight to eight. Daytime internal security was left to hospital personnel. In Harry's experience, people wanted to feel secure. They just didn't want to work at it.

He looked over his shoulder. He still had the corridor to himself. He smiled. This was going to be fun.

The hospital whites—jacket, pants, and T-shirt— were just part of his disguise. He also wore plain black shoes, brown contact lenses, and a brown wig. He wasn't entirely comfortable with the wig, but it did change his appearance, making his face look longer and exaggerating the size of his nose.

He wore whites from the same company that outfitted all Oakes attendants. They belonged to his collection of authentic uniforms from organizations like UPS, Con Ed, and the U.S. Postal Service. Each uniform had the proper ID, badges, and letters on company stationery, all identifying Harry, under various aliases, as a legitimate employee. He also owned rags worn by street people, including a WWII army blanket which reeked and which he kept in a plastic bag down in the basement. Along with his battered taxis, Harry had everything he needed to effectively change his appearance at any time.

Harry Earles. The ghost with the most.

He stopped in front of Chessy's room. He was composed and cool on the surface. Inside, however, he was tingling. His skin was flushed, and his eyes glistened as though reflecting light. And as always, when he anticipated being violent with women, he felt himself becoming sexually aroused. Pulling on the rubber gloves was the final step, with the *snap* serving as a starting signal.

A last look along the corridor. He was alone.

Opening the door, he quickly stepped inside and quietly closed the door behind him.

The room light was on. And the room was quiet, soundless, as though it had not been occupied recently.

At once Harry became alert. His brain told him something was wrong. Terribly wrong.

The room contained twin beds. But neither had been slept in. Both were neatly made up.

The room was empty. Deliberately and dangerously empty.

He had the right room. A framed photograph of Magellan and Chessy on horseback sat on a night table. The room itself gave every indication of being inhabited by teenage girls. The walls were hung with posters of rock stars, television hunks of the moment, London street signs, Islanders hockey pennants, and of all things, a huge color poster of President Clinton. A small desktop computer was running a screen saver of flying toasters. The air-conditioning was on low, and the room smelled of lemonish perfume.

Harry quickly went into action, his way of suppressing his anger.

He checked the bathroom. The closets. He looked under the beds.

No Chessy.

He crossed the room and stood with his back to the door. *She should have been here.*

He considered waiting until she returned. No good. She could come back at any time. Or not at all.

He reached behind him for the doorknob, then froze. Something on the nearest bed caught his eye.

He crossed the room and stood looking down at the object for some time. Long seconds passed before he could bring himself to pick it up.

When he did, his jaw tightened.

He was holding a CD of *Tosca.* The same recording he'd left in Magellan's apartment just days ago.

Timeline

Manhattan

Denny Rinko was waiting for Ross Magellan in the lobby of her West Side apartment building, holding a Kmart shopping bag and looking terrified. "We've never met. I'm—"

"I know who you are. You're Denny Rinko. Connie nearly died trying to save your worthless ass. You're under arrest for stealing wiretaps from police headquarters. Assume the position."

Denny put up his hands. "Wait. Hear me out. I did some bad shit to Connie. I know it and I'm sorry. That's why I come here. I want to make it up to him. The guy saved my life. I owe him."

Ross slid a hand into her shoulder bag. "You're also running out of places to hide. I said assume the position."

"Chill, OK? Just chill."

He held out the shopping bag. "I got something here. Two times Harry tried to kill me. That's how bad he wants it. This stuff is hot. I mean it is *hot*."

Ross took her hand from the shoulder bag. The hand was empty.

"I'm listening," she said.

"You know about the wiretaps—"

"And the kiddy porn."

"Harry's idea. All of it. What you don't know is, I never gave Harry all the tapes. The ones with him on them I kept. I think you're gonna want to hear them. Harry would kill anybody for these tapes in a heartbeat."

"He nearly killed Connie. Prigo pulled the trigger, but Prigo worked for Harry."

Denny Rinko took off a Mets baseball cap and nervously ran a hand over his shaven head. "How is Connie?"

Ross said, "I've spent the past six hours at the hospital. He'll make it. It was touch and go for a while, but he's going to make it."

Denny exhaled loudly. "Cool. Way cool."

"He took three bullets for you."

"People been shitting on me my whole life. Outside of being good with computers, I ain't got nothing going for me. The other shit I do, people don't like. Young girls, dope, messing up somebody's life like what I did to Connie. And I'm pissing away money on a film project that's probably heading right into the toilet. But I saw something today. I saw Connie take on Prigo. Saw him take those bullets for me when he didn't have to. Not after the shit I did to him—"

Denny began to weep.

Ross took the shopping bag from him. "And you'll never bad-mouth another cop, right?"

She didn't feel sorry for Denny. Compassion had no place in her world at the moment. Compassion would have turned Denny into a victim, something she wasn't about to do.

Denny said, "There's stuff here about some dead policewomen and Harry. And there's this guy who's covering up for Harry—"

Ross looked at him. "You've heard these tapes?"

"Oh, yeah. I tried getting a little extra cash out of Harry. I thought these tapes were worth something. I only ended up pissing him off."

Ross pointed toward the elevator. "Upstairs. You're going to play these for me."

They entered her apartment to find the phone ringing.

Fargnoli was calling. Ross was too tired to talk to him or to anyone else. She was exhausted, drained by what happened to Connie. And there was the possibility that Fargnoli was Harry's protector. Right now, a prolonged conversation with her lieutenant was on hold.

She also had something else to think about. One way or another, tonight marked the end of her relationship with Harry. Within hours one or both of them would be dead.

"Turn on your TV," Fargnoli said. "Your friend Judge Reiner made the news."

"What about him?"

"He's deceased. Son of a bitch just blew his brains out."

Queens

In the basement of his Queens home, Harry Earles finished shoving eight hundred thousand in cash into the floor safe. The safe was full, every inch packed with cash. There wasn't room for another dollar.

Which left him with a problem. Upstairs in his bedroom, in suitcases hidden under the bed, was another six million in cash. The wiretaps were selling like hotcakes. In fact, Harry doubted if hotcakes themselves had ever sold this well.

He closed the safe, then covered it with his old golf clubs. He considered hiding the six million down in the basement. In the oil tank under some old rags. The tank was empty and wouldn't be refilled until fall.

He shook his head. No good. The tank wasn't secure enough. It was too exposed, and besides, he'd scheduled it for a cleaning next week. The bedroom would have to do for now. If nothing else, it was under lock and key. Leave it be until he found somewhere better protected.

Ironic, he thought. You break your back acquiring money. Then you break your back trying to hold onto it. When, if ever, did one get the chance to relax and enjoy one's ill-gotten gains? Life, in his opinion, was one gigantic contradiction.

He locked the door to the storage room. He was in his robe and slippers, ready to call it a day. The business tonight with Chessy was annoying. He was still analyzing it. Had Magellan gotten lucky or had his contact at Oakes Institute gone over to the enemy?

Either way, Magellan had sent him a signal. The lady wanted to go to war.

So be it.

He intended to strike back with everything he had. The allotted time between Magellan's birth and death was about to come to an end.

He'd need two days to dispose of her. One day to plan her murder, another to carry it out. In forty-eight hours Magellan would be extinct.

Over and done with.

Her death must look like an accident or a suicide. That's why he needed time to plan. Planning had allowed him to effectively dispose of the others. Magellan may have saved her sister's life tonight, but in the process she'd forfeited her own.

Harry walked into the living room to find his wife watching the late news and shaking her head.

"Oh dear, oh dear," she said. "What a shame."

She looked at Harry. "It's on the news. Judge Reiner's dead. He just shot himself. Happened out on the island somewhere. What a shame."

Harry looked at the television screen, at a photograph of a smiling Judge Adam Reiner shaking hands with the governor at last year's presidential convention. Reiner, a fiftyish, stocky little guy. Gray hair parted in the middle. And a waxed mustache of which he had been inordinately proud.

Helene said, "I wonder if he learned you were after him. I'm surprised he'd do a thing like that."

Harry, hands in the pockets of his robe, rocked back on his heels. He wasn't surprised. Not at all.

12:15 A.M.

Manhattan

Ross Magellan, wearing jeans and a hooded sweat-shirt, stepped from the lobby of her West Side apartment building and walked to a limousine parked curbside.

She waited while Big Mac left the car and opened the passenger door.

Jackie Blue stepped out first. Lou Angelo followed.

Neither Jackie Blue nor his bodyguard said anything to Ross. Without a word they returned to the limousine and drove away, leaving Ross and Lou Angelo alone on the dark street.

Lou Angelo turned to Ross, confused and angry.

"Jesus, what is this shit? One minute I'm with Mercy, getting her settled in the new place. The next, I'm out here on the street with you. No wallet, no ID, and no idea as to what the hell's going on."

"We have to talk."

"Ever hear of the telephone? Every home has one these days. Jackie drops by. Doesn't call. Says it's an emergency, and the next thing I know, him and Tiny Tim are throwing me into a limo and driving me here. I want to know what the hell is going on. You want to talk to Leo? No problem. You pick up the phone, you dial, we talk. If you want, we meet. But not like this."

Ross reached into her shoulder bag, removed a string of black and red beads, then hung them from her neck. Her shield was attached to the beads. She didn't wear the badge on a chain anymore because the chain was too shiny. Perps could see it a block away and make her as a cop. Like Lou Angelo was doing now.

Under the streetlight, he suddenly looked older.

He shook his head. "You're a cop. I don't believe it."

Ross felt a drop of rain on her face. She looked at the sky.

"Starting up again," she said.

She looked at Lou Angelo. "My car's in a garage around the corner. Let's go."

Angelo seemed to shrink in front of her. There were tears in his eyes.

"We trusted you," he said. "Me and Mercy, we trusted you. Hell, I can't do jail. I'm too old. Wouldn't last a month inside. You might as well shoot me."

"Someone shot Connie today. Two in the chest, one in the shoulder. I'd like to talk to you about that."

Lou Angelo frowned. "Jesus, why does everything have to happen at once? Yeah, I would have talked to you. You should have called me. I'd have had the best surgeon in the city operating on him. He OK?"

The lawyer seemed genuinely concerned.

"He's fine," Ross said. "Lost some blood, but he'll pull through. Thanks for the offer, but I'm not interested in talking to you about doctors."

Angelo said, "Connie's the second person I know to get shot today. Friend of mine, Adam Reiner, committed suicide. Shot himself. He's the judge I'd lined up to help with your divorce. Adam's the last person I thought would put a bullet in his own head. He—"

Angelo looked at Ross. When he saw it in her face, his eyes widened.

"Shit," he said. "You were after Adam all along, weren't you? Your 'divorce' was bogus. You were using me to get to Adam. He found out and killed himself rather than go to prison."

Ross took his arm. "Bogus divorce, yes. And yes, we were after Reiner. We're running a joint operation with the FBI. That makes this a federal case, so pay attention. One more thing: Reiner didn't commit suicide. He was murdered."

"That's not true. Who'd have the guts to murder the state's top narcotics judge?"

"These days, everybody. In this case, Reiner's partner made the hit."

"But I'm—"

He stopped.

Ross said, "You were about to say you were his partner. Wrong. You were his bagman, his collector but not his partner. He didn't tell you everything. People with that kind of power never do. That's how they stay in power. Reiner's dead and that puts it on you. Payoffs. Passing along intelligence files. Witness tampering. The FBI had planned to discuss these issues with Reiner. Since he's not available, that leaves you. Speaking of friends, buddies, and pals, isn't it interesting how tight Albanians and Italians are? It's something you notice in organized crime. Lots of Albanians live in Italy. Maybe a third of all the Albanians in the world. Naturally they wind up doing deals with wiseguys over there as well as over here. Drugs, credit-card fraud, counterfeiting, gunrunning, stolen cars. Albanians and Italians. Closer than close. You speak Albanian, don't you, Lou?"

"Learned it from my grandfather. Albanian's a second language for Italians. Just like Italy's a second home for Albanians. Everybody thinks Albanese is an Italian name. It's really Italian for *Albanian*. You said with Adam gone I might have to take the weight."

"You collected for Reiner, but he wouldn't touch a dime until it had been cleaned. So you handed money to TV consultants, telemarketing people, and friends. They passed it on to the judge's phony campaign. And as we know, you cut yourself a slice before passing anything on. You're looking at a major tax problem right there. Plus there's the murder of Viktor Ramiz. He's the Albanian who got bagged by his friends before he could rat them out to the FBI."

Angelo shook his head. "I had nothing to do with that killing."

"You sure?"

"OK, I knew about it in advance. Adam said something, and I pretended I didn't hear him. Just pushed it out of my mind is all."

"Makes you an accessory," Ross said. "Add that to campaign fraud, mail fraud, money laundering, and tax evasion and you've got one hell of a jackpot on your hands. With Reiner gone, the people helping you launder money will jump at the chance to cut their own deals. I see all fingers pointing in your direction. You're running out of time in which to cover your ass. Now I can help you. Help you with everything, including the Ramiz murder. All you have to do is make one phone call."

"One phone call?"

"After you make it, forget we ever had this conversation. In fact, forget you ever made the call. Question: Did Jenn Sanchez ID this cop who was trying to kill her?"

Angelo shook his head. "No. She said knowing his name was too dangerous for me."

"She got that right. But that's not going to help you. He'll assume Sanchez has given him up, so he'll try to kill you. One more reason for you to make that call."

Angelo shook his head. "Who are you? I mean we never did get that straight."

"Detective Magellan. Detective Ross Magellan. I work in Organized Crime."

"Detective Magellan, I suppose it's asking too much to let me break the news to Mercy. The kid's high-strung and something like this, me being arrested, it could send her off the deep end."

He gave Ross a sad smile. "You were good, kiddo. I've seen cops work, and believe me, you're up there with the best. Had me fooled from the get-go. No hard feelings. You were just doing your job."

Ross said, "You don't have to go to prison."

"What are you talking about?"

"Make that call."

"Are you being straight with me? Because with you, I don't know if it's chickenshit or chicken salad."

"There's just us two out here in the rain. No task force, no U.S. Marshals, no prosecutors holding mid-night press conferences on the sidewalk. You and me. That should tell you something."

Lou Angelo used his palm to wipe rain from his bare forearm.

He said, "It tells me you're into something not kosher. Whatever's happening with you is happening off the books and under the table. You're working alone, right?"

"Do yourself a favor, Lou. Don't ask any more questions."

Lou Angelo had never seen a colder smile on a woman.

"You're asking me to trust you," he said. "This after what you just did to me. I should have my fucking head examined. Know what the worst part of this is?"

"What?"

"I still like you. That's the worst part."

Queens

Harry Earles entered his kitchen, sipping herbal tea. Across the room a broad-shouldered man stared through the screen door at the night rain.

The man looked at his feet. "Come through the back like you said. Sorry 'bout the mud. Rain surprised me. All day we had sun. So I figure that's it, we done with the rain." He nodded toward the rain-soaked yard. "Would you look at that shit?"

He held up a can of beer. "Brought my own. Hope you don't mind."

He had a pointed chin and impeccably groomed short hair.

Harry pointed to a cardboard box on the kitchen table. "You bring everything?"

"Everything there was to bring. I'll leave it to you to check it out."

"The money?"

"I made him open a safe in his living room. Found some more in the garage. Didn't stick around to count it. Just threw everything in the box. I take my half now and be on my way."

Harry looked into the box. "I assume the money's all there."

The man grinned. "Hey, homes, you think I'm some kind of chump? I seen you work. Anybody play you for a fool, you on them faster than Elvis chasing a peanut-butter-and-banana sandwich. You picked me 'cause you know I'd play the game. Also I figured since you paid the dude, you know how much *ought* to be there. I start making deductions, you gonna start asking questions. Then we got problems. I don't need that much drama in my life. Half of the money in that box is mine. Hey, half is cool. Plus, I figure we be doing more business together. No sense me messing up a good thing."

Harry nodded his approval. "Your share could come to four hundred thousand dollars. Not bad for one night's work."

The man cocked his thumb and forefinger in imitation of a gun, then pressed the tip of his forefinger against his temple.

He said, "The judge, he done retired."

Harry nodded in agreement. "I've said it before. Death is more than just an unfounded rumor. Not too many people die when they should. Judge Reiner, bless him, was one of the few."

He sipped his tea then said, "You'll replace Prigo. Sell the tapes, then bring me the cash. I'll set the price. No bargaining. Now, about Denny."

"He's at Magellan's crib. The one on the West Side."

Harry nodded. "He goes tomorrow. Get the wire-taps before sending him on to Jesus. And don't touch Magellan. I've got plans for her."

"I can dig it, homes," said the man. "Now let's seal

the deal. Start counting out my money. I got women I got to keep happy. No finance, no romance, as they say."

1:30 A.M.

Queens

Ross Magellan, smoking her first cigarette in three years, was parked beneath the Queensboro Bridge. The .380 was on the seat beside her.

She rolled down the window to let in fresh air. What had begun as a downpour was now just a drizzle. In passing headlights, the rain appeared to be a shower of glistening needles.

Waiting was turning her into a basket case. That's why she'd gone back to smoking. But just for tonight.

She'd quit tomorrow. Provided she was still alive.

She hadn't known how much she'd missed smoking until now. *Let's hear it for the soothing weed.*

Ahead of her, just past the bridge, lay a rain-slicked intersection. On the far side of the intersection, a Mercury, its tailpipe emitting gray smoke, slowly rolled into sight. At the corner of the block, it turned right, then headed down a quiet street of two-story redbrick houses. A red taillight on the Mercury was broken.

In keeping with the late hour, most of the homes were dark. Among a dozen or so houses, Ross counted just three lights. One light, in a bay window with green drapes and Christmas decorations, drew the attention of the Mercury. In front of the window, the Mercury came to a near stop, only to continue rolling until it reached the corner. A right turn and the Mercury was gone.

Ross took a drag on the cigarette and waited for her heart to slow down.

She was pulling surveillance on the house with the bay window and Christmas lights. Waiting for something to happen. If it didn't she'd have lost the biggest gamble of her life.

Meanwhile she was in a very depressing neighborhood. Even with darkness and rain hiding a great deal of the area, she'd seen enough to know she wouldn't be moving here anytime soon. She was in an area of cheap homes surrounded by railroad yards, factories, and public-housing projects. Not to mention cracked streets full of potholes. She'd just chased a homeless man away from her car, flashing her shield so the skell could see it. That's when she'd made sure the doors were locked and her gun was where she could reach it in a hurry.

She began opening and closing her lighter. The rain was having the effect on some locals that you'd expect from a full moon. One woman had opened her door, shoved her reluctant dog outside to do his duty and then slammed the door in his snoot when he tried to follow her inside. A man in shorts and anklets stepped outside to curse the sky before returning to his home, supposedly better for the experience.

Ross fingered the badge hanging from her neck. *Be patient, Harry always said. Most of the mistakes people make come from impatience, he said. Listen and wait, he told Ross. Be still and alone.*

Try doing that when you're up against the man who taught you those things.

She drummed on the steering wheel with her hands, keeping time to "And Sammy Walked In," the Michel Camilo tune. Michel on piano and Sammy Figueroa on conga, the two kicking it to the max. It was one of her favorite dance records. Not too fast, not too slow. It was in the tape deck, which was silent. Something else she'd learned from Harry. Sound carried at night.

Ross was playing the tune in her head, note for note, her eyes on the house with the bay window, broken flagstone walk, and Christmas decorations. Harry's house.

She stopped drumming and lit another cigarette. Lou Angelo had made the phone call. Saying what Ross wanted him to say. The faithful Italian friend counseling his Albanian homies.

Fear had lent an urgency to his voice. He sounded believable, though at times slightly incoherent. What mattered was that he'd followed orders. He'd lied his ass off.

It remained to be seen just how convincing he'd been.

Ross was reaching for her lighter when the Mercury reappeared. Again it turned the corner, heading down the quiet, rain-slicked street, tailpipe sending smoke signals. Ross tossed the cigarette out the window and reached for the .380. She felt fear and excitement. *It was going down.*

Then the Mercury passed Harry's house, disappearing into the darkness. She sank in her seat, disappointed and frustrated. Had she been wrong about the Merc? Had she been wrong about Lou Angelo's ability to talk shit under pressure?

No.

Terrified and elated, she sat up straight. She'd called it right.

They came jogging out of the rainy darkness. Out of the Mercury. Headed toward Harry's house. Four men in dark clothing, ski masks, and carrying what Ross assumed were automatic weapons. When they reached the house, they separated.

Two men disappeared around back. Two remained at the front door.

Ross, her heart beating out of control, gripped the .380 until her hand ached.

Opening the car door, she swung her legs out into the rain. She did not, however, leave the car. Instead she remained seated.

Listen and wait.

One invader stood at Harry's front door, looking at his watch. Then he raised one hand. Ross thought, *They've done this before.* In another country, at another time. And always with military precision. The man looking at his watch lowered his hand.

A signal.

Dropping into a crouch, he brought up his weapon and fired at the front lock. The door flew open.

Still firing from the hip, the invader entered the house.

Ross waited.

Inside the house a woman screamed. The bay window was shattered by gunfire, sending glass, wood chunks, and Christmas lights flying onto the lawn. Nearby car alarms went off.

Ross waited.

She heard the *pop-pop* of a handgun. Immediately a black-clad invader appeared in the doorway, then dropped to a kneeling position against the doorjamb. More shooting from the house, a mixture of small arms and automatic weapons. People in the houses around Harry's turned on their lights.

Ross waited.

The gunfire stopped. A man inside the house shouted in a foreign language. Two shots from a handgun and he was silent.

Now.

Ross stepped from her car. She had to get to the house before the police arrived. She had to make sure.

She jogged toward Harry's home, splashing across the intersection and holding the .380 under her sweatshirt to protect it from the rain. One of Harry's neighbors, a bald-headed Hispanic man in Bermuda shorts and espadrilles, stood on his front porch and stared at the space once occupied by Harry's bay window.

Ross identified herself as a police officer, held up her shield, and ordered him to return to his home.

She didn't point the gun at him. She simply let him see it.

He backed away, then hurried inside and slammed the door.

At the entrance to Harry's home, Ross felt the neck of the man kneeling in the doorway. He was dead. His ski mask had been pulled up to his forehead, revealing one gold earring and a thin, mustachioed face. An automatic weapon of some kind was half hidden under his knee. Ross couldn't make it out, but it appeared to be high tech. The kind of firepower carried by people who were serious about guns.

She stepped into a small foyer, turned right, and entered what should have been the living room. Except it had been turned into a makeshift bedroom, with a bed, wheelchair, bedpans, and makeup table. Bottles of prescription medicines rested on a night table; a Bach mass came from a tape deck beneath the table. The walls and furniture contained gaping bullet holes. In one corner, a Christmas tree, bright with blinking lights, had turned white under falling plaster. The bed, which had been placed by the open window, was now wet with rain. A dead intruder lay beside the bed, the carpet beneath his head darkened by blood from a neck wound. Somehow a blood-soaked origami frog had landed on his back.

Ross heard a sound behind her. Terrified, she spun around with her arms extended. A two-handed grip on the .380.

She saw Harry. Seated on the floor to the right of the front door, his back to the wall. She'd passed by without noticing him. *A mistake.*

He was bleeding heavily from the chest and legs. The left side of his face was also bloody. She thought, *Anyone else but you would have been dead.*

He wore a blue bathrobe and brown slippers. His eyes were half closed. The Glock was in his left hand now, resting on one thigh.

He slowly turned his head toward Ross.

"Think we got them all," he said. "I know there's one in the yard and one in the kitchen. The two here make four. I think that's all of them. My wife. Can't see her. Take a look and tell me how she is."

Ross walked to the bed and looked down at Mrs. Earles. She lay on her side, a plain-looking woman with curlers in her hair and a mole on her temple. She'd been hit twice. Her jaw had been shot away, and in her back was a hole the size of an orange. Her pulse was weak.

Ross turned to speak to Harry and froze. His Glock was aimed at her head.

"Lay your gun on the bed," he said. "Carefully."

She did.

He said, "Just happened to be passing by, right? Offhand, I'd say you set me up."

"You and your wife need medical attention," she said. "Let me call a doctor."

"How is my wife, by the way?"

Dying. Or dead. Just like you.

Ross took a deep breath. "She looks OK to me, but I'm no doctor. I do know she's unconscious and bleeding from a leg wound. My guess is she's in shock."

Harry grinned. "Ain't that a hoot. Helene gets hit in the one place she can't feel it. Fun things happen when your spinal cord's damaged."

"Harry, let me make that call."

She needed time.

"You set me up. Got these Albanians all hot and bothered over God knows what. Schmucks willing to come out in the rain on the say-so of some Cuban. Reiner's boys. A bunch of Neanderthals who did his dirty work for him. How'd you manage to manipulate these cretins? I know you're behind this little episode, so don't insult my intelligence by denying it."

He closed his eyes against the pain, then opened them wide. And he still held the Glock.

Ross wanted a cigarette. Badly. But any sudden move could be her last.

"Look," she said. "At least let me call an ambulance

for your wife. Police are on the way, but they won't be bringing an ambulance with them."

"You'll be dead when they get here. We both will. You and I are going to be together. If not in this world, then in the next. Meanwhile, talk to me. You're good at talking."

Ross said, "The Albanians worshiped Reiner. You know that. When they figured out you'd killed him, that was all the motive they needed. I'd like to call an ambulance for your wife. You owe her that much."

Harry yelled, "Helene! Helene!"

He pushed against the floor in an attempt to stand. But in the end he was too weak to move.

He closed his eyes. "This hurts. You wouldn't believe how much it hurts. Chest, legs. I feel like I've been eating ground glass for a week."

Ross said, "Helene's in shock and she's bleeding. She needs a doctor."

Harry looked at her. "I loved you. You knew that."

"You wanted to control me. It wouldn't have worked and we both know that. You'd have had to kill me. Harry, I'm going to call an ambulance for your wife. I'm reaching in my bag for a phone."

"You only carry one gun. I know you. Thought I did, anyway. Make the call."

She'd bought herself a little more time.

Ross put the cell phone to her ear. In the distance she could hear police sirens. She looked at Harry. He was going into shock. And bleeding. If he heard the police sirens, he'd kill her and die happy.

Ross raised her voice to take Harry's mind off sounds outside the house.

"Yes, 911? This is Detective Magellan." She gave her badge number.

"I have an officer down," she said. "Yes, one officer. Detective Harry Earles. He's attached to OCCB. I also have a woman who's been wounded. Mrs. Earles. Yes. Home invasion. That's right."

She gave Harry's address.

"Make it quick," she said. "The woman is paralyzed and needs immediate attention. Thank you."

She closed the phone and dropped it in her bag.

Harry grinned. "You've been a busy little bee. Everything in one night. Rescue your sister, then wait a couple of hours and put a few holes in Harry."

"Two days. That's how long you spend planning anything. I knew you'd want Chessy for payback. Nobody puts one over on Harry Earles. You'd strike back at me unless I moved first."

"So you attacked while I just thought about attacking. Shows initiative. Where is Chessy, by the way?"

"Some guys from Connie's company are keeping an eye on her. Couldn't go to the department for help, so I made other arrangements. I contacted Doctor DeCarlo. Spoke frankly. Told him you had somebody at the hospital you were squeezing for information on Chessy. I added that an incident might harm the institute's image. Doctor DeCarlo is very image-conscious. People in his line of work have to be. He cooperated to the fullest. I told him to leave you alone. Let you come and go, so long as you didn't get homicidal."

Harry looked down at his stomach. "Bleeding like a stuck pig."

Ross held her breath. *More time. I need more time.*

"I could go into the kitchen," she said. "Bring back a wet towel and—"

"I don't think so. Just stay put. Don't trust you out of my sight. It's Helene I'm worried about. I loved you. Why can't you understand that?"

"You mean because you stalked me and broke into my apartment and tried to frame Connie for murder? Did Reiner order you to do that?"

Harry took a couple of deep breaths. "Reiner had me follow you and—"

He stopped to take another breath.

Ross said, "You were following me on your own. It was strictly personal until Reiner learned we were investigating him. He then encouraged you to continue following me and report back to him. Our investigation of Reiner was doomed from the beginning. You've been his boy all along. You did the stuff he didn't trust Lou Angelo to do. The dirty stuff. In return Reiner protected you. Pulled certain cases from the department's databases. Destroyed evidence that might have sent you away for murder. You guys were quite a team. Why'd you kill him?"

Harry nodded, a teacher taking pride in a prize pupil. "I see you've been talking to Denny. He and Reiner had something in common. Greed. Denny wanted to blackmail me. And Reiner decided to take all of the money from the sale of the illegal wiretaps. Denny told me about the taps and I told Reiner. Figured I'd do him a kindness after all he'd done for me. I also figured he'd heard about them from his Albanian friends, so why not be up-front? But like they say, no good deed goes unpunished. The bastard wanted it all."

He coughed. "Every last dime. Thought he had enough on me to get away with hosing me like that. The man was a degenerate gambler. They're the worst. You ought to know that."

The sirens were getting closer. Ross said, "And you had him continue his gambling."

"That was for your benefit. So you wouldn't suspect anything. Where's that ambulance?"

"I think I just heard it. I could go outside and check on it if you'd like."

"Stay where I can see you. Denny is definitely the scum of the earth. Should have taken him out when I had the chance."

Ross nodded. "I heard those tapes he held back on you. The ones implying that all was not right regarding the death of certain female undercovers who worked with you. Denny said Reiner knew we were investigating him from day one, thanks to you. No matter what we turned up, Reiner knew about it because you were passing everything on to him. It was your way of thanking him for protecting you all these years."

"Gratitude is a form of courtesy."

"And you're nothing if not courteous. I suppose the judge figured even illegal tapes could make trouble for the two of you. So he said go get them. And you did. Reiner was taped when they tried to link him to receiving payoffs from the Albanians. Instead they got the two of you talking about dead undercovers. Nothing happened, though. The case files were removed, and no one pushed for an investigation. Reiner was too powerful. And you? You covered your tracks pretty well on your own."

Harry eyed the bed. "My wife—"

"I'll take a look at her."

Ross returned to the bed and felt Helene's wrist pulse.

She was dead.

Ross turned to Harry. "She's breathing but still unconscious. So Reiner got greedy. Is that what happened?"

"I had a friend pay him a visit."

"Friend?"

Harry gestured toward the back of the house. Ross looked over her shoulder and saw a dead black man on the couch with a 9mm in one hand. He was Cleveland Nobles, the cop who'd replaced Freddy Palacio as Reiner's driver.

Harry said, "The day I saw you going to the library, I knew you were checking on me. What tipped you?"

"I wasn't looking for you. I was looking for something on Sanchez. For anything that would tell me who was after her. How long had you been following me?"

Harry dismissed her with a wave. "Doesn't matter. The Albanians didn't come here tonight to make polite conversation. One did take the time to call me an informant. What was that all about?"

"Somehow they got the idea that you were going to the FBI tomorrow morning to cut a deal. To save yourself after having killed Reiner. You intended to buy your freedom with records, cash, and the illegal taps, which had information on the Albanians. The Albanians loved Reiner. And to have him killed by a man who planned to betray them, well, you can understand how they might feel."

"Who reached out for them? Wasn't you. You're not connected."

"Lou Angelo. He's their attorney, remember? And he speaks Albanian."

Harry nodded. "Many Italians do. Did you know the Albanians have thirty-seven alphabets? Not an alphabet with thirty-seven letters, but thirty-seven different alphabets. So you used Angelo. I'd take my hat off to you but I'm not wearing one."

"The Albanians were also told that there'd be a lot of money at your place."

"Denny told you the money was here."

Ross took a step toward him. "He did. Speaking of incentives, I told Lou Angelo you'd kill him one day."

"Reiner wanted him gone. Angelo knew too much. Except he didn't know about Reiner and me."

Ross watched the Glock slip from Harry's hand and drop to the floor. Harry, his eyes on her, picked it up again and pointed it at her.

"I loved you," he said.

"You kill the people you love. My turn would have come sooner or later."

"I don't want to kill my wife. Want . . . want to make sure she's OK. Ambulance. Where's . . . ?"

Ross said, "I've spoken to Jenn Sanchez. She said you and Reiner conspired to murder Viktor Ramiz."

Harry gave her a backhand wave. "Didn't kill Ramiz. Delivered him to Reiner. Reiner killed . . ."

"Did Reiner plan to use the illegal wiretaps to squash our investigation?"

Harry's eyes were almost shut. "Didn't Denny tell you that? Didn't Denny tell . . ."

Ross said, "Reiner was going to stop us with the illegal taps. He was going to lie and say we made them last week. That would put the department and the FBI on the defensive and—"

Harry took a deep breath. His hands slipped from his thighs and fell to the floor. He closed his eyes.

Ross made her voice as soothing as possible. "And with illegal taps tied to our investigation, Reiner would be home free. Our investigation would have to be shit-canned."

Harry opened his eyes to find Ross standing over him and holding his gun.

Harry whispered, "Albanians say breathing is not addictive but it would be fatal to give it up. My wife. Is she—"

Ross, who'd faked the ambulance call, said, "She's still alive. The ambulance just arrived."

I owe him that. One more lie.

Ross said, I'll see to her, and Harry smiled and tried to raise a hand in gratitude.

Instead, his hand slid to the floor, and he died.

Closure

They sat in Connie's hospital room. For a long time they held hands and remained silent. Eventually Ross said, "I love the sunset."

She pointed to the East River. "It sets the water on fire. Gives it a glow."

Connie squeezed her hand. "Watching you cross your legs in that miniskirt gives me a glow."

"I don't want to be responsible for a relapse. Didn't you just get shot not too long ago?"

"I'm told I'm well on the road to recovery. I credit that to your miniskirt. Maybe if I started wearing one, I might recover faster."

"Forget it," Ross said. "You're in no condition to shave your legs."

Connie said, "Speaking of close shaves, how did you explain your presence at Harry's house to Fargnoli?"

"I told him I'd gotten a call from Harry, who wanted to see me right away. Harry gave me no details.

Everyone knows he doesn't like talking on the phone. He was my ghost, so I assumed he had information I should know. I drove out to Queens but got there too late, it seems. Harry was dead, killed by some Albanians he'd once investigated. Cops found over nine million in cash in Harry's home. Reason enough for a home invasion, I'd say."

Connie inched his wheelchair closer to a night table, picked up a drink, and sipped through a glass straw. Then he said, "Fargnoli's no dummy. He'll think on this thing and he's going to have questions."

"He'll behave himself. The department doesn't want a scandal. Letting Harry get away with killing undercovers makes the department look dumb. So even if my story is shaky in spots, no one's going to press me. Not after finding that shrine to me in Harry's house. And his journal."

"So even if they suspect you set Harry up to get wacked, nothing's going to happen."

"You got it, sport."

Connie wheeled himself closer to Ross's chair. "What about the stuff from Reiner's house? The records and files Nobles took from the judge after killing him."

Ross shook her head. "What records? Everything disappeared. Harry died in a home invasion perpetrated by Albanians looking for payback. Reiner's a suicide and Cleveland Nobles just happened to be in the wrong place at the wrong time."

"And Lou Angelo?"

Ross took out a cigarette, looked at it, then threw the butt and the pack into a wastebasket. One day at a time.

"Big Lou will have to work out something with Labriola," she said. "It'll mean giving up his Albanian friends. I've talked to Labriola. If Lou does the right thing, he could end up in the witness protection program without going to prison."

"With Mercy to keep him warm on those cold winter nights. Won't Lou's testimony lead to Judge Reiner?"

Ross nodded her head. "It might. Labriola's happy to nail even a dead Reiner. But the feeling around the federal courthouse is, he's pissing in the wind. Reiner's now being held up as some kind of saint by his family, Jewish groups, the bar association, you name it. Labriola might have to settle for making a case against the Albanians."

"What about Freddie Palacio?"

"He does his year at Elgin and he keeps his mouth shut if he knows what's good for him. Lou Angelo keeps his mouth shut about the phone call I asked him to make. Otherwise, he could do time as an accessory to the Ramiz murder."

Connie touched the bandage on his shoulder. "Hope this doesn't mean I've lost my curve ball. Any charges being brought against Harry?"

There was a look of disgust on Ross's face.

"He's getting an inspector's funeral," she said. "Far as the world knows, he died a hero."

And I get away with killing him. That was the deal.

Ross said, "He goes out like a hero. The Blue Wall of Silence wins again."

Connie nodded. "True. But this time it's protecting you as well. Like you said, your story's a bit shaky. Seven people died in that shootout at Harry's place.

Two were cops. If you can walk away from that, you've won the lottery. I think the less said about Harry's funeral, the better."

Ross reached in her shoulder bag for a stick of gum. Connie was right. One more secret to keep.

And speaking of secrets, she hadn't told Connie she'd been ordered to investigate him. Fargnoli had suggested she keep quiet about that. He was right, of course. Connie, like most cops, had no use for a cop who ratted out a brother officer. Had he learned Ross had been ordered to spy on him, even against her wishes, he'd never trust her again.

And there was Sanchez. She'd called to thank Ross for helping Lou Angelo with the feds. She'd also said she'd like Ross to call her. I can help you, Sanchez said. You don't want to end up like me.

As she sat holding Connie's hand, Ross thought about inviting Sanchez to lunch one day. But afraid of what she might hear, she never made the call.

Visit the
Simon & Schuster Web site:

www.SimonSays.com

and sign up for our
mystery e-mail updates!

Keep up on the latest new releases,
author appearances, news, chats,
special offers, and more!
We'll deliver the information
right to your inbox—
if it's new, you'll know about it.

SIMON & SCHUSTER
A VIACOM COMPANY
www.SimonSays.com

2345

**Politics. Power. Murder.
And one detective you'll
never forget.**

FEAR'S JUSTICE

Also from
MARC OLDEN

POCKET BOOKS

2802